W9-AUO-220

SCRIPT FOR SCANDAL

Recent titles by Renee Patrick

Lillian Frost and Edith Head mysteries

DESIGN FOR DYING
DANGEROUS TO KNOW
SCRIPT FOR SCANDAL *

* *available from Severn House*

SCRIPT FOR SCANDAL

Renee Patrick

This first world edition published 2019
in Great Britain and 2020 in the USA by
SEVERN HOUSE PUBLISHERS LTD of
Eardley House, 4 Uxbridge Street, London W8 7SY.
Trade paperback edition first published
in Great Britain and the USA 2020 by
SEVERN HOUSE PUBLISHERS LTD.

British Library Cataloguing in Publication Data
A CIP catalogue record for this title is available from the British Library.

ISBN-13: 978-0-7278-8910-2 (cased)
ISBN-13: 978-1-78029-650-0 (trade paper)
ISBN-13: 978-1-4483-0349-6 (e-book)

All Severn House titles are printed on acid-free paper.

Severn House Publishers support the Forest Stewardship Council™ [FSC™],
the leading international forest certification organisation.
All our titles that are printed on FSC certified paper carry the FSC logo.

MIX
Paper from
responsible sources
FSC® C013056

Typeset by Palimpsest Book Production Ltd.,
Falkirk, Stirlingshire, Scotland.
Printed and bound in Great Britain by
TJ International, Padstow, Cornwall.

To Eddie Muller, for guiding us and so many others through the shadows

ACKNOWLEDGMENTS

We cannot extend sufficient thanks to our peerless agent, Lisa Gallagher, who never gave up on us or this series. Severn House is now home to Lillian and Edith, and the ladies have been made to feel so welcome by everyone there, especially Kate Lyall Grant, Sara Porter, and Natasha Bell.

Time to round up the usual suspects, the people we regularly rely on in writing these books. They include Edith Head's three biographers, Paddy Calistro, the late David Chierichetti, and Jay Jorgensen; the staff at the Academy of Motion Pictures Arts and Sciences's Margaret Herrick Library; the dedicated archivists at Paramount Pictures; and Deborah Nadoolman Landis of UCLA's David C. Copley Center for Costume Design, and her associate Natasha Rubin. We are in your debt.

Finally, our thanks to every bookseller and every reader who has supported Lillian and Edith.

'Every gal has her price. And mine's high.'

Joan Crawford, *Sadie McKee*, 1934

Los Angeles Register   *March 24, 1939*

LORNA WHITCOMB'S
EYES ON HOLLYWOOD

MGM has snapped up screen rights for Franchot Tone to star in his Broadway hit *The Gentle People*. Eligible ladies are asking if his long-brewing divorce from Joan Crawford will finally be final by the time the actor makes his way west . . . Rumblings around town that movie extras are again looking for a home of their own far from the Screen Actors Guild. Seems some of the milling multitudes who fill out the crowds for the cameras would happily part ways with SAG and form their own union. A vote on the matter is forthcoming . . . They sure do grow 'em big down South, if the diamonds flashing on the fingers of oil heiress Virginia Hill are any indication. Wonder if the flame-haired beauty gets tired carting those carats around the nightspots . . .

ONE

I had narrowed my options down to the corned beef hash or the turkey sandwich. I couldn't make the final decision, though. Not with the gears of seduction grinding away next door.

Him: a junior executive type, emphasis on junior. He'd coaxed a mustache onto his upper lip, but a few carefully placed drops of milk could have enticed a cat to lick it off. He sat with his jacket shucked, shirtsleeves rolled up, necktie loosened. Her: a dewy-eyed blonde. The peppy sailor hat perched on her head made her look even younger than he did.

And because we were in Hollywood – the Bronson Gate of Paramount Pictures a literal stone's throw from our adjacent tables in Oblath's Café – all the sweet nothings were about her career.

'I'm telling you, sweetheart, extra work is strictly from hunger.'

Junior leaned forward, the better to share the hard-won wisdom of his weeks of experience. 'Talents like yours deserve to be front and center.' The girl, whom I'd started to think of as Trixie, nodded solemnly.

I had no intention of eavesdropping. But Oblath's was quiet in the late afternoon, the lunch service over, the cocktail rush still hours away. Aside from the chipper chock of clean dishes being stacked in readiness, the couple's palaver was my only entertainment until my friend, the costume designer Edith Head, made her way from the studio across the street.

Trixie steepled her fingers, their tips painted Ingénue Pink. 'I'd still like to sign up as an extra. Just for the work.'

'What work? A day or two a month if you're lucky, and that's provided you get in. Central Casting keeps a tight rein on those spots nowadays. Meantime, how you gonna eat?'

Trixie looked utterly downcast, as if her balloon had just popped. Even her sailor hat slumped. That cued Junior to start pitching woo like Dizzy Dean. 'But it's like I always say. You start in the background, you stay in the background. You're meant for better things. Like a studio contract. Which is where I come in.'

Listening to his line made me happy I'd packed in the acting racket. I had come to Los Angeles from New York three years earlier, obsessed with pictures and harboring vague dreams of stardom. It only took a single disastrous screen test to convince me that if I did possess any talent it would have to be carefully excavated, like a mummy from one of those Egyptian tombs, and who had the time and manpower for that? I'd opted instead for gainful employment, relieved to be off the merry-go-round yet still close enough to enjoy the music and the swirling lights.

Still, Junior made a good point. If you'd travelled all the way to Hollywood seeking silver screen glory, you might as well aim for the top. I recalled the advice of my old roommate Ruby. *Don't wait for the spotlight to find you, mermaid. It'll hit someone else first. You have to run toward it, fast as you can.* Of course, the spotlight never found Ruby. Only trouble did.

Thinking of Ruby made me sad. I distracted myself with a newspaper left behind at lunch. Hungary had invaded Slovakia. Adolf Hitler had triumphantly sailed into the harbor of Memel on a battleship to crow over Lithuania's ceding of the seaport to Germany. Some suggested this would mark an end to Nazi aggression, but

English prime minister Neville Chamberlain warned the world not to hold its breath.

Say, how were our prospective lovebirds getting along?

'So what's doing this weekend?' Junior asked Trixie with exaggerated casualness.

'Nothing much. Rinsing out a few things, going to the pictures.' He shook his head, dismayed by her naïveté. 'No, you've got to go out! Make an impression! Be seen!'

'By who? Nobody knows who I am.'

'They'll never learn if you stay at home. You should let me squire you around.'

'Before I've had my screen test? I'm not sure I see the sense in that.' No babe in the woods, our Trixie. I was starting to like her.

As Junior fumbled for an answer, my thoughts turned to my own plans for this spring weekend. Saturday night I'd likely see a picture or two in the company of my beau Gene Morrow, unless Los Angeles' criminal fraternity demanded his attention; the LAPD never rested, no matter who had a premiere. Then I'd make a rare foray into work on the Sabbath. I was social secretary to Addison Rice, the semi-retired, movie-mad industrialist whose lavish get-togethers drew Hollywood's elite. Sunday's affair would be a croquet bash. I'd spent the morning walking the course with Addison's gardener Mr Ayoshi, who marked every place a hoop sullied his handiwork on a map of the grounds. Over each stake that had been hammered into the earth, he simply lowered his head in despair. When Addison's enthusiasm for the sport waned – around two-thirty Sunday after-noon, I'd wager – Mr Ayoshi would return the landscape to its customary Edenic splendor. The pending party had prompted my visit to Oblath's; I'd asked Edith to raid Paramount's extensive research library for books on the game.

I glanced across Marathon Street but saw no sign of my friend. Trixie looked over at me, Junior pivoting in his seat to see what had caught her eye. Back into the newspaper I dived. Ronald Colman would be replacing Ray Milland as the lead in Paramount's upcoming adaptation of Rudyard Kipling's *The Light That Failed*, a casting decision I approved of wholeheartedly. Not that anyone had asked.

Swinging her searchlight gaze around the otherwise empty restaurant, Trixie said, 'I don't understand why we're here. Couldn't we meet in your office across the street?'

Junior pressed a palm to his chest, playing aggrieved. 'What? You don't think I'm trying to take advantage of you?'

'No, it's nothing like that—'

He made to leave, and Trixie frantically waved him back into his seat. Junior raised both arms in the classic cardsharp's move: nothing up my sleeves, no tricks in my pockets. 'Can't say as I blame you. I could feed you some malarkey about wanting to keep you a secret until the contract is signed, or say that going on the lot can overwhelm people.'

It overwhelms me, I thought. Every time I go through that gate to visit Edith.

'But the truth is' – here Junior let out with a sigh meant to sound world-weary, but that only made it seem like the chicken croquettes weren't sitting right – 'the truth is you remind me of why I got into pictures in the first place. Finding talent the right home. I want to concentrate on that. Keep it pure, away from the greasepaint and Klieg lights.'

The kid had nerve, considering he still probably had his confirmation suit hanging in his closet. Trixie gnawed the inside of her cheek, her resolve wobbling. *Hold the line, Trixie. Don't fall for his bunk.*

But now I had to wonder why *I* wasn't on the Paramount lot, either. Edith never abandoned her post, yet the parley at Oblath's had been her suggestion. Her wanting to meet away from the studio implied she had news she didn't want the walls to hear. Perhaps she was leaving Paramount. Edith had been officially running the studio's Wardrobe Department for a year, but she'd intimated the steady procession of big names brought in to design various pictures made her feel as if she were understudying her own position. Her tenuous hold on the job could have finally worn her down. Or maybe the development was a sunnier one, and she was going to get married to Bill Ihnen, the man whose company she'd been keeping of late. A June wedding would make for a most pleasant affair. Thoughts of what I might wear to it sidetracked me from the temptation of Trixie.

I'd ordered the turkey sandwich when the café's door opened. Junior sat bolt upright. Trixie did likewise without even seeing who'd entered the joint and practiced batting her eyelashes. A bright girl. We'd all be working for her someday.

The man loitering in the doorway, hands deep in his pockets, surveyed the room with a puckish expression under his trilby. His mind, I knew, was already cranking out jokes. Junior signaled to him but the man breezed past his table in favor of mine, absently peering at me.

'Hello, Mr Wilder.'

A Continental sound of recognition emerged from Billy Wilder's throat. '*Ach*, yes,' he said. 'You are Edith's friend.'

'Lillian Frost,' I filled in for him. Knowing Edith and working for Addison, I was accustomed to being recognized purely by function. 'What brings you here?'

'Squabbling with Charlie.' Wilder waved in the direction of the Paramount lot, where his writing partner, Charles Brackett, was apparently still prisoner. 'My choices were taking the air or putting him out of my misery. This seemed the wiser option. Although why I ventured here I don't know. It's the only place in town you can get a greasy Tom Collins.'

'I heard that,' the waitress snapped as she deposited my turkey sandwich on the table. It looked like she'd spilled a Tom Collins on it.

'You are meeting Edith?' Wilder asked.

'Yes. Just passing the time listening to that junior executive make his pitch.'

Wilder glanced over his shoulder at Junior, flashing his pearlies our way. 'Executive? Bah. He's a messenger. Zips around on a bicycle delivering scripts. He doesn't have an office. I didn't even think he had a necktie.' Wilder peered at Junior again. 'Son of a bitch, is that my tie? One went missing from my desk.'

Junior seized the opportunity afforded by the eye contact to bound over, hand extended. Behind him, Trixie gaped. 'Hey, Mr Wilder, it's Jerry! You remember me, don'cha?'

'Of course.' Wilder's eyes twinkled, admiring the kid's moxie. He decided to play along. 'Your comments on the script were very helpful.'

'You're the scribe. I just try to think of the audience.' Junior looked at me askance, his expression indicating he thought Wilder could do better. 'I've got a talented little lady over here I'd like you to meet.'

'Yes, I see. Talented at what exactly?'

Trixie grinned at Wilder in a manner that seemed distinctly unwholesome.

Naturally, Edith Head bustled into the restaurant at that exact moment. She looked crisp and clean in a tan dress with a matching short sleeve jacket, its front unadorned by buttons. The books clutched to her chest and the spectacles beneath her precisely trimmed dark hair lent her the appearance of the world's most sophisticated schoolgirl. She stopped short, discomfited by the gaggle of guests around my table.

'Our Head of costume has arrived at last.' Wilder bowed gallantly in my direction. 'I couldn't allow your friend to be alone. Sadly, I didn't arrive in time to prevent her from ordering food.'

A loud clatter of cutlery followed. My waitress had heard that crack, too.

'Thank you, Billy,' Edith said. 'It's so nice to have you back from MGM.'

'I needed the break. I can't listen to Mayer anymore. And I can't play my little flute, because Brackett broke it over his knee in a fit of pique. I don't know why. It was almost in tune.' He pulled out the chair opposite mine for Edith. 'Don't let me keep you two. My young friend and I have some business to discuss.' Junior eagerly hooked Wilder's arm and dragged him toward the table where Trixie, so help me, curtsied.

Edith seated herself. She shooed the waitress away, using the gesture as an excuse to peer back at Wilder and his new companions. Adjusting her thick glasses by their temples, she said, 'Why on earth is he sitting with Jerry the messenger?'

'He sees some of his own pluck on display.' Since we'd met, Edith Head had become my staunchest ally, my fiercest advocate, and my most indispensable nag. Using the same gentle seismic pressure that had forged the mountains of California, she had pushed me to claim a place for myself in this new land. And solve a murder or two along the way.

'Congratulations on getting to dress Ronald Colman,' I said, eager to flaunt my fresh knowledge.

'What?' Edith fussed with the stack of books as I explained. 'Oh, *that*. I've known about that for weeks.' She slid two tomes across the table, leaving a script directly in front of her. 'The croquet books you asked for. Seems like a great deal of fun. The clothes certainly look comfortable.'

'You're welcome to come. You have a standing invitation to any and all of Addison's activities.'

'I'm tempted, but I'm afraid my Sunday is spoken for.'

Her every waking minute, as far as I could tell. I nodded at the script. 'Is that your latest masterpiece?'

'One of several on my plate at the moment. It's the other reason I wanted to see you today.'

Off the lot, I thought as I wiped my fingertips with a napkin. Edith threw another glance at Wilder then turned to look pointedly back at Paramount before pushing the bound pages over to me.

STREETLIGHT STORY

by

George Dolan and

Clyde Fentress

'Don't think much of the title.' I fanned the pages. 'Is it a musical?'

'Heavens, no. A crime story. A B picture, to be honest.'

'I often like those more than the featured attractions. So there's a big, juicy murder.'

'More than one. May I have some of your water?' Edith didn't wait for my reply. She helped herself to a sip, leaving a ghostly imprint of lipstick on the glass. I had never seen her so nervous. 'It recounts a bank robbery, and the pursuit of the men responsible. I'm afraid I only recently learned the truth about the picture.'

'What truth?'

Edith reached across the table and took my hand. 'The script is based on the California Republic bank robbery of 1936.'

I pushed my sandwich aside. I couldn't eat now. Or for the foreseeable future.

TWO

On April 14, 1936, I was still living in New York City with my uncle Danny and aunt Joyce. I couldn't say with certainty what I did that particular Tuesday, but I could hazard a guess. Odds were I went to work in the basement of the Empire State Assurance Company, where I was a mediocre typist but excelled at avoiding the wandering hands of my boss Mr Armbruster. On the train ride home to Flushing, it's possible I tried to talk myself into entering the Miss Astoria Park beauty pageant, with its grand prize of a Hollywood screen test, being touted in the newspapers.

Three things I could guarantee were true of that date, though.

I had potatoes with my dinner, I wondered if anything special would ever happen to me, and that night I went to the pictures.

On the other side of the country that morning, three men pulled up outside the California Republic Bank branch on Vermont Avenue near Franklin in a black Ford. One of the men, Leo James Hoyer, remained in the car while the others, Borden C. Yates and Giuseppe 'Gio' Bianchi, went inside brandishing guns. Several bank patrons said the belligerent Bianchi behaved like a mad dog while Yates was quiet, even solicitous, fetching a chair for an elderly woman who felt faint. The two men exited the bank with twenty thousand dollars in cash.

They made it as far as the Ford. A police car in the vicinity responded immediately. The officers exchanged fire with the bandits. Bianchi and Patrolman Wendell Starnes were both killed at the scene. Starnes left behind two young daughters. Patrolman Eamonn Murphy took a bullet in the leg but continued to fire at the fleeing Ford containing Hoyer and Yates.

Two days later, Hoyer was found dead of injuries sustained in the shootout by Los Angeles Police Department Detectives Gene Morrow and Teddy Lomax. Only Borden Yates remained at large, the stolen twenty thousand dollars still missing. Teddy got a line on Yates's location. He and Gene followed the lead to a rundown Victorian on Bunker Hill, not far from where Gene grew up. The tip proved out. Yates's gentlemanly days had ended at the bank; he emerged from the house guns blazing. Teddy Lomax fell at once. Gene, in turn, cut Yates down with a shot that an eyewitness described as 'worthy of Wild Bill Hickok'.

That should have brought the sordid saga to a close. Only the money was never recovered, a fact that set tongues to wagging. Gene found himself dogged by rumors that he and Abigail Lomax, Teddy's widow, were an item and had been for some time. Never mind that Gene had known Abigail since childhood, had introduced her to the man she would marry, had served as best man at the wedding. The rumors still dogged Gene, with Teddy Lomax almost three years in the cold ground. The whispers didn't stop Gene from remaining close to Abigail, or prevent him from doing his job. The Los Angeles Police Department had a reputation for corruption, after all. A little dirt only helped Gene fit in.

Just over eighteen months later, my path would cross with his. We had been together ever since.

Not that Gene had filled in these particulars. He seldom spoke about the worst day of his life. Once, at a police function, he'd pointed out Eamonn Murphy to me, walking with a cane and an old man's gait. I had looked up the details in newspapers myself, and committed them all to memory.

I returned the script to Edith's side of the table, banishing it to whence it came. 'So I'll sit this picture out.'

'There's more, I'm afraid.' Edith shifted in her chair and looked directly into my eyes. 'The film's producer, Max Ramsey, is an old friend. Yesterday he told me the writer, or one of them, at any rate, knows what actually happened.'

'What do you mean, "actually"?' The tension in my voice resounded in the relative quiet of the restaurant. Billy Wilder turned to check on me. Even Trixie offered a pitying glance in my direction. *Mind your own business, Trixie.*

Edith as always remained unflappable, her tone level. 'The writer in question is a former convict, one who served time in San Quentin and elsewhere. He specializes in underworld stories, based on his own experience and what he learns from his . . . cohort. This writer didn't commit the robbery, but says he knows who did.'

'So do I.' I muscled the words past my clenched jaw. 'Giuseppe Bianchi, Leo Hoyer, and Borden Yates. They're all dead.'

'That they are.' The lenses of Edith's glasses swung back toward Paramount's Bronson Gate and her adjacent office window. She'd gone out on a limb for me, and I had to remember that. 'But this movie will tell a different story when it goes into production next week. According to the script, the robbery was conceived by a police detective, although here he's left the force. His former partner is killed in the pursuit of the thieves, and this man takes up with his wife.'

Now I knew why we were here, on the neutral ground of Oblath's. I reached back across the table for the script. 'What's this character's name? This sinister mastermind?'

Edith paused. She'd led me right up to the landmine. Time to learn if it would go off. 'Jim Morris.'

Gene Morrow, Jim Morris. Only the thinnest of veils for the writing duo of Dolan and Fentress. The name JIM leapt up at me from the pages. At least they'd given him plenty of dialogue.

From the kitchen came an angry sizzle, Oblath's beginning the shift into evening when it would churn out steaks and chops for the hungry Paramount hordes. The scents of meat and smoke made my stomach clench.

'I'd like to talk to your friend,' I heard myself say. 'The producer of this epic. I want this from the horse's mouth.'

The waitress, sensing I'd abandoned my lunch, slapped a bill on the table. Edith paid it. I rose woozily, like a bushwhacked boxer who wanted to punch back but didn't have his legs under him yet. Teetering toward the door, I spied Junior sulking at his table while Trixie spoke animatedly with Billy Wilder. She gently swatted him with her sailor hat, feigning outrage at something he'd said. Without the hat she seemed older, more like a wised-up veteran trying to salvage her career than some waif hoping for her big break. She and Wilder didn't notice us leaving.

Good on you, sister, I thought. *But remember this lesson. No matter how good you think you have it, Hollywood will always find a way to sandbag you.*

THREE

We double-timed across the lot, facsimiles of Jerry the messenger boy zipping by on bicycles. 'Max is something of a veteran,' Edith said. 'He's been with Paramount almost since the beginning. He knew Jesse Lasky. To hear him tell it, he scouted the ranch in Agoura before the studio bought it.'

I wondered if that's where we were walking. The messenger boys had become few and far between. We passed a man in a Foreign Legion uniform clutching a canteen, and I told myself he was working on a picture. Max Ramsey might have had seniority, but judging from the remote location of his office he didn't cut much ice at Paramount.

'He's with the B unit now,' Edith said, 'but he's part of the history of this place. Clara Bow took his advice as gospel. And Max was so kind to me when I started. I doubt I'd be here today if he hadn't requested me for some of his pictures in those early years. Normally, we'd shop *Streetlight Story*'s costumes, perhaps borrow a few items from stock. But Max asked me for a favor, and I simply couldn't say no. I told him I'd stretch the wardrobe budget to give the picture some distinction. I'm glad I did. I'd never have learned about the script's history otherwise.'

Edith was unusually chatty this afternoon, I thought, chalking it up to nerves. Then another explanation occurred to me. She was merely filling up my silences. I usually blathered incessantly whenever I visited the lot, questions tumbling out of me, every set prompting a memory of some favorite film. But I'd said next to nothing since we'd left Oblath's. The enormity of what Edith had told me had shaken me to my core.

I'd lived for the movies since I was a child. I really didn't want to hate them now.

We reached the frontier outpost where Max Ramsey was now stationed. The blonde working in his outer office barely glanced up from her magazine. I got more eye contact from a grinning Sonja Henie on the cover of *Photoplay* as the receptionist hooked a thumb toward the next door. 'He's in there,' she said, popping her gum.

Edith and I proceeded on unannounced. As we entered his office Max Ramsey lurched forward and slammed a meaty hand onto his telephone. Whether the pantomime was to indicate he was expecting an important call or had just ended one, I didn't know.

'For the last time, Max,' Edith said, 'fire that girl.'

'But I can't! She's my discovery!' Max hoisted himself out of his chair and came around the desk to embrace Edith. He was an imposing, barrel-chested presence, his frame sporting what had to be close to three hundred pounds. But the head perched atop his bulk, dusted with hair the color of iron filings, seemed to belong to an earlier, smaller model. Perhaps one from his heyday in the 1920s; his dated gray suit, double-breasted with flared lapels and wide-hemmed trousers, was a freshly tailored relic. He gazed out through deep-set eyes like a man under siege. Only one thing in Hollywood was worse than a producer who needed a hit, and Max Ramsey was it: a producer beginning to suspect that even a hit wouldn't save him.

Edith introduced me as a friend who worked for the well-known Addison Rice. Max proved his producer bona fides by immediately applying this information to his own woes. 'An Addison Rice party! That's what the nightclub scene has to be like. Not just gaiety but scale! A rambunctious energy! The whole picture falls apart if our boys look like pikers there. Are you sure you can manage it, Edith?'

'Of course. I promised you my best. I wanted to ask—'

'Suppose I could try springing a few more shekels from the coffers.' Max returned to his desk and placed his hand on the telephone again. He didn't lift the receiver; clearly it was more talisman than tool. 'Let the front office know *Streetlight Story* requires a certain sheen.'

'About the picture, Max.' Edith spoke in a patient voice, indulging an old friend. 'Lillian and I wanted some information on the writer you told me about—'

'Fentress!' He thundered the name as if summoning a Norse god. 'Only reason I did this picture. It's not your usual programmer. Thanks to Clyde Fentress, it'll have the stink of real life.'

It certainly stank of something. 'I'd like to know a little more about this real-life business,' I said. 'Edith tells me Fentress has been in prison.'

'More than once. Used to be a thief. Occasional strong-arm stuff, but mainly he was a burglar. Even escaped from prison a time or two. Wrote a picture about one of his crashouts. I wanted to do it here, but there was no interest.'

'How'd he become a writer?' I asked.

'On his last turn up in Q' – Max shivered, thrilling at his own use of hardboiled lingo for San Quentin – 'he started writing for the prison journal. His scribblings came to the attention of a big name literary type back East.'

'H.L. Mencken, I believe,' Edith said.

'Mencken. He under contract out here? Anyway, Clyde was one of several fellows in stir who showed a knack for storytelling. Mencken became their advocate. They started selling ideas to the studios back in the twenties while they were still locked up. Jailbird scribes, can you imagine? Say, that'd be a good angle to promote this picture. Adolph, Jesse and I bought a few of Clyde's stories, but didn't make them. He was more of a Warners talent back then, grittier stuff. The kind of thing I could use right now, I don't mind telling you. The writing helped get him paroled, and Clyde's been cranking them out since.'

'Is *Streetlight Story* based on a real crime?' I asked.

'That's what drew me to it. A bank robbery over on Wilshire in 1935.'

'Franklin in 1936,' Edith said.

'Yes, well, the details don't matter. Liberties have been taken with the facts, but I have it on Clyde's authority we're getting the truth. He's done his homework. Scandalous, what happened, when you think about it.'

I wanted credit for my good behavior. I didn't scream, or cry, or wrench the phone from under Max's hand and hurl it at his tiny, tiny head. 'And your movie is just going to put Clyde's version of events out there, unchecked.' No matter who it hurts.' Max's gaze shifted to Edith in something resembling alarm. 'Lillian knows some of the people involved,' she said. 'Ah. I see. Let me assure you, you have nothing to fear. Names and locations have been changed.' 'Not enough.' I snapped off the words as if biting into pemmican.

I knew I was making Max uncomfortable when he turtled back and finally relinquished his hold on the telephone. He commenced his argument by blithely contradicting himself. 'The picture isn't based on fact, per se. The actual robbery's more of an inspiration. It's why we partnered Clyde with the other fella, Dolan, ex-newspaperman. To clean the material up. Fentress, you see, he knows that milieu, the characters, the way the environment shapes and bends these people. Again, Warners-type material. He's merely using the robbery as a framework. Just to give it—'

'The stink of real life,' I finished for him.

'Precisely. So you understand.' He beamed at me, now that we were speaking the same language. 'We need some of that realism for the nightclub scene. The glamour, the extravagance. Like one of your Addison's parties! Any pointers you can give?'

'I'll see what I can do,' I said.

My flat line reading didn't register in Max's ears. Having heard what he wanted to hear, he turned to Edith. 'You can work miracles. I've seen you do it before, Edie. I need it again.' He attempted puppy dog eyes, but only succeeded in looking like an aging hound trying to avoid another trip to the veterinarian's office.

Edith, to my surprise, played parrot. 'I'll see what I can do,' she said.

The needy Max required reassurance on several other scenes, so I made to leave. Edith squeezed my hand as we said goodbye. 'Don't forget this,' she said, pressing the copy of *Streetlight Story*'s script on me. I didn't want it, but I couldn't leave it behind.

As soon as Max's door closed, I took off running. Tracking down Clyde Fentress might take some time.

Writers' offices were scattered across the Paramount lot. I went to the closest building housing several of them and trotted along its length, reading the names off each closed door. There was a noticeable lack of clacking keys on this Friday afternoon. I'd probably have better luck locating Fentress if I went back to Oblath's.

On I went, mounting the building's exterior staircase and scouting the upstairs tenants. No sign of Fentress's name. Down below a bicycle rolled past bearing Jerry the messenger boy, formerly known as Junior. Feet braced on the handlebars, cocky grin smeared across his face.

I hollered down at him. 'How'd you do? The girl say yes?'

Jerry brought the bike to an effortless halt. 'Taking her to the pictures tonight. Who are you, anyway?'

'Cupid. Don't let the duds fool you. Where can a gal find a writer named Clyde Fentress?'

'Deep in the wilds of the lot. Southeast corner, over by Van Ness. End of the row.'

At the very least, I figured, all this walking had to be doing wonders for my legs.

I knew Fentress's office was empty. I sensed his absence as I approached and hammered on the door anyway. Nobody answered. None of the neighboring doors opened at the racket I raised either, including the one bearing George Dolan's name. Friday had indeed come to the lot early.

'We both musta missed him.' The voice emerged from the shadows at the corner of the somewhat shabby building. I turned toward it and instantly wished I hadn't.

The man had brown hair, neatly combed and parted. His suit was well kept, despite being the color of boarding-house wash-water. But no one, it was safe to say, took in these attributes, at least not at first. Not with the man's left eye commanding your attention. It drooped, as if it had been set lower in his face. Worse, because of some palsy or nerve damage it functioned independently of the right eye, never quite looking where its partner did.

Naturally, the man didn't comment on his condition himself. 'Clyde's probably out drinking, given the hour. Trying to avoid his missus. She's a piece of work. Sorry, where are my manners? Name's Nap.' He bowed slightly as he introduced himself, the left eye rolling up to leer at me.

Completely nonplussed, I blurted out the first thing that came to mind. 'Short for Napoleon?'

'Short for Aloysius. Aloysius Conlin, if this is a cotillion. They call me Nap, because, well . . .' He casually flicked a finger against his cheekbone, close enough to his wandering eye that I flinched. 'This tends to make me look sleepy.'

What was I supposed to say, that I hadn't noticed? Instead I nodded. 'I suppose it does.'

Conlin scanned the lot. His left eye sought me out. Like the picture of Jesus Christ hanging over my aunt Joyce's dining room table in Flushing, Nap Conlin always seemed to be looking at me. 'So who are you? You work on the lot?'

'Lillian. I came from Mr Ramsey's office. How do you know Clyde?'

'From around.'

'Around where? Maybe prison?' I scraped up a smile I didn't feel. 'Some of us have heard Clyde's story.'

'Figures. What, did this give it away?' Again he slapped a finger near his damaged eyeball and I almost screamed. 'Yeah, Clyde and I met in stir. Folsom, it was, years back now. I knew right away he was smarter than me, had it knocked. Caught on to this writer's racket. Me, I'm no good with words, so I'm just a humble actor.'

'You are?'

'Trying to make a go of it, anyway. Just extra work so far, but I'm signed on at Central Casting. You mighta seen me in *The Cornerman*, boxing picture RKO did. I'm one of a row of plug uglies in the gym. Roles like that are my specialty. Providing character, which I got to spare.' He waggled his eyebrows, the left one still responding to direct orders. 'My look helps me get on any lot I want, provided I come by after lunch.'

I stared at him, not understanding. For the third time, he smacked his face near his eye, this time with genuine hostility.

'I tell 'em at the gate this is make-up and I got to get back to the set. It's not like the guy's gonna come in for a closer look. Works every time. Worked today. I'm here, ain't I?'

I agreed with him. He certainly was. 'Are you hoping to catch on in Clyde's next picture?'

'Figure it never hurts to ask. *Streetlight Story* is sure to be a doozy.'

My hand began to ache. I realized I'd rolled up my copy of the *Streetlight Story* script, clenching it until my fingers had gone numb. 'What makes you say that?'

'Based on a real caper. Clyde told me the story. He's been carrying it around for years.'

'And he's always on the level?'

'Always. If he says something happened a certain way, you can believe it. He's got great respect for his whatchacall craft.' Conlin nodded crisply for emphasis. 'I help him sometimes. Keep my ear to the ground and my eye open.' He thrust his left orb toward me and chortled. I willed myself not to recoil. 'Anything I hear from the boys, any good stories, I pass 'em along, see if he can use 'em in pictures. He throws me a few bucks if he does. He's a good egg, Clyde. Had some choice scuttlebutt to share with him today, a real corker of a yarn, but I got here too late.' Conlin slid along the railing closer to me. 'Say, maybe we can find ol' Clyde together. You know where a fella might wet his whistle around here?'

I stared levelly into his right eye. 'Sorry,' I told him. 'I've got no idea.'

STREETLIGHT STORY

A-4 CLOSE SHOT — NEWSPAPER HEADLINE

The banner reading: 'STRING OF ROBBERIES BAFFLES POLICE.'

After a moment, THE CAMERA BEGINS TO MOVE BACK.

A-5 THE EXTERIOR OF THE CLUB MADRID

The marquee is dim. It reads 'Eric Richlieu and his Continental Orchestra — Dining — Dancing — Entertainment.' Many people bustle past during the lunch hour. They ignore the young newsie outside the night-club, doing his level best to sell papers.

NEWSIE
Read all about it! Get your paper!

Eddie Lawrence walks up to the lad, a nickel already in his hand. He flips it into the air. The newsie hands Eddie a

paper and snatches the coin. Eddie stops
to survey the front page.

>   EDDIE
> Baffled, it says. Who's baffled?

>   NEWSIE
> If the paper says it, it's got to be
> so.

Eddie grumbles and raises the newspaper,
making as if to swat the kid. The boy
sticks out his tongue at Eddie and scampers
away.

>   EDDIE
>   (talking to himself)
> Nobody's baffled. We're just stuck.
>   (yelling after the kid)
> We're just stuck, that's all.

He walks toward the entrance of the Club
Madrid. A sign dangles from the door reading
'Closed.' Eddie smirks at the sign, nudges
it aside, and goes into the club.

A-6 INSIDE THE CLUB MADRID — FULL SHOT

The elevated stage is bare. Most of the
tables arrayed around it have been draped
with cloths.

A-7 EDDIE

He walks into the club and stops at the
only table that has been laid out for
the evening. He picks up a linen napkin
and inspects it, then waves it daintily
in the air, finding it a bit frou-frou.
He tosses the napkin back on the table.

A clatter erupts behind him. Eddie turns around and sees a trio of chorines in their rehearsal togs coming down from the stage. Eddie doffs his hat as they walk past, goggling at him.

>   EDDIE
>   Afternoon, ladies.

The first of the dancers giggles at Eddie, her laughter spilling like toppling dominoes through her compatriots as they continue out. Eddie shrugs at their reaction and begins inspecting the flatware.

A-8 JENKINS — BY THE KITCHEN DOOR

Jenkins, the nightclub's general dogsbody, limps in from the kitchen dragging a mop and bucket. He sees Eddie lifting a fork to the light and scowls at him.

A-9 JENKINS AND EDDIE

>   JENKINS
>   Help yourself, why don't you. We're
>   closed.

>   EDDIE
>   Yeah, I know. The sign on the door
>   told me.

>   JENKINS
>   (angrily)
>   You don't listen too good, then. Why
>   don't you take it on the arches, pal?

>   EDDIE
>   Supposing I was invited.

                    JENKINS
                (confused)
        Well, were you?

Eddie puts the fork down, taking care to
arrange it neatly. Jenkins fumes at him.

                    EDDIE
        I'm looking for Jim Morris. Understand
        he's the head man around here.

                    JENKINS
                (belligerently)
        Who's looking for him?

                    EDDIE
        Eddie Lawrence is.

                    JENKINS
        And who's Eddie Lawrence when he's at
        home?

Eddie pulls back his suit jacket, revealing
the detective's shield clipped to his
belt. Jenkins gulps.

                    JENKINS
        Why didn't you tell me you were a
        cop?

                    EDDIE
        You were busy telling me you were closed.

A-10   ARLENE — AT THE CLUB MADRID'S DOOR

        Arlene pulls the door open to find Eddie
        and Jenkins.

A-11   CLUB MADRID — FULL SHOT

Eddie spots Arlene entering and doffs his
hat with a small smile. Jenkins sees her
and shakes his head.

                    JENKINS
  You're too early.

                    ARLENE
  Excuse me?

                    JENKINS
  Auditions for the chorus are after
  lunch. Two o'clock.
        (looking her up and down)
  I'd definitely come back if I were you.

                    EDDIE
  Good thing you're not.

He walks over to Arlene and chastely kisses
her on the cheek.

                    EDDIE
  Hello, sweetheart. They're closed.

                    ARLENE
  I know. The sign on the door told me.

Jenkins stares from one to the other and
back. He starts beating a retreat to the
kitchen.

                    JENKINS
  I'm going to—

                    EDDIE
  Yeah, why don't you?

Jenkins vanishes through the kitchen doors.
Arlene shakes her head at Eddie.

                    ARLENE
Do you have to pick on everybody?

                    EDDIE
Sure. Part of the fun of the job.

He pulls Arlene close to give her a real
kiss. As they do, Jim Morris emerges from
the kitchen. He is being fitted for a
tuxedo, the jacket still covered with
chalk marks. He sees Eddie and Arlene in
the clinch and shakes his head.

The kitchen door flies open again and a
tailor comes out, his hands knotted in worry.

                    TAILOR
Meester Morris, I no-a finish your suit.

                    JIM
We've got time, Carlo.
     (yelling at Eddie and Arlene)
Easy over there! Around here people
pay good money for that kind of show!

Eddie and Arlene laugh. The tailor toddles
back into the kitchen in agitation.

                    EDDIE
That fella who greeted me new around
here?

                    JIM
Second day on the job.

                    EDDIE
Might want to give him the sack.

                    JIM
Good help's hard to find. Haven't you heard?

                    EDDIE
Yeah. We've lost some good men down
at the department lately. You're one
of them.

                    JIM
Starting this number again. And me
without the violins here yet.

                    ARLENE
        (quickly playing peacemaker)
It's a beautiful club, Jim.

                    JIM
It is now that you're here.

                    EDDIE
Old Silver Tongue. Probably helps in
your line.

                    JIM
Didn't do much for me when I was on
the force. Fella could make a living
but not any money.

                    EDDIE
Fella could also do some good, if he
wanted.

                    JIM
I do plenty of good here. Time away
from your cares and woe is a service
too. I could use a partner.

                    EDDIE
Sez you.

                    JIM
                (seriously)
I mean it, Eddie. I could use someone

who knows this city the way you do.
Who can stop trouble before it starts.
The Club Madrid is coming up flush. You
could finally make some real money.

                    EDDIE
The city pays me enough.

Jim smiles at Arlene.

                    JIM
I'm talking about enough money to treat
your lovely wife the way she deserves.

                    ARLENE
Eddie's always taken good care of me.

                    EDDIE
                (testy)
You heard the testimony, Your Honor.
Is that why you brought me here, to
make your big pitch? I thought the
three of us were going to load up on
chow mein, like in the old days.

                    JIM
Table at Chao Lin's is already waiting.
I just thought I'd ask again because
of what I read in the paper this morning.

                    EDDIE
                (annoyed)
Baffled. Nobody's baffled. We're—

                    JIM
—just stuck, that's all. Sure, I remember.

                    EDDIE
We'll crack this one, I promise you.
Reminds me, I should call downtown.

                    JIM
Got a hot tip in the fifth race, do
you?

                   EDDIE
Yep, and I placed that bet this morning.

                    JIM
Of course you did. Phone's at the
front desk. Tell them I said it's OK.

                   EDDIE
Mighty white of you.

Eddie leaves to make his phone call.
Arlene smiles at Jim.

                  ARLENE
Do I get the grand tour?

                    JIM
Sure thing. In a minute.

A-12 CLOSE SHOT — ARLENE AND JIM

    Jim moves closer to speak to Arlene in
    confidence.

                    JIM
I could use your help convincing him.

                  ARLENE
Eddie's his own man. Always has been.
You knew that when you introduced us.

                    JIM
He's never faced a united front before.
If we both worked on him . . .

                    ARLENE
Would it really make a difference?
Being a police officer is all Eddie's
ever wanted. Who am I to take that
away from him?

                    JIM
          (after a long pause)
I never should have let you get away.
Ready for that tour?

                    ARLENE
              (nervous)
I should see what's keeping Eddie.

She hurries off after her husband. Jim
watches her with a crooked smile on his
face. He shakes his head and heads for
the kitchen.

                    JIM
              (shouting)
Carlo! Get out here and finish my suit!

              END OF SEQUENCE 'A'

FOUR

I read *Streetlight Story* in a hamburger joint far enough from
Paramount to minimize the chance of encountering familiar faces.
I didn't want any interruptions. The movie unspooled across my
mind's eye with the aroma of onions instead of popcorn as
accompaniment.

I hated it. *Streetlight Story*'s script was, to use a word I'd learned
back in New York, *dreck*. One hundred and four pages of claptrap
with the occasional snappy wisecrack and spots for two songs.
Another version of me – the one who'd stayed in Flushing, perhaps

– would have enjoyed the movie made from it. But I wasn't that me. I was this one, and the notion of this picture playing in theaters shrouded me in dread.

In the script, Gene – sorry, *Jim* – was a sharpie with a surplus of charm and a quick line forever at his disposal. He bankrolled the nightclub he'd opened after quitting the police force with proceeds from a string of robberies he'd masterminded by exploiting his knowledge of both sides of the law. He also carried a torch for Arlene, who was most definitely *not Abigail*, the girl he'd foolishly introduced to his tough-as-nails heart-of-gold ex-partner Eddie. Any similarity to Teddy was purely coincidental.

After a big, glamorous nightclub scene that was clearly the cause of Max Ramsey's fretting, Jim steers Eddie toward a confrontation with his handpicked hair-trigger crew. Following a bank robbery, Eddie is shot and killed – only he isn't, playing possum so he can get the drop on his old friend, busy with his designs on the (presumed) widow Lawrence. I didn't buy the plot twist. It seemed needlessly cruel to poor Arlene, a character I didn't want to feel sorry for. It was crueler still to the gods of plausibility, the whole megillah grafted on to give the enterprise a happy ending. I understood the logic, though; *Streetlight Story* would be the second half of the bill, meant to send audiences home on an up-note.

Max hadn't lied. The details *were* different; as far as I knew, the California Republic bank robbery had never been tied to any other crimes. But I still loathed the tale they told. Clyde Fentress was positing that Gene had not only orchestrated the heist, he'd arranged Teddy's death to get Abigail. The very thought pained me. What pained me even more was having to tell them about it.

Gene had inherited Teddy's seat at a cops' poker night. He said he'd be happy to back out of it. He'd lost enough money lately.

Abigail told me it was a pleasure to hear my voice. She only had a quiet evening at home with the radio planned, so getting together would be no imposition at all. Fun, even. It had been too long since we'd seen each other.

The prospect of being hemmed in by exhausted strangers on streetcars drove me mad, so I splurged on a taxicab to take me to Gene's house on Bunker Hill. The taxi pulled up outside the ramshackle Victorian, and I couldn't bring myself to go in. I hiked past the Shell station on the corner to a drug store I didn't like and ordered a coffee I didn't want. I let it cool in front of me, then drank it out of spite. Having summoned Gene and Abigail, I was the one who would be late.

I finally knocked on Gene's door. He answered at once. His brown hair and his shirt collar hung limply at the end of a long day, but his eyes crackled with life. 'It's our mysterious mistress of ceremonies,' he said loudly, then pulled me inside his home and his arms.

'Hello,' he whispered in my ear.

Making sure we remained in the privacy of the tiny entry alcove, he kissed me. The stubble on his chin scraped my face, the corner of a table dug into my back, my knees buckled. For a moment I thought about taking his hand and rushing out into the night, leaving Los Angeles and the picture business behind us.

Abigail waited in the front room. She hadn't changed after work, wearing a navy blue straight skirt, an ivory blouse, and a baby blue cardigan with an openwork pattern on the front that she'd probably knitted herself. She flitted over and embraced me, so delicate I could feel her heart beating against my chest. She was right; it *had* been a while since I'd seen her. Gene and I had withdrawn from her over the past few months after deciding – mutually, I reassured myself – that the three of us were spending too much time together. She was her usual lively presence, the little girl breathlessness of her voice making you want to draw her close and protect her.

I hadn't missed that quality, I had to admit. Not at all.

A few moments of idle chatter and snacks foraged from Gene's poorly stocked kitchen followed. Schoolteacher Abigail was already looking forward to the summer but needed another job; did I know if Tremayne's, the department store where I'd once worked, was hiring? Gene groused amiably about work, sending me reassuring glances. I'd convened this little meeting. He'd hold the floor until I felt ready to address it.

My nerves frayed, I placed the copy of the *Streetlight Story* script onto the coffee table, the pages beginning to curl up like waves from my constant worrying of them.

'I should have guessed,' Gene said with a smile. 'You visited Edith.'

'You already know the story in her new picture,' I said. 'Just not told like this.'

I laid it out from start to finish. I rued my decision to have a cup of coffee, the liquid congealing in my stomach, but with determination I saw the tale through. Finally, I sat back, the silence broken

only by the rattle of ice cubes as Gene massaged a tumbler of
whiskey between his palms. He stared at his reflection in the bay
window, the better to admire his sideways grin of disbelief.

Then Abigail unleashed a huge, wrenching sob.

I didn't wait for Gene to console her. The sisters at St Mary's
had trained me well. I ran to Abigail and she flung herself at me,
hot and trembling, the shudders wracking her frail form coming
from a deep and contained place.

'Why are they doing this?' she asked through tears. 'Why can't
they leave us alone? Teddy's gone and we want some peace.'

Us? I thought as I tutted and stroked her head. *We?*

'Maybe no one will make the connection,' I said. 'But people
involved with the movie are touting it as a true story and I thought
you both should know.'

'What's this jailbird writer's name? Clyde Fentress?' Gene's voice
was even. 'Don't know the man. But I'll find out all there is about
him by tomorrow.'

Abigail turned toward Gene. 'You have to tell Lillian.'

I fought off a shudder of my own. 'Tell me what?'

'More big news!' Gene set his glass down. 'Our esteemed district
attorney Buron Fitts has quietly reopened the investigation into the
California Republic bank robbery. Specifically they're looking at
the circumstances of Teddy's death.'

'What? Why?'

'Because we have a new reform-minded mayor and the DA's
looking to curry favor. He thinks he has a tiger by the tail with this
one. It's got everything. Missing money and the possibility of a
police officer murdered by his partner.'

The air rushed out of my body. A moment later, I felt Abigail's
hand cradling my face. We had switched roles; now she offered
comfort to me.

'It's still in the early stages,' Gene continued matter-of-factly. 'All
being handled on the QT directly out of Fitts's office. Rumor is
they're reviewing every aspect of the case, but paying particular
attention to me.' He laughed; the sound was hollow. 'Amazing I still
have friends who'd pass along rumors to a stone-hearted blackguard
like myself. Must be after some of that twenty grand I have stashed
away.'

'How can you joke about this?' My voice cracked and my eyes
sought out the *Streetlight Story* script. I wished Gene hadn't sealed

up his fireplace, so I could consign its offending pages to the flames. 'Why now, after three years? Is this because of the movie?'

'No,' Gene said. 'This is the first I've heard of *Streetlight Story* or Clyde Fentress, so it's unlikely. Something else lit a fire under Fitts.'

'We don't know what it is.' Abigail had at some point taken both of my hands in hers.

I couldn't give shape to my next question, but then I didn't have to bother. Abigail spent every day working with children. She was accomplished at divining what was on the minds of those who couldn't properly string words together. 'As soon as Gene heard about the investigation, he let me know. We've spent the last few weeks figuring out how to handle it.'

'Weeks?' I said. 'When did you find out?'

'It's ridiculous.' Gene paced the perimeter of his well-worn rug. 'Fitts has enough skeletons in his closet to fill Forest Lawn. And the brother of our last illustrious mayor was just found guilty of cooking the city books to sell jobs. But what are they doing? Coming after me. At least I'll go out in glory. I'm getting a damn *picture* made about me.' He gestured at the script and the title page fluttered.

Abigail instinctively smoothed it flat. 'Lillian? Would it be all right if I borrowed this? I'd like to read it.'

'What for?' Gene asked.

'Well, if Teddy's a character . . .' She hesitated. 'It would be like having him back for a while.'

'He's not a character,' Gene said. 'The script's nothing but bushwa.'

'Of course you can have it!' I assured her. 'If that's what you want.'

'It is. At least, I think it is.' Abigail lifted the script uneasily, as if expecting it to snap at her. 'Who's playing in it, anyway?'

It was a sign of how rattled I was that I'd never thought to ask Edith. 'I'll find out,' I promised.

'Tell them it's Gable for me or bust.' Gene clapped his hands. 'I don't know about you ladies, but the condemned man could use a hearty meal.'

'Don't call yourself that,' Abigail said. 'And I couldn't possibly eat.'

'Me, neither,' I added.

'While I could eat a horse, jockey and saddle included. Let's go up the street to Tony's for some spaghetti. I'll polish off what you don't finish.'

I excused myself to powder my nose. As I started down the hall, Gene walked over to Abigail. His arms enfolded her slight frame. I ran the rest of the way to the bathroom.

I understood perfectly why Gene had confided in Abigail regarding the DA's investigation. Had he told me about it, I would have immediately asked if she knew.

But he hadn't told me. He'd known about the DA's interest for weeks, Abigail had said. We'd seen how many movies and shared countless cups of coffee in that time without Gene breathing a word of his troubles. Why hadn't he brought me into the fold too? Gene and Abigail were a united front, while I was excluded.

United front. Where had I just come across that phrase?

In a line from *Streetlight Story*. I cursed the script again as I locked the door behind me.

FIVE

I was scrubbing my apartment with hot water in a cold fury when a downstairs neighbor shouted that I had a telephone call. Gene sounded in deceptively high spirits. 'Happy Saturday. Are we still stepping out tonight?'

'I'd understand if you'd rather cancel.'

'I promised you, didn't I?'

'Is that what I am to you? An obligation?' I chided playfully. 'You know where I am. Come get me.'

When he did, I was garbed for gaiety in a navy crepe dress with a white linen bib collar and matching ruffle cuffs, and liberally spritzed with Coque d'Or, the perfume that had been one of Addison's several Christmas gifts to me. I waited until we broke our clinch to ask, 'Did you learn anything?'

'About what?'

'Clyde Fentress. Last night you said you'd find out all there was on him.'

Gene wearily rubbed his eye, which roused disturbing images of Nap Conlin. 'I asked around.'

'And?'

'And Fentress robbed a dance hall in Oakland at the tender age of fourteen. Graduated from youth camp to matriculate at several other fine California institutions. Plied his trade around San Francisco mostly. Would resort to violence only when necessary, but on those occasions took to it with aplomb. Can't gauge him as a writer of pictures because I haven't seen his work, but by all accounts a tough customer.'

'I don't like the sound of him.'

'Clyde doesn't worry me.'

'What does worry you?'

Gene couldn't conceal his exasperation. 'It's Saturday night, Frost. I'm trying not to worry about anything. You aren't making it easy.'

I responded by making the ultimate sacrifice. 'OK. You choose the picture.'

'Jesus, I'm not in that much trouble.'

'I want you to enjoy yourself. What haven't you seen?'

'*They Made Me a Criminal.*'

'Be serious.'

'I heard it was good. There's another one called *Sergeant Madden.* Cops and robbers.'

It would not have been my first choice, not with *Midnight*, a new romantic comedy co-written by Billy Wilder and featuring costumes by Edith Head, playing. It wouldn't have been my fourth or fifth, either. But when the name Josef von Sternberg appeared in the film's titles I relaxed, Gene's fingers entwined in mine. Von Sternberg had directed all those gorgeous pictures starring Marlene Dietrich, who I could attest was even more swoon-worthy in person.

Only here the object of Von Sternberg's attention wasn't Dietrich's exotic mystery but the blunt features of Wallace Beery. He played a stage-Irish cop, forever puffing on his pipe and lecturing the good-looking but pigheaded son who'd followed him onto the force.

By the time young Madden, framed for a crime he didn't commit, was shipped to Sing Sing, my hand and Gene's had long gone their separate ways. As the son died in a hail of gunfire, a victim of hard luck and his own stubbornness, I shrank into my seat while Gene chuckled darkly through the onslaught.

Outside the theater, I mentioned dinner knowing Gene would instead suggest an early night. On the ride home I berated myself for not insisting we see *Three Smart Girls Grow Up*. Nobody ever got railroaded in a Deanna Durbin picture.

*   *   *

I arrived early for Sunday mass to say a prayer to Saint Raymond Nonnatus, patron of the falsely accused. Gene hadn't officially joined their ranks yet, but as my uncle Danny said, it never hurt to put a word in with the right man. Confession was being heard at that hour, and I briefly considered joining the queue. *Bless me, Father, for I have sinned. It's been fourteen days since my last confession. I have told white lies, coveted my neighbor's cute jumper, and wished ill on everyone involved with a Paramount production except the costume designer, who really should have shopped the picture's wardrobe.* I resisted the impulse because I feared ending up in the confessional opposite Father Nugent, and when he asked if *Streetlight Story* had a good role for Pat O'Brien, I'd have to say the actor would make a perfect Eddie.

The good father's homily explicated the Sermon on the Mount by drawing repeatedly on *Angels with Dirty Faces*. My kind of sermon.

I emerged from church to find the sidewalk speckled. It was raining. Drizzling, to be precise, the light precipitation a pleasant change of pace – unless, of course, you were hosting a croquet party.

Addison's Cadillac waited at the curb as scheduled. I let myself in, knowing Rogers, Addison's chauffeur, wouldn't budge from the car to aid me, even under postcard-perfect conditions. He harbored a childish grudge simply because during an ill-advised driving lesson I'd almost gotten us both killed.

'Better get going, and don't spare the whip!' I cried. Rogers spent the next minute and a half adjusting mirrors, then rolled the car slowly forward.

The rain hadn't intensified by the time we reached Chez Rice. Still, the household help transported tables from the lawn to the lobby. My benevolent boss Addison Rice supervised from a doorway. He had donned a festive tam o'shanter, the matching argyle vest stretched to its breaking point over his stomach. 'It's not much of a sport if it's at the whims of the weather.' He pouted.

I took the croquet mallet that dangled from his hand, noticing the smashed pane of glass at ankle level. 'I'll send the league a strongly worded letter. What's the plan?'

'We'll have an indoor picnic instead. I've requisitioned blankets from the linen closets.' I fell in and set about my tasks. Within an hour the fun was in full swing, a phonograph filling the foyer with music as Dorothy Lamour demonstrated a suggestive dance

from one of her jungle movies. I didn't join in the appreciative
hooting, though, preoccupied with Gene's predicament and my
complete inability to help him. Through the window I watched
Mr Ayoshi, wearing a slicker and trailed by an assistant carrying
an umbrella, as he carefully removed croquet hoops and reclaimed
what was his.

The rain slacked off by evening. I would bid farewell to this disap-
pointing weekend by luxuriating in the splendor of Edith's creations
for *Midnight*. As I contemplated which friend might accompany me,
a knock came at my apartment door. Soft but insistent, a mouse
carrying an important message.

Abigail retreated from the threshold when I responded, then
laughed at her own timidity. I waved her inside. 'This place is
darling,' she cooed. 'I've always wanted to see it.'

That's right, I thought, Abigail hadn't visited my humble
Hollywood abode before. For that matter, she and I had never been
alone together without Gene in a nearby room. Absent his gravity,
which had pulled us both close, we'd never really bonded.

'I'm sorry to drop in, but I thought you might need this back.'
Abigail thrust the *Streetlight Story* script toward me. It looked
like she'd run a warm iron over the pages. 'Thank you for letting
me borrow it.'

'You didn't have to trouble yourself. You read it, then.'

'I did.'

The lengthy ensuing pause sent my movie-going plans out the
window. 'The drug store up the street does Dutch apple pie on
Sundays,' I said idly.

'With crumbs on top?'

Ensconced in a booth with flaky goodness to fortify us, I broached
the subject of *Streetlight Story* anew. 'What did you make of the
script?'

'It was strange. Like looking in one of those mirrors at a carnival
that warps your reflection, so it's close to but not quite you.'

'That must have been unsettling.'

'On the contrary. Every once in a while, there'd be a glimmer
of my Teddy. It was nice to see him again.' Abigail chased strudel
around her plate with a fork. 'They got his attitude right. Lots of
bluster. And he did love betting on the horses, although that wasn't
always funny like it is in the script. And the way he and Gene ribbed

each other. I'm not sure I can watch two actors do that.' She discreetly dabbed her eyes with a handkerchief. I hadn't seen her reach for it, then realized she'd kept it wadded in her palm as a precaution in case she needed it during our talk. She seemed awfully young to be a widow.

I scrambled to change the subject slightly. 'I thought you came off well.'

'Really?' Abigail wrinkled her nose. 'My character seemed kind of thin.'

'You have two men in love with you!'

'I suppose that's the way to look at it.' She tapped her fork against porcelain. 'That Jim was a real louse.'

'Charming, though.'

'True. He has all the best lines, which should make Gene happy. He's so frustrated by the district attorney's investigation. He has no idea what prompted it. He wants it to become public or dry up and blow away. Until then, he'll joke about the sky falling.'

And what if it did fall? 'I wish there was some way I could help.'

'But you did. You spared us a rude surprise by telling us about this movie. It's not like you could investigate the bank robbery.'

The thought struck with such force it drove me back into my seat, almost knocking the fork from my hand. Abigail reached toward me. 'Are you all right?'

'I'm fine. I just realized we can have these pies *à la mode*. What do you say?'

Monday morning posed a major problem. I was trying to make a musical with George Raft.

'The Trocadero!' Addison announced as he moved his token around the board. 'Excellent! I could use a rest.'

Faced with finding a Christmas gift for Addison, the man who literally had everything and could invent whatever came next, I opted for silliness. I'd purchased the Transogram Movie Millions board game, the object of which was to mount a production by building the right hand of cards. Addison had insisted we play as soon as he opened the box on Christmas Eve, and dealt a hand to me several mornings a week. Photographs of Hollywood luminaries adorned the cards and most of them had been guests in Addison's home, a fact that tickled my employer no end. I shuffled my hand. Joan Blondell and Shirley Ross smiled up at me, but unless I swapped out Raft with Bing Crosby, my dream of making *The Runaway Cinderella* would die aborning. I didn't worry about who was behind the camera; according to the game's rules, a good director could tackle pictures of any stripe but Ray Milland could only appear in westerns, a fact that undoubtedly came as news to him.

As we played, Addison plotted his agenda for the coming months. 'Springtime in Los Angeles! Let's celebrate! A season of soirées! I'm toying with a Zodiac theme to start. It might require hiring some farm animals, though. And some twins. But be sure to schedule Thursday afternoon workshop time for the next few weeks. Hedy and I are on the verge.'

'Is Miss Lamarr's idea panning out?'

'It's intriguing, to say the least. Still a few wrinkles to be worked out, but she's onto something.' Only my employer, a man who'd made a mint designing radio parts, could meet the actress billed as 'The World's Most Beautiful Woman' and wind up collaborating with her on some harebrained engineering scheme.

I jotted down a note about Addison's lab time on the pad I kept handy. With frustration, Addison tossed down a card bearing the handsome face of Fred MacMurray. 'That tears it. I give up on romance. But I love a mystery.' He chortled. 'Just like that show on the radio.'

'From the makers of Fleischmann's Yeast.' Time to present my own harebrained scheme. 'On the subject of your parties. When I saw Edith on Friday I met the producer of her next movie. He told me your parties inspired a scene in the film.'

'You don't say.' Addison absently laid his cards on the table face-up. Yep, he held Crosby. I was never getting my musical off the ground. 'What's the fellow's name?'

'Max Ramsey. An old hand at Paramount, knew Jesse Lasky. Said your parties had great energy and tasteful opulence.'

Addison repeated the last two words, relishing how they felt on his tongue. 'When did we have him here?'

'We didn't. That's purely his impression from the columns.'

'Remedy that, Lillian. Invite Max to the next one. In fact, let's schedule one so we can invite him to it.'

'Consider it done.' I shuffled my cards and, with an exaggerated sigh, threw down Gail Patrick. Addison's mystery needed a leading lady. 'Max even asked for details on your parties to help plan the scene.'

'Did he?' Addison was so pleased he didn't notice I'd surrendered

Gail Patrick. I had to nudge the card again. 'Feel free to share whatever he'd like to know.'

'Good. I didn't want to say anything without your permission.' Now to bait the hook. 'It did occur to me you should receive something in return.'

Addison smiled and gestured at his ornate office. 'There's nothing I need.'

'That may be true, but there is something you want. I know it's your dream to appear in a picture.'

A sharp intake of breath. 'You don't think that's possible?'

'It could be, as you're providing technical help. It only seems fair. I'm not saying you'd end up on one of these cards like – who is that? – Gail Patrick. You wouldn't have a speaking role. You'd be an extra. But you'd be in the picture.'

Addison leaned back to mull the notion while I fussed with my remaining cards as if his decision didn't matter. But it was the key to ending my malaise and helping Gene. Abigail had been correct. I couldn't investigate a years-old bank robbery. The District Attorney's office had that charge.

But I *could* investigate the script based on that robbery. I could find out what Clyde Fentress knew and how he knew it. I only needed Addison's blessing to spend the necessary time at the Paramount lot.

'Could such an appearance be arranged?' Addison asked with the voice of a boy inquiring about the Christmas gift he dared not hope for.

'If I enlist Edith to help grease the wheels.'

'Then grease away! At once!' He beamed at me, his grin stretching further when he finally spotted the Gail Patrick card on the table. 'And I have my cast! Lights, camera, action!'

SIX

T he man in Edith's office had broad, impossibly straight shoulders and a figure tapering to a point, his ankles pressed together. He looked like he'd been built to be driven into the ground – or, I thought once I heard his German accent, a vampire's heart.

Edith, every color of springtime captured in the scarf draped over her pale gray suit, made the introductions. 'Your timing is perfect,' she said. 'This is Aaron Ludwig, who will be directing *Streetlight Story*.'

Ludwig moved with the restrained grace of a ballet dancer. He gazed at me through disinterested blue eyes beneath a lacquered swoop of black hair. I said it was a pleasure to meet him.

'You are a liar, Miss Frost.'

Not the reply I anticipated. The air rushed out of my lungs as if it had remembered other plans. Watching me fumble for a response, Ludwig's expression softened marginally.

'If it truly were a pleasure, you would recall we have already met, if briefly. At the home of Salka Viertel.'

I should have considered that possibility. Salka was nominally a screenwriter – Greta Garbo scripts a specialty – but of late she'd taken on a more important role, doyenne of the community of European emigrés fleeing fascism. Her Santa Monica home had become a gathering place, her Sunday salons a refuge where exiles could exchange news, advice, and word of job opportunities, Salka serving as an informal Works Progress Administration to help her colleagues get hired on at the studios. I still stopped by some Sunday afternoons when I craved Continental company and a slice of *gugelhupf*.

'My apologies,' I said, a faint memory stirring. 'You were called something else.'

'Luddy.' He spoke the sobriquet with mild distaste. 'My given name is Ludwig Aaronofsky. Salka advised me to Americanize it. My friends always called me Luddy, but as this is such an informal country, that courtesy is now extended to one and all.'

'I so wanted to see your film. Salka described it to me in detail.'

He sniffed. 'I'd ask which one, but here I am known only for *Serpent in the Garden*. A trifle of a love story involving mesmerism. Paramount threatens to make an American version, but with your Production Code the more . . . intimate scenes would be impossible to recreate, and without them the film has no point. Do not allow me to detain you ladies. I am here to reacquaint myself with Edith's handiwork.' Luddy – now I was calling him that, too – swept an aristocratic hand over the sketches strewn across Edith's desk.

'Take your time, Luddy. If you have any questions, don't hesitate to ask.' Edith drew me toward the window. I could see Oblath's, where my ordeal began, across the street. 'How was your weekend, dear? What did you think of *Midnight*?'

A short, dismissive sound came from Luddy's throat. I couldn't tell if it was directed at Edith's sketches.

'I haven't seen it yet,' I said contritely. 'It wasn't a very romantic weekend. We saw *Sergeant Madden* instead.'

Another noise emanated from Luddy, this one indicating interest. 'If I may ask, what did you think of the film, Miss Frost?'

It wasn't one of Paramount's, so I felt free to give it both barrels. 'The story was rather silly.'

'Ah, but a film is not the story, is it? A film is the mood. The story merely the frame. Von Sternberg is without peer at creating mood, filling the screen with interest. I have seen this picture. You are correct about the story.' He waved his manicured nails at me as if they were roses to be cast at my feet. 'But the images! The long shadows, the agony the father feels about his son's fate taking physical form on the screen. Most instructive.' He held up one of Edith's sketches – a woman rendered in bold, vivid strokes wearing a long black dress with delicate double straps crisscrossing over the open back – and raised a judgmental eyebrow. 'For the nightclub, *ja*?'

'Yes. We can, of course, make adjustments, bearing in mind our budget and time constraints—'

'Always it is money in America, or the lack of it. Every decision made on that basis.' He let the sketch fall to the desk and shrugged. 'I, too, will use shadows on this next trifle. Mainly to conceal the lack of money, but also to evoke. To build the landscape of our story, such as it is. It is a dark, urban nightmare, all driven by the torment in Jim's head.'

I started. Luddy pronounced the character's name with a soft 'J' and an elongated 'E', making it sound like he'd said *Gene*. At least to my overly sensitive ears.

Luddy raised another sketch aloft. It depicted a cute house dress, pastel pink with a pattern of blue daisies. Edith held her tongue, awaiting his comments.

'I confess this one eludes me, Edith. I suppose I pictured the woman as more of a wanton.'

'Again, I'm happy to make alterations that suit your vision of the character. Based on my reading of the script, I saw her as a policeman's wife. Loyal, devoted to her husband.'

'Yes, yes, but every woman has desires. A repressed desire is still a desire. On some level we must understand this woman wishes to be ravaged by *Gene*.'

There was that mangling of the moniker again. I refrained from correcting his pronunciation, chewing my cheek instead.

Luddy tapped Edith's insufficiently immoral sketch against her desk. 'Always we must remember *Gene* is the infection in this picture. A sickness. He taints the virginal wife and the city itself. The city's shadows reach out for him, to destroy him, and always he runs. The city, it distorts itself around *Gene*. Fighting him as a healthy body fights disease. We have shadows to save money, and to cut at him. This . . . *Gene*.'

Please stop saying that name, I thought, unable to look at Edith.

'This is why we must have someone likable to play him,' Luddy continued, oblivious to my distress. 'They insist I cast a villain in the role. A "heavy". But I ask you, what kind of devil introduces himself by slipping his hand in your pocket?'

'Who is playing the part?' I blurted desperately.

'Chester Clement,' Edith said.

I couldn't help wincing. Chester Clement as Gene? That plodding Paramount staple who'd been menacing actors from behind plaster boulders since the 1920s? Who wound up in jail at the end of every picture? Luddy, I hated to admit, had a point.

'Better to use the actor playing the detective, Eddie. This Robert Preston has a garrulous quality I like. Better still to cast someone else entirely.' Luddy shook his head. 'To my mind this *Gene* is a disease. Always a disease introduces itself subtly. A cough, some fatigue. You never see the disease until it has claimed you, when you slice open the body and find the tumors. *Gene* must be a friendly man, charismatic, handsome. We like *Gene*. We wish for him to succeed. But then, when the truth of his character is revealed, when we learn who *Gene* truly is, we are devastated.' He picked up a discarded sketch. 'I do not care for this nightclub gown at all.'

I spun away from the window. 'Would you excuse me? I have to go.'

Edith took me by the elbow and spoke into my ear. 'Are you all right?'

'I'm not sure. But I should do what I came here for and talk to that bum writer. And while this is hardly the time, I also wanted to ask a favor.'

I raised the subject of Addison appearing as an extra in *Streetlight*

Story. 'If I know Max, he'll get a kick out of the notion,' Edith said airily. 'I'll put it to him today.'

As I took my leave, Luddy never glanced at me. Edith walked to her desk, reasserting her dominance. 'Tell me how you see this dress,' she said to Luddy, 'and I will move heaven and earth to bring it to life. Within our budget, of course.'

Typewriters thundered at Clyde Fentress's building, the Underwood army definitely on maneuvers this Monday morning. But no sound emerged from his office. The blinds were closed, too, not a promising sign. Maybe he'd holed up inside to wait out a hangover, I thought, recalling Nap Conlin's words. I pounded on the door loud enough to wake the dead drunk.

It flew open instantly. 'Judas Priest, sister, you knock the door like the fuzz.'

Taken aback, I uttered the only thought in my head. 'You're not drinking.'

'Not yet, anyway. Why, who you been talking to? Unless we've met before?' Clyde Fentress's voice was reedy and raw, as if he didn't use it much. He had the close-cropped haircut familiar from countless prison pictures, scalp and temples shining aggressively under a tight bristle. I wondered if his maintaining that style meant he planned on returning to stir, or if he'd simply gotten used to it. To provide contrast, he wore an obviously silk purple necktie knotted with a four-in-hand along with a matching silk pocket square. He'd cultivated an image, I understood now, of a man from the wrong side of the tracks now riding those rails first class.

While I puzzled all this out, he appraised me with eyes the color of a file baked into a cake, eyes that made it clear nothing I might say or do would impress him. I swallowed hard.

'We haven't met, Mr Fentress. I'm Lillian Frost from *Modern Movie*.' I blew the dust off a can't-miss dodge I'd deployed before. The prospect of talking to a fan magazine cracked many a stony Hollywood heart. 'I thought I'd try to catch you while I was on the lot. We wanted to feature you in a story about former convicts who have rehabilitated themselves by writing for pictures.'

Fentress grunted. 'You talking to all the brethren? Bob Tasker and Ernie Booth, too?'

Knowing everyone appreciated a solo turn in the spotlight, I said,

'This would mainly be about you. You're the true success story. A happy marriage, a new picture about to start shooting.'

The second-story man turned second story man waved me into his office. 'Come into my cell. Better appointments than the ones I'm used to.'

The room smelled fusty, and Fentress didn't bother to open the blinds. When he shut the door the office immediately felt close, an ominous charge hanging in the air.

I needed a moment to get my bearings. 'I read the script for *Streetlight Story*.'

'Whadja think?'

Don't give him an ounce of satisfaction. 'Very interesting. Max Ramsey tells me it's based on an actual bank robbery.'

'Yep, back in '36. Truth of the thing was hushed up. It's being hushed up again thanks to those yard bulls at the Breen Office. Those censors live to take the teeth out of a story. Then my partner George Dolan got a hold of it, put in too many goddamn jokes. Lots of comic relief.'

'I like comic relief,' I said.

'Then hell, maybe George is right. What say you leave those remarks out of your little article?' He auditioned a smile. I envisioned it on the far side of a gun and suppressed a shiver.

'Let's talk about the truth of the thing, then, and get the facts on the record. How did you come by them?'

'The brotherhood. Guys like me, living on the outside now. You can walk out of prison but you never leave that world behind. It's a world that's often ignored. So I file reports on it. Like George used to do when he was a reporter, only I put 'em in pictures instead of in print. More people see 'em that way.' Another vulpine flash of teeth. 'Everybody likes pictures.'

'Who told you about this particular robbery? And what really happened?'

'It's a funny story.' He stretched out his arms as if yawning, then abruptly seized the cord on the blinds. Sunlight flooded the room, forcing me to blink. I squinted through the dancing dust motes and realized it hadn't been the darkness giving the room an aura of danger. That sense of menace emanated directly from Clyde Fentress, who now studied me curiously.

'My guys tell me almost everything, y'see. Plenty of them are still working, if you understand me. And the ear I got to the ground brings me the rest. All of which means . . . I know who you are, Miss Frost.'

A rattle as he flicked the blinds shut again, prompting a new round of frantic blinking. He was playing me like a fiddle, and I couldn't figure out how to stop him.

'Not just that you pal around with that costume lady, always wears dark glasses. And not just that you had a bit of luck with some crimes came up and got a taste for sticking your nose where it doesn't belong. I also know you're Detective Gene Morrow's girl. Or at least you think you are.' His laughter sounded like chains being dragged across a stone floor.

Every instinct told me to flee, but my legs wouldn't follow instructions. And some dim, stubborn part of me refused to leave empty-handed. 'You're so smart. Much smarter than me. Why not just tell me what you know? Tell me the truth about the California Republic bank robbery of 1936.'

Fentress shook his head. 'Sorry, sister. Wait for the picture. Go see it with Morrow. But I'm telling you right now, don't watch the screen. Watch Morrow's face. That's where the story is.' He pointed at his typewriter. 'Now if you don't mind, I've got to get back to work. Put some hardboiled stuff down on paper, make it so tough even George and the Breen boys can't neuter it. You can show yourself out.'

I headed off the lot in a hurry, away from the grim specter of Clyde Fentress and his death rattle laughter. Without thinking I left through the nearby Van Ness gate. The shortest route back to where Rogers waited with Addison's car meant passing within view of Fentress's window. On the off-chance he was peeping through the blinds – he seemed the type – I instead took the long way around. The stroll gave me the opportunity to settle my nerves, and to purchase a newspaper for the ride back to work. I needed a distraction, and my usual one-sided conversation with Rogers wouldn't turn the trick.

My stratagem worked for all of twenty seconds. Then I saw Nap Conlin's eye gazing out at me from one of the inside pages. Someone had closed it for good. Saddest of all, the story never mentioned his acting career.

Los Angeles Register   March 27, 1939

EX-CONVICT MURDERED

LOS ANGELES, MAR. 26 (AP) – The body of Aloysius
Conlin, age 42, twice convicted of armed robbery, was discovered in the downtown Los Angeles hotel where he was living.
A Los Angeles Police Department spokesman said Conlin's
body was found on Saturday evening in his room at the Hotel
Maitland on East Fifth Street, where he was also employed as
handyman and night clerk. Initial reports indicate he was beaten
to death sometime late Friday night or early Saturday morning.
Police are pursuing several lines of inquiry. Conlin had served
terms at San Quentin and Folsom State Prisons.

SEVEN

T he hard stare I sent to my friend Violet Webb conveyed a
simple message. *Choose your words carefully.*
'Well,' I said. 'What did you think?'

Vi bought herself time by taking a long pull on her ice cream
soda. Finally, she closed the *Streetlight Story* script and pushed it
back across the drug store counter toward me.

'Honestly? I kind of liked it.' She slumped forward, her blonde
ringlets drooping. 'I read it awfully fast, though, with you hanging
over me like a vulture the entire time.'

'I was reading a magazine.'

'You pretended to read a magazine. Whenever I laughed you
looked to see what page I was on.' She drew on her straw again,
downing the dregs of her dessert with a thirsty slurp. 'But don't
listen to me. I'm probably wrong.'

'That's what annoys me. I kind of like it, too.' I flicked the script's
cover, now sticky with drops of Royal Crown cola. 'You knew Eddie
was still alive at the end, didn't you? That part's pure hokum.'

'Sure. But grade A hokum.' She rubbed her shoulders with excite-ment. 'Couldn't you just see the look on that big dope Jim's face when his old pal Eddie waltzes in and arrests him when he's trying to make time with Eddie's wife?'

'Yeah. That'll be some swell moment.'

I braced myself against the countertop and considered the unthink-able: another ice cream soda in which to drown my rapidly multiplying sorrows. Vi chucked me on the arm. 'Chin up, Lillian. Let's talk about the picture we did see instead of the one they haven't made yet.'

That picture had been a poultice on the wound of my afternoon. Having spotted the article on Nap Conlin's murder, I'd telephoned the police from Addison's. I was eventually routed to a bored detect-ive named Tate, who spoke in a garbled tone that sounded like he'd bolted a glass of Bromo-Seltzer just before lifting the receiver. He was unimpressed by my tale of encountering Nap on the Paramount lot a day – if not mere hours – before his demise, looking to relay some juicy criminal tidbits to a man who could spin them into studio gold. I spelled Clyde Fentress's name and told the detective about his criminal record. I heard no pencil scratching on Tate's end of the line. He said in a patronizing voice he'd look into it, reassuring me Nap had likely met his end at the hands of a fellow tenant at the flophouse where he'd breathed his last. 'It's the kind of place where you scrape the soles of your shoes on the sidewalk when you step outside. Still, thanks for the tip.' Tate didn't bother to conceal his earth-rattling belch as he hung up.

Despondent at this reaction, I sought comfort where I always did, at the pictures. Another telephone call summoned Vi. The petite blonde had been one of the flock of lost sheep I'd met at Mrs Lindros's boarding house, and we'd remained friends after I'd moved out and she'd found a modicum of success singing with a dance band. She had readily assented to a late matinee of *Midnight*, set amidst Paris society with repartee courtesy of Messrs Wilder and Brackett and wardrobe by Edith Head. Except in the case of Claudette Colbert, who for some reason insisted on having another designer, Irene, tailor her togs. ('She simply hasn't taken a shine to me,' Edith once said with a shrug.) Vi joined me in hissing La Colbert's every appearance, much to the consternation of those around us, although I had to admit to myself, if never to Edith, that she looked divine.

'It was all just heaven,' Vi said dreamily. 'Her hotel room, her clothes—'

'Her Don Ameche, coming to her rescue.'

'I won't look as good when my Don Ameche comes for me, although I'll bet my Don comes in his own taxi, too. You're lucky you have Gene.'

I made a faint sound of agreement and glared at the *Streetlight Story* script. Vi flicked the cover. 'Put this silliness out of your mind. Gene's going to be fine.'

How I wanted to believe her.

Miss Sarah Bernhardt was waiting on the porch when I returned home, but I knew that to be purely coincidence. The imperious Burmese cat had paused while touring her kingdom and our paths happened to cross. She had been through a crisis around New Year's Day, shunning her food and losing weight, and my landlady Mrs Quigley had allowed the building she owned to fall into near-ruin as she nursed the companion that had been more faithful to her than any of her late husbands. Miss Sarah was back in the pink now, her brief brush with death not making her any more congenial; if anything, she'd only become haughtier, determined not to squander any of her remaining time on those beneath her station. Judging from the flick of her tail as she strutted past, I'd failed to make the grade.

I called out a good evening to Mrs Q. She bustled out with a flush in her cheeks and her reading glasses tucked in the gray cushion of her hair, like an errant bird that had crash-landed there. From within her first-floor apartment came the scrape of utensils. She had company.

'I've been entertaining your friend,' she chirped in her too-loud voice.

A long, lean shadow fell across the hallway behind her. Then the silhouette of the man who cast it appeared, almost as lanky. He placed a hand on the doorjamb, aiming for a debonair insouciance, but I could tell it was because he was well into his cups and needed the support. Only someone half-deaf and almost blind like Mrs Quigley would be unable to tell Simon Fischer had been drinking most of the day.

'There you are,' he said, his voice lightly amused. 'I was beginning to fear you'd gone out on the town.'

I suggested we take a stroll. Simon scratched the scarred skin at his left temple, an unwanted souvenir from his service in the Great

War. The flesh around the stark white patch had flushed red, proof he'd taken a few glasses of the homemade wine Mrs Quigley bought from the DiStefanos across the street as she'd plied him with the stew perpetually bubbling on her stove.

'Why not? I could use the exercise,' he said. The bow he offered Mrs Quigley almost toppled him, and she laughed as if it were a pratfall staged for her amusement. I tugged him toward the door.

The cool night air sobered Simon up at once. He took a flask from his jacket, his two-tone shoes echoing hollowly against the sidewalk. 'How are you?' I asked.

'Tired. I'm supposed to be at a Bund meeting. Some speaker from Chicago on fire with news from the Führer. But I'm not in the mood to listen to that nonsense tonight.'

He offered me the flask. I took it, mainly to keep it away from him for a few moments. Simon made his rent working as a driver for Lodestar Pictures, the position merely a pretext for his true job – clandestinely gathering intelligence on Nazi sympathizers in Los Angeles operating within the German-American Bund. He was part of a ring of agents initially bankrolled by the studio moguls and now funded by the city's broader Jewish community. Simon had spun a web of lies out of necessity when we'd met last year, then I'd suspected the worst when I'd learned about his Bund associates. I was suffused by a curious sense of relief once I'd been vouchsafed the truth; I had wanted to like Simon, and now I could – although not in the way he would have preferred. What's more, I'd been entrusted with his secret. That made me a lifeline for him, one of the few people around whom he didn't have to wear a mask.

I felt a bright tension whenever I was with him, a mixture of unease and excitement. Simon treated me like a woman of the world who knew something of the perils of the modern age, not a blinkered Catholic schoolgirl who buried her nose in movie magazines. I was deeply flattered but feared in my heart he'd miscast me. No Marlene Dietrich roles for yours truly. I'd been cut from character cloth, fated for sidekick turns. I wasn't up to the challenge of this part; the isolation of his double life took a toll he'd increasingly been treating with liquor, and I didn't reciprocate his romantic interest because Gene and I were keeping steady company. Still, I could on occasion help him shoulder his burden, an assignment I took seriously.

I raised the flask to my lips without taking a sip. 'Are you hungry? How about a bite at Cavanaugh's?'

'Mrs Quigley fed me. Could feed a regiment on what she dished out. Would you like to go someplace?'

'I'm happy to walk. How's work? Driven anyone exciting lately?'

'The usual gaggle of money men. Caught a glimpse of Cagney when he was on the lot.'

'I'm surprised you recognized him.'

'It's only because I know how fond of him you are.' He gestured for the flask, which I reluctantly returned. 'How's you these days? How's Prince Charming?'

Simon had his own woes. I didn't need to share mine about Gene. That I did so anyway only reinforced I had no business being on his call sheet. 'He's under investigation,' I said, telling him everything about the pending movie and the murder of Nap Conlin.

'Don't worry about Morrow,' Simon said. 'I don't care for the man but there's no way he's low enough to have killed his own partner. He'll come through this smelling like a rose. His type always does. Though I admit I'm happy to see him sweat. Have to tip my cap to this fella Fentress. He's someone I'd like to talk to.'

'What on earth for?'

'Pointers on how to crack the writing racket. Something I've been thinking about.'

I peered at him. 'No fooling?'

'I've been toying with turning some of what I've seen into stories for the pulps, maybe even pictures. They're making that *Confessions of a Nazi Spy*, after all. Gotta have some way to foot the bills once they find me out.'

'I think that's a fine idea.'

'Maybe you can help me when the time comes to get off my duff.' He stopped abruptly, squinting into the dark as if searching for assailants. The light from a streetlamp slashed across the ivory patch on his face and the slick of perspiration on his forehead. 'Shall we go somewhere? Into Hollywood proper?'

'I can't. It's been a long day.'

'I suppose mine's about to get longer, then. If I leave now, I can make it for the second half of this big talk at the Bund, maybe hear something I can pass along to the mucky-mucks. Stay in their good graces a week longer. Can't have bad reports circulating about me.' When we reached his car he kissed my forehead, maintaining a

distance by placing his hands on my shoulders so as not to bring
any trace of me to his next destination. He smelled of whiskey. I
lingered on the sidewalk and watched his Buick lurch into the night.
Simon could feel himself drifting away, and I wasn't enough to
keep him tethered. I genuinely wished him well, and thought
considerably less of myself.

The downstairs phone rang as I was rinsing a few things out. Mrs
Q hollered my name, and I fought my way through the jungle of
damp stockings without benefit of a pith helmet.

'Greetings, kid! How goes the war?' Kay Dambach's voice rattled
down the line in best Walter Winchell fashion. It had grown a touch
fulsome of late, rehearsing for the radio show she didn't yet have.
Another veteran of Mrs Lindros's boarding house, Kay – Katherine,
professionally – was a budding gossip columnist, constantly on the
prowl for scoops and pestering me for dirt from Addison's parties.
Her aggression had put a chill into our once fast friendship. She
was the last person I felt like speaking to now.

'You caught me at a bad time,' I said. 'Most of my wardrobe is
in the sink.'

'There's no sink big enough. This'll be a short call. I only wanted
your reaction to the story of the day.'

I waited. 'And what story is that?'

'Easy on the coy routine. Spill what you know and I'll get out
of your hair, which I'm sure you just washed also.'

'You're going to have to enlighten me.'

A melodramatic gasp followed, no doubt accompanied by the
clutching of Woolworth's pearls. 'Heavens, is it possible you
genuinely don't know?' She couldn't suppress her glee, coiled
around her words like a snake. She knew full well she was the
bearer of bad tidings, and had pretended to assume I'd already
been informed so I'd feel even worse when she told me. I braced
for the bulletin.

'Word is Gene got into a set-to this evening. At a *bowling alley*.
With a *nobody*. A *writer*, if you can imagine. Why would anyone
tussle with a scribe, especially Gene?'

If I knew Kay, she already had the answer to that question.
'What's this writer's name?'

'Clyde Fentress. The way I have it, Gene stormed into a Paramount
party at the Highline Bowling Court – you know the place, we went

there a few times – and chewed this Fentress out in front of several notable names. Then Gene started throwing punches.'

'That's not true,' I protested. 'If there was a fight, then Fentress started it.'

'So you *do* know him.' I heard her scratch down a note. 'My people tell me he's one of those suspect scribblers lately liberated from the hoosegow and selling squalid stories from therein, so maybe you're right. Anyway, both injured parties are at Saint Luke's right now. Quite the donnybrook.' Her voice dropped to a more hushed level. 'I'm not going to quote you, sweetheart, you have my word. But do you have any comment?'

I let the click of the receiver speak for me.

EIGHT

L os Angeles did a booming business in private hospitals, secluded sanitariums where notable names could recuperate from whatever maladies afflicted them – including ones they'd brought on themselves – far from the public eye. St Luke's put on no such airs. It was open to whoever required comfort. Not that many would seek it there; along with an antiseptic sting that singed the nostrils, an aura of doom hung over the place. Maybe it was the nuns around every corner, walking in tandem, their habits billowing, as if presaging some demented Busby Berkeley number.

I raced in, searching for Gene. The first familiar face I spotted wasn't one I expected. Preston Sturges loitered by a water cooler, grinning at a pair of passing sisters in a manner implying he'd just conjured the perfect gag for them to add to their act. Paramount's top writer – and friend to Edith Head – looked spiffy and wholly out of place in a mustard-colored sportscoat with a pattern of faint brown checks along with trousers the shade of Brazilian coffee. His impressive crown of hair stood in becoming disarray. 'Miss Frost! You join the party in time to aid in the tidying up. The festivities and fisticuffs are over.'

I stumbled through a greeting and asked why he was there.

'Made the mistake of joining a studio bowling expedition. Normally wouldn't go, but this new script has me addled and I

needed a break. Used to roll the odd line with Philip Dunne and
Harry Cohn. Did you know Harry once worked the Midwest lanes
with a partner, grafting rubes out of their hard-earned? A writer
name of Clyde Fentress was the cause of the hubbub. Do you know
him?'

I allowed that I had made his acquaintance.

'Fentress tells a great story. I'm sure most of them are bilge water
but at least they're not about battling for a table at Earl Carroll's.
Makes for a change of pace at any rate.'

Gently, I urged the writer to recount what had happened.

'The damnedest thing, if you'll forgive my coarse language.
Fentress was coming back from a telephone booth when this other
fellow stormed in and pulled him aside. Quite roughly, I should say.
Their conversation grew heated and came to a peak when the fellow
called Fentress a liar, prefaced by a compound word I'm electing
not to repeat. Fentress simply smiled at the man. I'm told it's difficult to stare down a man who's been in prison. Then again, Fentress
is the one who told me. The confrontation became physical. Not
particularly graceful, but physical. Mostly half-hearted haymakers
and some rather sad grappling. The police were called, and as I
hadn't yet spoken to them, I agreed to accompany Fentress here.'

'How did it become physical?' I labored to keep my voice neutral.
'Who threw the first punch?'

'Couldn't say, although Clyde would certainly have been in his
rights. Calling a man a liar in public isn't cricket, no matter how
noisy the venue. They're both contending with the *gendarmerie* now.'

Shouting my thanks over my shoulder, I ran down the hall.

After passing another covey of nuns, I spied police officers in the
doorways of two adjacent rooms. I sat down to wait. Nearby a young
woman about my age maintained a solemn vigil. A clip kept her
chestnut hair from falling into her freshly scrubbed face. She wore
a straw-colored blouse and a brown skirt with a front box pleat to
allow for ease of movement. That, along with the bowling shoes
she'd neglected to remove, made me think she'd been part of the
Paramount party. She possessed the wary stillness of an athlete,
the tang of perspiration her only fragrance.

One of the police officers moved and the woman craned her neck
to peer into the room. Clearly she was awaiting news of Clyde
Fentress.

'Excuse me,' I said in appropriate hospital tones. 'I just got here. Is Clyde OK?'

The woman's eyes narrowed, suspicion coming so easily to her the lids practically clicked into place. 'They haven't said. Do you know him?'

'Slightly. My name's Lillian. I met him at the studio.' I was in close proximity to too many nuns to lie.

The woman said nothing in reply. 'Anyway, I'm sure he's fine. I haven't seen you around the lot,' I went on cheerily.

'I don't work there.'

'Oh. Then how do you know Clyde?'

She shifted in her chair to face me, eyes down to slits, bowling shoes flat on the floor in preparation for launching herself at me.

I leaned back in honest supplication. 'I don't mean to pry. Hospitals always make me nervous.'

One blink, then another, then the woman relented. She crossed her legs, left foot bouncing. 'My name's Sylvia. Sylvia Ward. Clyde's my . . . we're friends.'

'From San Quentin?' Her foot froze. 'Sorry. Bad joke. Clyde told me about his alma mater.'

'He did?' Sylvia flashed a nervous smile. 'Clyde is – he and I – well, I'm his protégée, I suppose.'

'You don't say. Don't think I've met a protégée before.'

'You can't let him know I used that word. He'd tell me not to get above myself.' Another smile, this one more genuine. 'I wanted to learn to write pictures. Clyde sort of took me under his wing.'

'I should find a mentor of my own. Have you written anything I might have seen?'

'Oh, no. I'm not—'

'*Sylvia!*' The voice boomed down the hallway. Nuns turned, the heads of many a nurse snapped up in alarm. What they saw merited the effort: a redheaded woman in an emerald green satin gown, the color showcasing her hair, the exquisite tailoring complimenting her curves. Matching evening gloves leant her appearance a regal quality, which she undercut with an abundance of jewelry. She struck me, at first glance, as a woman who'd wear diamonds by daylight.

Wordlessly, Sylvia rushed over to her, the woman folding her in her arms with a gentle tutting. 'It's your lucky day, sweetheart. You caught me on my way out for the evening. And I always come when called.' Honeyed strains of the South sweetened her somewhat harsh voice. She stepped back to look Sylvia up and down, the two of them an almost comical contrast. 'First thing we do, sugar, is replace those shoes. You see him yet?'

'No. And I have to before . . . before she . . .' Sylvia trailed off, eyes moistening, a hint of tears all she was prepared to show.

Her crimson-topped companion required no further prompting. After caressing Sylvia's arm, she sashayed to the door of Fentress's room and targeted her feminine wiles on the police officer standing guard. The poor man didn't have a chance.

The redhead proceeded to put on a show worth a pretty penny. She leaned in close to speak to the officer, never quite touching him even though some part of her form or another was forever on the verge of grazing his. She gestured toward Sylvia and then Fentress's room, every movement bigger and more suggestive than it needed to be. When the officer said something, the woman tossed her head back to laugh raucously, offering her throat to him, the square-cut neckline of her gown presenting her pulchritude for his delectation. By this point, even a heavily bandaged man on a nearby gurney had propped himself up to admire her performance.

The officer's resolve was waning. The redhead slipped a hand into her emerald clutch, and I heard a soft snap. It took me a moment to recognize the sound of a rubber band around a sizeable wad of bills letting one slip. The greenback moved to the woman's gloved hand, which shook the officer's, no doubt in tribute to his steadfast devotion to duty. The policeman looked pointedly at Sylvia, then glanced up and down the hallway before sauntering off.

Sylvia knew a cue when she saw one. She scampered into Fentress's room. The redhead commandeered Sylvia's seat. An almost physical force shot through me as she crossed her long legs, like the crackle of electricity before a storm hits. Here was a woman, I thought, who took center stage wherever she went, who carried herself more like a movie star than any movie star I'd ever met. And I'd met my share.

'Always amazes me hospitals don't have bars,' she drawled. 'The one place you really need a drink. Think one of these here nuns could rustle up a stinger? I left mine warming up at home. You part of this Paramount crowd, honey?'

'Sure.' I invisibly crossed myself in case that answer constituted a lie. 'You look like you're going to a better party.'

'The best party's one you throw for yourself. Tell you the truth,

I dress like this to listen to the radio.' She punctuated the comment with another husky laugh. I had no choice but to join in. I introduced myself.

'Glad to know you. I'm Virginia. Sylvia didn't give me the whole story. Who threw a punch at ol' Clyde?'

'I don't know. I missed it.'

'I guarantee whoever it was, Clyde likely deserved it.'

Sylvia flitted into view in Fentress's doorway, pacing nervously. Virginia clucked with sympathy. 'The poor little flibbertigibbet.'

'She's bearing up better now, thanks to you. Is she really Clyde's student?'

Virginia hooted so loudly that the police officer stationed outside what I took to be Gene's room glowered at her. She winked at him. 'Sure, I reckon you could put it that way. Clyde's teaching her, all right. School's always in session. And Clyde covers every subject in detail.' Sylvia, rubbing her hands together, vanished from view. Virginia shook her head. 'It takes talent to live at night. I sometimes wonder if Sylvia has it.'

She then swung her stems toward me, eyes glittering like the baubles adorning her neck. 'Say, you work at Paramount, maybe you can tell me. What are these studio types looking for? What's the magic trick for getting a screen test?'

The notion that Virginia would require help from anyone, much less me, in securing attention deserved one of her throaty guffaws.

As I formulated my answer, another woman approached. A rail-thin thirtyish brunette with a finishing school carriage and a strikebreaker's eyes. Those chilly orbs categorized me as unimportant – but swept over Virginia and reserved judgment. The brunette's trim figure suggested her exercise came in the form of horseback riding and harboring grudges. Her devastatingly simple black evening dress had been conceived and executed with a quiet dinner in the company of friends in mind. Her evening was winding down, even as Virginia's was gearing up.

The brunette breezed into Fentress's room as if it were one of her many closets. Virginia gave out with another whoop of laughter. 'Lucky us. Good seats for the fireworks.'

'What do you mean?'

'I do believe that was Mrs Fentress come to call.'

I gazed at the still-untended door. 'Think I want a closer look.'

'You're a girl after my own black heart. Report back.'

A few steps had me close enough to the door to hear voices. A patrician one I took to be Mrs Fentress's: 'I'm confused. Are you two meant to be working? There's no typewriter. Unless – don't tell me you can carry an entire scenario around in that pretty little head of yours, dear.'

Then Fentress himself, sounding abashed. 'Don't be like that, Josie.'

And finally Sylvia, her words barely audible. 'I'll leave you two alone. Good night, Clyde.'

I darted back to my seat a split-second before Sylvia emerged stiffly from the room. Virginia hung a crooked smile on her face. 'How is he? All in one piece?'

Sylvia glanced back at the open doorway. Her voice remained chastened, low. 'I'd like to go now.'

'Fine idea. Let's make a party somewhere. It's always one when Virginia Hill shows up.' Virginia rose and hooked Sylvia's arm in her own, while I stared at her in astonishment. She took my thunderstruck expression in stride. She'd encountered such looks before. 'Care to join us, Lillian?'

'I – no thank— Did you say Virginia Hill?'

'Only my family and my enemies call me anything but. Oh, dear. Does my reputation precede me?' She batted her eyelashes so broadly I felt a breeze. A screen test, I thought, would be a waste of everyone's time.

'How could it not? You're in all the columns.'

'Don't believe everything you read. Myself, I only believe what Sylvia here puts to paper. Not that there's enough of that to keep me busy.' She cackled. Sylvia grimaced, which only made Virginia laugh harder. 'What do you say? Shall we hunt down those stingers together?'

'Thank you, no. I'll stay here.'

'Suit yourself. Come along, Sylvia. Let me minister to your needs.' Virginia blew a kiss to a nun as she led Sylvia away. The nun sternly shook her head and continued on.

I ventured back to Fentress's room and caught my first glimpse of the man himself since the dust-up. He sat on the edge of the bed, looking pale but not too much the worse for wear with a yellowing bruise on his face and a matching collection on his right hand. He seemed more embarrassed than in pain.

Josie Fentress spotted me first. She appeared disconcerted only because she'd already decided I didn't merit attention, yet here I was intruding on them.

'Who do we have here?' Her jaw-clenching technique would give Katharine Hepburn a run for her money. 'Another protégée?'

Fentress wearily glanced at me. 'No. A busybody. Tell your boyfriend he can't throw a punch.'

One of Josie's meticulously manicured brows levitated at the comment. Perhaps I deserved consideration after all.

I forced myself to speak in the hushed quiet of the room. 'I wanted to ask you about Nap Conlin.'

'So did the police this afternoon. You must be the one who blabbed to them.' Fentress pushed himself off the bed. He winced with the effort. 'Told them I never saw Nap on Friday. He showed up on the lot uninvited, probably to promote himself a part in *Streetlight Story*. I had no idea he was coming. The gate guard backed me up. End of story.'

'And if there's one thing you know, dearest, it's stories.' Josie eyeballed me the way she'd consider a coat she'd chosen to donate to charity. 'Would you excuse us? My husband is still recuperating from his foolishness.'

I left, her tone like unseen hands ushering me from the room. Quite the coterie of women had shown up to see Clyde when word of his altercation with Gene had gotten out. Sylvia, Virginia, Josie. An impressive trio.

Plus little old me, rounding out the quartet.

The police officer posted outside Gene's room had wandered off. I seized the moment and ducked inside.

Gene lay on the bed. To my amazement, he looked worse than Fentress did. Raw scrapes on the backs of both hands, purpling around his slightly swollen nose. Clyde, I knew at once, had cheated.

Gene caught sight of me. His lips twitched but never quite made it to a smile. 'Lord. Did I make Hedda Hopper's column?'

'No. A friend told me. What happened?'

'A free and friendly exchange of ideas.'

'Are you in trouble?'

'Nah. A cop and ex-con swapping blows – and a cheap headbutt on Fentress's part? Just another Monday night. Anyway, I wasn't there as a cop. More as Fentress's subject. His muse.'

'But he could make problems for you.'

He shrugged and shifted his gaze to the window. 'If he does, he does.'

I'd never seen him like this before. Cold. Fatalistic. Impassively anticipating his impending ruin.

'I almost called you about Fentress this afternoon.' I told him about the screenwriter's connection to the late Nap Conlin.

My story only warranted an uninterested grunt. 'Hadn't heard any of that. I just wanted a word about that script of his.'

'What did you want to say about it?'

'Whatever it was, I said it. It's up to him to listen.'

He clearly intended that statement to be the finale of the conversation. I didn't receive the memo. 'Just tell me it wasn't you who threw the first punch.'

Gene snagged his fedora off the table by the bed. 'I'm afraid it was. Unless you count the screenplay as a punch, like I do. And I count that headbutt as two. If you don't mind, I'm going to grab some rest before they make me go over it again.' He dropped the hat over his face, hiding his eyes from me and the world.

Once again I found myself scurrying by nuns on my way to the exit. I needed the night air and some clarity, a fevered part of my brain already convinced I'd never find the latter. I couldn't make sense of Gene's distance toward me, or his actions toward Fentress. Why publicly confront him about his script unless there was an element of truth to it? And if there was, did that mean Gene had feelings for Abigail he'd kept buried all this time?

One of the sisters I rushed past wished me a good night, and I almost burst into tears.

San Bernardino Lamplighter   March 28, 1939

KATHERINE DAMBACH'S
SLIVERS OF THE SILVER SCREEN

The strikes weren't only on the alleys last night at the Highline Bowling Court when a party from Paramount was interrupted by a man looking to settle a score of his own. Scribe Clyde Fentress, a product of San Quentin, found himself confronted by Detective Gene Morrow of the Los Angeles Police Department. Heated words soon turned to fisticuffs. Morrow's fellow boys in blue ultimately broke up the brawl and ferried the fighters to St Luke's where the good sisters stitched up the scrappers. What caused the beef? We hear Fentress's latest filmic foray isn't as fictional as some would like. Remember that California Republic Bank heist that garnered the detective headlines he'd rather forget? Seems Fentress's scenario for Para's soon-to-shoot *Streetlight Story* details the unsolved crime, painting Morrow as the villain. Doth the detective protest too much? . . . Lodestar ingénue Frances Lander turned heads at the Troc Saturday night wearing her current husband on one arm and her former spouse on the other. Those Hollywood gals, so democratic!

NINE

'Y ou met *the* Virginia Hill last night?' Addison asked. 'The Alabama oil heiress who's always in the papers?'
      'Yes,' I said. 'It's sort of a funny story.'
   'Then let's hear it!' Addison leaned back from his mid-morning snack of sugar atop half a grapefruit, ready to be regaled. Which posed a problem.
   I'd arrived at work fearful the morning's gossip columns would prominently feature the previous evening's brawl. But the story

hadn't gotten much play, likely because only a writer had been involved. When mentioned, it was in oblique blind item style; Lorna Whitcomb discreetly asked whether 'Paramount's touted new production is hitting too close to home for some.' Alone among her tribe, my old friend Kay had spelled out specifics. If she'd set out to get my goat, she could consider my goat got. I'd hidden her column so Addison wouldn't see it.

Then my employer genially inquired how I'd spent my evening, and without thinking I let slip about Virginia. Now Addison sat opposite me, hands folded across his considerable belly, awaiting my spellbinding yarn.

'It was at a bowling alley,' I said. Addison blinked several times before understanding the tale was told and the lights were coming up.

'Ah,' he said, then repeated the sound with a nod. 'What kind of person is she? One can't help wondering from reading about her. Out every night swaddled in diamonds and furs, spending a thousand dollars at a clip. They say she dated Errol Flynn when she first came to town and they quarreled at the Brown Derby. She threw a drink at him in front of everyone.'

'I heard it was a raw egg.'

'Journalistic standards have certainly fallen. Shall I invite her to something so I might meet her myself? Do you think she would come?'

'Wild horses couldn't keep her away. She'd probably bring some of her own. Just have plenty of stingers on hand and do whatever you can to help her land a screen test.'

'Right. And a stinger is—'

'French brandy and crème de menthe. I looked it up this morning and took the liberty of ordering some of the latter.'

'Splendid. Now, on the subject of screen tests . . .' Chortling, he rubbed his palms together so vigorously I feared he'd start a fire. 'I haven't been able to sleep with the prospect of my motion picture debut. I've been thinking I should prepare for my performance.'

'But you won't have a line,' I said. 'I thought I made that clear.'

'Oh, you did, but nonetheless I want to be ready. How does one convey emotion on screen? I'm unschooled in the art of acting. Aye, there's the rub. A theatrical expression, you know.' He nodded emphatically, momentous decision made. 'I should practice. Perhaps we could rehearse some lines from the *Streetlight Story* script.'

'Oh, I don't think—'

'I confess I found it on your desk and paged through it. This Jim character has a lot to do. Including some scenes with Arlene, a part you can read.'

No. My brain ceased functioning, its TILT sign lighting up. Addison paid me well, but nowhere near enough for him to play my boyfriend while I voiced the lines of the woman for whom he supposedly still carried a torch.

'I'm no actor, either,' I said reasonably. 'I've told you about my screen test. It was so bad the projectionist walked out of the booth and directly into a monastery. You don't want to rehearse with me. You want a teacher. A private coach. Shall I make some calls?'

I had no sooner uttered the words when my office telephone rang, the universe possessing a farceur's sense of timing. I left Addison to his grapefruit and soon heard Edith's voice.

'I thought you should know, dear, there's a detective on the lot interviewing Mr Fentress.'

My heart sank. Of course the police would treat last night's melee like a third Louis/Schmeling bout. 'Do you know why he's there?'

'To speak to Mr Fentress about a Mr Conlin. It seems you provided information that Mr Conlin visited the studio shortly before he was murdered. The detective's under the impression you work here, and I thought—'

'I'll be right over.'

I hustled back to Addison, who gave me his blessings to depart. 'I quite like your suggestion of an acting teacher,' he said, tipping more sugar onto his grapefruit rind. 'But I'll make all the arrangements myself. I have some people in mind.'

I was about to enter the Costume Department building when a voice hollered my name. Jerry the messenger skidded to a halt alongside me.

'Oh, it's you. How'd your big weekend date go?'

'Swell, swell.' He fussed with his flyaway hair, obviously fibbing. 'We're planning a June wedding. How was your weekend?'

'Spent in solemn reflection. You stopped me to ask about my weekend? Wait, how do you even know my name?'

Jerry hemmed, hawed, and continued rearranging his hair. The mystery was solved a moment later when Barney Groff appeared, his obsidian gaze already locked onto my eyes. 'Miss Frost, a word?' At that request, Jerry vanished from sight.

Groff was Paramount Pictures' head of security and all-around man in a pinch. When problems arose, be they physical, financial, or legal, Groff dealt with them, often with nothing more than his telephone. I suspected he'd been on the horn the night before, finessing the Fentress fiasco. As he brushed non-existent specks from his trim black suit, I realized he'd dispatched Jerry to waylay me, because raising his voice or accelerating slightly in my direction wouldn't befit a man of his stature.

'I understand,' he began slowly, 'once again I have you to thank for unwanted attention. It's not enough your hot-headed detective friend is the reason there are all these items in the newspapers today.' He raised his hand, forgetting he wasn't actually holding said newspapers. It didn't matter; I saw them anyway. 'Now the police are grilling one of my writers about a murder. Why are you here, Miss Frost?'

I swallowed my pride around the considerable lump in my throat. 'To apologize to Edith, and to you,' I said.

Groff never showed surprise, either. That would mean admitting he hadn't known something. Instead, he stepped back and smoothed his permanently slick hair. 'See that it doesn't happen again,' he said, and strode away.

Jerry circled back. 'So what are you doing next weekend?'

'I don't know yet,' I answered soberly.

Edith's office usually coursed with focused energy, creativity harnessed to some particular project. But on this day it sputtered and popped everywhere, the atmosphere chaotic.

She greeted me in the outer office almost apologetic. 'Max is here,' she said softly. 'And in high spirits.'

She wasn't kidding. Max, in another new suit freshly shipped from 1923, radiated enthusiasm. He marched around Edith's desk like a general who'd received a dispatch that the enemy's lines had been broken; his joy might be contained at the moment, but he'd be ordering the champagne and dancing girls soon enough. He didn't remember my name, and he didn't care. 'I told you they'd come around, Edith,' he said, picking up their conversation where it had left off. 'They're finally treating the picture with the respect it deserves. I've been banging my head against a brick wall and it turns out all I needed was some gossip in the newspapers!'

Oh really? 'What's the good news?' I asked.

'Just the fact that overnight *Streetlight Story* has become the hottest ticket on the lot!' With deceptive grace, Max scooted over to Edith and planted a kiss on each of her cheeks. Edith replied with one of her toothless smiles and waved him away. 'Barney Groff himself offered a *mea culpa* this morning! He said all the mentions the picture rated because of the true story angle completely turned him around! *Carte blanche*, anything I want!'

Typical Groff, I thought, haranguing me out of spite while capitalizing on the publicity I'd unintentionally generated. I wondered if I was entitled to a share of the profits.

Max bubbled on, his ardor undimmed. 'The real proof Paramount sees the picture's potential is they've relented on my casting choice. We'll have to monkey with the production schedule to accommodate him, but he'll be marvelous as Jim! We're no B picture any more!' He embraced Edith and began pirouetting her around the office, Edith smiling at him even as she squirmed in his grasp.

I wanted to interrupt and ask who this chosen thespian was, but I didn't need to. Edith's secretary knocked on the door, took in the scene without comment, then ushered Fred MacMurray inside. The handsome face that had gazed out at me from many a romantic comedy – and a card in Addison's Transogram Movie Millions game – wore a mask of concern.

Edith greeted him warmly and introduced me. I stared at the actor and tried to envision him as Gene. After what seemed like several hours, Edith nudged me and I eked out a hello.

'It's a great day, Fred.' Max pumped his hand. 'For both of us. Turning point in your career, you know. And mine.'

MacMurray did not look like he agreed. 'I'm not sure about this "casting against type" business,' he said. 'Period dress is one thing. I don't mind telling you I felt silly in those clothes from *Maid of Salem.*'

'You wore them well,' Edith interjected.

'But the character I'll be playing in your picture . . .' MacMurray shook his head. 'He's a heel.'

'Which is the point!' Max bellowed. 'The role needs your charm. You'll make the audience fall in love with you.'

'And they'll hate me by the end of it. Honestly, look at this character. He quits the police force, robs banks, tries to kill his best pal and take his woman . . .' MacMurray shrugged helplessly. 'I'm just a saxophone player.'

'Then you're a rogue with a song in his heart! You have my word, Fred, this is going to open up whole new roles for you.'

'Or shut me completely out of the old ones.' MacMurray sank into a chair, genuinely conflicted.

Max perched on a footstool opposite him. I feared it would collapse under his weight. 'You talked to Luddy this morning, didn't you?'

MacMurray nodded. 'He told me I was going to play a tumor, and the city would cut me to pieces. That can't be right, can it? Maybe it was his accent.'

'You can't pay attention to what he actually says. That's his intellectual side. German, you know. But we need that! We're going for the highbrow as well as the hoi polloi with *Streetlight*. That's why you've got to do it.' Max slapped his putative star on the knee. 'You saw the press the picture got today. Barney Groff was singing its praises just this morning! Tell you what. You and I will talk to Luddy again. Let me handle the translations.' He chuckled. 'By the time he's done, he'll have won you over and you'll be champing at the bit. *Streetlight Story* needs you, Fred. And you need it. You've got to keep audiences guessing. You can't laff it up with Carole Lombard forever.' He somehow said 'laff' so I could hear both Fs in it.

MacMurray remained unconvinced. 'What do you say, Miss Frost? Should I play this louse of a guy?'

I looked into his fetching features and imagined him next to me at the fights. At the movie theater. On Gene's lumpy sofa, which slanted so much to one side I always tumbled into him.

Edith leaned forward, her eyes pleading. 'Lillian.'

Jolted from my musings, I uttered the first thought that came to mind. 'The Transogram Movie Millions game says you're a romance star.'

Max rolled his eyes as MacMurray turned to him. 'There you have it,' the actor said. 'This sax player's not going to argue with that.'

TEN

E dith's farewells to Max Ramsey and Fred MacMurray spilled
into her outer office, where a man waited through them with
a hugely amused smile. Fortunately, he had the jutting jaw to
support it, along with the craggy features of a stone gargoyle. More
remarkable than his face was his tweed suit, a rarity in Southern
California, the fabric a warm, full-bodied gray. His hat, held behind
his back, bobbed with a tick-tock regularity as he studied the illus-
trations on the walls. Whoever he was, he projected the mechanical
entitlement of one accustomed to receiving undivided attention. He
could afford to be patient.

As Max and MacMurray left, the man waved Edith's secretary
off. Tall as well as thickset, he loomed over Edith. I longed to fetch
her a slant board so she could look at him without risking her neck.

'You must be Miss Head. Byron Frady, Los Angeles Police
Department.' He showed her his badge like a jeweler presenting a
necklace he knew the customer couldn't afford. 'I'm told I might
find a Miss Frost here.'

Meekly, I raised a hand.

Edith led the way back to her office. 'May I say, Detective, that's
a handsome suit. Authentic Scottish tweed, if I'm not mistaken?'

'That it is. Quite the eye you have. But then I suppose that eye
earned you this grand office.'

'Tweed's more affordable now, isn't it, with the tariffs coming
down last year?'

'At least we can credit President Roosevelt with doing one thing
right.' Frady chuckled at his own comment. 'It's still quite dear, but
a suit like this lasts forever, so you save money in the long run.'

'A wise decision. How can I help you?'

As Frady took a seat, I saw his flamboyance didn't end with his
suit; his crossed legs revealed fine lisle socks of meadow green with
contrasting clocks. The detective was a man whose vanity went
from the ground up.

'I was visiting with Clyde Fentress. I felt the personal touch was
required.' Frady swung his green socks toward me. 'I'd like you to

tell me about your encounter with Aloysius Conlin, known to friend and foe alike as Nap.'

I did, Frady frequently interrupting with questions.

'You've told me more than Fentress did. A man of his background isn't exactly inclined to assist the authorities.' Frady had yet to stop smiling, apparently delighting in all things. 'He did say, Miss Frost, you misrepresented yourself to him. Is that correct?'

'Yes.' Catholic school had conditioned me never to lie, while from both Gene and Simon I'd learned to say as little as possible when being questioned.

'You shouldn't have done that, young lady.' Frady wagged a finger at me. I felt myself flush with shame even as I yearned to bite the admonishing digit down to the knuckle. 'But then you had your reasons. You wanted to learn about Fentress's script and its relation to Detective Gene Morrow.'

'Do you know Gene?'

'Not as well as you do. He and Fentress came to blows yesterday, I believe.'

Edith frowned. 'I hadn't heard that.'

'Don't concern yourself. All a misunderstanding,' Frady said. 'Clyde informed me he wouldn't be pressing charges.'

Relief surged through me. Frady's smile finally dimmed. 'I also knew Nap Conlin, as it happens. I used him much the way Fentress did, as a source of information. He'd turn up for a chinwag with bits of news to barter.'

'Fascinating,' Edith said. 'Would he offer the same material to you and Mr Fentress?'

'Unlikely, ma'am. Aloysius, God rest him, took this acting business seriously, even though he was only an extra. He was good in that boxing picture, mind. Aside from what he overheard at the hotel where he worked, which wasn't much, he'd completely lost touch with the criminal element. It got so most of what he tried to foist on me was gossip column stuff, better suited to Lorna Whitcomb. An actor smoking marihuana cigarettes on location. Rumors of an auto accident covered up by a studio. Not this one, I'm pleased to report.' He patted Edith's leg, and she flashed a tense smile. 'Even tried to convince me gangsters were muscling in on bit players like him. Beating some of them up, demanding money in exchange for jobs. Not a scrap of proof, of course. Should've told him to sell that one to Clyde. Sounds like one of your pictures.' He laughed again, one of those men who thought himself blessed with an easy charm simply because it spread like leaking oil.

'It sounds as though you knew him quite well,' Edith said. 'I'm sorry for your loss.'

'I don't mind telling you, it was sad seeing him in his shabby room down the hall from the hotel's front desk. Lying on the floor, buttons all around him. Tea gone ice cold. He'd laid out two cups, so his killer was likely known to him.'

'Forgive me,' Edith interjected. 'Did you say buttons?'

'Yes, ma'am. From Aloysius's shirt. We found several on the floor. Not to be indelicate, but he'd been finished off with a heavy object, sort of a bookend, from a table in the hall outside his room. Alas, the Hotel Maitland is the kind of establishment where witnesses are in no hurry to come forward. May you ladies never find yourselves there.' Another knowing chuckle.

'If I may ask, what sort of buttons?'

'Shirt buttons. Not quite mother-of-pearl, but close.' Flummoxed, Frady peered at Edith. 'Why the interest?'

She shrugged girlishly. 'Occupational hazard.'

'Ah. My interest in poor Nap's death is an occupational hazard as well. I owe it to him to pursue every lead. It's why your report about his visiting the studio sparked my curiosity, Miss Frost.'

'Do you think it will be helpful?' I asked.

'Can't rightly say. The Maitland's a true den of iniquity, so smart money's there. Still, in Nap's memory, I shall leave no stone unturned.' He slapped the tweed on his legs. 'I've taken enough of your time. I'm sure there's sewing to be done, Miss Head. And give my regards to your Detective Morrow.'

A glorious silence descended on Edith's office. We took a moment to revel in it, letting the fog of Frady's condescension dissipate.

'Buttons?' I asked.

'Force of habit,' Edith said.

'I'm definitely persona non grata to Fentress. How can I find out about the script now?'

Edith canted her head so the sunlight reflected off her glasses, concealing her eyes. I'd long suspected she'd marked precise locations on her carpet so she could find such a spot no matter the time of day. 'His writing partner, Mr Dolan, must be familiar with his working methods.'

'Do you think he'd talk to me?'

'Possibly, provided Mr Fentress hasn't yet warned him about your penchant for deception. You really shouldn't have done that, young lady.' She almost smiled. 'Shall we try him? It might be better if I accompanied you.'

The long hike to Dolan's office commenced with good news. 'Please let Mr Rice know he's invited to appear in *Streetlight Story*. In the nightclub scene, at Max's request.'

'You mean yours.'

'I knew Max would agree if I asked.' Edith stated this with such certainty I wondered how deep their connection ran.

'I can't thank you enough. And Max! There must be something I can do for him.'

'You could have reassured Mr MacMurray with more zeal.'

'I know. But they can't use someone I like to play Gene. Not this script's Gene, anyway.' I sighed. 'What do you make of the idea?'

'Assuming Mr MacMurray brings his usual charisma to bear, it's enormously effective casting.'

'I just want an actor with a hunchback and a harelip in the part. Doesn't Paramount have anyone like that under contract?'

'I'll make inquiries.'

'How's Bill these days?' I hadn't seen Edith's friend and colleague Bill Ihnen, an in-demand production designer, for several weeks.

'Busy. We had coffee in the commissary recently and he asked after you.' Edith nodded at two passing actresses. They clutched hands excitedly at this recognition. 'I was thinking about your friend Mr Fischer. Have you heard from him?'

Edith was one of the select few who also knew about Simon's covert work spying on Nazi sympathizers. She admired him for his efforts, but I couldn't shake the feeling she neither liked nor trusted him. At least she'd referred to him as 'Mr Fischer' instead of informally, as she once did. He had risen, however grudgingly, in her estimation.

'No,' I lied, for reasons I didn't fully understand. 'Not in ages.'

Edith nodded somberly. 'Perhaps that's for the best.'

The typing emanating from behind George Dolan's door had a steady, soothing rhythm. Here inspiration punched a clock. We were loath to intrude.

Dolan was the rare man who seemed to be balding amiably. The retreat of his sandy hair de-emphasized what would otherwise have been a prominent forehead, on which was perched a pair of wire-rimmed glasses. He'd ditched his jacket to work in his shirt-sleeves, which suited his disposition. His front pocket sagged under the notebook he'd tucked inside, a greasy fingerprint on its cover.

He raised a hand midway through Edith's introduction. 'I know who you are, Miss Head. I never join a team without knowing the major players. It's a pleasure to make your acquaintance.' His face betrayed no sign of recognition when Edith said my name. Fentress hadn't yet poisoned the well.

'In or out, ladies?' Dolan sparked a cigarette. 'Happy to have you in the office, but the studio keeps us galley slaves in tight quarters.'

Fentress's adjacent office was again as quiet as a crypt. 'Inside would be good,' I said.

I yielded the office's other chair to Edith and stood by the door so I could hear Fentress should he return. 'We wanted to learn about *Streetlight Story*,' Edith said as she settled herself. 'Given all the attention it's getting.'

'I wouldn't know about that.' Dolan gestured at his typewriter. 'Too busy whipping the next one into shape.'

'Mr Fentress mentioned the picture's based on a true story,' I said.

'It is, somewhat. But you can't take Clyde too seriously. Unless you found him in your house. That used to be his specialty. You heard about that, I suppose. Seems everybody on the lot except me knew he'd been in prison when the studio threw us together. For some reason, we clicked as a team. I rewrote Clyde's story pretty heavily, so much so I'm amazed he's still talking to me. No way was that yarn of his running the gauntlet of the Hays Office.'

'What was wrong with it?' I asked.

'In a word? Everything. In his version, the bad guy was still a cop, setting up bank robberies. That's a Production Code no-no right there. Then he kills his partner, and the partner stays dead. And only the Gillette people would have gone for the ending. It'd make you want to slit your wrists, so it would have sold plenty of razor blades.'

He chuckled. I slumped against the door, feeling faint.

'Clyde's version was too depressing. The studio loved the betrayal angle, which has been kicking around since Cain v Abel. My job was to provide a little pep, some uplift for the ride home. I gave our heavy a nightclub, wrote in a few jokes, added that ridiculous twist so man and wife could live happily ever after. Clyde grumbled but the studio signed off, which means my own wife and I can live happily ever after, too.' Dolan shook his head in grim admiration. 'Clyde's original version would have been something to see, though. They'd maybe make it in France. I'd pay two bits to watch it.'

'If only we could have read it,' Edith said.

'Would you like to?' Dolan opened a drawer in his desk. He nodded, and his glasses fell into position on the bridge of his nose. His fingers moved dexterously over neatly organized files. 'I should still have a copy of his story. Again, I don't necessarily buy his version of what happened back in '36, even though he swears he's got the inside dope. You hear the police talked to him this morning? Only topic of conversation in the commissary. He took a powder before I could ask him about it. Apparently he got in some kind of fight last night?'

'Do you know where Clyde got his information?' I asked, struggling to scrape the anxiety from my voice.

'He's very mysterious about it. Which has me convinced he's making it all up like the rest of us are. Always nipping off to meet cronies from the old days, comes back cackling and full of ideas. I'm never invited, and wouldn't go anyway. I've got work to do. Here we are.' He extracted a slim folder and handed it to Edith, who in turn gave it to me. 'Again, don't assume that's according to Hoyle. I certainly didn't. I did my own research.'

'Oh? What kind?'

'I didn't come here until '37, so I talked to a reporter who had the skinny on the actual robbery. Which I proceeded to ignore, because again, the picture business is all about make-believe. I just wanted to know the facts before I started. When in doubt, ask one of us hacks.'

'Is that your background?' Edith inquired.

Dolan nudged his glasses back up. 'Yes, indeed. From Philadelphia P-A. Started in sports, which they say is the only real writing in newspapers because all you need to know is who had the most points or knocked the other fella down. Moved into politics and cut my teeth covering William Vare. Wrote a play about him that didn't steal from *The Front Page* too much. When it caught Paramount's attention I came running, because I like money and the missus likes gardening year-round.'

'I daresay that makes you a marked contrast to Mr Fentress,' Edith said.

'Part of me can't help winding Clyde up and listening to him tee off on the picture business. "They don't want the truth! Everything's got to have a song in it!" He calls me The Bartender. Always watering down the whiskey. But like I say, I've developed a fondness for financial security.'

'Clyde seems to be doing all right for himself,' I said. 'I've met his wife.'

'Josie? Then you've met the source of Clyde's income. The fair Josephine was hatched from the Hatcher family. One of the genuine California clans. They were building palaces out here when the place was all Mex. What Clyde and I earn combined is mere tip money to Josie.'

'One of the Hatchers married to a former convict?' Edith raised an eyebrow. 'However did they meet?'

'At a Hatcher family soirée for prison reform. Clyde was guest of honor, a jailbird who'd taken flight thanks to the power of the written word.' Dolan rolled his eyes. 'He's got a whole party piece he'll do on the subject if you pay him and serve dinner. Anyway, he meets Josie, the black sheep of the Hatchers, and they hit it off. Clyde starts in with his hardboiled tales of San Quentin and realizes Josie's old man steals more money every morning before breakfast than Clyde did his whole career. And Cupid's arrow doth hit its mark. Josie married him partly to prove her political bona fides and mainly to irk her family. They make a fun couple. Good dancers, surprisingly.'

I opted to press my luck and question him on one other subject. 'Marriage seems to have done wonders for him. Sylvia Ward told me he's taught her a lot.'

'You've met Sylvia, too? Yeah, she's often flitting around while we're trying to get our stories straight.'

'She's also trying to make a go of writing for the pictures?'

'Why else would you spend time with Clyde? At least I get paid to do it.' Dolan grinned. 'She's a talented kid. Gave me some pages she hammered out on the sly at work, answering phones over at Central Casting. Have to say they were damn good.' He flipped his eyeglasses back down and returned his attention to the drawer. 'Thought I had them here. Anyway, she could easily make something of herself in this business. Provided she takes after me and not

Clyde. The rate he's going, he'll drive himself to drink. Even more, I mean. Good thing he's got a wife to cover his bar tabs.'

I asked Dolan if it would be possible to speak to his reporter friend about the 1936 bank robbery – 'for the purposes of verisimilitude in the costumes', Edith amended – and he said he'd try to put us together. Edith and I let him return to work.

'Mr Fentress's original story might shed light on his sources,' she said as we walked back toward her office.

'Interesting to learn Sylvia works at Central Casting. Nap Conlin mentioned he was registered there.'

'So is every extra in Hollywood, in their multitudes. Which is how Mr DeMille typically requests them. I wouldn't attach any significance to that fact.'

'You have to admit it's an interesting coincidence.'

'And likely that's all it is.' Edith examined me as if I were a child insisting I had a fever on a school morning. 'You heard Detective Frady. Mr Conlin led a harsh life replete with unsavory characters. He met his end in a rather squalid environment. His murder is, in all probability, unrelated to the production of this film.'

What she said made complete sense, and I told her so. I just left out that I didn't believe her.


```
           'THE BIG STEAL'

              Story by
           Clyde Fentress

      Property of Paramount Pictures


THE ACTION OPENS in a SMALL BANK. A
SQUIRRELLY MAN enters, wipes the sweat
from his face, and looks around. No one
pays him any mind, least of all two fellows
in the corner, EDDIE LAWRENCE and JIM
MORRIS, kitted out for a fishing trip. They
```

josh with each other, Jim clearly a good-time Charlie always up for a laugh. The squirrelly man goes to a teller window and draws a gun. Before he can finish saying 'THIS IS A ROBBERY', Eddie and Jim nab him. They're police detectives, and they have been lying in wait.

LATER, Eddie and Jim leave the police station. Jim is happy with the day's work, but Eddie says Jim's tip wasn't so hot because the fellow they arrested isn't part of the gang they're after. Jim asks how he knows this. Eddie says it's because the gang knocked over a bank that very after-noon on the other side of town. Jim shrugs and says they did the best they could. Besides, they have a date to fill up on chow mein like they did in the old days.

Eddie and Jim meet ARLENE, Eddie's wife, at the restaurant. Jim and Arlene try to buck Eddie up but he is having none of it. Jim says the old carnival has returned to town for the season. It comes out Jim and Arlene were childhood sweethearts and he used to bring her to that carnival. He reminds her about a token he won that he didn't turn in for a prize because he was saving it to win her heart. Then he intro-duced her to Eddie, and she married him instead. His two best friends together. Eddie grumbles about hearing the sappy story again. Jim suggests they go to the carnival for old times' sake, but Arlene reminds Eddie he promised to take her dancing.

Eddie and Arlene in a shabby dance hall. Arlene says if he took the job her father offered him they could go somewhere better, but Eddie wants to stay a cop.

Jim goes home. He has an evening paper. The successful robbery is the banner headline, the one they foiled below the fold. Jim opens a drawer and fishes out a carnival token. He still has his little keepsake. He then telephones a girl to ask her out.

CUT TO ANOTHER BANK ROBBERY. The hoods pulling it are vicious and quick. One of them walks out of the bank with a limp.

A WITNESS reports one of the bandits had a limp. Eddie says it could be LEFTY HERMAN. Eddie and Jim split up to look for him.

Lefty Herman limps down the street to his apartment. Inside, he finds Jim waiting. Lefty is relieved — BECAUSE JIM IS HIS PARTNER. Lefty gives Jim his share of the robbery money. Lefty's little boy comes into the room, but his father shoos him away. Jim watches the boy go and tells Lefty to get out of town for a while with the kid.

Eddie is frustrated because it looks like Lefty has taken a powder. Jim says he can't find him either, but has a new lead.

In a dive ('disreputable') bar, Jim buys a drink for PETERS who is quite the rumpot. Jim gives Peters some money and says there will be more for him when he gets out if he does exactly as Jim tells him. First, walk into the bank with a limp . . .

Peters limps into a bank and is arrested
at once. In the police station, he tells
Eddie and Jim he robbed all the other
banks. The POLICE CAPTAIN is very happy
with the confession. Eddie is not.

Eddie, Arlene, and Jim go to dinner. It's
supposed to be a celebration but Eddie is
in a mood. He goes to use the telephone,
leaving Arlene alone with Jim. Jim says
he could use a woman like her and he
wishes they would have stayed together.
Arlene is flattered and says the right girl
is out there somewhere. Jim says the right
girl is looking at him now.

Eddie returns to the table, in a good
mood at last. His horse won the eighth
race and one of his informers told him
where he might find Lefty Herman. He asks
Jim to come with him. Jim says he's off
the clock and would rather see the lady
home. Eddie rushes out. Arlene's feelings
are clearly hurt. Jim goes to settle the
bill, but first he ducks into a telephone
booth and calls Lefty, telling him to get
out—

Eddie paces outside an apartment house.
He has just missed Lefty and is angry.
Lefty watches from an alley across the
street, holding his little boy's hand.

Jim brings Arlene home. She is upset when
she sees the door to their house open.
Jim goes inside and finds no one. Arlene
is embarrassed to admit the lock is broken
and they cannot afford to fix it. She says
they need money. Jim tells her she needs
someone who can take care of her. He

shows her the carnival token he has saved
all these years. Arlene is distressed and
asks Jim to leave.

Jim meets Eddie at the police station and
says he has a new lead. He brings in
SLEEPY RIORDAN, so-called because of a
drooping eye. Sleepy tells them he has
heard about the Lefty Herman gang's next
robbery. When Sleepy steals a look at Jim,
Jim gives a secret nod back — BECAUSE
THIS IS A SET-UP. Eddie and Jim make plans
to watch the bank.

Jim meets with Lefty Herman and a gunsel
named NOLAN. Lefty's son is there and
wants to play cops and robbers. Lefty
sends the boy away but keeps the tiny
police badge he gives him. Jim tells the
men to be ready to come out of the bank
with their guns blazing.

The robbery takes place. When Lefty and
Nolan come out, there is a CLOSE-UP SHOT
of Jim firing his gun into the air. Shots
fly from all directions. Nolan is able to
escape with the money. Lefty and Eddie
shoot each other. Eddie dies in Jim's arms
after making Jim promise to look after
Arlene. Lefty also dies. Tumbling out of
his pocket is the tiny police badge his
son gave him. Jim kicks it into the gutter,
not wanting to be reminded of the little
boy he has just orphaned.

LATER, Jim escorts Arlene home from Eddie's
funeral. The lock on the front door is
still broken. Jim tells Arlene they should
both leave, and start over together in a
place where no one knows them. He says,

'We will remember Eddie and sometimes we will forget him, and that will be OK, too.' She tells him no but Jim is very persuasive. She is thinking about the idea.

The captain tells Jim he is off the case, but not to worry because they are close to finding Nolan and the loot.

Jim meets in secret with Nolan to split the money. Jim shoots Nolan, takes all the swag, and leaves. But Nolan is not quite dead. He drags himself to a telephone.

Jim stashes the money in his car and picks up Arlene. He suggests they go to the carnival for old times' sake.

As they walk along the midway, they are spotted by a beat cop.

Jim and Arlene walk through the carnival together. Arlene rests her head against Jim's shoulder. He smiles, because he is winning her over. He notices a cop watching them. Then another. And another.

Knowing the jig is up, Jim turns on Arlene. He is cruel to her and says he does not want to be with her after she has been with Eddie. She begins to cry and he laughs at her. Arlene runs away. Jim runs in the opposite direction with the police officers in hot pursuit.

With no place else to go, Jim flees into an office building. The officers chase him upstairs. He fires his gun at them until it is empty. Not wanting to be captured,

he takes the coward's way out and jumps
from a window, falling to his death.

Outside, the police captain finds the robbery
money in Jim's car. He consoles Arlene
and shields her from the sight of Jim's
mangled body. But Arlene can still see the
old carnival token that has fallen from
Jim's hand. She picks it up and pockets
it, the only souvenir she has of the two
men in her life who are now both gone.

THE END

Property of Paramount Pictures

ELEVEN

F entress's story moved, I had to admit that. Its coal-black heart
kept a lively tempo.

Aside from that, I hated it. Even more than the screenplay
it spawned.

Here, Gene's proxy was an out-and-out devil, rendering children
fatherless and turning wives into widows. If Paramount needed to
pad the running time, he could always kick a few dogs and push a
kindly old woman down a well.

Plus Fentress had taken pains to highlight that the character of Jim
had chosen 'the coward's way out.' A fitting fictional fate given Jim's
inspiration had, by Fentress's lights, gotten away with murder.

My head throbbed. I belatedly realized it had been throbbing for
days.

I could understand why the story had been substantially revised;
Fentress could curse George Dolan until the air turned a lovely shade
of blue, but the ex-newspaperman had done the job Paramount wanted,
and done it well. The Motion Picture Production Code, rigorously
enforced since 1933, would never permit a criminal to evade the hand

of justice via suicide. By altering the particulars and adding ludicrous twists of plot, Dolan had done Fentress a great favor. He'd also caused me – and Gene, and Abigail – no end of woe.

But most importantly, in the original story Nap Conlin had a featured supporting turn. Sleepy Riordan was undoubtedly based on him; he *had* to be. Fentress had set down what he claimed was the definitive version of events. In it, Nap played a role in setting up Teddy's murder.

Was that part of the story true? Was it why Nap had sought to see Fentress? Was it why he'd been killed?

The recesses of my brain murmured other questions: *If it is true, is the rest of the story true as well? Could Gene truly be guilty?*

The headache intensified, spreading into my eyes. At least Paramount had made Fentress change his title. I should have known he'd never have christened a script *Streetlight Story*.

I read the story twice on the brief ride to Western Avenue and Hollywood Boulevard, where Rogers piloted Addison's Cadillac Fleetwood to the curb. I gazed up at a four-story sandstone structure, concrete landings for the fire escapes protruding from each floor. The balconies were bedecked with bas-relief sculptures depicting the making of motion pictures, a director in a canvas chair issuing instructions into a megaphone. It didn't escape my notice that the members of his acting company were, ahem, unclothed. They were nude in the classical tradition – one even wielded a spear – but nude nonetheless.

What better decoration for the building that housed Central Casting, employer of Sylvia Ward? I wanted to speak to her, and again had to hope Fentress had not yet blackened my name. Dismissing the surly Rogers for the day, I ventured inside.

A directory indicated Central Casting was on the third floor; to my surprise I discovered the Motion Picture Producers and Distributors of America, enforcers of the Production Code, could be found on four. Maybe if I tipped off Joseph Breen about the *au naturel* adornments on the edifice, he'd return the favor and lower the boom on *Streetlight Story* for moral reasons.

The lobby was thronged despite the late afternoon hour. Cowboys in full western regalia loitered as if expecting to be summoned to a posse. Women lined the hallway leading to the elevators, their dresses well-kept but slightly dated. Thinking me a casting agent, many bravely made eye contact, their bright smiles a dam against their desperation. One hopeful in faded gingham bustled over, the infant in her arms wearing an immaculate sailor suit and a colicky expression. 'Looking for babies today, ma'am?' Her voice had the high, flat tones of someone who'd stopped expecting to be heard over the horde. 'She's real talented. Cries on cue.' Proving the point, the child uncorked a full-throated wail. I shook my head and stumbled into the sanctuary of the elevator. The action never stopped in the Hollywood & Western Building: dramatic dreams dashed on three, artistic visions nibbled to nothing on four.

Central Casting's door was heavy and windowless. The peephole only added to its forbidding quality; slap an oversized knocker on it and it would be fit for duty in one of Universal's horror films. I tried the knob only to find it locked.

I bruised my knuckles and the peephole snapped open, revealing a tired green eye. 'Yeah?' came a guttural male voice.

I swallowed the urge to say 'Moe sent me' and order a whiskey sour. 'I'm here to see—'

'Name?'

'I – Lillian Frost, but I'm looking for Sylvia—'

'Nothing today. Try later.' Before I'd even registered that the peephole had closed, it reopened. 'How tall?'

'Come again?'

The thick door didn't prevent me from hearing the man's weary sigh. 'Your height, sister. How tall are you?'

For some reason I told him. 'Five foot eight.'

A grunt vaguely signaled approval. 'Can you dance? Ballroom stuff. And play badminton?'

At the same time? I wondered. 'Yes on one, no on two.'

Another low rumble from the man. 'There's maybe something. What's your name again?'

'Hang on a second. I'm looking for Sylvia Ward. I'm not registered here.'

'Why didn't you say so?' The peephole closed again, this time for good.

The drug store on the ground floor had plenty of coffee and a dearth of costumed desperados. I took a seat by the window and waited. I tried rereading Clyde Fentress's screen story, but stopped when it dawned on me I was envisioning Fred MacMurray as Jim and realizing how good he'd be in the role. I was halfway through a *Times* item on Eddie Cantor's post-radio show jibes at Adolf Hitler prompting a fistfight between a cast member and some of the audience when I spotted Sylvia.

She walked so briskly I had to run to catch up to her. She wore a brown and yellow plaid jacket over a dark blue dress, and had replaced her bowling shoes with brown peep-toe pumps. The footwear didn't prevent her from covering a lot of ground; she moved with the purpose of someone determined to put distance between herself and her workplace. I called her name and was embarrassed to find myself out of breath.

Sylvia turned toward me, her innate suspicion returning to her face. 'It's Lillian. We met last night.'

'I remember.' Her voice was guarded.

'How's Clyde doing? I didn't see him today.'

Sylvia didn't respond, instead peering at me like something that had scuttled out from under her icebox. I threw myself into the situation and on her mercy. 'Look, it's no coincidence I ran into you. Somebody at the studio told me you worked at Central Casting and, well, I wanted to pick your brain.'

She didn't turn on her heel. That counted as progress, so I kept talking. 'A few minutes at the drug store. Coffee's on me.'

Finally, she shrugged. 'Sure.'

Once inside, she dispensed with any chitchat. 'What did you want to pick my brain about?'

I had to ease my way into the meat of the conversation. 'Central Casting. A friend of mine wants to sign on for extra work and I was hoping you could give me some pointers.'

Sylvia looked dubious, undoubtedly suspecting I'd invented this acquaintance as a blind for my own dreams of silver screen glory. 'This friend of yours. She have a job?'

'Yes, a good one.'

'Tell her to keep it. You don't want to roll the dice on acting when you have steady work. You definitely don't want to pin your fortunes on being an atmosphere player.'

I made note of the term. 'I suppose it was more an idle daydream for her than anything else.'

'Let it stay one. Whatever she's doing, she's better off.' Sylvia gripped her coffee cup as if warming her hands with it, never lifting it to her lips. 'You know how they choose performers nowadays?

With a machine. We make up a punch card for every actor in our files. Height, weight, description. Are they knock-kneed? Bow-legged? Do they have buck teeth? Punch another hole in the card. Then a request comes in from one of the studios.'

'Tall girls who can ballroom dance and play badminton,' I murmured.

'Exactly. And the machine just . . . anoints actors for the job.' She trembled in awe, like Bernadette seeing the Blessed Virgin at Lourdes. 'People come all this way, and they're reduced to a handful of traits on a card. So they can get picked by a contraption that's meant to be used for bookkeeping. Some outfit called International Business Machines built it.'

'Is that what you do? Organize punch cards?'

'No. I have an even worse job. I'm the bearer of bad news. I'm the voice on the other end of the line, telling actors "No" when they call in to see if there's any work. I'm lucky I didn't have the hot seat today. That's from four to eight in the evening, people hoping to line up a job for the next day. Almost two thousand calls an hour sometimes, when there's only nine hundred jobs a day.' She chuckled darkly. 'We have a poster on the wall that says, *Do You Understand Figures?*'

'I can see why you want to talk my friend out of it.'

'I'd like to talk plenty of my regulars out of it. It's getting so I recognize them when they call. Some of them ask me for advice, or word on what jobs might be coming up.' She spun the mug in her hands, still not drinking from it, the coffee cold now. 'It isn't the young ones who get to me. It's the ladies with children to support I worry about. Then there are times the actors just scream down the wire at me.'

'That's hardly fair. It's not your fault.'

'Yes, but I'm the one on the phone. And I have what they want, which is a job.' She nodded at the counterman. 'They'd just as soon holler at him if they had the money to come in here.'

'It makes sense you'd want to be a writer.'

'That's letting myself in for a whole different set of disappointments. I don't care. I know pictures are seen as silly, disposable entertainments. But they're not. Movies are what people remember. When you're sitting in the dark, you let yourself be vulnerable. You allow things in. And those things you carry with you.'

She spoke with an earnestness that would sway any cynic. But then I already agreed with her. Movies had long held me in their thrall, which was why I couldn't abide Fentress using that power to spread falsehoods about Gene.

Provided they *were* falsehoods.

'Besides,' Sylvia continued, 'a writer can work anywhere. All you need is a pencil, some paper, and an idea.'

'Sounds like something Clyde taught you.'

She smiled down at her coffee, the affection not directed at the skim of milk on its surface. 'One of his pet phrases. He took me seriously when nobody else did. Can't put a price on that.'

I couldn't resist steering the conversation to another topic. 'You know lots of interesting people. Not only Clyde, but Virginia Hill. How'd you meet her?'

'Happenstance. Virginia tends to pull people along in her wake. I got caught up, I guess.'

'Easy to understand. She makes quite the impression.'

'Virginia lives the kind of life I aspire to.'

'I'll say. Make me an oil heiress any day.'

'I don't mean money,' Sylvia said sharply. 'She's carefree. Doesn't put any limits on herself, doesn't give a damn what people think of her. She's like a character in a script.'

'Maybe one you'd write,' I said, aiming at flattery.

Sylvia nodded, distracted. 'Maybe. Whatever gets me away from the switchboard and telling stories drawn from real life.'

Like *Streetlight Story*, I thought.

I could sense Sylvia's waning interest. I had to put my main question to her.

'Do you happen to know a sometime-actor named Aloysius Conlin?' I asked quietly.

'Never heard of him,' she said, the sudden tension in her face providing the true answer.

'He's also called Nap, although he's not billed that way.'

Sylvia shook her head. 'Doesn't help.'

'He was killed the other day. I saw him on the lot right before it happened. He mentioned he was registered with Central Casting.'

'So are nearly ten thousand other actors.' Sylvia's words were hot enough to singe.

'How many of them also know Clyde Fentress?'

'Thanks for the coffee.' Sylvia gathered her purse and left without a backward glance.

I sat where I was, watching night gather on the far side of the window. A woman came into the drug store, her face several years too old for her gaily colored dress. She beelined for the telephone booth. I heard her ask for a Garfield number, which meant she was calling Central Casting. Her eyes tilted upward, as if trying to influence the operators a few floors overhead.

'Hello? Lois Emery calling.' She hung up a moment later without another word. I wondered who'd been on the hot seat breaking the bad news to Lois, now that Sylvia had gone home.

TWELVE

A new day dawned, with diligence as my watchword. I hurled myself into Addison's social calendar, relieved he wouldn't be hosting a party this weekend; only the Friday bash he'd been invited to loomed on the immediate horizon.

'Hello, Lillian!' My employer's voice boomed so loudly I sprayed ink from my fountain pen across the envelope I'd just addressed. Addison took several ungainly steps into my office, then stopped and declaimed in an orotund voice, 'How goes this fine day?'

'No developments in the last hour. Are *you* all right?'

He advanced again, a beleaguered expression on his face as if he were counting and feared losing his place. He paused next to my desk. 'Why, yes. I am – actually, no.' He returned to his normal tones and slumped slightly. 'This acting business is playing havoc with me. Since you confirmed I'll be in the movie, I've been working on my articulation – it's vital, you know – and I wanted to practice it while walking. Only now I'm, well, thinking about it. Walking and talking simultaneously. Deuced difficult when you *try* to do it.'

I didn't have the heart to remind him he wouldn't be delivering a single line. Instead I said, 'I've seen you walk and talk before. You're very good at it.'

'Thank you, Lillian. I always thought so.' He cleared his throat and resumed his sonorous timbre. 'I also wished to inform you I have secured instruction in the dramatic arts. My lessons commence on the morrow.'

With that, he exeunted. Curtain.

*   *   *

Addison wandered about rehearsing for the better part of the morning like a ghost haunting his own house. He was moaning theatrically about *Mabel, little Mabel, with her face against the pane* when Edith telephoned.

'I wanted to— Good heavens, what's that caterwauling in the background?'

'Some half-baked radio drama, I think.'

'It should be taken off the air at once. George Dolan left a message, thinking you worked for me. He'd like you to come by his office.'

I wanted to go at once, but I'd shirked my responsibilities at Addison's enough. I told Edith I'd work through lunch and be at Paramount mid-afternoon. She asked me to visit her. As if I wouldn't have done so anyway.

After hastening through the day's labors, I sought out Addison. 'Fare thee well, dearest Lillian,' he rumbled. 'Parting is such sweet sorrow.' He bowed deeply and backed away into the shadows. I didn't tarry for an encore.

No sound came from Fentress's shuttered office while Dolan's door was ajar, his steady typing spilling out like music. I crept forward with fingers crossed.

My breath caught as I saw Clyde Fentress sprawled in the chair opposite Dolan's desk. He fired a plume of cigarette smoke upward as if the ceiling had wronged him. Dolan virtuosoed over his keyboard, eyeglasses down.

I had to assume Fentress had badmouthed me to Dolan since he'd left his message. I wanted to back away, but at that moment Dolan stopped typing. They spoke to each other in a crackling cadence similar to their own scripts.

DOLAN

We have to get these guys out of the casino somehow.

FENTRESS

Doors are always good.

DOLAN

Whatever we do, it's got to land them in the soup.

                    FENTRESS
They're not already in the soup?

                    DOLAN
Yeah, but right now it's cold soup.

                    FENTRESS
So they're in the vichyssoise.

                    DOLAN
Or at Oblath's. Say, listen to you
with the vichyssoise reference. They
ladle that out at Folsom regularly?

                    FENTRESS
          (embarrassed)
Josie likes it.

                    DOLAN
Something chilly and pale? Can't
imagine why.

Fentress sat up to put some English on his retort and saw me. His expression hardened. 'There she is. Who are you today? Reporter? Wardrobe girl?'

Knowing I'd never win him over, I concentrated on Dolan instead. 'Technically, I never said I worked for Paramount. Neither did Edith.'

Dolan laughed. 'Spoken like a lawyer or a fellow Catholic.'

'She lied to me,' Fentress said.

'I have it on good authority you've done worse, old thing.'

'It doesn't matter. I don't want you talking to her.'

Apparently I had become invisible. Which only angered me further. 'Why not? What are you afraid of? If your information on Gene is good, why not tell me where you got it?'

'Because I don't owe you a damn thing.' Fentress grinned with indecent pleasure. 'I owe Morrow and the LAPD even less. You think I give a damn if I hurt your boyfriend's feelings?'

Dolan scribbled on a notepad. 'He hurts mine constantly.'

'That's because it's easy to do. Look at the set of you, George. You went from hard-bitten newspaperman to California dandy overnight. Buying salmon-colored shirts for golfing. Coming in here every day smelling like a barber shop.'

'Shirt. I bought one salmon-colored shirt. And I didn't marry an heiress last time I checked.' Dolan nudged his glasses up to pinch the bridge of his nose. 'Just tell her what she wants to know, Clyde. It won't hurt the picture. We've got MacMurray, for Pete's sake.'

'That lightweight. He's all wrong. Morrow's a heel.'

'No, he's not,' I said with all the force I could muster. 'And your picture's helping to ruin him.'

'George ruined it first. Watering down the whiskey.'

'Here we go. It's not our job to tell the truth. It's our job to get paid.' Dolan tore off the sheet he'd written on and crumpled it. 'As for my writing, I'd give anything to see the scripts you pounded out while you were on parole.'

'George.' Fentress wielded the name like an icepick. Dolan, unconcerned, turned to me.

'He was prohibited from writing about crime and criminal matters for two years when they set him free. I'd love to see how much truth was in those pages. Westerns where the cowboys talk like they're on the yard at San Quentin. Costume pictures where Lady Wetherby has the vocabulary of a cooch dancer.'

Sulking, Fentress pivoted so I was banished from his sight. 'We gonna write this one? Let's get back to work.'

Dolan cocked his arm and made to throw the ball of paper at his partner. Fentress ducked. When he did, Dolan eyed me and tossed the paper in my direction. I bobbled it, then dropped it into my purse. Fentress had missed the exchange entirely.

'You'd better go, Miss Frost,' Dolan said. 'Clyde gets fussy when the muse beckons.'

'Shove it up your ass,' Fentress said.

'Lady Wetherby couldn't put it better.'

Two steps from the door, I uncrumpled the paper. Dolan's neat handwriting proved he'd been to Catholic school.

Meet me at Stanley Rose Bookshop after five. My reporter friend will talk to you.

Behind me, Dolan's typewriter started up again, as steady as ever.

One of the many Costume Department assistants told me Edith had stepped out briefly and led me not to Edith's office but the fitting salon next door.

Inside I found a lithe brunette of about twenty pirouetting on the pedestal before a trio of mirrors. The outfit she wore, a pale green and tan checked dress with a matching jacket likely pulled from her own closet, did not warrant the treatment. But I understood her enthusiasm. I had taken a turn or two on that pedestal myself.

The woman blushed when she spotted me and hopped down, determined to take possession of her own embarrassment. She had wide green eyes and a grin that gathered in the corners of her mouth.

'I must have looked a fool,' she said, her voice a touch husky. 'But who cares? I can't believe I'm in this room.'

'It always feels like a dream to me, too.'

The woman shot me a sly look. 'You wouldn't happen to be Lillian Frost, would you? Edith's been talking you up all afternoon. My name's Nora. Nora Hegerty.' She peered at me, holding out a distant hope. 'Edith says you're from New York?'

'I am. From Queens.'

'No kidding! Where?'

'Flushing.'

'Sunnyside Gardens!' Nora practically leapt in the air. 'Finally, someone who doesn't think I'm talking about darkest Africa when I mention those places back home.'

'Such as?'

'Ever go to the Astoria Pool?'

My smile blazed new trails, reaching almost to my ears. 'You're talking to Miss Astoria Park of 1936.'

We fell on each other then, chattering about favorite shops. At one point our conversation was simply a list of fondly remembered streets on the other side of America.

Edith entered, breaking up our babel. 'As I predicted,' she said. 'I knew you and Brenda would get along splendidly.'

'The bonds of our shared stomping grounds run thick,' I declared. 'Now who's Brenda?'

Nora slapped her forehead. 'I keep forgetting. *I'm* Brenda. The studio renamed me when they put me under contract. Nora Hegerty sounds like someone who waited on tables at Tully's Tavern in Woodside. Which I was very good at, by the by. But I'm Brenda Baines now. Brenda Baines. Come on, call me Brenda or it'll never stick.'

I laughed. 'Glad to know you, Brenda Baines.'

'An honor to dress you, Miss Baines,' Edith chimed in.

'Miss Baines! Miss Baines! May I have your autograph?' I cried.

'This is good. This is working. I'll turn around when I hear that name now.' Brenda planted both feet firmly and gazed at the trio of reflections before her. 'I'm Brenda Baines, about to appear in *Streetlight Story* with Fred MacMurray and Robert Preston!'

The world spun away from me. I felt dizzy and saw double, knowing the mirrors weren't to blame. It took me a moment to form the question, another to croak it aloud.

'You're playing Arlene?'

'Yes!' Brenda – not Nora, never Nora, Nora was dead to me now – glowed with excitement. I felt myself grow cold, as if she were drawing all her energy from my body. 'The biggest part I've gotten, and by far the best.'

At least act happy for her, mermaid, my old roommate Ruby purred in my head. *She'll meet you on the way down, too.* I couldn't follow the advice. The smile kept falling off my lips, the paste on it dry.

'Would you excuse me?' I beckoned Edith into the outer office, not trusting myself to walk any farther.

'Lovely girl, isn't she?' Edith said. 'You two should have much to talk about. She reminds me of you.'

'We're nothing alike.' I looked back into the salon. Brenda stood at the window, watching the traffic on Marathon Street. That's how the world will see Abigail, I thought. While no one would be playing me at all. I hadn't even been written out of the story, because I'd never been written in. I had no role, at least not on the screen. I'd be the fool out in the audience, shoveling popcorn into my mouth and rooting for Jim and Arlene to kiss, hoping to win a gravy boat at the intermission bingo game.

Edith removed her glasses and gazed directly into my eyes. Her own had the distant compassion of a doctor's. 'You're both bright young women who have traveled a long way and created opportunities for yourselves. I wanted you to meet her now. It will make matters easier when the picture comes out.'

Yes. Because the picture would be coming out. Not due to spite, but because it had to.

'I hate that I wish it wouldn't.' The words came out of me in a rush. 'Normally I'm so excited about pictures. This one is bearing down on me like a train. It's too much to take in. And now . . . Brenda.'

'I understand. But she's only doing her job, as am I. Max insisted on redoing her wardrobe now that we have additional resources, even though the picture starts shooting tomorrow. He's asking for opulence.' Edith darted into her office and returned with a sketchpad. The topmost sheet bore a revised illustration of Arlene's nightclub dress, the one Luddy had dismissed. This new rendering had opulence in abundance. While the long skirt maintained the same lines, the simple bodice had been replaced by a beaded top with a jewel neckline and short sleeves. I yearned for it at once.

'It's unusual to make these changes so close to production, so we're working non-stop,' Edith said. 'This while I'm fitting Paulette Goddard for her new film with Bob Hope, and preparing a dozen more pictures besides. Max is reading scripts, Mr Dolan and Mr Fentress are writing another one. It's all just so much sausage being made.'

'Is that meant to make me feel better?'

'Yes, it is. In a few months, *Streetlight Story* will be in theaters. If we've done our jobs properly, it will provide an evening's entertainment. A few weeks later, it will be gone. It won't change who Detective Morrow is, or how you feel about him. It's only a movie. There'll be another one to see the next day. And everyone will have worked very hard on it.'

I thought of my uncle Danny, who'd painted backdrops at the old Paramount Studios in New York, and felt myself growing teary. But Edith had no time for such nonsense. She had opulence to organize. 'Did you see Mr Dolan?'

I relayed my plans for the evening. An assistant interrupted to hand Edith a slip of paper. She frowned as she read it.

'Speak of the devil. Miss Goddard has taken issue with her wardrobe. Again. I must dash. Do call with the latest. And say goodbye to Brenda.' She flew to her office, already girding herself for the next crisis.

Brenda smiled when I returned to the salon, offering a preview of the pearly whites she'd flash at Fred MacMurray. 'You don't happen to know where a girl could get good pot roast, do you?' she asked. 'I could use a New York meal to celebrate.'

I studied her, Nora effortlessly adjusting to the role of Brenda who would be playing Arlene, based on Abigail. While I regularly muffed my lines as Lillian Frost, a part some critics said lacked dimension.

'I have no idea,' I replied. 'It was lovely meeting you.'

THIRTEEN

I'd been in the Stanley Rose Bookshop before, idling away a few minutes on a lively length of Hollywood Boulevard; Grauman's Chinese Theatre was only a few blocks distant. On this visit, I took it in anew.

It smelled dusty and close, that intoxicating perfume of all bookshops, but with an additional tangy note of furtiveness; a tome or two, I'd wager, had left the premises in a plain brown wrapper. The store had drawn a goodly number of customers for a weeknight. Virtually all of them were men, scholarly sorts equipped with eyeglasses and sportscoats of varying degrees of shabbiness. One paused in his perusal of the shop's wares to point the stem of his pipe at a book as if posing for an academic catalog. A cloistered space at the top of a flight of stairs suggested an office. Chuckles emerged from an area at the store's rear walled off by a shelf of colorful art books. Not seeing George Dolan anywhere, I began nosing around the stock.

The spell cast by any bookstore soon fell over me. I'd surface every few minutes to scan the room for Dolan, then dive back under seeking treasure. I was trying to make head or tail out of a book on Kandinsky when the man stationed at the cash register beckoned to me. He had a spare frame that seemed more the result of disposition than diet, and the faint agitation of one striving not to appear agitated.

'Pardon me, miss,' he said with a Texas drawl. 'You look trustworthy. Might I ask you to watch the till a moment? I'll be right back.' He then started for the rear of the store without awaiting my reply.

'What?' I hollered after him. 'Who's in charge here?'

The man spun back to me. 'Nominally? Me. Stanley Rose, at your service.' He bounced his fingertips off his prominent forehead and continued on his way.

I glowered at the now-abandoned cash register. Tending to it was in no way my responsibility. Had the proprietor left the drawer open, exposed bills wagging like tongues, I'd be under no obligation to close it. Let the learned clientele rob the place blind. It'd serve Rose right for running a business this way.

But I found I couldn't vacate the front of the store, either. My finely honed Catholic guilt kept me in the vicinity, just in case. As my uncle Danny said, life tests us constantly, and you don't learn your grade until after you graduate.

A man in a sweater vest and red bowtie sauntered past the register with several volumes under his arm. He didn't speak to me so much as the spirit of the store. 'Tell Stanley to put these on account.'

I waited for someone to speak up. No one did. 'Hold on!' I yelled at his receding back. 'What's your name? What account?'

'Any of the brothers Warner.' He vanished out the door.

I stomped over to the register to scribble a description of the man for Rose's presumably non-existent records. *Sweater vest. Smug. One of many.*

Stepping behind the register proved my undoing. A queue instantly formed, and instincts forged during my Tremayne's Department Store stint took over. I wrapped a book for one customer, and told another when I didn't have change to break his hundred-dollar bill that he'd have to come back and no, he couldn't have the book in the meantime. A man standing off to the side said 'Excuse me, miss' during this discourse and I took great pleasure at snapping 'In a minute' at him. Only when he left in frustration did I identify him as Edward G. Robinson.

Still reeling from telling Little Caesar to blow, I said, 'Next!'

George Dolan stepped up, squinting at me through his glasses. 'What are you doing?'

I flapped my arms. 'Working the register!'

Understanding and a grin broke simultaneously across his face. 'Oh, I get it. You must have come in the front door.'

'How should I have come in?'

He hooked his thumb. 'Through the back. It's where the parking is. I've been waiting for you. Let's go.'

'But who's going to watch the till?'

Dolan grabbed a walrus-faced man eating an apple over a copy of *Great Expectations*. 'Hey, Milt, hold the fort, would you?' Milt grunted and carried both dinner and diversion behind the register.

'Thank you for agreeing to help me,' I said.

'Anything to irritate Clyde.' Dolan chuckled. 'Plus I recognized that crazed look in your eyes. Used to get it myself when I couldn't let a story go. Like a dog with a bone.'

We reached the stairs to the mezzanine. I started up, but Dolan delicately took my elbow. 'Stanley keeps his special collection upstairs. Material's a little more . . . artistic.'

'Oh,' I said, chasing it with a worldlier, 'Ah.' Dolan gestured toward the store's back room.

It was another largely masculine environment, more pipes and eyeglasses. The men scattered around laughed raucously, their camaraderie buttressed by whatever liquid was in the pitcher on a side table. Dolan offered me a glass but I demurred, drawn instead to the lithographs on the walls. The artwork was interesting, audacious, probably scandalous. I didn't know enough to be sure.

Talk flew around the room at a furious clip. One man spoke of the Nationalists' victorious march into Madrid ('Spain's just the coming attraction, the feature hasn't started yet'). Two more concentrated on matters closer to home. 'Mark my words, the extras will make a go of it on their own. Break away from the Screen Actors Guild.'

His conversation partner refilled his glass. 'Better run over to the Writers Guild and tell 'em to man the barricades.'

'How are we gonna man barricades without extras?'

A man slouched against the wall, unlit cigarette bobbing in time to his words beneath an unkempt mustache. 'Give me the bank robber over the banker. At least we know what the bank robber's doing and why.' The words 'bank robber' seized my attention, but before I could horn in Dolan spoke.

'I've got something for you.' He snatched a file off the side table before it was appropriated as a coaster. 'Found those script pages Sylvia wrote.'

One of the men made a scoffing sound. 'You mean Brother Fentress's "discovery"? He doesn't actually make her type, does he?'

'These pages are better than anything you've produced since you tumbled off that train, Lou.' Dolan handed me the file. 'Honestly, they're good. For a historical. Always skip that kind of pageant myself, but I liked this enough to offer to show it to DeMille's people. Sylvia wants to finish it first. She's savvy, all right. Clyde and I bounced the wife's dialogue in *Streetlight Story* off her, and she convinced me to keep that business with the thief's kid from Clyde's story in the script. I pegged it as maudlin, but she swears women will go for it.'

'Those pages better be good,' Lou said drunkenly. 'Otherwise, Comrade Josie will haul Clyde up before the People's Court for a People's Divorce.' He fished a flyer out of the wastebasket and gave it to me to pass along to Dolan. The paper reeked of oranges. 'You see she's doing another of her pass-the-fur-hat dinners?'

'Christ, again?' Dolan skimmed the broadsheet. 'Most of what Josie knows about politics she learned from books bought in this store. Got half her art here, too.'

'The next thing getting hung in that house is Clyde if he keeps fooling around with that girl,' Lou opined, nodding at his glass in confirmation.

A woman entered through the shop's rear door, like everyone in the know apparently did. She was approaching the half-century mark in age but her hair retained its reddish tinge, albeit with some chemical assistance. She possessed sharp features, particularly her eyes, which took in the back-room scene with glee. 'The standard troop of miscreants at assembly,' she said in an unplaceable accent, vaguely western but broad enough to scoop up traces of every place she had ever lived. 'Who's this innocent you lot are attempting to corrupt?'

Dolan greeted her warmly. 'Lillian Frost, may I present Florabel Muir.'

Had I been drinking whatever liquid the pitcher contained, I would have spit it out. Florabel Muir's byline had appeared on many of the most sensational *Daily News* stories of my youth. My blood still curdled at the memory of my uncle Danny reading aloud her account of the murder of gangster 'Legs' Diamond. Now she covered the Los Angeles beat for the same New York newspaper.

'You're the one whose curiosity I've come to sate,' she said.

'And I'm the one taking my leave.' Dolan donned his hat. 'I beat a hasty retreat homeward so I don't upset the little woman.'

'Are you married to Josie Fentress, too?' Florabel surveyed the room again as Dolan exited. 'As usual, nothing but orange wine. Shall we adjourn next door for some real refreshment?'

Florabel and I took a shortcut through the parking lot and entered another back room, this one in the adjacent restaurant, Musso & Frank Grill. More intellectual imbibers had gathered here. Among them stood Stanley Rose, swirling an empty cocktail glass. He nodded genially at me. 'How's it going over there?'

After a dumbstruck moment, I said, 'Milt's covering for me.'

'Good. Milt's a square fella.'

Florabel bantered with assorted well-wishers but never stopped leading the way into Musso's long, narrow front room. She ignored the dark wooden booths in favor of the bar, a massive structure that looked hewn from a Spanish galleon that had run aground in Santa Monica. Diamond patterns adorned each of its panels. We settled ourselves and ordered martinis. I took advantage of the moment to get a better look at my companion. Florabel had a pioneer woman's sturdy face; I could readily picture her raising livestock and a dozen overall-clad young'uns somewhere in Wyoming. Instead she'd become a chronicler of the city, dressed in a functional navy suit that had clearly served her well on many a lengthy night with the boys awaiting a verdict in the courthouse. A brooch on the lapel provided her sole nod to frivolity, a bunch of red enamel cherries dangling from a stem with bronze leaves. 'What do you do at Paramount, exactly, and why do you care about this years-old bank robbery?' she asked.

I heard presses rolling when she spoke. No way would I attempt to hoodwink this woman. I told her the truth – I didn't work for Paramount, I was involved with Gene, and I had to know how Clyde Fentress had come by the version of events he'd shilled to the studio.

Florabel took pity on me, patting my hand. 'This new investigation by the DA is a tough break for your friend.'

'Then you've heard about it?'

'That's my job. Word is, Detective Morrow is the target, but I have no idea why – or what prompted DA Fitts to reopen the case. They're being awfully tight-lipped over there, especially for them, so they must have something. Detective Morrow doesn't know what it is?'

'He has no idea. This is so absurd. Gene never planned any bank robbery. He couldn't have. You know that, don't you? Mr Dolan said you had all the ins and outs of this story.'

'George is the press agent I never needed.' She sipped daintily at her drink. 'I didn't cover the story, you understand. I'd only been out here a few months. I'd actually quit the newspaper game. Was trying to make a go of it in pictures, like friend Dolan, over at Fox. It didn't take. Mary Astor's scandalous little love diary came out that summer and I was the only one who knew how to play the story. Don't know why I ever tried to leave the business. No sense fighting your nature. I should have known when I started following the California Republic caper instead of churning out script pages.' Another, longer sip, to prepare herself. 'You know who's responsible for the robbery, yes?'

'Bianchi, Hoyer, and Yates.'

'Good girl. But there was always talk, even back in '36, of a fourth man. A Svengali, pulling the strings. He chose the bank, chose Bianchi, Hoyer, and Yates. I was never completely sold on the idea. I think it came about to explain where the twenty thousand dollars disappeared to. *Somebody* must have it. Over the years that notion became sort of accepted wisdom. There was a fourth man, the brains of the operation, who ended up with the money and is biding his time.' She reached for her glass but didn't pick it up, turning it on the surface of the bar instead. 'One of the names bandied about was Detective Morrow's.'

'It's not him.' My vehemence startled even me. I wondered who this resolute girl was, and why she didn't come around more often. 'If there is a fourth man, which nobody seems to know for sure, it isn't Gene.'

'For what it's worth, I agree. But he makes a convenient subject for speculation.' She ticked off the reasons on her fingers, one of them literally ink-stained. 'He's alive, he knew the principals, and he was and remains close to his partner's widow.'

That relationship with Abigail, forever threatening to drag Gene down. An image of her formed in my mind and I realized, to my dismay, I'd pictured Brenda Baines.

'Again, I don't cotton to the notion myself,' Florabel continued. 'But Fitts is operating under the idea Morrow's the fourth man. I'd like to know why that is.'

You and me both, I thought.

'Maybe there is something to this fourth man angle,' she said. 'It makes a kind of sense.'

'Then it has to be someone else.' I sampled my martini, and like that half of it was gone. 'What about Fentress? He seems to know an awful lot about what happened.'

'That he does. So why write a script confessing to everything once you've gotten away with it? Although . . .' She trailed off, as if lost in the rhomboid patterns behind the bar.

'Although what?'

'I'm thinking about Clyde. We've rubbed elbows a few times. Always check for my wristwatch after. I'm all for a man turning over a new leaf, but he's not going to do it at my expense. Anyway, back in 1936 Clyde was on the ropes. He hadn't boarded Josie's gravy train yet, and his career in pictures had hit the skids. He didn't turn it around until Paramount paired him with George.'

'So he might have returned to his old trade. Kind of like you did,' I added without thinking.

'Don't lump me in with Clyde.' Florabel smiled. 'But I can see it. As for why he'd put pen to paper on the subject now, well, I heard the boys in the back room next door cracking wise on how the Fentress union has hit rocky shoals. If Clyde's looking to go his separate way . . .' She shrugged, mulling the possibilities.

'Can I ask about another name? Aloysius Conlin.'

'The late Nap. Now taking the big sleep. Damn, that reminds me, I meant to pick up a copy of that book next door. I'm familiar with Nap's work.'

'And Nap was familiar with Fentress. Any chance Nap could have been the fourth man?' *And, as such, not at all keen on Clyde's script reviving interest in the case?* I thought.

'I haven't heard that before, but I reckon it's possible. Then anything is possible out here under the golden sun.' She sat back to reconsider me. 'I may have to do some digging now. Either find the missing money or figure out what bee got into the district attorney's bonnet that made him delve into this business again.'

'Use your feminine wiles,' I said.

'Those withered some time ago, alas. All I have left are tenacity and skill. Though in my day . . .' Her chuckle blossomed into a guffaw. 'There are things in this business only a woman can get away with.'

'Such as?'

'This goes back to one of my first jobs, in Salt Lake City. We were covering a murder trial and the July Fourth weekend was coming up. Beastly hot. I had an invitation to go to the mountains, but I couldn't leave during deliberations. The jury was deadlocked.' She glanced at me. 'Six good men and true. All of them married.'

I nodded encouragingly.

'Somehow I found my way into the jury room during lunch. Brought an entire bottle of perfume my beau had given me for my birthday. Narcisse Noir.' The name conjured a pleasant memory for her, and she smiled. 'I chose to sacrifice it. Spilled the whole thing under the table. Said it was an accident, of course. Those half-dozen men came back from lunch, caught a whiff of what they'd been missing, and acquitted the man in under an hour. Never underestimate the power of a fine perfume.'

'Was the man guilty?'

'No idea. But six of his peers said he wasn't, and I got to cool off in the mountains.'

She laughed again, and I couldn't help joining in. 'I met Virginia

Hill the other day, the heiress? She strikes me as someone who'd try a gambit like that.'

'You don't say. Is she somehow wrapped up in this California Republic business? You didn't fall for that heiress bunk, did you?'

'It's not true?'

'Not in the least. She's what they call a courier. Runs money for gangsters out of Chicago. It was common knowledge when she lived in New York, which is partly why the boys sent her out here. She has to explain how she came by all that cash somehow, so she cooked up this Alabama heiress line.' Florabel leaned in, confidence-close. 'Here's a little story. I was at Westmore's Salon of Beauty getting my hair done – this color doesn't linger on its own – when a package comes in for Miss Virginia Hill. She's due in that afternoon, fresh from Mexico City. The package is thin. I get a gander at the sender's name and recognize it from Chicago circles.' Her eyebrows shot up suggestively toward that crown of preserved red. 'So I dilly-dally until Miss Virginia arrives. She opens the bundle. What's inside?'

I couldn't make myself answer.

'Ten one-thousand-dollar bills. I know this, because she asks Perc Westmore to break one for her. He does, and she tips everybody in the place fifty dollars. Even the gals who *aren't* doing her nails. What does this tell me? For one thing, I'm in the wrong racket if Perc Westmore has a thousand in change in the till. It also tells me that while Virginia Hill may be a fellow redhead, she's a dangerous woman, and one best avoided.'

I was still marveling at the story when I noticed Florabel had at some point surreptitiously taken out a small notebook. I could make out some of what she'd scribbled—

Morrow CalRep Va Hill???

She had told me plenty. But I'd revealed more, to an inveterate newshound who already sensed a scoop.

'I can't thank you enough for your time,' I said, dropping a few bills onto the bar. 'But I should go. Work tomorrow.'

'Pity you don't work at Paramount. I was going to ask about rumbles I've heard. Studio big shots footing the bill for an operation spying on the German-American Bund.'

I grabbed my purse. 'Sounds far-fetched to me.'

FOURTEEN

On the streetcar out to Bunker Hill I watched the lights flicker to life. They illuminated once-grand Victorians now subdivided into rooming houses, and hastily constructed apartment buildings that looked seedy on the day they welcomed their first tenants. I had a soft spot for the no-longer-fashionable neighborhood. Elsewhere Los Angeles teemed with starlets and millionaires, the aspiring and the arrived. In Bunker Hill, no one dwelled on the glorious past or planned for a hopeful future; they simply aimed to make it through another day. The stubborn pride of the occasional neatly tended lawn and the scent of home-cooked meals heavy on cabbage and carrots reminded me of Queens, where I'd grown up. Like most indomitable things, it wasn't pretty, but it didn't need to be. In Bunker Hill, life was looked square in the eye. I had come to look longtime resident Gene square in the eye, too.

I'd caught him in the middle of something; he wiped his hands on a rag as he kissed me on the cheek. 'Hello, stranger,' he said. The bruises on his face had faded, noticeable only if you knew to look. 'Sorry I haven't called. Been busy. Abigail's here.'

He led me inside, detouring to the garage. Abigail waved to me. She looked wan, or maybe it was her tan shirtwaist dress. Gene's ancient lawn mower lay on a workbench, its blades too dull to gleam in the light. He glared at it. 'Started to cut the grass, but the damn thing stopped working. Trying to fix it.'

Abigail widened her eyes at me and suppressed a grin. We both knew Gene had no mechanical inclination whatsoever, approaching common household tasks with dread. 'And I dropped in to see if there's any news.'

'Is there?' I asked.

Gene's tongue pistoned against his cheek as he studied the machine's innards. 'Nope. Still twisting in the wind.'

'On that morbid note, I'll leave you two. And you should hire a neighborhood boy to cut the grass.' Abigail paused at the door. 'I nearly forgot. I had a question about summer jobs at Tremayne's. Can you walk me out, Lillian?'

The scents of jasmine and barbecue jostled on the night air, proof that spring had indeed sprung. 'I can call my old manager Mr Valentine if you think it'll—'

'Never mind that,' Abigail interrupted. 'I wanted to make sure you're OK.'

'Why wouldn't I be?'

'Gene said you hadn't called since he got into that silly fistfight. I was afraid you were avoiding him.'

'He hasn't called me, either.' The petulance I heard in my voice indicated Abigail might be right. Perhaps I had been steering clear of Gene, at least until I'd unearthed some truffle of useful information. I wondered what his excuse was for keeping his distance.

Abigail, naturally, already knew. 'That's Gene pretending to be stoic. This is tearing him up inside. Not that he'd ever say so. You know men. They have to appear strong at all costs.'

'And we have to let them?'

She cracked a smile. 'It worked with Teddy.'

She took out her keys as we reached a roomy dark blue Hudson Terraplane. 'It's twice the car I need. Should sell it and get a smaller one, but it was Teddy's. Big and flashy, just like him.' When she spoke again, her gaiety sounded forced. 'It does wonders for my posture. Have to sit up straight so I can see over the wheel. Go easy on Gene, will you? And make sure he doesn't hurt himself on that damned lawn mower.'

I found him looming over the offending apparatus, holding a screwdriver in each hand as if they were a knife and fork. 'Want to take a break?'

'Probably a good idea.' He doused the light before he finished the sentence.

We moved into his drafty kitchen. I imagined Gene as a boy, sprinting through on his way to build a fort in the backyard. The thought made me weepy, and I pushed it away realizing I hadn't eaten anything aside from the olive in my Musso & Frank martini. In the icebox I found some cold cuts teetering on the edge of edibility and set about making a sandwich. I'd been in Gene's house often enough to feel comfortable doing that.

'I need to ask you something,' I said as I foraged for mustard. 'It's been bothering me. Why didn't you tell me you were in trouble?'

'I didn't want you to worry, Frost.'

'I'm Catholic. I'm going to worry no matter what. You might as well harness that power and put it to use.'

Gene laughed, the sound as refreshing as water in the desert. 'Fair point.'

'I understand why you told Abigail. I suppose I've been wondering why you didn't think I needed to know, too.'

'I have an answer. You're not going to like it.'

I set my sandwich on the table. It could wait.

'I didn't want you trying to help me,' Gene said flatly.

'Why not?'

'Because you can't. No one can.' He started to speak, fell silent, started again. 'This investigation is one of two things. Either the fix is in, and I'm on my way out because I've made enemies. Or it's a show, being staged for reasons I can't fathom. In which case, it'll be over soon enough. Those are the only choices. I know you, Frost. You can't help getting involved, so I wanted to spare you.' He looked at me across the table, his eyes exhausted. 'But I didn't, did I? You've been helping me.'

I chafed at how he said 'helping'. Like a patience-strained mother in a flour-strewn kitchen speaking to a child. *What a good job you did helping Mommy!* But now was not the time to object.

Gene pushed himself to his feet and fetched a beer. When I declined one, he poured a glass of water and put it next to my sandwich. 'I suppose I should thank you for adding Nap Conlin to the equation. I gather it's one reason Fentress didn't raise hell about our tête-à-tête. He suddenly had a more pressing problem.'

'A detective talked to Edith and me about Nap at Paramount yesterday.'

'You got Tate to leave his desk?' Gene rocked backward. 'I didn't think a stick of dynamite could do that.'

'No, another man came to the studio. Frady.'

The legs of Gene's chair slammed onto the linoleum with a sound like a gunshot. 'Byron Frady? A knight in tarnished tweed? *He* showed up at Paramount?'

His intensity was such that I could only nod.

Gene howled with laughter. 'Byron's no detective. He's a captain.'

'He never mentioned his rank. He just passed along his regards.'

'I'll bet he did.' Gene set down his Pabst, the better to brace his head with both hands. 'He hates my guts.'

'Why?'

'Because Teddy was his fair-haired boy. Frady spotted him early on, earmarked him for big things. When Teddy was killed, Frady blamed me.'

'But – what does he think you did?'

'I don't know. Maybe he heard the same bullshit rumors about me and Abigail as the rest of the department. Maybe it's enough I was there when Teddy died. Since then, he's made his displeasure known every chance he gets.' He pressed both palms to his forehead. 'Captains generally don't undertake solo interrogations, Lillian. Remember when I said I made enemies? Frady's gunning for me.'

'Why now?'

'Because the whole department's being shaken up by Mayor Bowron's election and his reform push. This month they forced out dozens of senior men. All with over twenty years of service, all of them loyal to the old chief, Two-Gun Davis. But not Frady. Wily Byron survived the purge.'

I felt many steps behind. 'So . . . couldn't that mean he's honest?'

'Sure, if you're Pollyanna. Downtown, the stories run a little darker. They say he's so bent not even the new broom crowd can lay a hand on him. He's crooked in ways they can't even see. Frady's paying for those tweed suits somehow. He's cagey. And he's got plans.' He chuckled, the sound like something rising from a drain. 'Mayor Bowron's Police Commission decided the department's promotion list was so tainted by corruption they tossed it out. Started from scratch. Every test for the next rank has to be taken again – only this time they're including chief of police. Frady's let it be known he's throwing his hat in the ring. Bastard could actually land the job. This could all be in preparation for his big move. It'd be just like the son of a bitch to settle my hash before he tries ascending to the highest office in the LAPD.'

'Wait, so if Frady's on some personal vendetta—'

'No. I *hope* he is. I'm praying for it. Because the alternative is worse.'

I didn't understand, and said as much.

'The other explanation is the department is sufficiently concerned about the DA's investigation they're looking to torch me before Fitts can do it. Better to clean your own house than let someone else call it dirty. And Frady's just the man to drop the hammer.' He took a hearty pull on his beer. 'However you slice it, it doesn't look good for your Mudville Nine.'

I thought I'd scream, or cry, or slap the beer can out of his hand. Instead, I found myself thinking of everything Florabel Muir had told me. Find the money or find the evidence.

'The DA wouldn't reopen the California Republic investigation unless he had a witness or something explosive. You don't know what it could be? You can't even guess?'

'No.' He sensed my frustration and took pity on me. 'But whatever it is, it's a lie.'

That put me slightly at ease. 'Do you think the robbery could have been planned by someone else? A fourth man, still at large?'

'"At large?"' Gene grinned at my use of the term. 'No. I've heard that cockamamie theory. There's no one else.'

'Then what happened to the loot?'

'Yates or Hoyer hid it before they died. Some homeowner will turn it up decades from now when they start putting in a swimming pool, and the last California Republic mystery will be solved. Probably after I'm dead. I'm having another beer before Frady breaks my door down. You sure I can't interest you?'

'No. Could gangsters have been involved with the robbery?'

'Gangsters? What brought this on?'

'I met Virginia Hill the other day when I talked to Clyde Fentress's protégée.'

'I don't know the name.'

'I thought she was an oil heiress, but it turns out she moves money for some gangsters in Chicago. It seems strange she should turn up in the middle of this.'

'All manner of strange things turn up in cases like this. The trick is focusing on the right ones. No gangsters are involved, from Chicago or right here. This was about three strong-arm men, all of them long gone. Any other questions?'

I took a breath. 'Yes. What can I do for you?'

'I already told you. Nothing.'

'That's ridiculous. There must be something.'

He smiled genuinely then for the first time in the conversation. 'One thing. You can believe in me.'

'Done.'

'I have a question now. You going to eat that sandwich?'

'It can wait.'

He stepped around the table. I stood up and melted into his arms, inhaling the faint aromas of beer and grease, the ghost of the after-shave he'd put on that morning, the jumble of familiar scents he carried in his hair and skin and clothes. I fell into it all. As I did, a part of me wondered how many more times I'd be able to do so.

The sounds of a radio quiz show came from Mrs Quigley's apartment, including Mrs Q calling out incorrect answers to her Philco. I hollered in a greeting.

'There you are!' she replied. 'Have you eaten?'

'Yes, thanks.' The sandwich wasn't much, but it counted.

My landlady shuffled into the front hallway, wrapped in a dressing gown she swore had been a gift from Flo Ziegfeld himself. The garment had turned shiny with age, so maybe she was on the level. 'Your friend was here.'

I hoped desperately she meant Vi. 'Who?'

'The fellow who eats me out of house and home, bless him.'

'What time?'

'Around two, two-thirty, so he only took a bit of lunch.'

Simon at liberty in the middle of a workday. Not a promising sign.

'*And* you had a phone message. Such excitement!' Mrs Q fished a scrap of paper from her dressing gown pocket, replaced it, then found it again. 'Yes, here it is. A detective telephoned, but not your nice Mr Morrow. Yes. A Mr Farrell.'

She'd written down *Frady*. I didn't bother making note of the number. I had no intention of returning the call.

I was bidding Mrs Q goodnight when her head snapped toward the radio. 'Oh, what's his name? McKinley's vice president! You know who I mean. Hobart! Garrett Hobart!' She smiled angelically at me. 'He died in office, you know.'

Miss Sarah sidled past with a look that said, *I've been dealing with this all day.*

Upstairs, I changed into my own dressing gown and retrieved the file George Dolan had given me, containing Sylvia Ward's fledgling attempt at writing for the screen. A brief note had been clipped to the first page, the handwriting with nary a trace of girlishness.

Mr Dolan,

Here is a sample of my scribblings. Thank you for taking the time to look at my work. Please blame any shortcomings on your partner Mr Fentress.

> *Regards,*
> *Sylvia Ward*

I fixed a cup of tea, sat in my favorite overstuffed armchair, and dimmed the lights in the theater of my mind.

Sylvia hadn't titled her nascent script of twenty or so unnumbered pages. The action began in 1760s Philadelphia, with a young Quaker seamstress named Betsy Ross learning she has been apprenticed to an upholsterer. She finds herself instantly smitten with a fellow laborer, a non-Quaker named John; by page four she was sewing tiny hearts into her work where only he would see them. Betsy and John soon marry against their families' wishes and open their own upholstery shop. The excerpt ended with a customer inquiring if they could make bed hangings for a newly arrived delegate to the Continental Congress named George Washington.

I let the final page flutter to the floor. Sylvia's efforts surprised me for several reasons. The subject matter seemed a tad grandiose for her. The young lovers' dialogue had a playfulness that came as a contrast to Sylvia's brittle nature.

The biggest shock, though, was understanding I'd heard every word of it before. I suspected it on page one, but needed to skim the others for the realization to sink in.

Sylvia, as far as I could tell, had retyped the opening pages of *The Stars and Stripes*. Lodestar Pictures had released the mighty pile of patriotic hooey the previous summer in the hope of sparking Fourth of July box office fireworks, but the film had fizzled. Critics praised the meticulous recreation of Washington crossing the Delaware and the cast of thousands used in the epic Battle of Trenton scenes, but those garlands couldn't overcome the titters in the gallery when Lodestar icon Madge Granger, too old to play the now-widowed Betsy Ross, seduced a Hessian colonel on the eve of the skirmish.

I'd always loved Madge Granger, though, and I teared up when a tattered Old Glory caught the breeze in the closing shot.

To impress George Dolan, Sylvia had passed off as her own work pages from a produced script, one that had likely come through the offices of Central Casting in order to fill out those lauded battle scenes. Why, I wondered, would she do that? No time like the present to find out.

I stepped into my slippers and trotted downstairs. Mrs Quigley's radio droned on as I leafed through the White Pages. Sylvia – all praise to the Archangel Gabriel, patron saint of telephony – was listed. But apparently not at home; the phone trilled hollowly five times. I had pulled the receiver from my ear when I heard someone pick up.

'Who is it?' More than annoyance registered in Sylvia's voice; it sounded hostile, as if I had joined a pitched argument already in progress.

'Sylvia? It's Lillian Frost. We—'

'You. I know all about you. I know who you are now. You and your boyfriend.' Whatever heat had been in her words drained away. She spoke coldly now, a minister presiding over a stranger's funeral. 'He took a swing at Clyde, and you're a liar. You're no Paramount employee, and you have no friend interested in extra work. I'll bet you have no friends at all, you witch. Why on earth should I talk to you?'

I'd somehow ended up on this side of the accusation when I was the one who'd called in high dudgeon. 'Three words. *The Stars and Stripes*.' OK, that was four words, but still, it made a worthwhile rally.

After a moment Sylvia's muffled voice came down the line; she wasn't alone, and whoever she was speaking to found themselves at the sharp end of some pointed instructions. When she addressed me again, she seemed wholly unperturbed. 'I don't know what that means, and I don't want to talk to you.'

'Neither of us has been honest. How about we both come clean?' I heard another muted comment directed at her visitor, this one emphatic. 'Sylvia?'

'How about you go to hell.' Her slamming down of the receiver was emphatic, too.

I turned on my radio, hoping music would soothe me after a long day. So I'd caught Sylvia in a lie. I'd lied to her, too. Whatever it meant could wait until tomorrow.

The sounds of the King Cole Orchestra washed over me. I waited for them to still the voice in my head insisting something was off and needed to be tackled at once. *Silence, little voice*, I instructed, remembering Gene's words. He didn't want or need my help.

Then Abigail's comment came back to me. *That's Gene pretending to be stoic. This is tearing him up inside.*

I donned a coat for my second trip downstairs. I noted Sylvia's address in the telephone directory, then arranged a taxicab.

She lived in a newer boxy building, close enough to Central Casting for her to walk to work. A scattering of potted petunias lining the entryway made a meager bulwark against the building's drab brown brick. Buzzing Sylvia's apartment yielded no response. I stared at the faux stained glass inlaid in the front door, the lobby's single bulb refracted through varying shades of amber and green. I would wait until Sylvia returned home. The silly little fears rampaging through my head were baseless, and certainly not worth rousing anyone else from their bed.

The building's manager padded out in answer to my ringing his doorbell, his grotesque shape through the mosaic of glass resolving into a hairy-shouldered man chewing an unlit cigar. I waved Sylvia's script pages and mouthed some nonsense about a Central Casting emergency. Somehow I convinced him to lead the way to Sylvia's second-floor apartment.

The manager slowed as we reached her door. He pushed on it and it swung open, spilling light into the hallway.

Fingers instinctively smoothing his unruly hair, he ordered me in broken Slavic-accented English to wait. I nodded that I was happy to oblige.

The man's wracked gagging came first, followed by a faint, almost ghastly hint of perfume, as if the fragrance had been used to mask more unspeakable aromas.

As the manager emerged from Sylvia's rooms, I rushed forward. Pop-eyed, he waved me off. 'Is not good for woman,' he said with a thick tongue. Peering past him I glimpsed an overturned mule next to the sole of Sylvia's bare foot as she lay on her bedroom floor, and I wondered which woman he was referring to. Both of us. Maybe all of us.

From somewhere in Sylvia's apartment came the ringing of a telephone. No one made a move to answer it.

FIFTEEN

A police station close to midnight – complete with sporadic, jackal-like cries from the bowels of the building and coffee that tasted like it had been boiled in the can – made an improvement over my vigil outside Sylvia Ward's apartment.

The building's hirsute manager had a neighboring tenant alert the police while he guarded Sylvia's door, arms folded and shoulder hairs at attention. He glowered at me as if informing him of Sylvia's death were a greater crime than killing her, because my offense upset his night's sleep.

I indicated I felt faint and needed water. He grumbled and stepped into Sylvia's apartment, shielding her body from my view with grudging gallantry, and gestured toward the bathroom.

I took in the tiny front room's décor, spare enough to suggest vacancy. I could almost convince myself that's what had happened: Sylvia had packed a grip and lit out for parts unknown, an occurrence so commonplace in Los Angeles that one of the newspapers should have run a column tracking such hasty departures to spare people undue grief. She had made so little impression on her quarters I imagined even Clyde Fentress, newly sprung from San Quentin, would have found them austere.

Sylvia had trod equally lightly in the bathroom, like a secret boarder hoping not to be discovered. A lonely lipstick and a container of blush next to a sliver of soap, a bottle of shampoo in the shower stall. Relics that could have been left by anyone, anytime. A makeshift clothesline had been rigged between two exposed pipes, the still-drying personal items dangling from it the truest testimony Sylvia had, in fact, been here.

I splashed water on my face, using the single threadbare towel still smelling of detergent to blot it away. *It would have made no difference if I'd read those script pages earlier or gotten here faster*, I told myself. *There was nothing I could have done to save her.* Like all catechisms, I'd have to repeat it many times before it had any effect.

I averted my gaze as I left the bathroom, out of respect for Sylvia. I noticed something I had missed earlier, several shards of glass gathered by the baseboard, as if a bottle had shattered. Other odors now emanated from the bedroom, the last of the phantom perfume dissipating. The manager snapped his fingers and signaled me back into the hallway.

The first police officer on the scene had the manager – whose last name, I learned, was Bostic – and I stand next to each other like co-conspirators. A Mutt and Jeff detective duo arrived next. Obergfell, made up entirely of gristle and resentment, peppered Bostic with questions. Jeffries possessed the physique of the precinct's Christmas party Santa Claus. He rested his bulk against the wall and grumbled about the climb upstairs. He grilled me, his approach growing more direct even though Bostic confirmed my account. When I suggested they call Detective Gene Morrow, the partners glanced at each other and shooed us downstairs.

At the station, I watched Obergfell unpack Sylvia's purse. I'd never seen a woman travel so light: the barest quantities of make-up, some tissues, a single hard candy. The thought she'd never enjoy it now made me excuse myself to collect my wits at the water cooler.

When I returned to Obergfell's desk, the detective had retreated to the chorus while another man took center stage, bending over the contents of Sylvia's bag with his hands behind his back. I didn't see his face. I didn't need to. His tweed suit, this one a dazzling heather, gave him away.

'Miss Frost,' Captain Frady said without turning, my shadow announcing my presence. 'I'm disappointed you didn't see fit to return my telephone message.'

Despite my trip to the water cooler, my throat went dry. 'I, uh, I didn't get home until late.'

'Yet you then went gallivanting to Miss Ward's.' He faced me. Head on, his double-breasted suit was even more striking. His eyes made me think of that infernal machine clicking away at Central Casting. 'I'd have taken your call no matter the hour. All I have is my work. Did you extend my regards to Detective Morrow?'

I nodded.

'May I assume he responded with a litany of grievances?'

'He said you don't like him.'

'An assessment both accurate and admirably brief.' He flashed a newspaper-thin smile. 'I will explain, so there will be no confusion. I have no ax to grind. I do have a great many questions about the death of Detective Lomax. A man whose career I stewarded personally.

When I heard of a motion picture purporting to tell the true story of the incident, naturally I was interested.'

'You can't possibly believe that "true story".'

The man bucking to become the next chief of police of Los Angeles paused, resenting my interruption. 'I have made a study of the California Republic bank robbery. I am intimately familiar with the men involved. Borden Yates, who repeatedly took advantage of young women like yourself, Miss Frost, fathering a string of children out of wedlock and thus destroying those young women's reputations. Leo Hoyer, who learned to drive at speed outrunning outraged fathers because of his predilection for school-age girls. As for Giuseppe Bianchi, I had the pleasure of apprehending him in the year of our Lord nineteen hundred and twenty-nine. When they hauled that brute off to prison I'd have sworn sunlight would never strike him as a free man again. But our penal system works in mysterious ways.' He shrugged, helpless. 'These men were more than capable of murdering officers of the law, each possessed of the low cunning of the habitual criminal. Did they have the audacity to plan the robbery that took place in 1936?' Another shrug, this one less help-less. 'I myself have always wondered. Hence my interest in Clyde Fentress's film script, and his friendship with the late Nap Conlin. Now another person tied to Fentress has been killed, with you again the one informing us. Shall we discuss your evening in detail?'

He proceeded to interrogate me at length, Obergfell lurking like an unfunny jester before the king. Frady probed my story, pinpointing small inconsistencies and pressing for details. He was, I hated to admit, thorough.

'This person in Sylvia's apartment when you spoke with her on the telephone,' Frady asked. 'You never heard a voice?'

'No, only Sylvia speaking to them. She'd cupped her hand over the receiver.'

'You understand this person was likely her killer.'

The thought had arisen, but I'd shunted it from my mind. 'What happened to Sylvia, exactly?'

'She was strangled. With a length of the cord she used as a clothesline. We found several of them in her bedroom along with fragments of glass, some object broken amidst the struggle.'

Like a bottle of perfume, I thought.

We reviewed the events again, Frady stopping to appraise me across Obergfell's desk. 'You read these script pages and knew

Sylvia had misrepresented someone else's work as her own? From seeing the picture in question last July?'

Taking my cues from him, I shrugged.

'I commend you. A tidy piece of detective work.' He didn't sound particularly impressed, but as I expected no further hosannas I accepted the compliment gratefully.

After another round of questions, Frady extracted a gold pocket watch from his waistcoat. Even in the station's scant light, it gleamed. 'I believe we've covered this enough. I understand your chariot awaits. Permit me to escort you out.'

He made a show of scanning the scantily populated lobby. 'Dear me. I hope I wasn't misinformed. Shall we check outside?'

Gene's car waited at the curb, Gene slumped behind the wheel. He'd forgotten his hat, revealing the furrows he'd plowed through his hair. He spotted us and emerged warily.

'Eugene!' Frady called. 'Is this how you greet a young lady at this ungodly hour, one toiling on your behalf to boot?'

Gene opened the car's passenger door. 'I'm taking you home,' he announced. I stepped forward. Frady threw out an arm, checking my progress.

'Really, now, not even the decency to wait inside and walk the lady to your car. I have to question how you were raised.'

'It's fine,' I said, avoiding Frady's arm and trotting to the car.

Gene ignored me. He stared placidly at Frady, who in turn made with a vaudeville shudder.

'What's that sudden chill in the air? I do believe if I didn't outrank you, Eugene, you'd take a swing at me.'

'If you didn't outrank me, Byron, you'd be laid out on the sidewalk.'

'That sounds like a threat.'

'Only if you're planning on demoting yourself, sir.'

An explosive laugh from Frady. 'Good thing for you, my son, the only steps I take are up. Miss Frost. Do me the courtesy of responding promptly the next time I call. Thank you again for your assistance.' He bowed to us both and returned to work.

His car pointed toward Mrs Quigley's, Gene said, 'Tell me what happened.' I complied. I didn't realize the interview had ended until he said, in the same quiet voice, 'You were still trying to help me. After I told you not to only a few hours ago.'

'I don't regret it,' I said. 'I found out Sylvia concocted this elaborate lie about writing somebody else's script pages and I wanted to know why. I still do.'

'You could have waited until morning. You could have called me.'

'After you'd told me not to help you?'

Using his own argument against him stung. 'There's a perfectly good reason for her to fob off those pages as her own.'

'I'd like to hear it.'

'If Sylvia wasn't Fentress's protégée, but his mistress. They'd need cover for their affair, so they concoct this jazz about her learning to write at the master's feet. Fentress's partner Dolan is the stickiest wicket, so she dummies up a few pages for appearances' sake.'

'I suppose that could be true. Is it?'

'With a captain personally involved, people get woken up all over town. Even in Hancock Park. Fentress told a detective he and Miss Ward were romantically involved. He says she visited him at the studio until around six. He then stopped for several drinks and saw several pictures. He can't recall their names and said it made no difference, because they were all terrible. I've heard better alibis.'

'What did his wife say? Josie?'

'Nothing. She wasn't home. Before we start suspecting her, will you admit that explains those script pages?'

'Yes. But those pages don't explain why Sylvia was killed.'

'That depends. How bad were they?'

'You remember the picture. You took me to see it.' I shifted closer to him on the seat. 'Two people connected to Clyde Fentress have been murdered in the past week.'

'I'm aware of that.'

'But he wrote this dreadful movie about you! This has to help your cause somehow.'

'All it does is warn people not to have anything to do with Clyde Fentress, which anyone paying attention would have known already. It doesn't affect what's happening to me. I told you that before, when I expressly said not to help.'

I nodded. The most eloquent response I could think of.

Gene kept mum, too, all the way to Mrs Quigley's. He wished me goodnight and drove off into the darkness. Inside, I glimpsed Miss Sarah's tail as she slinked out of sight. Even she wanted nothing to do with me.

Los Angeles Register   March 30, 1939

LORNA WHITCOMB'S
EYES ON HOLLYWOOD

The Countess Dorothy Dentice di Frasso – Dottie to her friends (and that's half of *Who's Who*) – is planning a Friday night soirée that's the talk of the town. Invitations are scarce, but we know one famous face who won't be attending. It seems Kay Francis's fiancé Baron Raven Erik Angus Barnekow (just call him Erik) failed this week in his bid to file a complaint of slander against the Countess. He claims she falsely called him a 'Nazi spy' but the Countess denied it and said she's not interested in politics. That's probably wise when your villa in Rome is leased to the Italian Ministry for Foreign Affairs . . . Not for yours truly the train to San Francisco for the premiere of *The Story of Alexander Graham Bell*. I'll tour the Golden Gate Exposition in warmer weather, thanks. So what if the cars will carry the movie's stars Don Ameche and Loretta Young, not to mention Sonja Henie, Preston Foster, Tyrone Power, and— Hey, conductor, is it too late for me to buy a ticket?

SIXTEEN

N ix on my usual morning debate about lingering in bed a few extra minutes. I didn't want to risk outtakes from the bad dreams that punctuated a fitful night's sleep. Awake if not alert, I managed to attire myself in what the saleslady had called a 'hug-me-tight' jacket. Sister, she wasn't kidding. I may have bruised a rib buttoning the form-fitting top of my suit. But it looked smart with a flared skirt of matching Juliet blue and mid-heel ribbon-tied oxfords.

First stop at Addison's: the kitchen, for a large cup of coffee liberally doctored with sugar. In my little office I angled the chair toward the French doors so I'd have an excuse to leave on my sunglasses. Despite my best cosmetic efforts, the strain showed on my face. Even a pilgrimage to Westmore's Salon of Beauty wouldn't have helped.

I had my back to Addison, his correspondence receiving my attention, when he entered. 'Lillian! Meet my acting teacher!'

'Just a moment.' I finished addressing an envelope, pivoted in my seat, then nearly fell out of it. Next to a beaming Addison stood Bette Davis, eyeing me with a hefty dose of skepticism. The concentrated New England variety.

'Is this woman your social secretary?' Davis said, her inflection planting flags in syllables and transforming the question into an accusation. 'I thought perhaps she was some highly touted starlet unknown to me.'

I didn't comprehend her comment. Then it hit me: *sunglasses.* I whipped them off, the sight of my haggard face only hardening the actress's judgment. Clearly, I was some addle-brained late-night reveler taking advantage of her friend. She'd probably pull Addison aside and advise him to proofread the letters I'd typed.

'It's a pleasure to see you again, Miss Davis,' I said brightly, determined to revise her impression of me – and remind her we'd met before, at one of Addison's parties. Her smile in response indicated she had no recollection of that historic encounter. Davis had won her second Academy Award a month earlier for *Jezebel*, a film in which her character almost starts the Civil War prematurely by wearing a red gown to a formal ball, the scene so powerful I could still envision the dress's scandalous shade of scarlet even though the movie's black-and-white photography never showed it. Davis was not garbed so elaborately now, in a straight gray skirt and tan brushed mohair cardigan with wooden buttons. She moved to light a cigarette and I saw that, as usual, she had opted not to wear a brassiere.

Davis fired a stream of smoke into the room like an arrow. I told myself I wasn't the target. 'As I was saying, Addy,' she declared, 'I'm just back from Philadelphia. Sam Harris's wedding, you know. What fun!' Her delivery of the two words made me question how much enjoyment was had. 'Then I went right into my next picture, so this little break you're providing is a *treat*.'

'We can't thank you enough for helping Addison,' I said. I was going to participate in this conversation, by God. Davis cocked her head at me, then pointedly glanced down. The force of her gaze compelled me to do likewise, and I saw one of my shoelaces had come undone. Worse, I could hardly stoop to tie it now. I had cemented my status as a rank incompetent, the battle lost. Her opinion of me couldn't sink much lower, so only my respect for Addison prevented me from inquiring if her alleged affair with world-famous flyboy filmmaker Howard Hughes had prompted her recent divorce.

She turned to Addison. 'You're going to tread the boards, so to speak. How wonderful.'

'I won't be attempting anything like you do, Bette,' Addison said, one toe bashfully circling the floor. 'Basically I'm going to stand around.'

'Stand around?' The words echoed so loudly the chandelier rattled. 'That is not how the work is done. Now. What kind of character will you be playing?'

Addison worked his jowls several times before committing to an answer. 'I must admit I don't really know.'

'You don't know?' She laughed, a great raucous bark.

Addison looked imploringly at me. *You're on your own, fella*, I thought, before rolling up my mental sleeves and diving in, Davis's scorn be damned. 'Addison will be playing a man about town enjoying himself at a nightclub.'

Approval registered in the actress's features for the first time that morning. 'Now we're getting somewhere! So. What do we know of this man about town? Is he celebrating? Has he closed the deal of a lifetime? Or is he putting on a brave face because his marriage is ending?' Another loud guffaw made me step out from under the chandelier. 'Is he cavorting with the young chippie who will cost him his wedded bliss?'

Addison offered an impressive selection of contemplative noises. 'Well. Those are all splendid, viable suggestions. But I don't really think—' He spun toward me like a clockwork soldier. 'Correct, Lillian?'

'Indeed.' *Indeed what?* 'The precise nature of the character hasn't been determined yet. Addison will be an extra. Forgive me, an atmosphere performer.'

I anticipated my gaffe to warrant another blast of disdain from Davis, but she waved off my comment. 'I know a thing or two about *that*. When I first came from New York and signed my contract, the studio had no use for me. So I became a *test girl*. I lay about a divan like a prop while a dozen or more hopefuls, young men fresh from football teams and beanfields, swept me up and said they *adored* me, they *worshipped* me, they must *possess* me. Can you imagine? What an introduction! Still, I gave each of those aspiring actors something to work with. You'll be in a nightclub, you said. How are you going to dance?'

'Dance?' Addison's eyebrows reared back. 'Badly, I suppose.'

'So he's awkward! Why? Is he uncomfortable or has he sustained some sort of *physical injury*?'

Addison's hands fanned out behind him in search of a chair. Finding one, he sank wearily into it. 'I was making a joke. I mean, I have no idea what kind of band will be playing.'

'I must say, this production sounds very disorganized. Who's making this picture again?'

'Paramount,' I said with wholly unearned pride.

'Lillian's friend Edith Head is doing the costumes,' Addison chimed in.

'I haven't worked with her,' Davis sniffed. 'What's required of any production is precision. When we were making *Jezebel*, dear Willie Wyler had miniatures built for all of our sets. After dinner each night, he'd place the next day's set on the table and use toy cameras and actors to plan every shot while I spoke the dialogue. All timed with a *stopwatch*. Nothing to chance. It sounds as if you're being abandoned to your own devices to create a character out of whole cloth. So you must ask yourself, who is he? What kind of impression does he want to make? A man about town pours champagne one way when he's happy and another when he's sad. How shall your man about town pour?'

Addison spoke meekly, his voice waving a white flag of surrender. 'Honestly, I'm just hoping to fade into the woodwork.'

'Nonsense!' Davis thundered, her eyes widening. 'If that's all you're going to do, you'll simply be blocking some talented craftsman's woodwork!'

'I believe what Mr Rice means,' I said, wondering at what point I'd become Addison's legal representative, 'is he's taking his position in the background to heart. He doesn't want to call attention to himself, but does want to contribute to the seamless whole of the picture.'

Addison nodded in frantic agreement. Davis appraised me anew. 'Your point is well taken, dear.' She leaned forward as if planning to lower her voice, then spoke at the same volume. 'Incidentally, you have some lipstick on your teeth. Even in the background, Addy, you've got to know who you're playing so you can offer consistency to that . . . seamless whole.' She made the faintest bow in my direction.

I looked at Addison. 'She's right.'

'Naturally I'm right! You can't hide, not even in the background. Not when the camera is rolling. Edmund Goulding – we did *Dark Victory* together, and we're working on *The Old Maid* now – told me to only offer hints to the audience, not to give them everything at once. Isn't that *absurd*? What on earth does he think they paid for? To do some of the work themselves? No, we do the work, we *actors*. You and I must work now, Addy. We must learn about your character and decide how his being affects his actions. Like dancing. Must he be coaxed onto the floor? I rather like the idea of a war wound. We must *figure this out.*'

'Yes, of course. And we shall. Would you excuse us a moment?' Addison hoisted himself from his chair and, waxen smile on his lips, maneuvered me into the hallway. He whispered in my ear as if we were spies behind enemy lines. 'I don't suppose she'd let you sit in on this session. I'm a bit terrified of being alone with her.'

'That seems unlikely. Anyway, it's best if I go to Paramount this afternoon.' I summarized my previous evening and, after expressing his concern for me, Addison insisted I head to the studio at once.

He then turned his gaze back on Bette Davis. So did I. Her smoking alone in a sunlit room contained more drama than most battle scenes. 'I can tough it out. Besides, this lesson can't last forever. I have my lab time with Hedy this afternoon.'

'If I may ask, why didn't you go to Miss Lamarr for help with your acting?'

'She was the first person I called! She said she only wanted to discuss engineering with me. Then told me she didn't know anything about acting other than find your key light.' He peered fearfully at Davis. 'Probably shouldn't ask Bette about that.'

SEVENTEEN

Edith had suggested we meet at Stage 13, to mark the first day of shooting on *Streetlight Story*. I'd learned enough about how pictures were made from my uncle Danny – 'Nothing stops a crew from getting the job done, pet, except the possibility of food' – to schedule my visit for lunchtime.

Inside the soundstage's open elephant doors there was no sense of occasion, of some great undertaking being launched. Only an anthill industriousness, clusters of people intent on specific tasks, transmitting and receiving intelligence via unseen antennae. A police station set had been erected under the lights. Funny how little resemblance it bore to the genuine article I'd been in only hours earlier. I marveled at the fact I'd likely seen every one of the set's component parts in other Paramount films. But the flats, furniture, and props had never been arranged in this exact combination before. Thus had an entirely new location been born.

Max Ramsey and Luddy were having it out on the set. Max sat in a chair looking diminished. His director loomed over him like a browbeating cop, his long shadow somehow possessed of weight and menace.

'Maybe you were used to something different at UFA,' Max said wearily. 'But I'm telling you the brass loves us now. We're on velvet. You don't have to pinch pennies. You can light this set properly.'

'Brass? Velvet? These I do not understand.' Luddy smiled through a veil of cigarette smoke. 'But this set is properly lit. More light will only reveal less.'

'Luddy. Sweetheart.' Max began pleading his case again. I walked a lap around the soundstage and didn't see Edith. Time enough for a quick stop elsewhere.

The trek to Clyde Fentress's office seemed to take longer, as if extra yards had been edited into the lot. I was not surprised to find his door shut, and no answer to my knock. I tried George Dolan's door anticipating the same result, but he softly called out, 'Come in.'

He wore a cream-colored shirt and a snazzy gold tie bisected by an ivory stripe, reminding me of Fentress's 'California dandy' jibe. But if Dolan had selected the clothes to spruce his spirits, they'd failed to turn the trick. He slouched at his typewriter, not having bothered to roll a sheet of paper into position.

'I won't ask if you've heard,' he said. 'Clyde told me you're the one who found Sylvia.'

I nodded solemnly.

'I'm sorry you had to deal with that. I can't get over it. What a loss. She was such a talented girl. Those pages she showed me had real promise.'

I couldn't bring myself to reveal what I'd discovered about those pages that had led me to Sylvia's apartment. I opted for the kinder gesture and returned those same pages to him. 'I thought you'd want them back.'

He accepted the file gratefully and started to open it, only to drop it on his desk, the burden too great. 'Did you like them?'

I didn't have to lie. 'Yes. I could see it all playing out on the big screen. Is Clyde here?'

'No. I telephoned this morning to find out why he was late. We had plans to crash the opening day of *Streetlight Story*. Provided we could get past security.' He smirked as he sparked a cigarette. 'Writers, as a rule, aren't typically welcome or even necessary once cameras are rolling. That's when Clyde told me what happened and said he wouldn't be coming in. I stayed to hammer out a few pages, but . . .' He reached for the typewriter and sarcastically struck a few keys. 'Inspiration's in short supply today.'

'That's understandable. How's Clyde taking the news?'

'Same way he takes everything. To him, all of life's some big joke. Don't misunderstand me. I know he's hurting. But he acts like he's not. I blame that mordant big house sensibility of his. Can't break character even when tragedy strikes, the poor bastard. Pardon the language.'

'It's quite all right. I heard someone say Clyde was at the pictures last night?'

'Was he? That'd be a rarity. At times I'd swear he actively loathes movies.'

I knew my next question was clumsy, but I couldn't concoct a better angle. 'I imagine his wife Josie will be a big help in the coming days, now that he's lost his protégée.'

'You'd be the only one to imagine it.' Dolan chuckled. 'I

sometimes think those two tied the knot just so they'd have the story to tell. Clyde and Josie lead very separate lives. Not a lot of love in that marriage. Plenty of money, though, so maybe it all balances out. The wife and I only have the former, so we wouldn't know.'

I told him I was on my way to the *Streetlight Story* set. 'Please convey the writers' warmest regards,' Dolan said loftily. Then, 'I hope this script isn't upsetting you too much. I didn't know the whole story when I started working on it. No one will connect this with your detective friend. Anyway, who remembers movies?'

No one but me, I thought.

Halfway to Stage 13, I spied the familiar figure of Bill Ihnen ambling toward me. The art director and Edith's old friend called to mind the phrase 'neat as a pin', always splendidly attired and with a permanent lively quality in his eyes. He hugged me in greeting, and I found myself clinging to him. Bill took my neediness in stride, gently patting me on the back.

'What brings you here?' I asked. 'Are you working on the lot?'

'A friend's trying to coax me into a job. I'm happy puttering for the moment, but sometimes it's easier just to hear them out.'

'Were you with Edith? I'm on my way to meet her.'

'No. She told me she had a lunch appointment. I should have known it was you. Can't keep my prospective non-employer waiting. Give Edo my love, would you?' With a peck on the cheek, he bounded off.

The crew, sated and on guard for the post-lunch doldrums, began filing back in earnest. Luddy now had sole dominion over the police station set. He stood with his arm around a sandy-haired man with high-waisted pants and his eyes pressed into a perpetual squint. Luddy addressed him in a low, seductive tone. 'The question, Norman, is can you make those shadows even darker?'

'They're plenty dark as is,' the other man, whom I took to be the cinematographer, ventured carefully. 'And Mr Ramsey wants us to bump up the lights.'

'I saw him take you aside earlier. I would put it to you, Norman, that a well-lit wall remains exactly that. A wall. Whereas this . . .' He extended his fingers toward a band of blackness creeping across the set. 'This can add interest. But only when sculpted by talented hands.'

Norman hiked his pants up even higher, which I would have thought an impossibility, as Luddy's flattery took effect.

'Wouldn't it be intensely interesting,' the director continued, 'if the very thing Jim is fighting is *already* within these walls?'

Norman rubbed his chin with his knuckles, entranced. 'Yeah, yeah . . . I feature it. He's shadowboxing, but for real.' He emerged from his haze, now resolutely practical. 'I can deepen the contrast, but it means resetting half the rig. It'd take a few minutes.'

'They have given us money. Let them give us time.' Luddy clapped Norman on the shoulder, sending him on his way.

The cinematographer exchanged nods with Fred MacMurray, wearing a suit that likely cost more than the entire stock of the haberdashery where Gene bought his clothes. The actor took in the set in its current configuration. 'Awful dark, isn't it?' he asked Luddy.

'This is why we have you, Frederick. To illuminate the scene with your incandescent performance.'

MacMurray laughed. 'You know best, Luddy. As long as someone tells me where to stand, I'm happy.'

From close by came a faint gasp. I realized I'd been holding my breath since MacMurray had appeared. *Snap out of it, Frost. He's not Gene. He's not even playing Gene. He's an actor who specializes in wisecrackers with handles like Crick and Buzzy. You've already met him. Just go over and say hello.*

Breathing steadily in and out like the nuns had taught me, I approached him. 'Hello, Mr MacMurray.'

'Hello,' he replied in the time-honored tradition, and looked at me expectantly.

'It's nice to see you again.'

'Yes. Likewise.' He projected the essence of affability, but that couldn't conceal the fact he didn't remember meeting me in Edith's office a few days ago.

Are you sure you're ready to play Gene? I wanted to ask. *Because Gene remembers everybody.*

'Just here to say break a leg.' As I walked away I passed Luddy, staring into the shadows as if he'd mesmerized himself.

I had planned to walk the perimeter of the soundstage one more time searching for Edith when I spotted the woman. One could hardly miss her, dressed to make an impression in a wide-brimmed veiled hat and a tapered black dinner suit with pleated silk lapels. Belatedly, I recognized the woman as Brenda Baines. Next I found myself bolting toward a neglected corner of the soundstage. I was

apparently in no mood to talk to the actress, my subconscious seizing
the reins and sending me into hiding. I was close enough to hear
Brenda's heels click against the floor as I waited for her to pass—

'Hello, Daughter!'

'Hey, Ma!'

I risked a peek. Brenda had been hailed by an older woman
whose refined features clashed with her homely wool coat and cloche
sporting three forlorn flowers. They embraced heartily.

'Who are you supposed to be?' Brenda asked. 'Has your poor
little Johnny been scooped up by the long arm of the law?'

The older woman hooted. 'Got it in one.'

'Been busy? Lining up jobs?'

'Nerk since I played your sainted mother for the blink of an eye
months ago. What was that picture called? When does it come out?'

'*College Capers*, and it's been and gone. Laid such an egg I
didn't tell my real mother about it.'

After another moment of commiseration, Brenda said her goodbyes.
I turned away and busied myself with my purse.

'Lillian?'

Bette Davis had been right. There was no point trying to fade
into the woodwork.

Brenda tottered toward me in careful heel-toe fashion, not having
mastered the towering shoes assigned to her by the wardrobe department. She gripped my hand, both as a greeting and a means of
stabilizing herself. 'The studio gives you acting, singing, and dancing
lessons, but nobody teaches you how to walk in these shoes. What
are you doing over here?'

'Staying out of everyone's way.' Edith had turned Brenda out in
high style, the outfit tasteful and not in the least ostentatious. Yet I
couldn't help thinking I'd never seen Abigail in anything that sophisticated. And Brenda, after all, was playing a character inspired by
Abigail.

'Can you tell how bad my jitters are? I can't believe we're shooting
already. It's happening so fast.' Her fingers were ice cold and still
entwined around mine. To put her at ease, I changed the subject.

'I overheard you talking to—'

'Ida. Ida Jarvis. She's a swell gal, isn't she? Been an extra for
almost twenty years.'

'That's amazing. Did she say "nerk"?'

'Central Casting slang. When you telephone, the operators say "nerk" for "no work". Or "tralay" for "try later". Takes less time to say, but it still hurts to hear.' Brenda wobbled a step closer. 'Ida used to be a dress extra. That's where the money is. Somebody has to sit in all those nightclub scenes sipping champagne.'

'Used to be?'

'You have to have your own evening gowns, dinner gowns, formal afternoon clothes. Costs a pretty penny to keep those duds up. And you have to stay fashionable. That's what did in poor Ida. Her best outfits were too horse-and-buggy. She was drummed out in a dress parade back in '35. Tells the story all the time. Central Casting put out the call and nearly a thousand actresses turned out in their finery, or what passed for it. Half of them sharing the same chinchilla wrap, handing it from one contender to the next. Anything to get that bump in pay.' She shivered. 'It's so demeaning and unfair. I felt awkward talking to her when I'm kitted out like this.'

She pirouetted. 'What do you think?' she asked, the second glances she merited from a passing pair of grips apparently insufficient evidence. 'Is this how I should dress to meet my police detective husband for dinner?'

All rationality fled my brain. Did she know about my connection to Abigail? Had Edith told her the reason for my interest in the movie?

'I don't understand,' I said, my smile fixed in place.

'I love the clothes, but are they too fancy for a policeman's wife? Maybe they're just too fancy for me. I'm more of a Gimbels girl. Honestly, tell me what you think.'

Why ask me? I longed to scream. My head throbbed. I had to say something. I was curious to hear what it would be.

'So . . .' I began. 'You don't like Edith's designs?'

'What? No!' Panic flooded Brenda's face. 'I love them! Don't tell her I said that!'

The poor girl was already terrified, and I'd managed to ratchet up her nerves even more. *Brava, Lillian.*

I took her hand again. It had turned clammy. Unless mine had. 'You look grand. Speaking of Edith, have you seen her?'

'She had to run to the Costume Department for something.'

'I'll look for her there. Break a leg.' I squeezed her hand and took my leave, not looking back until I'd stepped into the sunlight. The elephant doors were trundling shut, and outside Stage 13 the red wigwag light blazed to life. The world of *Streetlight Story* was being hermetically sealed off.

Brenda truly did look grand, doing Edith's efforts proud. Still flustered, she had fallen into conversation with Fred MacMurray. His commentary elicited a giggle from her. I'd seen Gene provoke similar laughter from Abigail. My last glimpse was of the two of them stepping into the shadows that Norman the cinematographer could never render dark enough.

EIGHTEEN

M y traitorous shoelace had come undone again. I tied it with a double knot stout enough to support a ship's anchor, visualizing Bette Davis rolling those oh-so-expressive eyes, as I waited for Edith outside her office.

'There you are!' She beetled in, fussing with her hairpins. 'I must have missed you.'

'That's OK. I ran into everyone else. Did you see Bill?'

'Bill? Ihnen? Is he here?' She checked her hairpins again. 'I didn't see him, either. Now. What's going on?'

I told Edith about my fateful evening. She expressed sympathy over my ordeal. 'A dexterous piece of deception on Sylvia's part. She not only knew what pages she could pass off as her own without discovery, but developed sufficient acumen to offer Mr Dolan suggestions on *Streetlight Story*'s script.'

'Suggestions he actually took,' I said in wonder. 'Do you buy Gene's notion of why she'd do it?'

'Given Mr Fentress told the authorities Miss Ward was his mistress, it's entirely plausible.' The telephone interrupted her. She uttered a string of crisp syllables into the receiver, then set it down. 'I have a thought about one aspect of this matter. I'll elaborate after a trip to the workroom. Care to come along?'

Not one of the dozen or so heads bent over sewing machines looked up when Edith entered the expansive workroom. But somehow those machines thrummed faster, the seamstresses operating them instinctively sensing their boss's arrival. Edith strode over to a shapely dress form, the gown draped upon it familiar yet foreign.

'Is that Brenda's dress for the nightclub scene?' I asked over the machines' murmur.

'We reused the original skirt. The production may have a higher budget, but that's no cause to waste the studio's money.'

Atop the long skirt of soft black crepe, the newly constructed bodice shimmered in pale pink beading with darker bands on the collar and sleeves. The height of elegance, the dress guaranteed all eyes would be on Brenda well before Luddy called 'Action'.

'It's beautiful,' I breathed.

'Presentable, perhaps. With a few alterations.' After exchanging sentences in Spanish with a nearby seamstress, Edith patted her shoulder in commendation. The woman's evident pride nearly bore her aloft.

A sight across the workroom made Edith blanch. To my amazement, I heard her curse under her breath before she sprinted toward a woman who appeared to be proffering a box of chocolates to a pair of seamstresses.

Unable to resist, I trailed after Edith.

My first surprise came when I recognized the mystery woman as Paulette Goddard. The raven-haired actress had made an impression as the barefoot waif who wins Charlie Chaplin's heart in *Modern Times* – and another when she pulled off the trick in real life. The exact nature of the cohabitating couple's relationship remained an enigma; the gossip columns regularly speculated on whether Chaplin and Goddard were in fact married, and if so when and where the ceremony had been performed. Land or sea? Catalina or China? There was certainly an Oriental influence on Goddard's bewitching silk shantung dress in navy and rose, the navy bolero jacket trimmed in rose braid.

Bombshell no. 2 was realizing Goddard was not sharing candy with the Wardrobe Department but holding open a cigar box overflowing with jewelry. Necklaces, to be precise, a few of the baubles rubies and emeralds but the bulk of them the sob sister of stones, plain old white diamonds. Goddard waved the box at a panic-stricken seamstress, chirping, 'Ignore the colored ones that snuck in there. They're worthless. That's usually where men start, so those you have to send right back.'

The seamstress's eyes flicked to Edith, who presented the final, most staggering surprise: the almost icy tone with which she addressed Goddard. 'Done with your wardrobe tests, Paulette. And back in that lovely dress.'

'I bought the fabric while Charlie and I were touring China. Had it made at Mainbocher's in Paris. You know that's where the most skilled silk hands are. Just thanking the ladies for their work by passing along a little hard-won advice.' Goddard thrust her trinket trunk at another terrified tailor. 'Never take anything from a man that goes bad.'

'Rubies go bad?' I blurted.

Pity elevated Goddard's sculpted eyebrows. 'Oh, honey.' One of the seamstresses mustered up the nerve to lean forward and peer into the jewelry box. Goddard pulled it back, snapping the lid shut.

The sharp sound proved the straw that fractured the dromedary's dorsum. Edith briefly closed her eyes before speaking. 'We've taken enough of your time today, Paulette.'

'I don't mind. Who else wants a gander?'

None of the seamstresses moved. The mercury in Edith's voice tumbled. 'I'll call when we've arranged the next test. Thank you.'

The last two words sent Goddard scurrying from sight. Edith stood still as if guarding against the actress's return. Then she declared, 'I'm sorry you were subjected to that, ladies,' repeating the line *en Español*. The wardrobe staff kept their eyes on their work.

As we mounted the stairs to her office, Edith said wearily, 'Miss Goddard will be appearing in *The Cat and the Canary* opposite Bob Hope. We've shot two dozen wardrobe tests and she's rejected the clothes in each one. This for a movie that takes place over a single night, requiring limited costume changes.'

'Maybe she's still smarting over losing Scarlett O'Hara to Vivien Leigh,' I said.

'No. She just enjoys showing off her jewelry. Even to women who work long hours for too little pay.'

Edith had banned the brouhaha from her mind by the time we reached her door. She asked me to wait in the outer office while she used the telephone. When she fetched me several minutes later, I detected an element of triumph in her customarily inscrutable expression.

'I was struck by Florabel Muir's assessment of Sylvia's friend Virginia Hill. Not to suggest Miss Hill is involved in Sylvia's death, but given her alleged underworld associations she may warrant a closer look.'

Having had the same thought, I nodded vigorously.

'A woman of means has only so many options in Los Angeles when it comes to clothes. I made inquiries and, as befits our putative heiress, struck oil right away. I telephoned Howard Greer. Do you know him?'

'By fancy label only.'

'Howard once occupied this very office. He gave me my start. An original Greer gown from his salon is proof you've arrived. Naturally, Miss Hill is one of Howard's best clients. I thought perhaps he could provide insight into her character.'

'There are no secrets in a dressing room. It's a wonderful idea. When can I see him?'

'How about now? I'll arrange an introduction.'

One of Edith's secretaries cracked open the door. 'Mr Ramsey is calling again.'

'Tell him I'm out.' Edith adjusted her spectacles. 'You know, it's been too long since I've seen Howard in person.'

We took Gower to Sunset. A mere two turns, but with Edith at the wheel the ride felt like a spin in a Tilt-A-Whirl. As she drove, she briefed me on Howard Greer.

'He began by designing for Lucile, Lady Duff Gordon. A testament to his talent that that should be his first position. Paramount brought him out in 1922. He hired me, but he did so much more than that. He endured my insecurities, taught me everything I know. Smoothed the way for me to work with Travis.' Travis being Travis Banton, Edith's predecessor and the man she eventually replaced. 'Howard left the studio in 1927. His salon has been a roaring success from day one. Nothing but bespoke garments for the carriage trade.'

'And apparently couriers for gangsters.'

Edith wrenched her roadster around a truck. 'Howard always was an egalitarian.'

We coasted to a stop outside a low white stucco structure with a red tile roof. Pepper trees cast architecturally perfect shadows over the building. An attendant in plum-colored livery greeted us, the words GREER, INC. in gold on the brim of his hat. Angels sang as Edith and I crossed the threshold.

A circular staircase spiraled us up to a desk. Behind it stood a bluff-featured man with graying hair save for a black widow's peak. He had the demeanor of a modestly successful businessman pressed by the city fathers into running for mayor – only any businessman who wore such an immaculate suit would immediately be suspected of graft. Howard Greer welcomed Edith effusively. His broad

Midwestern accent had acquired a few plummy tones, the customary adornments for those who had conquered Los Angeles. Edith introduced me, and Howard waved toward a mammoth book on the desk.

'I insist you both sign our guest register to commemorate this splendid occasion. Don't worry, you don't have to buy anything.' I added my best schoolgirl scribble under Edith's, noting the top entry on the page was a princess I'd never heard of from a country unknown to me.

Howard led the way into the main room. At the sight of it, my fingernails sank talon-like into Edith's shoulder. She gracefully shook them off, having visited this outpost of paradise before. A fire crackled, more for the sound effect than the warmth. The walls had been swathed with burgundy satin. Strategically placed divans could accommodate fainting anywhere in the room, a low plaid desk next to each one suitable for the writing of sonnets or checks. Through the open patio doors I spied green tables and chairs underneath awnings. From the adjacent room drifted soft classical music, accompaniment to the mannequin parade staged for the paying customers. I glimpsed a statuesque blonde in curve-hugging gold lamé as she passed a redhead in a black cocktail dress, a garden of embroidered pink roses framing the neckline. I pirouetted in place, unsure where my gaze should linger.

Howard beamed at the effect his establishment had on me, then turned to Edith. 'If it weren't for that silly fashion board set up by the Mojud Hosiery people, my dear, Travis and I would never clap our weary eyes upon you. You're like some half-remembered dream. Has it really been fifteen years since you slinked into my office, looking like a pussy cat drawn by Fujita, with a clutch of borrowed drawings you claimed were your own? So clever, our dear Edith.'

Edith's smile was indistinguishable from a wince; she had no interest in rehashing past crimes, at least not her own. 'How is Travis?'

Howard responded with a hand motion that meant nothing to me but communicated volumes to Edith, for she shook her head sorrowfully. 'How about some tea?'

'We don't want to be a burden,' Edith said.

'Nonsense. This place essentially runs itself. I'm scarcely needed when Miss Wong is here.' He gestured at an elegant Oriental woman in emerald green observing the mannequin parade like its watchful grand marshal.

'We wanted to ask about that client I mentioned,' Edith said. 'Virginia Hill.'

'Then I insist we go outside. In springtime, all my conversations take place *al fresco*. With tea.'

Gray-clad retainers manifested on the patio from some unseen kitchen. They poured piping hot tea into china cups bearing the same tartan pattern as the desks inside. The extravagant touches did not strike me as excessive in the least. The oasis Howard Greer had created was not predicated on luxury but grace. *This*, each perfectly calibrated detail proclaimed, *is how life is meant to be lived. And it can be, with only a miser's bankbook and a savant's style.* My stay in Hollywood's premiere palace of couture glamour might be brief. But I vowed to enjoy every sumptuous minute of it.

The tea, need it be said, was delightful.

'Lillian!' Howard said my name as if he were thrilled beyond repair to find me in such surroundings. 'Do you work with Edith at Paramount?'

'No, I'm the social secretary for Addison Rice. I feel as if I see your gowns on a weekly basis.'

'His parties keep the doors open, bless him!' Howard pressed his palms together and cast his eyes heavenward. 'I haven't relied on anyone like him since Ethel Barrymore walked in soon after we opened and laid out sixty-one one-hundred-dollar bills for an entire wardrobe. The wolves weren't only at the door, they'd counted out their cutlery in the lobby.'

'I still think of that opening night,' Edith said with a laugh.

'The night before!' Howard crowed. 'That's the one that haunts. There I am, convinced we're going down the drain before one customer has set foot inside. So certain am I of ruination I begin downing martinis. Not at Travis's pace, but then I'm only a mere amateur by comparison. I head home that night in the company of some of the girls, and as we're racing through the intersection of Hollywood and Vine a police officer pulls us over. I open the car door and in a moment of unsurpassed suavity drop my cocktail shaker to the curb, where it lands with a pronounced *clank*.'

'What did you do?' I asked.

'Let it be known the first Greer original to go forth into the world was a print silk chiffon tailored for the considerable frame of Mrs O'Leary, wife of Patrolman O'Leary, for her to wear to many a policeman's ball. Long may it wave.' He saluted in the general direction of Hollywood and Vine.

'Are you still naming the gowns?' Edith asked. 'The Biarritz, the Baccarat, the Balmoral—'

'And those only the Bs! We had other monikers, too. Whoops, Get Her and Blind Nuns Under Water come to mind, but those were only for internal use.'

'If I may ask,' I ventured, 'why did you stop designing for the movies?'

'Ornamentation!' he thundered. 'I would complete a gown and be told by starlet, director, and executive alike, "Exquisite! Now add ruffles and some fringe and we're off to the races."' He shook his head solemnly. 'My designs, for good or ill, require a third dimension to be appreciated. The subtleties of color, of fabric, of draping that speak to me don't register on the screen, while the clothes that make an impact there are too grandiose for everyday use. I lack the unerring camera eye that Travis and dear Edith possess.'

She clucked at the compliment. 'Say it as many times as you like, Howard, I'll never believe you. I steal from you to this day. Much as we'd love to revisit that bygone time, we're here on something of a mission.'

'I know. That's why we took the air.' Howard's eyes flitted about the patio. 'She's here.'

'Who's here?' I asked.

'Your quarry. Virginia Hill. She's attending a party this weekend and requires a dress. She also requires lingerie, and that's where I left her. In the lingerie room.'

The words made sense individually but not collectively. 'The – I – you have a lingerie room?'

'*Mais bien sûr.* The salon's fitting rooms are styled to make each woman look like the best possible version of herself based on her native coloring. Blonde, brunette. A room for ladies who have embraced the gilding of silver in their hair. Each of those *chambres de magie* has been designed to eliminate distractions and place the focus squarely where it belongs: on *la femme.*'

'Genius,' Edith said. 'A towering idea.'

I had so many, many questions. I started with the obvious. 'What does the lingerie room do?'

'Puts one in the right mood.' Howard smiled devilishly. 'Steel yourselves, ladies. Virginia has been in there for quite some time.'

NINETEEN

A gray-clad attendant was dispatched to the lingerie room. She returned to whisper in Howard's ear. 'Virginia is still being fitted, but she has chosen to grant you an audience,' he informed us. 'I wish you both Godspeed.'

The attendant led the way to a door and knocked. 'Come on in and don't be shy,' Virginia called back.

She waited inside Howard's *chambre de magie* in a borrowed green satin robe and mules. She hadn't cinched the robe shut, revealing swaths of ivory skin and delicate fabric almost the same hue. The gleam in her eye made it plain the dishabille was a deliberate decision to discombobulate us.

She needn't have bothered, and not only because Edith had seen those with more notoriety wearing even less. Virginia in a state of semi-undress could not possibly compete with the room itself. Cushions erupted from the French day bed that served as the centerpiece. A green dressing table crowned with a trio of mirrors was complemented by matching tufted chintz chairs. Rose-shaded lamps cast a beguiling glow over all – save the fur rug that lolled lasciviously off the day bed onto the floor. Aside from its black trim, it had been dyed the fervid green I associated with arsenic. No flood of rose light could pacify its effect.

'Ain't it grand the way Howard takes care of you?' Virginia grinned and hoisted her drink. No afternoon tea for her. 'Got a pitcher of stingers, so help yourself.' She embraced me, and I was enshrouded in a lush cloud of Chanel No. 5. At my mention of Edith's name, Virginia decorously pinched her robe closed.

'I know your name from the movie magazines,' she said.

'As I know yours from the gossip columns,' Edith replied.

'What say we set all that nonsense aside and really get to know each other?' Virginia toasted her own idea with a sip of her stinger.

'I can tell you have excellent taste if you're allowing Howard to provide, one might say, a complete wardrobe.'

'The French know a lot about lingerie – it's their word, after all

– but nothing about the lines. I want 'em snug. It should look like you're not wearing any.'

Edith sniffed. 'I can attest from my years in fitting rooms there are many women who make that very choice.'

'You mean stars?' Virginia's eyes sparkled. 'Do tell.'

Edith responded by sitting in one of the tufted chairs. Her discretion evidently earned Virginia's respect. She, too, took a seat, crossing her long legs. 'Now why are you two interested in little ol' me?'

'I wanted to express my condolences about Sylvia,' I said.

'Likewise, sweetheart. I hear you're the one who found her.'

'That's right. I'd learned she'd deceived me.'

A grin sidled across Virginia's face. 'Let me guess. You learned I deceived you, too. Found out the source of my income and the company I keep.'

'I don't know any of that matters,' Edith said. 'From the outset you've presented yourself as a woman who appreciates – and can afford – lovely clothes.'

'Oh, I *do* like you,' Virginia cooed. 'Yeah, I could always parlay a buck into a bundle. It's the only talent I have. Well, that and one or two others. I got that skill from my old man. A worthless bastard even by Alabama standards, but one hell of a trader. He could leave in the morning with nothing but a pocketknife and come home at night with a horse.'

'How did you know Sylvia?' I asked. 'Did you meet her through Clyde Fentress?'

'No. I don't move in Clyde's circles. His old ones or his new ones. I only know what poor Sylvia told me about him. I've never properly met Clyde. Or his wife. She sounds like hell on wheels. Have you made her acquaintance?'

'Not formally. So how *did* you meet Sylvia?'

Virginia cast her eyes demurely about the room. 'Do you think these walls can keep secrets?'

'Considering the wares purveyed in here,' Edith said, 'they'd better.'

Virginia sat back. 'I met Sylvia through her boyfriend.'

'You mean one other than Clyde,' I said.

'Yes.' Another glance at the walls. 'Have you ladies ever heard of Ben Siegel? The papers usually call him a "Hollywood sportsman", but that's not exactly what he is.'

The name did clang a chime. 'Then what is he? And I thought he was called Bugsy.'

'I'd advise you not to use that nickname.' Edith kept her voice low, perhaps wondering herself about the walls' ability to stay mum.

'Yeah. Sends Ben right into a rage.' Virginia considered Edith. 'How'd you know about that?'

'Mr Siegel has been mentioned in my salon a time or two. Mainly as a clotheshorse, the first man to sport maroon and dark green evening wear on the West Coast. I understand he's quite the debonair figure.'

'And how. Best-dressed man I ever saw.' Virginia's eyes danced at some memory. 'You know how he pays for those fancy threads?'

'One hears stories.' Edith shifted on her chair. 'That Mr Siegel is a gangster. The New York underworld's emissary to Los Angeles.'

'All true. But take it from me, Ben's really here because he's nuts about pictures. Thinks he should be in them. He'd walk away from the rackets in a hot minute if he could get in front of a camera.'

'Hang on,' I interjected. 'You're saying Sylvia was involved with Ben Siegel? How'd that happen?'

'I told you. Ben loves pictures. Sylvia wanted to write them and works for Central Casting. You know, common interests.'

'But Sylvia *didn't* want to write pictures,' I said.

Virginia shrugged. 'Then they developed other common interests.'

'So Mr Siegel introduced you to Miss Ward,' Edith said.

'Not exactly. Let's say Sylvia and I were members of the same club.'

'Ah. You, too, were involved with Mr Siegel?'

'No need to pretty it up, Edith. Ben and I had fun in the feathers. He's good at it. So am I. One of the other talents I mentioned earlier.'

Her brazenness brought a ferocious blush to my face while Edith took it in stride. Virginia kept talking.

'We had a few laughs back in New York, where we met. I came out west, saw Ben and Sylvia together one night, and decided to size up the latest flavor Benny was sampling. Sylvia and I hit it off. Again, chalk it up to common interests.'

'What was your impression of poor Miss Ward?'

Virginia cocked her head, an actress who wanted her audience to know she was thinking. 'A sweet kid. Kind of "out of her depth", if you know what I mean.'

Not like you, I thought.

'About Ben— Mr Siegel,' I amended, not permitting myself any informality when it came to transcontinental hoodlums. 'When did you meet him?'

'First time? 1937. Early in the year, because I was wearing a fur. I remember that. It was in Brooklyn. I was going around with another fella then, Joey, but Ben has a way of commanding the attention. We had a memorable night. Actually, two. No, three. Then he went home to the wife and kids. Ben's been here part of the year since the '20s. He's always had business out this way. Never stopped talking about Los Angeles the whole time we were together.' She moistened her lower lip. 'Well, that ain't entirely true.'

Edith let the innuendo lie. 'If I may ask, Miss Hill, where were you last night?'

'When Sylvia was killed? I was in Lorna Whitcomb's column.'

'I see. I haven't read today's newspapers. I don't suppose you'd know Mr Siegel's whereabouts.'

'I don't keep tabs on him. We're no longer on intimate terms.' Virginia turned to me and batted her eyes. 'If you tell the police about Ben and Sylvia, honey, I'd appreciate it if you left the source of your information out of it.'

A soft knock on the door preceded the Oriental woman we had noticed earlier. She nodded at Virginia. 'Pardon the intrusion, Miss Hill, but we have the garments ready for you to try.'

'Thanks, Karen. Send 'em on in.'

Edith and I rose as Karen slipped out of the room. I spied a book on the dressing table, a slim volume entitled *Forever* by Mildred Cram. 'Howard's thorough when it comes to the props,' I remarked.

'Oh, no. That's mine.' Virginia clutched the book to her breast like a young girl defending her diary. 'It's my favorite. I've read it over and over. It's about fate and destiny and a love greater than death.'

'Sounds intriguing,' Edith said. 'Has there been a film version?'

'No picture could do it justice. Someday I'll find my soulmate, like they do in the book.' For once Virginia didn't come across as wised-up and worldly. She sounded like she believed every word she said.

In the corridor, Karen directed a battalion of attendants bearing filmy garments into the lingerie room. 'Excuse me, Karen,' I began.

'Yes, Miss Frost?'

We had not, I recalled, been introduced. 'I know this is an imposition—'

'You would perhaps like to visit our brunette room? But of course. This way, please.'

She escorted us to a slice of amber heaven, a room with walls a subdued shade of gold. Sunlight streamed in through vermillion curtains. I caught sight of my five-foot-eight-inch frame in the mirror and gaped in disbelief. I was still too tall, with long arms that seemed positively simian. But in this room, within these walls, bathed in this magnificent light, I looked . . . not hideous.

'Can I live here?' I asked.

'The wallpaper was imported from Austria,' Karen said pleasantly. 'I can inquire about securing more for you, if you'd like.'

'You should see what Howard calls the Black Room,' Edith said. 'He had tiny mirrors embedded in the ceiling. It's like you're under the stars. What did you make of Miss Hill?'

'I wish Sylvia really had written a movie about her. She's quite a character. How did Sylvia put it? She lives life on her own terms.'

'That is beyond doubt. I agree with Florabel Muir's assessment. Miss Hill, I believe, is quite the dangerous woman.'

'Speaking of dangerous women, the one I'd like to talk to is Josie Fentress. If only I could find her.'

Karen cleared her throat. 'Forgive me, Miss Frost.'

'Yes?'

'Mr Greer indicated I was to assist you and Miss Head any way I can.'

'What is your name, dear?' Edith asked.

'Karen Wong. It's an honor to meet you, Miss Head. I am a great admirer of your work.'

'As I am of yours, Miss Wong. I have reason to believe you are responsible for the smooth operation of Howard's salon.'

'I'm honored to be part of Mr Greer's vision.' Karen deflected the compliment as deftly as Edith delivered it. I felt as if I were watching a tennis match between two gifted athletes. 'I could not help overhearing your conversation, and thought it might interest you to know Mrs Fentress is hosting an event this evening at the Ebell Club.'

Her pass-the-fur-hat dinner, I thought, remembering the circular I'd seen at the Stanley Rose Bookshop.

'Mrs Fentress is a client of Howard's, I take it?' Edith asked.

'As are a number of her guests,' Karen said.

'I stand by my earlier comment, Miss Wong. You are an integral part of this salon's success.'

'Thank you, Miss Head. Could I perhaps interest either of you in a gown?'

TWENTY

The Ebell Club boasted such a glorious edifice it saddened me the building had lately become associated with endings. The Italianate clubhouse in Hancock Park had been the site of Amelia Earhart's final public appearance before she vanished in 1937. The Ebell bravely shouldered its cameo in the tragedy; a cornerstone of Los Angeles civic life, it regularly hosted events like this evening's dinner in support of the Global Refugee Alliance, organized in part by Josephine Hatcher Fentress. As Edith inched her red roadster past a state funeral's worth of black cars lining Wilshire Boulevard, I devoutly wished she'd driven the entire way at that speed.

'This is a pretty pulled-up affair if half the guests are in Howard Greer originals.' I watched a gaggle of socialites sweep into the clubhouse. 'How are we supposed to waltz in?'

'I'm sure we'll think of something.' Edith brought the car to an ungainly halt a few blocks away. She rummaged in the trunk, emerging with a long black garment bag she draped over her arm.

'What's that?'

'A coat.'

'It's not that chilly.'

'One never knows.'

A spectacular entryway wrought of wrought iron made adequate preparation for the lobby. Chandeliers dangled from a coffered ceiling garlanded with rosettes. I was mid-marvel when an officious woman strode over, already preparing to give us the distaff bum's rush. 'I'm sorry, this is a private event.'

Edith's hand snapped up, presenting a card reading GREER, INC. in gilt letters. Her other hand hoisted the garment bag. 'Mr Greer sent us,' she said, in a voice implying we were being stayed from the swift completion of our appointed rounds. 'Mrs Winslow's replacement gown. There was an incident with a wineglass.'

'Oh. Of course. Yes. Carry on.' The woman waved us toward the assemblage and hurried away.

'Who's Mrs Winslow?' I asked Edith, chasing after her.

'The woman in the wineglass incident. It's all anyone's talking about.'

We followed the procession into a courtyard, verdant under a purpling sky and ringed by a colonnaded walkway. Around a fountain depicting a woman bearing a bowl, clusters of conversation had sprung up. I spied a number of dazzling dresses I was prepared to credit to Howard Greer, along with a few that looked like they'd last been liberated from mothballs when the Armistice had been signed.

Then I noticed someone staring, if not daggers, then letter openers at me. I alerted Edith we were about to have company.

Kay Dambach, my occasional friend and gossip's queen bee without a court, made her way over with that new girdle gait. As usual, Hank 'Ready' Blaylock had her arm. Her cowboy consort, one of the finest stunt riders in Gower Gulch, served as Kay's escort in part to stanch stories about his preference for male companionship. He greeted me with authentic affection while Kay's eyes took on a more mercenary cast.

'I don't believe you've officially met Edith Head,' I said.

'Yet I feel Miss Dambach is a friend from her column. And Mr Blaylock's facility with horses is of course well known.' Edith, firing the first salvo of flattery.

'How's Vi these days?' Ready asked, angling for a friendly conversation. But Kay had long since stopped having those, and plunged into the business at hand.

'Some crowd at this bash. A passel of Bolsheviks and a dowager who claims to be a Civil War widow. From the looks of her, I can guarantee the South isn't going to rise again, no matter how big a smash *Gone with the Wind* is. What brings you ladies out tonight?'

'I'm interested in learning about' – frantically I scanned the closest placard – 'the plight of the refugees.'

'In a pig's eye.' Kay cackled. 'You're here because tonight's picnic is the handiwork of Josie Fentress, whose husband traded blows with your man Gene. A fracas *I* told you about, so you owe me. I want the truth. Is that why you're here, Miss Head? Does this event have any bearing on the picture you're designing? What's it called? *Searchlight* something?'

'I hate to correct you, Miss Dambach, but neither would I want you to commit an error to print. I'm here to assess the viability of the Ebell Club for a charity costume event planned for later this year. I can't provide details yet, but when it's announced I assure you it will be the event of the season.' She leaned in slyly. 'You've netted an exclusive. Congratulations.'

Kay, bewitched by visions of a scoop, had forgotten me entirely. 'You can't whet my readers' appetites?'

'Not about the event, but there are some tidbits about upcoming Paramount films I'd be delighted to share.' As she stepped closer to Kay, Edith flashed me a look: *scram!* Ready made an able accomplice, blocking my departure from Kay's view as Edith commenced holding forth.

I slipped into the dining room. Standard practice at such soirées was to have some form of entertainment open the bill, but Josie had chosen to firebrand it up by booking a speaker. A tiny, wizened man fulminated at the front of the room in an impenetrable accent, the few older ladies scattered at the tables exchanging looks as if the band were playing unfamiliar music too loud and too fast. I snatched a few hors d'oeuvres from a passing tray and returned to the courtyard. Edith continued expounding, her hand on Kay's arm for emphasis but also to prevent her escape. I continued searching for Josie.

Her husband hove into view first. Embarrassment flickered across Clyde Fentress's face when he realized I'd caught him in full soup and fish. Then he stalked toward me like a beast on an African veldt, nostrils flaring as if he'd caught my scent on the wind. 'What the hell are you doing here?' he growled.

I took an involuntary step back, then some low instinct commanded I hold my ground. This was how Fentress and his criminal cohort functioned, forever hunting for weakness. I couldn't afford to show him any.

'You already know. I'm the one who found Sylvia.'

'Why were you even looking for her?'

'I read her script pages. Found out she wasn't your protégée.'

'I already volunteered that to the cops.' He smirked. 'Beat you to the punch.'

'And I reminded them Sylvia's death was the second in your circle this week.'

'You still trying to hang Nap's murder on me? I hadn't seen him in weeks.'

Around us, the courtyard filled with some of the city's most distinguished citizens. 'At least the sad news about Sylvia didn't force you and your wife to scale back your social obligations.'

Fentress's entire body tensed, like a dog's awaiting the signal to pounce. 'You're not on the lot anymore, girly. You're making trouble out in the real world. Where there are consequences. What do you want?'

'I was hoping to talk to your wife.'

'What for?'

'I understand the police couldn't locate her last night. As you and Sylvia were romantically involved, your wife had reason to want her dead.'

Fentress looked momentarily startled; had the prospect of Josie's guilt never occurred to him? Then his customary swagger reasserted itself. 'What Sylvia and I had did not involve romance. That why you're pestering me? Romance? You're twisting yourself into knots over Gene Morrow. He worth it?'

'Yes.'

He surveyed the crowd, then pulled me behind a pillar and aimed his gray eyes directly at mine. It still felt like staring at a wall.

'OK. Tell you what,' he said. 'You help me clear my name and I'll dish out every detail about the California Republic job. The whole truth, not that malarkey I wrote for those tin-pot dictators who run Paramount.'

'Why do you need me? Just level with the police and let them do their job.'

His laughter was showy and broad. Any decent director would have cut it. 'Even if I was inclined to play fair with John Law, it wouldn't help. I'm an ex-con. One who's made good twice over. Decent job, married into money. The cops hate my guts. They won't bend over backwards to do right by me. Then there's Josie. She may be rich, but politically she's racked up enemies. The woman's essentially a Red. She knows just because the city elected a mayor who hums along with the reform tune doesn't mean he knows the words. Corruption ain't going anywhere, especially when it comes to the LAPD. As for you, well . . . you've got an in with the department, don't you?'

'No, I don't. Gene's in trouble. You know he is.'

'True. But cops close ranks around their own. People are gonna be working on his behalf. You may hear about it. And who knows? Maybe your clowning around on your own might turn something up.'

I ignored his slight. 'This is more malarkey. You don't mean any of this. You just want me to leave.'

'*Yes*, I want you to leave! My wife's here! That's why I'm being on the level. What do you say?'

I considered his proposition. What Fentress suggested meant not only working against the District Attorney's office but Gene himself, albeit on Gene's own behalf. Provided Fentress's 'whole truth' exonerated Gene.

'If I do this,' I said slowly, 'will I like what I hear?'

'Of course not. It's the truth. Nobody likes the truth. The entire picture business exists because people would rather be told lies. But once you hear the truth, you know it. And you can't unhear it.' Fentress peered around the pillar in a modest panic. I wondered if he'd been that agitated when he'd been pinched by the police. 'Do we have a deal?'

What choice did I have? 'Sure.'

'Swell. Now *beat it*. Before Josie . . . dammit, it's too late. Here she comes. Don't say a word about Sylvia.'

'You want me to clear your name, don't you?'

He threw me one last alarmed glance as Josie Fentress glided toward us, the impeccable hostess smile yielded by years of breeding her sole welcoming feature. Not for Josie the exposed shoulders and décolletage of the evening gown. Her dinner suit – floor-length deep blue skirt and elaborately embroidered jacket, its gold thread flashing in the light of the pillar candles – covered her from swan-like neck to high heels, demonstrating the depth of her commitment to the evening's cause.

'Clyde, darling.' Had the champagne been as flat as her voice, she'd have burned the club to the ground. 'You deserted Mrs Cowan at the table. We discussed that.'

'Sorry, dear.' Fentress attempted a chuckle. 'Just stretching my—'

'Return to her at once, would you? Before she begins spouting the Hearst line to her dinner companions.'

Fentress skulked away without a word. Josie's gaze fixed me in place as surely as a pin used to mount a butterfly.

'Tell me, are you Clyde's new conquest?' she murmured. 'The one in the hopper, or is it the chute? Clyde associated with all these rodeo sorts and I never could get their patter down.'

'No, Mrs Fentress. I know your husband from the studio.'

'One doesn't necessarily preclude the other.'

I could follow Josie's direct approach, too. 'I wanted to ask you about Sylvia Ward.'

'The late Sylvia.' She almost savored the words. 'I saw you with her the other day.'

'Yes. She and your husband were having an affair.'

She craned her neck to squint at me, and still managed to look elegant doing so. 'Who are you, exactly?'

'A busybody minding other people's business.'

'Oh, yes, *now* I know. My husband told me. You're that girl intent on sabotaging his movie. Because you're so bound to your man. Not at all independent.'

I smiled. 'That's me. Sylvia was—'

'Clyde told the police he was romantically involved with her. He told me some time earlier. He doesn't keep secrets from me. He knows how pointless that would be.' She nodded toward him, seated at a table, tilting his head so the elderly woman at his side could pour her bile directly into his ear. 'We do lead separate lives for the most part. I request his presence at these events from time to time so he can regale my friends with a few unvarnished stories about his various incarcerations. He's always good for a few laughs. Isn't this a lovely venue? Such history. It's why I wanted it for this occasion. That, and having the event here makes everyone happy. The old guard feels they're doing good. My political confreres think we're putting one over on the stuffed shirts. And Clyde is utterly miserable.'

He certainly seemed forlorn, bantering with the battle-ax at his table. I doubted his spirits would improve once he headed to home and hearth with Josie.

'Could I ask where you were last night, Mrs Fentress?'

'When poor Sylvia was killed? Why not ask your policeman boyfriend for that information? I can only assume he has it, because I suggested to the officer I spoke to that he take a good look at your Detective Morrow. After all, he was bested in physical combat by my husband the other day, with Sylvia as witness.'

I swallowed hard. 'I believe they fought to a draw.'

'He didn't tell you he'd beaten Clyde? Maybe he *is* honest. I can see why you hold on to him.' She patted my arm, the sensation like being comforted by a Frigidaire. 'I'll tell you what I told the good captain in the company of my family's attorney this morning. I spent yesterday afternoon putting the finishing touches on this event, then relaxed by taking a long drive alone while my husband went to the pictures by himself. No one can verify either of our stories, alas. But I'm not particularly worried.'

I almost missed much of what she said. One of her words derailed my attention. 'Did you say captain?'

'A high-ranking member of the department attended to the matter personally. Sought me out on his own initiative, out of deference to my family. A change may have come to the police force at last.' She waved over my shoulder at someone. 'Can't recall his name at the moment. Wore a most striking tweed suit.'

'Frady.'

'That sounds right. Determined as well as distinguished. A man who can produce results. Speaking of which, would you mind if I left you, dear? I must circulate and ask those assembled to dig deep.'

A helpful member of the Ebell Club pointed me toward a pay phone and asked if she could fetch me anything. I looked, she informed me, deathly pale. I hadn't considered that Gene could be linked, however tenuously, to Sylvia's murder.

And Frady, the implacable Frady, remained on his trail. The man turned up everywhere.

Gene picked up the call. 'Are you in trouble?' I blurted.

'Always. Were you asking about something specific?'

'Did you have to answer questions about Sylvia's murder once it came out she was Clyde's mistress?'

'It raised an eyebrow or two downtown, but no one's taking it seriously. Other rocks are more likely to fall on my head first.'

'About Sylvia,' I said. 'Would it make a difference if I told you she was sleeping with Bugsy Siegel?'

I took the lack of glib reply as a victory. Gene pressed for details, which I provided as succinctly as possible.

'I'll pass this info along to the investigating officers.' He paused. 'It sounds like you're still trying to help, Frost.'

'Nope,' I lied. 'I spent today looking at clothes. Honest.'

Edith was so pleased with herself you could almost see her teeth when she smiled. Almost.

'I talked Miss Dambach's ear off about Paramount's slate of pictures without giving away any trade secrets. Did you find Mrs Fentress?'

'I think she can give Virginia a run for her money in the danger department. Can we get out of here before I'm compelled to make a donation?'

'I already made one. A few dollars slipped into one of the boxes. We can pretend it's from both of us.'

San Bernardino Lamplighter   March 31, 1939

KATHERINE DAMBACH'S
SLIVERS OF THE SILVER SCREEN

Talk is swirling around town about the death of a young woman who spent her days behind a desk at Central Casting and her nights – well, *that's* the question that has tongues wagging. Young Sylvia Ward, found murdered in her apartment this week by Hollywood hanger-on Lillian Frost, manned the floodgates against the tidal wave of extras hoping for their big break. Did she have her eyes on bigger things herself? Some are saying a seasoned scribe was giving the girl a leg up in the screenwriting game. I suppose that's one way to crash the movies . . . Paramount costume designer Edith Head is thrilled to see more musical films go into production. Brightness and joy are what we need these days, the wardrobe wizard believes. She'll be making music with her sketchpad designing the wardrobe for a Victor Herbert biography set to start filming later this year.

TWENTY-ONE

L ife, I knew, was not all furbelows and canapés. After a day spent summiting the Social Register, I rose vowing to put my shoulder to the wheel. Granted, my labors would consist of organizing Addison's 'Come as Your Childhood Dream Job' party featuring two orchestras, a far cry from running laundry service at a leper colony. But at least I'd be at my desk.

I had started with the day's correspondence when the doorbell sounded. An all-atwitter Addison buzzed into my office. 'My acting teacher has arrived!'

'Miss Davis is back for round two?' I'd worn shoes without laces. I was bound to make a better impression today.

'No! Another friend became available. Would you mind greeting her? I need a moment to prepare.'

I reached Addison's spacious lobby and immediately retreated. Joan Crawford stood admiring the flowers. I'd need a moment to prepare as well. With a deep breath I strode forward, poised to reintroduce myself—

'Good morning, Lillian!' Crawford, whom I'd met twice in my reception duties at Addison's parties, had somehow remembered my name. What's more, she rushed toward me with hands extended. I gripped her butter-soft pink suede gloves. Her black jersey dress floated around her knees as she walked, topped by a fingertip jacket outlined in white. 'You'll have to give me the name of Addison's florist. It's so good to see you again.'

'Likewise, Miss Crawford.'

'It's funny, I thought of you the other day.'

'I can't fathom why.'

She laughed uproariously at my honesty. 'The World's Fair! It's to be in Flushing, where you're from. You must be excited, everyone's attention on your old neighborhood. I read the most darling article about it. I'll have it sent over to you.'

I flailed for a response. I knew for certain I'd never told Crawford I was from Flushing in the forty-five or so seconds we'd spoken. The actress was simply that organized. She had a system for dealing with various factotums while I had difficulty recalling the name of the person who delivered Addison's champagne. Although to be fair, there were three of them.

'Addison is so pleased you're able to help him,' I said as I led the way to my lord and master.

'As am I. I had been in New York, about to sail to Brazil. But . . . I'm sure you know about my pending divorce.'

I nodded gravely, as if she'd mentioned a death in the family. The severing of the marital knot binding her to actor Franchot Tone had populated gossip columns for months. 'I was under the impression that had happened.'

'Oh, it's all over bar the shouting. Merely a matter of paperwork. Divorce by deposition, they call it, so I made plans for my holiday. But at the last minute the judge decided not to do it by absentee and I had to race back to Los Angeles. Most inconsiderate of him. I had my stand-in ready to go.'

I blinked. 'Your stand-in?'

'Yes, Kasha. Used to be married to my brother. Stands in for me on all my pictures.'

'So – I'm sorry, I'm confused. She was going to stand in for you in divorce court?'

'Yes, all perfectly above board. She knew her lines, but they never called "Action".' She laughed, finding the whole business queer. As if asking the former sister-in-law you hired to spell you under the soundstage lights to also take your place in a legal proceeding were a commonplace occurrence.

The divorce was primarily how the actress got press in the wake of being branded 'box office poison', along with Marlene Dietrich, Katharine Hepburn, and others, by a group of theater owners the previous year. I had high hopes for her next picture, already the talk of the town even though it co-starred Norma Shearer, another name on the toxic list.

'I'm so looking forward to *The Women*,' I said. 'May we expect a full fashion show?'

'Literally and figuratively. Adrian has outdone himself. I trust him implicitly. He toned me down in color and line, taught me not only to accept but to emphasize my shoulders.'

Crawford greeted Addison with a few questions about 'your lovely wife Maude' that sounded almost sincere. He thanked her for agreeing to tutor him.

'I'm not sure what I can teach you about acting,' she said, then paused so her audience could protest. 'I've never studied it, although Franchot says I have what the French call "intelligence of the heart". All I can offer is what Johnny Arnold at MGM told me the day of my screen test. Don't be afraid of the camera. It's only got one eye and it can't talk back.'

'You won't have to show me many pointers,' Addison said. 'I'm only an extra.'

'An atmosphere performer,' I amended.

'Then I might be able to provide some help. I got my start through Central Casting. I played a party guest, then ended up dancing in *The Merry Widow*.' Crawford removed her gloves. 'I can tell you this much. It's no place for the timid. Shyness gets you nowhere. You've got to scheme to get ahead.'

'Fortunately, there's no need for that.' Addison chortled. 'Thanks to Lillian, I already have the role.'

'Yes, but now the real finagling begins.' Crawford appraised

Addison. It felt like a bored tigress had just wandered into the room. 'For instance, does the scene involve the principal actors going through a door? If so, try to place yourself by it, so when the scene picks up on the other side they have to use you again for continuity. It's another shot, maybe on another day, and that's more money in your pocket.'

'But Joan.' Addison raised his arms to encompass his palatial abode. 'I don't need the money.'

'I thought you were interested in the experience of being a background player. That's a huge part of it, Addy, how to get noticed. How to squeeze everything you can out of every second on set. Money, attention, time. That's the extra's lot.'

Addison's brow furrowed. 'But I thought it was . . . talking while walking. Or walking while talking. And figuring out if I'm meant to be happy or sad.'

'That matters, too! But you've got to get the job before you can do it. I'm always about getting the job. As for doing the job, I'm happy to help you. I can begin by sharing the best advice I've ever gotten on acting. It's from the man who directed me in *Grand Hotel*. Edmund Goulding.'

Addison kept a straight face at the name. Perhaps he didn't require much coaching after all.

'He took me aside.' Crawford pantomimed the gesture. 'And told me, "Give the audience a taste of what you're thinking, not the whole meal." Isn't that wonderful? The idea of practicing that kind of restraint changed the world for me.'

The same tip didn't knock Bette Davis on her heels, I thought.

Crawford clapped her hands. 'Now! Where shall we rehearse?'

'The library, I should think. Lillian, we're not to be disturbed. Oh, and one more thing.' He moved closer so he could speak to me in confidence. 'I'm attending that party this evening. The one being held by Countess di Frasso.'

'Yes, sir. I confirmed the particulars yesterday.'

'Her man telephoned this morning and extended the invitation to you, as well! Lillian Frost, by personal request!'

'Me? But why?'

'Some mention of seeing your name in the newspaper. You've become a celebrity in your own right. Such fun, isn't it?' He turned to Joan. 'Shall we begin?'

Crawford blew me a kiss. 'Bless you, Lillian. Bless you.' She managed to leave the room without taking a bow.

Various vocal exercises and the occasional thunderous cry erupted from the library for the rest of the morning. La Crawford eventually departed, promising an even more vigorous follow-up session. I turned my attention to the most pressing matter: what to wear to the evening's function. I telephoned Paramount and left a message for Edith, who didn't return my call until after lunch.

'Your friend Miss Dambach scarcely used any of my commentary,' she said.

'Did you really expect her to?'

'It was fairly slim pickings at that event.'

'Speaking of soirées, I've been invited to one and seek your sartorial support. I'm tagging along with Addison to a party at Countess Dorothy di Frasso's this evening.'

Edith spoke in a hushed voice. 'Rather last minute, isn't it? Do you know why you were invited?'

'My appearance in Kay's column, apparently. Who figured the Countess read it?'

'That could be the explanation. But I did some research this morning and . . . do you recall the *Metha Nelson* affair?'

'Who played the lead? Did you do the costumes?' The joke didn't land. I racked my brain. 'Vaguely. Isn't the *Metha Nelson* a boat? I remember the Countess was involved.'

'Correct on both counts. The vessel took a pleasure cruise down the coast late last year with a literal motley crew, as the newspapers reported it. The boat was chartered by Jean Harlow's stepfather, something of an unsavory character. Another passenger was a relative of the British Foreign Minister, Anthony Eden. By all accounts, the jaunt became rather debauched and there was a question of mutiny.'

'Mutiny? As in *On the Bounty*?' A picture that starred Joan Crawford's soon-to-be-ex-husband Franchot Tone, I thought, wondering who he'd sent to divorce court in his stead.

'Yes,' Edith said. 'There was a grand jury hearing, although surely that's a maritime offense, and no bill was returned.'

'And Countess di Frasso was onboard for it all? At least I won't be at a loss for a conversation starter.'

'The problem, Lillian, is who else was aboard.' Her voice found an even softer register. 'Benjamin Siegel was also on the *Metha Nelson*. It would appear he and the Countess are . . . intimates.'

I gripped the phone more tightly. 'But what about Sylvia? I thought Bugsy was seeing her.'

'Mr Siegel is evidently not exclusive, as I'm sure Mrs Siegel could attest. My point is while your invitation could stem from your recent notoriety, it's also possible Mr Siegel is using the Countess to gather information on you. I wish you'd bear that in mind as you weigh accepting this invitation.'

'It seems like the wrong time to ask you for fashion advice.'

'We'll come back to that subject. I planned on calling you to pass along the latest rumor. Max tells me Clyde Fentress is about to be fired.'

'Why?'

'There's always been some noise about his wife's politics, but Max says the police attention of late has riled the studio's chieftains. They're prepared to cancel his contract.'

'They can't do that!' I exclaimed. 'What if Clyde takes a powder and I need to talk to him? I can't exactly leave a message with Josie.'

'I'm afraid there's nothing to be done if the studio sees fit to release him. Now. Do you plan on attending the Countess's party?'

After hawing, then hemming, I said, 'Yes.'

'I assumed as much. Nothing from your closet will suit such an occasion. You're a guest, not the staff. I'm sending your measurements to Howard Greer. We'll see if he has something you can borrow. If I know him, Karen Wong will meet you later this evening with a gown for the ages.'

It bothered me, the prospect my party invitation was a put-on. Yet knowing Clyde Fentress could be in the wind perturbed me more. I had to keep track of him if I was to have any chance of clearing Gene's name. But I couldn't do it myself, and it wasn't like I could ask Gene to do it.

Then another possibility came to mind.

I left a message at Lodestar Pictures. I was packing my purse to leave when Simon telephoned back. He sounded genuinely happy to hear from me.

Might as well disabuse him of any illusions up front. 'I need your help,' I said, and explained I wanted him to follow Clyde Fentress once he left the Paramount lot.

'Why?'

'I can't go into it now. But it has to do with Gene.'

'As if I couldn't have guessed. Why should I lift a finger for that guy?'

'I should have guessed too,' I said. 'Never mind. I—'

'Follow him where and for how long?'

'Home, and until you're sure he's staying there. I can tell you what he looks like.'

'Don't bother. I've got a pal at Paramount who can point him out to me. I'd better leave now.'

'Thank you. I'm in your debt.'

'Forget it. You should know I'll do anything for you.'

He hung up. The phone rang again as soon as I set the receiver down.

'Good afternoon, Miss Frost.' Karen Wong's serene voice purred down the line. 'I'm so fortunate to have reached you. Tell me, do you prefer crimson or violet?'

TWENTY-TWO

My uncle Danny possessed a soulful singing voice, a mischievous twinkle in his eye, and a truly murderous sense of class. He remained eternally vigilant for any signs of airs or pretensions. 'Don't be getting above yourself out there in California, pet, becoming one of them lace curtain Irish,' he'd warned me before my westward trek. 'Walk around with your nose in the air, and you can't see what you're about to step in.'

As I climbed out of Addison's Cadillac in a borrowed Howard Greer gown outside a Beverly Hills mansion ablaze with light, I knew with certainty I was in danger of getting above myself.

The gown, ferried to me by the redoubtable Karen Wong, was violet with a parachute skirt so voluminous it could sweep the grand staircase at Radio City Music Hall clean. I feared it wasn't my style, but as Karen diplomatically observed, we didn't have time to debate. As for the mansion, it sat just north of Sunset Boulevard in Beverly Hills. It had been designed in the Spanish Revival style, the archways on the second floor protected by delicate iron railings, each one suitable for a senorita to be serenaded. Lampposts punctuated the pathways extending across the sprawling property, the farthest pool of light a horseback ride away. The house and grounds did not conjure up a sense of Old Mexico so much as a movie set there, which to my mind only made it more beguiling.

'The Countess staged boxing matches here for one of her parties.' Addison couldn't help sounding slightly impressed. 'What do you think of the idea?'

'I think Mr Ayoshi wouldn't care to have blood on his rhododendrons.'

Addison and I entered the foyer, where Countess Dorothy di Frasso may have been holding court but her dress called the meeting to order. The ruby pillar gown featured a gathered bodice, thin straps securing it over a considerable bosom. The dramatic look had been softened with a shawl of gauzy white silk, a necessary sop to the Countess's age. Her skin bore the synthetic suppleness of expert pampering, while her dark hair only fooled those willing to be fooled; it was apparent she had borne witness to a good half-century. Her eyes were small and active, practiced at scouting a room and assessing each new arrival's place in the hierarchy. They locked in on Addison and me, calculation of such ferocity commencing behind them that I half-expected smoke to plume from her diamond-studded ears.

Addison had emptied his dossier on the Countess on the ride over. 'This is a diplomatic visit. The Countess and I tend to throw competing parties, so it's good to have a bit of a truce. She's from back east. Married an Italian count, but that's only on paper. She gets to have a title, he gets a share of her inherited millions. She came to Los Angeles with Gary Cooper, believe it or not. They met in Europe, she introduced him to society and fancied herself his manager. Well, you can imagine the rest. Their parting was, they say, not amicable, so best not mention him.' He had only a vague recollection of the voyage of the good ship *Metha Nelson* – 'unpleasant business, what I remember of it' – and closed with his standard advice: 'Just have fun!'

When we reached our hostess, the meeting was as fraught as one between warring heads of state. 'Addison! What a delight! You realize I only did this so you would return the favor and invite me to one of your fabulous parties. It's utterly ridiculous we should be feuding.' Her accent, East Coast tempered by her time on the Continent, made her sound as if she'd grown up in a bank vault.

'Who says we're feuding, Contessa?' Addison made a show of kissing her hand. 'Maude sends her regrets. In Arizona for her health, you know.'

'Do give her my best. And you've brought a charming replacement.' The Countess's gaze settled on me. 'You must be Lillian Frost. I've heard tell of you, my dear. Marlene used to live here – she's a close friend – and she speaks so highly of you.'

I didn't let the deeply gratifying praise dull my defenses. 'Thank you for inviting me, Countess.'

'I'll want to know everything that's happening at Paramount. Here's a piece of trivia for you. Have you seen their new picture *Midnight*? My car makes a cameo appearance in it! Had the right look, they said.'

'I'm about to make my dramatic debut myself, thanks to Lillian. Background player in a film.' Addison puffed out his chest. 'I've been studying acting with Bette—'

'Oh, what a smashing idea! I wonder if I could get my friends a bit part in a picture, to round out their California experience. What fun that would be! I have the Duke and Duchess of Sutherland visiting now – great bearing, would be divine on camera, I'll introduce you – and I've got Prince Brindi staying with me shortly. Addison, perhaps you can put in a word.'

My employer bristled, but quietly. A self-made man, Addison had little use for aristocrats and their ilk. That attitude partly accounted for his fascination with the film colony, an entire society of people who had invented their identities and blazed their own trails.

'Enjoy yourselves. And Lillian, we must talk later!' I didn't anticipate lively chatter about Claudette Colbert pictures. The Countess had invited me under false pretenses; at some point, she'd buttonhole me and endeavor to pick my brain.

With Addison waylaid by well-wishers, I proceeded into the house alone. The riot of perfumes worn by the Countess's guests commingled into a single intoxicating scent. Addison had said the famed decorator Elsie de Wolfe, Lady Mendl – another of those blasted titles – had been given a blank check in accoutering the house, and the result proved worth it. Hand-painted green wallpaper. Mirrors that doubled the size of the dining room and quadrupled the light and gaiety.

Everywhere chinoiserie and bamboo lending a touch of the exotic. I could picture Marlene Dietrich prowling the grounds, feeling completely at home.

I circuited the house twice, finding new treasures each lap. I thought about taking a seat, but feared my parachute skirt would resemble a tent upon sitting down. Instead I paused in a room near the small orchestra and pondered my uncle Danny's disbelief at my referring to any orchestra as 'small'. What a long way I'd come since leaving Flushing.

The Countess appeared on the far side of the room. Not yet ready to face her, I drifted along the edge of the dance floor.

'Lively band. Would you care to take a turn?' The offer extended with a clipped New York delivery better suited to asking, 'Where to?' over the front seat of a taxicab.

A 'buzz off' was poised on my lips when I looked into the eyes of George Raft. The actor best known for his tough guy roles – and his card in the Transogram Movie Millions game – wore a tightly tailored tuxedo with narrow lapels. His hair gleamed under the lights. I knew he'd broken through as a dancer, so I wasn't about to spurn him.

He was even lighter on his feet than I'd expected. A few steps in, I said, 'I imagine we have some friends in common at Paramount.'

'You mean the studio I just parted ways with?'

Damn. In my excitement I'd forgotten Raft and Paramount had mutually agreed to end his contract, largely because Raft racked up repeated suspensions for refusing to play villains and brutes. I scrambled for a recovery. 'Really the only person I know there is Edith Head.'

Raft brightened. 'I always liked Edith. Not that she had much to do with me. Only so many ways to cut a prison uniform. She never had to put me in a suit of armor or anything.'

And if she did, I thought, *you'd ask for tight tailoring and narrow lapels.*

That well having run dry, I switched the subject to our shared New York heritage and the upcoming World's Fair. Raft talked about some hoofers he knew who'd hired on at various venues in Flushing.

'Thanks, Georgie,' another voice said. 'I'll take it from here.'

The owner of the voice wore the most immaculate tuxedo I had ever seen. He also had blue eyes. Blue the color of the ocean in your dreams. You knew that blue contained sharks and other dangers, and you didn't care.

Raft chafed at the interruption, even though he clearly expected it. 'I thought I'd get to finish the dance at least.'

'You need to share your gift. You're in a garden of wallflowers. Spread it around, Twinkletoes.' Raft backed away and the interloper took me in his arms the way you'd pick up a fork, or a hammer, or a gun. Like a tool, meant to be used.

'I enjoyed our dance, miss. Save me another one.' Raft's words were a small defiance, and he spoke them with sincerity.

My new partner pulled me close. I couldn't look at him. I concentrated on the green wallpaper. The man smelled of talcum powder and various lotions, which should have made him seem comical. My fingers moved involuntarily on his tuxedo jacket, because it felt so extraordinarily smooth. If my tongue hadn't dried up, I might have asked him where he'd gotten it.

The orchestra wound down the song. I prayed for them to play something with heat that would keep us apart. 'Flat Foot Floogie with a Floy Floy', maybe.

But no. In the cruelest of jokes, they struck up 'Thanks for the Memory', a tune Paramount made famous. The man lassoed me even closer, his arm coiled around me like a snake preparing to squeeze.

'You enjoying the Countess's party?' he asked breezily.

Somehow, I eked out a yes.

'It doesn't sound like it. I'd say it doesn't look like it, but I can't see you.' He paused, hoping I'd take the hint, then instructed, 'Look at me.'

I obeyed. I looked into those eyes of so-deep blue. The blue of the water at the base of a cliff, with some wild voice in the back of your head whispering 'Jump.' I couldn't be certain, but I thought I spied a hint of strategically placed eye shadow, meant to highlight that blue, make it shine.

'Thing is, we need some entertainment.' He continued to speak casually, as if we were on an elevator together. 'This lousy band ain't cutting it. So. Parlor tricks. I am going to guess your name. I've been able to do this forever. You ready?' He closed those blue eyes, and I drew in a breath. The lids slammed back open. 'Lillian Frost. Am I right?'

I nodded. The man gave himself a round of applause by tapping his fingers against the small of my back.

'Uncanny, isn't it? Think I've got a little gypsy blood in me. Now. An even greater demonstration of my talents. I am going to communicate my name to you. Like a brainwave. They call it telepathy. I read about it in a science magazine. When it comes to you, when you know the name of your dance partner, you will say it. OK?'

The blue eyes bored into mine. You'd need a whole new word to describe that shade, I thought.

'Benjamin Siegel,' I said, in what sounded to my ears like a perfectly normal voice.

'Please. Ben. To a woman in my arms, it's always Ben.' To prove the point, he spun me around, a little too fast for my liking. 'That gypsy blood is working well tonight. It's astonishing. I should be in pictures. You can use your pull at Paramount to get me in the door, now that George has loused it up over there. I admit, maybe this talent won't play very well onscreen. But if they can put a ventriloquist on the radio . . .'

Siegel considered himself in the mirror. He lifted his hand briefly from my back to adjust his hair. 'Now, Miss Frost,' he said, then repeated the words like an actor unhappy with his line reading. 'We know people in common. Like Dorothy. The Countess. Also my friend Sylvia. In fact, I know you found her. After she passed.'

Another spin and we moved through French doors and outside, onto a patio. We could hear the music but no one could see us. Siegel had engineered for us to be alone and in shadow, at a brightly lit and crowded house.

I didn't shudder. I didn't want to give him the satisfaction. And I feared if I started, I'd be unable to stop.

'What perplexes me,' he said into my ear, 'is that I never heard my friend Sylvia mention you. Yet you show up at her home late at night, looking for her. And find her dead. That's not the natural order of things. The person who finds you should be known to you, even if it's your neighbor or your mailman. The person who finds you should be somebody. You are nobody.'

We stopped dancing, though the music went on. Siegel opened his arms and released me. I turned away from him. In the grounds beyond, I noticed one of the lamps had burned out, creating a patch of darkness somehow blacker than that which surrounded it. *That's where he's going to kill me*, I thought. *If I worked here, I'd have had that lamp fixed.*

'Actually, Miss Frost, that's unfair. I apologize. You're not a nobody. You work for a well-respected man. You come from good stock, back in New York, where I'm from. Uncle Danny, Aunt Joyce, out there in Flushing.'

He stated these facts without menace. Yet fear scalded my stomach.

'But you're nobody to Sylvia. Yet you found her. And I want to know why. My gypsy blood, it's failing me on that score. So. You have to tell me.'

And I did. I told him everything. I babbled a little as I explained about *Streetlight Story*, and Gene, and Clyde Fentress. Tears leaked from my eyes but my voice remained level, if low.

Siegel interrupted me once, when I first mentioned the bank robbery. As soon as I said California Republic, he said, 'Right. The twenty grand.'

He knew about it. The crime wasn't news to him.

When I finished, those blue eyes moved over me as dispassionately as a butcher's. 'What did you think you were going to accomplish?'

I blinked frantically to buy myself a few seconds, but after they passed the question still didn't make sense. 'I don't understand.'

'When you showed up on Sylvia's doorstep, what did you think was gonna happen? Did you think she had the twenty grand?'

'I – no. I thought we could talk.'

'Talking doesn't settle anything. It didn't settle this.' He took a step closer to me. I took two steps closer to the shadows. 'I don't believe you. I think you're holding out.'

'I'm not. I swear. I only wanted to help my friend.'

'Sorry, I'm not buying it. You were up to something. Maybe Sylvia was, too. You and she—'

'Did the fun move out here? Or am I being a fifth wheel?' Virginia Hill sashayed out of the house but remained close to the French doors. Not out of a sense of safety, but so there'd be sufficient light to showcase her gown. Howard Greer had pulled out all the stops for this one, binding her in sable satin so tight it was obvious she'd left her lingerie purchases at home, packed neatly in their tissue paper. The dress descended to a puddle of ruffles on the floor, a flare at the knee the sole concession to human locomotion. She used it now to thrust her right leg insolently forward. Diamonds sparkled from a collar around her neck.

Never had such a flamboyant display made me happier. I let a tremble of relief run through me as Siegel retreated, peering at Virginia quizzically.

'All my pals in the same place. Ben and Lillian. I'd introduce you, but you seem to have already met.' She held a glass in each hand. She sipped daintily from one and offered me the other. I scampered over to accept it. 'There you go, sweetheart. A stinger for the stung.'

'Where's mine?' Siegel asked playfully.

'You don't drink, Ben. We established that back in New York.'

'We established a number of things there, as I recall.'

'Yeah, it was a regular conclave. Only Pope Pius wouldn't approve some of what you and I came up with.' Virginia glanced at me. She still hadn't moved that bared leg, pointed at Siegel. 'Drink up, dear.'

I gulped down half the stinger, the rush of heat and mint making me choke. 'You're meant to sip those,' Siegel said.

Virginia ran a manicured fingertip around the rim of her glass. 'You still seeing the Countess, Ben?'

'I'm a married man.'

'But you were on that boat with her for, what, a couple months? Your wife didn't mind that?'

'That's different. That was a business opportunity.'

'Business.' She slipped her fingertip briefly into her mouth. Siegel tugged on the collar of his shirt. I was confident the two gestures were unrelated.

'Yeah, business. Sharks. We were after sharks. For their livers. Because shark liver is a rich source of Vitamin A. Which is, as you know, hard to come by right now.' For some reason, Siegel addressed this explanation to me. I nodded politely.

He decided to seize the conversational wheel. 'How do you know the Countess, exactly?'

'Me? Oh, I don't.' Virginia smiled. 'Just what I read in the papers. She seems like an interesting gal, one I wanted to meet, so I invited myself. Walked right in. Who's going to say no to a dress like this?' She pivoted her hips around that unmoving leg. Siegel licked his lips. Apparently, he wasn't about to say no.

Virginia drained her glass. 'Come on, Lillian, let's go get a refill.

See if the Countess has scared up these layabout limey houseguests of hers.'

Siegel stepped forward. 'Lillian and I aren't done talking.'

'Yes, you are, Ben. Your gypsy blood is tired. Let it rest.' Virginia laced her arm through mine and guided me toward the house. I polished off my stinger before we reached the French doors.

'You all right, kid?' she asked. 'You look a touch peaked.'

'What do you mean, kid? Aren't we about the same age?'

'Not even close. I'm way older.' She patted my arm. 'I died a million deaths before I reached eighteen.'

For some reason, I believed her. 'Thank you for coming along when you did.'

'Ben wouldn't have done anything to you. Not out there. The location's all wrong. Ben likes a certain mood, wants his lighting just so. He thinks he's in a movie every second of the day. Unlike me. I at least know when I'm off camera.' She smiled, whether at someone across the room or at the absurdity of the situation, I couldn't say. 'It takes a talent to live at night. I hate to say this, kid, but I don't think you have it. Sylvia thought she did, and that's worse. Her dalliance with Ben was just a fling to him. It wasn't to her. Ben doesn't understand that. He never will.'

The orchestra had packed the dance floor. Addison was talking to a stodgy twosome I took to be the Duke and Duchess of Sutherland. I turned to alert Virginia, but she had slipped away, leaving only my empty glass and a trace of perfume behind.

George Raft approached, a sheepish expression in his eyes. 'Hello again, miss. I wanted to apologize. My friend Ben, well . . . he can be headstrong.'

'That's one word for it.'

The actor offered me a cigarette, which I declined. He ignited one of his own with a gold lighter. From the way he turned it in his hand, I expected him to flip it like the coin he used so memorably in *Scarface*.

'Sentimental about this,' Raft said, holding the lighter aloft. It bore an inscription I couldn't read. 'A gift from King Edward, back when he was just a prince. Before all the business with that woman. Taught him how to do the Charleston, if you can imagine that.'

'I can. Didn't you promise me another dance?'

He smiled. 'It would be my pleasure. Would now be all right?' He took my arm and led me out onto the floor. He was so nimble I almost didn't notice how sick I felt.

LORNA WHITCOMB'S
EYES ON HOLLYWOOD

At least one Hollywood denizen can't wait for next Monday because it means the mothballing of that ten-foot-tall Easter bunny on Wilshire Boulevard. He says the buck-toothed behemoth provokes heart palpitations every time he turns the corner . . . What a brilliant bash at Countess Dorothy di Frasso's home last night. There was champagne, dancing and many beautiful ladies flaunting their finery. The only gloom cast on the glamorous proceedings was when a guest asked the Countess about her upcoming European trip. Stalwart Dottie laughed off concerns about the voyage, but later confided she's crossing fingers she won't be caught in a war zone . . . Strife abroad and strikes at home? That's the word being whispered on studio lots. Those extra players haven't backed down from their talk of giving SAG the boot and forming their own union.

TWENTY-THREE

I approached my closet with an unusual sense of calm. After the previous night's excesses, I could keep things simple. Dungarees being too informal, I went with a white blouse, tan skirt, and red scarf. Addison wanted to compare notes on the Countess's fête while strategizing for his next party. I was happy to devote Saturday morning to the campaign before visiting Edith.

Addison greeted me at the door looking flustered. He stepped outside so we could speak in private, even though whoever might overhear us was several rooms away. 'I'm afraid I made a bit of a faux pas,' he said, whispering into the bargain. 'I forgot about my acting lesson! Joan arrived promptly on time. Would you mind waiting?'

I said not at all and he escorted me to the library so I could say hello. Joan Crawford had come garbed for her taskmaster role. Her navy twill dress had a militaristic air, fashioned like a frock coat with three gold buttons on the wide waistband.

'Lillian!' Again she charged toward me with hands outstretched, like I was a legionnaire come to liberate her. 'Addison tells me you wore a Greer last night! Isn't Howard's salon magnificent? You must try the Vibrant Room. It's what Howard calls the space for us redheads. Every wall painted the most bold, electric blue! I never feel more beautiful or more alive than when I'm in that room. I'm telling you, it's worth dyeing your hair for. Now, Addison. Did you practice your vocal exercises?'

'Yes, Miss Crawford.' He sounded like a sulky schoolboy.

'This is where I leave you.' I bowed to my employer. 'If you need my help, recite a soliloquy from *Hamlet*.'

I heard the doorbell en route to my desk and decided to spare the butler's bunions. To my astonishment, I found Bette Davis waiting. She wore an expectant expression that perfectly accessorized her sensible slacks and sea-foam green blouse flecked with tiny polka dots.

'Good morning . . .' She paused for me to fill in the name she hadn't bothered to remember. It took me a moment to think of it myself. 'What a cute outfit. Very casual. But then I suppose it is Saturday. Where would Addison like me?'

Oh, no. Oh, dear God, no.

'The solarium.' I blurted the name of the room farthest from the library. Davis pulled a face. 'It has wonderful acoustics,' I added.

'Acoustics. Will he be singing opera?' She laughed and let me show her into the house.

I trotted back to the library, calling on every patron saint I could think of to intervene. Something told me we'd need a full complement of them.

Rapping gently on the door, I leaned into the library. Crawford looked irritated, whether at Addison's aptitude or my interruption I couldn't be sure.

'Might I borrow Mr Rice for a moment?' I said sweetly.

In the hallway, I explained the imminent train wreck. 'Good Lord!' Addison braced himself against a table not prepared for the task. 'I completely forgot I asked Bette for a second lesson as well!'

'If only you had a social secretary to keep these matters straight for you. What would you like to do?'

Addison stood up, as stoic and brave as a man requesting a blindfold from a firing squad. 'We have a master class.'

It was my job to fetch Davis. 'Perhaps Addison should have sent a car,' she said as we walked. We reached the library door. Crazed grin on my face, I swung it wide.

The instant Davis and Crawford clapped eyes on one another, I wanted to get a sweater. Addison chuckled weakly and slumped against a reading stand, looking a trifle woozy. 'Good morning, Bette! It, uh, it appears we have you ladies double-booked.'

The actresses in tandem turned their gazes upon me, and I felt all the moisture leave my body. Naturally, they would assume the error was mine, and for Addison's sake I let them. He nodded his profound thanks to me, then coughed out another ghastly chuckle. 'And I thought, why shouldn't I take advantage of all this talent?'

A pause followed. Icicles formed in the room's distant corners.

'Why not indeed?' Crawford came out of the gate fast, gunning for an Academy Award of her own. She beamed at Davis. 'I'm happy to see you again, Bette. The last time was when I visited you while you were working with Franchot on *Dangerous*.'

'Yes, you two were so *affectionate* then. He would always return from lunch with his face covered in lipstick.' Davis lit a cigarette. 'Speaking of Franchot, I was *so sorry* to hear your union had come to an end.'

'As was I to hear the same of yours. But Franchot and I will be seeing *Dark Victory* at the premiere in New York.'

Davis brayed a laugh. 'What on earth for?'

'I'm a tremendous admirer of your work.'

'No, why see it with him if you're divorced?'

Crawford stiffened, then ratcheted up her good cheer. 'It's our way of being civilized.'

'That's not civilization, Miss Crawford, it's cruelty. But by all means see the picture. I haven't yet seen your most recent effort. What is it called? *The Ice Queen*?'

The reading stand groaned under Addison as he wavered on his feet. Crawford strained her cheeks to their very limits. '*The Ice Follies of 1939*. Just fluff, a fun little romp.'

'I enjoyed it,' I squeaked, determined to steer the conversation onto a steady track.

'You sing in that one, don't you?' Davis asked. 'I seem to remember reports to that effect.'

The question broke Crawford's spirit, her broad shoulders sagging. 'Yes, but the numbers were removed.'

'Ah. I remember reports to that effect, too.'

Enough was enough. 'Why don't we start Addison's lesson?' I announced to every room in the house, and most of the garden.

I expected both women to leap down my throat, but instead they simultaneously said, 'Yes, why don't we?'

And then, for what seemed like an hour and a half, no one spoke. Addison gestured at me helplessly, the man who'd created this mess unable to get himself out of it. Someone had to captain this vessel and maneuver it between two icebergs. That someone, apparently, was me.

'Again, Addison will be a background performer in a nightclub scene. We're not sure yet how he'll be used.'

Crawford nodded. 'Background is so critical. Even aspects the audience is unaware of. We're about to start work on *The Women* and everything about it will be female.'

'Sounds dreadful,' Davis said.

Her fellow actress went cheerfully on. 'Every book on the shelf, written by a woman. Every animal in a scene, female. That kind of detail can't help but create a mood, a sensation that will be communicated onscreen.'

'Cukor's directing, isn't he?' Davis sniffed. 'That sounds like one of his ideas.'

'Yes, he is.' Crawford kept her countenance angelic. 'I understand you were in his theatrical company, back in your early days. You were let go, weren't you? George said something about your being aloof.'

'There's a pleasant word for it!' Davis gave as good as she got in the seraphic smile department. 'I refused to fraternize with my colleagues. And George longs for sycophants, you know, worshipful types who take every one of his harebrained notions for genius. I'm sure you'll have a *marvelous* time. Now, Addison, what are we doing?'

He moved tentatively into the center of the room. Crawford raised her hand.

'Edmund Goulding suggested when we made *Paris* that I work barefoot. Draw in the earth's energy directly. I still do many scenes that way. Gives me a great strength and stillness.'

'How about it, Addy?' Davis cracked. 'Kick off your shoes and let your feet do their stuff.'

'I don't think that will be necessary.'

'Especially if there's to be dancing. Remind me, will there be dancing in this nightclub?'

'Yes, physical expression is key.' Crawford widened her eyes to demonstrate. Davis shielded hers so we couldn't see them rolling.

Addison stammered. 'Again, I'm not sure—'

'Let's go. Take a spin.' Crawford clapped her hands.

'Yes. Dance with—' Davis gestured at me.

'Lillian. That's a wonderful idea,' Crawford chirped.

'Is it, though?' I asked with only a hint of desperation. 'I won't be in the picture.'

'It's just for rehearsal. Come along now.' Davis's manner brought to mind every nun who'd ever instructed me. I had no choice but to obey. Addison placed his arms tentatively around me. Crawford leaned forward, visualizing us in a nightclub.

'Let's get you two moving,' Davis ordered. 'Shall I hum some music?'

'That's right, your husband's a bandleader, isn't he?' Crawford maintained her honeyed tone. Davis swiveled her head toward her.

'We don't need any music,' I yelled, dragging Addison through a basic box-step. I could feel him trembling in fear. As partners went, he was no George Raft.

'He's holding you as if you were a live grenade, dear.' Davis hooted. 'Relax, Addy. Take your time and get comfortable.'

Addison finally started to lead, his movements becoming smoother. I smiled at him, egging him on.

'You see what Maude's been putting up with for decades,' he said. 'Three left feet, I've got.'

Crawford nodded. 'Good, good. Now be aware of the camera.'

'What kind of extra looks into the camera?' Davis asked.

'I didn't tell him to look into the camera, Bette. I suggested he be aware of it.'

'There's a difference?' The question was followed by a long drag on Davis's cigarette.

'Of course there is.' A tremor of doubt crept into Crawford's voice. She sat even straighter to compensate for it. 'A performer always wants to know where the camera is, what it's pointing at.'

'The camera is not the actor's concern. The performance is.'

'What good is a carefully wrought performance if the camera

doesn't see it? Addison can work out the most nuanced character-
ization and if his back is to the camera it's all for naught.'

'The camera sees *everything*, Miss Crawford. It notices all.
Particularly body language. Didn't you yourself say physical expression is key?' Davis lapsed into a savage singsong when she quoted
Crawford's words back to her. 'Acting is more than just the face,
the widening of the eyes.'

'When has anyone ever paid to see someone's back?' Crawford
protested.

A sinister spark blossomed in Davis's own eyes as she relished
her upcoming rejoinder.

'I think I'm getting the hang of this!' a frantic Addison cried.

'You're not,' both actresses said at once.

For the next twenty-seven agonizing minutes my genial employer
was subjected not so much to an acting clinic as a vivisection, his
esteemed guests critiquing his every move. Davis and Crawford
offered contradictory advice that came within a hair's breadth of
compatibility, their dueling sensibilities closer than they at first
appeared. Together they made the ideal mentor, provided you could
ignore the cutting remarks. Addison perspired profusely while I
stumbled over my own feet as well as his. At one point Crawford
made a suggestion to me, prompting Davis to retort, 'Lillian is not
in the picture!' When I realized she had finally remembered my
name, I refrained from bursting into tears, keeping the morning's
one genuine display of emotion under wraps.

When the actresses found themselves at loggerheads over how
Addison should pull out my chair after our dance, he put his foot
down – but discreetly, as only he could.

'This has been quite the education!' He mopped his brow
theatrically. 'I feel I should stop now so I can absorb all you ladies
have taught me.'

'It was *so* helpful having the benefit of your wisdom,' I
cooed. 'Is there any possibility we can arrange to have you both
again?'

'That's doubtful,' Davis said.

'I'm afraid I'll be frightfully busy,' Crawford echoed.

'Cukor, you know.' Davis lit another cigarette. 'All that femininity.
The screen just lousy with it.'

We walked the ladies out, Addison and I forming a wedge to
keep them separate until we reached the front door.

Crawford again offered her impossibly toothy smile. 'It's been a lovely morning. I can't remember when I've enjoyed myself more.'

'Yes, a veritable slice of heaven.' Davis slipped on a pair of sunglasses.

'We'll have to do it again,' Crawford gushed.

'Why?'

Crawford lunged to embrace Davis, who chose that very moment to turn to Addison, leaving Crawford to stop awkwardly, arms extended in a stance resembling a dinosaur's. 'Do tell me how your debut goes, Addy,' Davis said blithely. 'Must dash.'

Addison and I waited in the entryway as the two actresses left, making sure they didn't drive their vehicles headlong into each other. Davis, I was fairly sure, considered the idea. We said nothing until the sounds of both motors had faded, leaving us in blessed silence and sunlight. We basked in the combination for some time.

'Well,' Addison finally said. 'I'm sure everything will be fine.'

'Are you taking wagers on that?'

'Is it too early to open a bottle of champagne?'

'It never is.'

TWENTY-FOUR

I enjoyed every trip to Paramount, but particularly savored those rare occasions when I stole onto the lot over a weekend. These visits reminded me of the fairy tale of the elves and the shoemaker, of work being done in secret. I'd glimpse flurries of activity in office windows or hear hammering from some remote corner of the studio, knowing the efforts would pay dividends come Monday.

Still, I steered clear of Stage 13, lest anyone involved with *Streetlight Story* – specifically Brenda, the Baines of my existence – was afoot.

The usual soft drone of sewing machines filled the Wardrobe building, but no secretaries were on duty at Edith's suite. Voices tumbled out of her salon, animated and tinged with laughter. I hesitantly announced my presence and Edith summoned me inside.

To my surprise, Florabel Muir greeted me first. The newspaperwoman wore the same suit she'd had on when last we'd met, now decorated with a lily-of-the-valley brooch, each bud a freshwater pearl. My response to her sounded notably guarded.

'Don't mind me,' she said. 'Just looking up your friend Edith while sniffing around *Streetlight Story*. I reacquainted myself with the cast of characters from the California Republic robbery. Square-jawed Teddy Lomax. Soft-hearted soft-touch lothario Borden Yates. Bianchi the wild man and Hoyer the degenerate. With the Hollywood angle as the cherry on top.'

'Miss Muir hasn't spared a sordid detail.' Edith was in her version of weekend wear, a twill skirt and a jewel neck blouse printed with colorful sailboats. 'How are you, Lillian? More importantly, how was the party?'

'Yes!' Florabel crowed. 'I hear you called on the Countess di Frasso.'

I faltered, unsure how much to reveal in Florabel's presence. The best move, I reasoned, was to play it conservatively. 'You were right,' I told Edith. 'Mr Siegel was there.'

'You'd think he and the Countess would have had enough of each other on that boat trip,' Florabel said.

'Can somebody please fill me in about that?' I asked. 'The *Metha Nelson* came up again last night and I was in the dark.'

'The full scoop on that voyage of the damned is known only to those onboard, and they won't talk. Paramount ought to scrap *Streetlight Story* and make a picture out of what we do know.' Florabel settled herself, her delectation evident. 'It begins, believe it or not, with a treasure map and a life-size golden statue of the Virgin Mary.'

'Hold on.' Edith reached for her telephone. 'Let me raise the Story Department.'

'Somehow Dorothy's husband, the Count, acquired this map and gave it to her. A little project to keep her occupied. It purports to reveal the location of buried pirate booty including the statue. Which, did I mention, is also covered with diamonds and rubies.'

'No,' I said. 'You did not.'

'Legend has it some priests and nuns slipped it out of Peru on a ship bound for Spain. Pirates butchered the lot of them and swiped the statue, so if you ask me the thing is cursed. Which may explain what transpired when Dorothy decided she was going to find it. She got Benny Siegel involved, along with Marino Bello, a conniver who used to be Jean Harlow's father-in-law. They assemble a jolly band and go off to the islands on this map. They dig until they get sunstroke, then they use dynamite. They find not a thing.'

'I have to say,' I had to say, 'this screwy proposition doesn't sound like something Bugsy Siegel would be involved in.'

'It's Benny, sweetheart, and that's because maybe it isn't.' Florabel grinned wickedly. 'The alternate explanation is the voyage was cover for a smuggling racket, Benny and the boys bringing contraband from the Pacific. Narcotics and French perfume, what every girl wants. The police raided Benny's house back in January after a hot tip he'd stashed the perfume there, but came up empty.'

'That sounds infinitely more plausible,' Edith said.

'But you haven't heard the *other* other explanation. Are you ladies familiar with the name Lepke Buchalter? Gangland figure out of New York, wanted on multiple charges and currently the target of an international manhunt. Nobody's seen hide nor hair of Lepke in two years. There are rumors he's hiding out on a South Seas island.'

'No,' I said, anticipating the next twist.

Florabel nodded with glee. 'This version of the *Metha Nelson* saga, by far my favorite, says Benny was dispatched by his New York cronies to bring provisions to Lepke so he doesn't turn himself in and spill all he knows to Uncle Sam.'

I shook my head. 'To think he told me it was about shark livers.'

'I've heard that one, too. Who knows, maybe that's legitimate. Anyway, debauchery broke out on the boat almost at once. The captain officiated a wedding between Bello and the ship's nurse, some thirty years his junior, with Benny as best man and Dorothy as bridesmaid. The problems really start when the *Metha Nelson* breaks down on the trip back and goes adrift. They're at sea for over four months. I can't imagine being on a barge with the Countess for four hours.'

'Edith mentioned something about a mutiny,' I said.

'Curiouser and curiouser.' Florabel cackled. 'The men were being kept separate from the women – the Countess, her maid, and the newly hitched nurse. Except for Benny and Bello, of course, who had special privileges. The crew members felt the ladies could stand to be more diplomatic. The half-hearted uprising was put down, but the *Metha Nelson*'s captain is a true old salt who insisted on following the law of the sea once the ship was towed back to terra firma. He got laughed out of court for his trouble. Here endeth this whale of a tale.'

'Remarkable,' Edith said. 'Perhaps you can enlighten us on Mr Siegel. He's shrouded in rumor, and unpleasant ones at that.'

'Like I was saying, Benny's New York's man in Hollywood. He's been coming out since the twenties, and really settled in a few years back.'

'So he was making hay here in, say, 1936?' I asked, thinking of Siegel's familiarity with the California Republic robbery.

'He'd definitely established his bona fides by then. He was sent out in part because the Chicago outfit had sewn up much of the town and gotten fat off it. They'd taken over IATSE, the International Alliance of Theatrical Stage Employees.'

'Really?' I gasped. 'That's my uncle Danny's union.'

'It's the union of any craftsman who works behind the scenes. IATSE's president, George Browne? Hand-picked by the boys in Chicago. His man in Los Angeles is a bruiser named Willie Bioff, and given his alleged business practices, it's as apt a handle as I've run across. Bioff goes to the studio bosses and threatens a strike. He then says it can be averted with a generous cash donation. The studios figure they're out the money one way or the other, so they take the deal.'

Edith, I noticed, had cast her eyes down in shame.

'And the money lines pockets in Chicago instead of going to the stagehands as increased wages.' My gorge rose on Uncle Danny's behalf.

'Exactly. Same difference to the studio chiefs. Some IATSE members have been after Bioff and Browne for years, claiming they sold out the workers' interests and turned IATSE into a de facto company union. They even dug up Bioff's past thanks to the Chicago Crime Commission. A sweet boy, Willie. Arrests for burglary and pandering. Vagrancy charges. *And* he was suspected of murder.'

'Then they had proof,' I said.

'Yes, but "they" are a pack of rabid reformers in league with those radicals in the CIO.' Florabel smirked. 'A stink was raised back in '37, but investigators cleared the union. Then came last year's look into influence peddling in Sacramento, and people started asking whether that IATSE report was a whitewash. Bioff left his job for appearances' sake, but he'll come oozing back. His type always does. Unless . . .'

'Unless?' Edith nudged.

'There are whispers the Screen Actors Guild sicced detectives on Bioff and took what they learned straight to the Treasury Department. Maybe that will ruffle the right feathers. Meantime, the Chicago boys are making a mint. New York says, "We want a piece of that" and unleashes Benny Siegel with orders to get them a union of their own. Benny works fast, grabs all the Teamster operations at the studios. Then he starts pressuring the extras. That's his dream. You see, Browne and Bioff can call a strike against any studio behind the camera. Benny aims to do the same in front of it. Always a showman, Benny.' She shook her head at the incorrigible scamp. 'Right now the background players are pushing to have their own union, separate from SAG. I imagine the enterprising Benny is out stirring the pot and capitalizing on the uproar. If the extras form their own union, Benny will be in position to have his hooks in it. In the meantime, he's probably shaking down the studios promising to tip the election. He doesn't miss a trick. I hear he leans on his celebrity friends for loans he never bothers to pay back.'

Like George Raft, I thought. 'Virginia Hill seems to know Ben.'

'Why do you say that?' Florabel's eyes narrowed. 'Was she at the Countess's last night? Did she and Benny talk?'

I played it coy. 'I got the sense they have history.'

'That's the trouble with these gangland types. Few hard facts. I believe I mentioned Virginia's tied into the Chicago outfit. The story is they sent her to Los Angeles to keep an eye on Benny, see what he's up to. They know Benny likes shiny things. The Chicago boys polished Virginia up and planted her in Benny's path.' She angled her head toward mine, just-us-girls style. 'You sure Benny and Virginia didn't have words?'

'Nothing worth repeating,' I said.

The three of us chatted about the Countess's party a while longer, Florabel's questions rather pointed. At long last, she rose to leave.

'Wonderful meeting you,' she told Edith. 'But the missing Mr Fentress isn't about to find himself.'

I tried to pass off my next query as idle curiosity, but – even with every Davis and Crawford pointer at my disposal – I couldn't make 'What on earth are you talking about?' sound casual.

'Clyde's gone,' Florabel said. 'Flew the coop. Maybe he's on that island with Lepke Buchalter.'

'Mr Groff asked to see him late yesterday,' Edith explained. 'Mr Fentress never arrived for the meeting. It would seem he heard the rumors about his head being on the chopping block and made himself scarce to put off the inevitable.'

'Trying to stay on the payroll until next week?' Florabel asked.

'As I understand it, he's not going to be terminated. Mr Groff wanted to ask about his, shall we say, research methods in light of recent events.'

'I'm assuming Mrs Fentress has no idea where he is,' I said.

'That's where the story gets juicy. No one knows where Josie is, either. They both bolted, maybe separately, maybe together.' Florabel practically salivated, already scenting the chase. 'I don't know which of them to search for first, but I'd better pick one instead of whiling away the afternoon.'

'Let me walk you out,' I said, feeling tremors of anticipation all my own.

I returned with an extra bounce in my step, enough to call my stride a swagger. Not that Edith noticed. She slaved over her sketchpad, her hand a blur.

'Paulette Goddard is pressing for more panache in her wardrobe,' she said with a sigh. 'I enjoyed speaking with Miss Muir. A most formidable woman. I had to be on my guard with her, but I wanted to pick her brain about Mr Siegel's enterprises. She's very smart.'

'Not as smart as I am.' My bravado was almost too much for me to take. Edith finally peered up at me. 'You said no one knows where Clyde Fentress is.'

'Yes. Mr Groff deployed every tool at his disposal to find him last night.'

'But poor Barney came a cropper. Ah, well. And Josie Fentress missing, too.' I tutted in shame at the world's laxity.

Edith set down her pad. 'What are you driving at?'

'I know where they are. Clyde and Josie. Both of them.'

'What? But how?'

I buffed my fingernails on the front of my blouse. 'I put a man on them is all.'

'You had Clyde followed?' Edith frowned. 'You couldn't have had Detective Morrow's assistance.'

Too late, I spotted the hidden cost of my gloating. I paid it in full. 'I asked Simon to help.'

Edith stood up so swiftly her petite frame seemed, for an instant, several inches taller. 'I thought we agreed you weren't going to see him anymore.'

'No, we didn't. We never spoke about that. You asked if I still saw him and . . .' I faltered, but made myself continue. 'And I lied to you about it.'

'I see.' Edith pressed her lips together, possibly to keep more damning words from escaping.

'We're not . . . involved or anything. I see him on occasion. Give him someone to talk to.'

'If that's the case, why lie about it?'

'Because I know you don't like Simon.' Although now that Edith had asked the question, I had to wonder about my answer. Maybe I did feel something for Simon, something I didn't care to admit even to myself.

'I like Mr Fischer, Lillian. What's more, I respect him. But I don't like him *for you*. Not that it's my place to make such judgments, much less share them. It's your life to live as you see fit.'

'Then I'd better go to where Clyde is, before he leaves. I'm going to call Addison and see if I can borrow his car.'

'If I may go back on what I just said, I strongly suggest you learn to drive. You can't keep relying on others to save the day.' She closed her sketchpad and picked up her purse. 'Now where are we going?'

TWENTY-FIVE

It was a good thing we had the roar of the Pacific to keep us company. My conversation with Edith had come to an awkward end once I'd relayed Clyde and Josie Fentress's whereabouts. We stayed mired in our own thoughts on the drive, the dueling rumbles of the car's engine and the ocean's waves filling the silence.

As Edith's roadster motored west along Roosevelt Highway toward Malibu, I recognized a building from many a fan magazine. 'Isn't that Thelma Todd's restaurant?'

'Please, Lillian,' Edith said. 'One murder at a time.'

I'd telephoned Simon from Edith's outer office once Florabel Muir had left. He'd answered after six agonizing rings. 'You're lucky. I just locked up my apartment, on my way to the Bund for the usual Saturday session of beer and megalomaniacal chatter. I was starting to think this errand you had me run wasn't that important.'

'No,' I told him. 'It's hugely important. Did you find Clyde yesterday?'

'He left the lot and immediately stopped for an afternoon bracer. My kind of guy. Then he drove home. Big, fancy pile in Hancock Park. Really fancy. What kind of pictures does this Clyde write?'

'The kind where he lives off his wife's money.'

'That makes sense. She came tooling home shortly thereafter in a dandy Cord Phaeton. Figured I'd wait a while, make sure they were tucked in for the night. Then man and wife came out, tossed two suitcases in her car, and took off. Per your request I followed them. Have to say, she drives like she's been followed before. I thought he was the one who'd been in jail.'

'He is. Her political bedfellows are probably why she's got eyes in the back of her head. Where did they go?'

'A cozy little mansion out toward Malibu. I had to let them turn off because traffic gets thin out there. I grabbed a bite at a fish shack, then looped back till I spotted the Cord outside a place with the name Graves on the mailbox. They could be gone by now or they could be there for the weekend. That's all she wrote.'

He reeled off the address.

'I can't thank you enough, Simon. I'm going out there now.'

'If you wait a while, I can take you.'

'I couldn't ask you to do that on top of everything else.'

'Run the conversation back. You didn't ask. I offered.'

'No. You've done enough. More than enough. I don't want to get you in trouble.'

'Worse than you have tried. The offer stands, should you want to save me from another afternoon of bratwurst and braggadocio.' He paused to let me reconsider, then threw in the towel. 'Let me know what happens. I'm invested in this business now.'

Josie's Cord Phaeton, indeed a dandy vehicle, was still outside the isolated splendor of a house on the hill above the Roosevelt Highway with a glorious view of the water. Simon hadn't exaggerated; traffic and neighbors were sparse in this still fairly wild stretch of Southern California. As Edith parked the car, I almost mentioned we could easily be made to vanish in such secluded country. Then opted to hold my tongue.

No one responded when I knocked on the front door. I was about to go exploring when the Fentresses circled around the house to surprise us. Josie the viper in a cute patterned sundress, Clyde looking hopelessly out of place in knee breeches, argyle socks and a golfing cap. If the boys at San Quentin could see him now.

'At least it's not the fuzz,' he grumbled. 'I told you this wasn't the place to hide out. Neighbors probably phoned the police on account of they didn't like the kind of cheese we brought with us.'

'Don't be ridiculous,' Josie said. 'Who would complain about Brillat-Savarin cheese? Besides, Louisa gave us loan of the house.'

'It's too conspicuous! We should've stayed in town to lie low, some place where there are people.'

'Like a flophouse?' I asked. 'Your friend Nap died in one of those.'

'Don't you know how to put a damper on a conversation,' Josie said.

Clyde peered around me at Edith. 'I know you. I read about you in the studio newspaper. You're the costume lady. Why are you here? Do I have a fitting?'

Edith smiled at him. 'I'm here because you're about to spin a yarn, Mr Fentress. I didn't want to miss it.'

The Brillat-Savarin cheese was delicious, its creaminess almost decadent. It made a lovely centerpiece to the impromptu picnic the Fentresses held inside their borrowed abode. Josie, it seemed, refused to go on the lam without toast points.

'We're not on the lam,' her husband stressed. 'We just wanted a few days away. Too many questions lately.'

Josie patted his hand, the affectionate gesture coming off as sarcastic. 'We should have holed up at some noisy motor court. Taken our meals at Clifton's Cafeteria so you could eat off a tray. Anything to recreate that jailhouse ambience you're used to, my darling.'

Fentress grimaced as if the repast didn't agree with him. Josie, it was now apparent, could say anything to him and he wouldn't raise his voice in response.

'Mr Fentress.' Edith dabbed the corners of her mouth with a linen napkin. 'What exactly was the basis for your *Streetlight Story* scenario?'

'You haven't cleared Clyde's name yet,' Josie said. 'I thought those were the terms of the deal.'

He'd told Josie about our arrangement, then let her stick up for him. Fentress looked distinctly queasy as he uttered a half-hearted backing of his wife's defense: 'Yeah.'

'You're hardly in a position to be making demands, Mr Fentress,' Edith said. 'After all, you've been sharing a mistress with a notorious underworld figure.'

Fentress scoffed. 'That's the story you've got? Pass.'

'It's no fabrication, I'm afraid. Although the initial reference to Mr Siegel's involvement was pure hearsay.'

A breath lodged in Fentress's throat, his eyes briefly becoming unmoored from logical thought. Josie's orbs, meanwhile, flashed dangerously. '*Bugsy* Siegel?' she gasped.

'Don't call him that,' I said. 'He doesn't care for the nickname. I had no cause to believe what I heard about him and Sylvia, until Mr Siegel contrived to meet me and demanded to know why I was interested in her.'

Fentress sat back and rubbed his face. He seemed genuinely taken aback by this revelation. Josie, too, had been temporarily struck dumb.

'It puts you in a difficult position, being linked romantically to – what's the term? – a gangster's moll.' Edith then took an elaborate pause. 'Only you're not, are you, Mr Fentress?'

This time I had trouble breathing. I'd had no advance notice of Edith's line of attack; what she was saying came as news to me.

'It's only speculation on my part,' she explained slowly, taking her theory for its first spin. 'But once Lillian discovered Miss Ward was not a writer, I realized you likely expected that information to come to light. How, then, to explain your relationship with her? Suppose you told a story people would readily believe.'

'A story people already believed,' Josie said.

'Precisely my point. Once Sylvia was murdered, you knew you would come under suspicion. Perhaps the wisest course of action would be to embrace the gossip commonly accepted as fact on the lot. Namely, that your putative protégée was, in truth, your mistress. A fabrication now considerably complicated by Mr Siegel being her actual paramour.'

Edith did not target her words at Fentress but at Josie. Josie, after all, wore the pants in the marriage. Clyde Fentress, looking ludicrous in his knee breeches, was ready to crawl off. The hard case, holed up in a glamour pad.

'What, then, was the late Sylvia Ward to you?' Edith continued. 'She was not your student. Neither was she your lover. Yet you lied to protect her – and yourself. Who, exactly, *was* Sylvia Ward?'

'Too bad you can't ask her,' Fentress said churlishly.

'I don't have to. Considering her relationship with you and the fact she was well informed about the California Republic bank robbery, I can hazard a guess. Sylvia Ward was the daughter of one of the thieves. Likely Borden Yates.'

From the look the Fentresses exchanged, I knew Edith's guess was on the money. I somehow prevented myself from yelping 'What?' aloud.

'A thief in your original story has a child, Mr Fentress,' Edith said. 'That detail remained in subsequent drafts of the script. Mr Dolan, in fact, said Miss Ward lobbied for its inclusion. That's because it's a detail drawn from life. *Her* life. When I learned Mr Yates fathered multiple children out of wedlock but maintained ties with those children, I drew that conclusion.'

Borden Yates, who repeatedly took advantage of young women like yourself, Miss Frost, Frady had said. And how had Florabel described him? *The soft-hearted soft-touch lothario*. Damn.

Fentress finally nodded. 'I've known Sylvia since she was knee-high to a grasshopper. That bit in my original story where Lefty's kid wants to play cops and robbers? Sylvia did that when she was little.'

'Then *she's* the one who told you Gene was behind the bank robbery?' I asked.

'No.' Fentress hammered the syllable home. 'I'd sold the story and was working with Dolan on the script when she came to me. She'd heard I'd written it. A mutual acquaintance I'd stupidly shot my mouth off to tipped her I'd spun the robbery that killed her old man into a picture.'

'Nap Conlin,' I said.

'Another pal from the old days. Used to run with Bord Yates and me. Sylvia tried to find the poor bastard work once he'd caught on with Central Casting. I'd lost touch with her. But once Nap told her about the picture she showed up at my door, demanding to know who killed her father. She never bought the official story, always believed there was another man involved with the job.' Fentress's brow furrowed, the first indication of remorse I'd seen from him. 'Sylvia gave me hell for not going to the law with what I knew and cashing in on it instead.'

'Yes, and why didn't you?' The only thing more astonishing than Josie's endless stream of jibes was her husband's martyr-like ability to absorb them without complaint.

'I had no choice,' he said flatly. 'I didn't have any evidence. And the cops would never go after one of their own.' Fentress looked directly at me. 'Because Gene Morrow planned and executed that bank robbery.'

'You're a liar,' I spat. 'Who told you that?'

Fentress leaned closer to me. Out of the corner of my eye, I saw Josie's rapt expression. Even she didn't know this part.

'Who told me? Sylvia's father. Bord Yates told me. He talked to me before the job. Didn't give up any particulars, because Bord was a good egg and a solid thief. But he let on he had something in the works, something big that would net him a decent payday. He made it plenty clear whatever this thing was, it had been planned to the last detail by someone else – and he'd be protected. Who could protect him other than a cop?'

'Wait a minute,' I said. 'Then he never gave you Gene's name.'

Fentress glowered at me before resuming his story. 'I didn't give it much thought at the time. Then, when the whole deal went belly up and Bord died, I looked at it with fresh eyes. Picked it apart. And realized Morrow's the only cop it could be. He got the money, offed his partner, and took up with his wife.'

'It's not him,' I said.

'Believe whatever you want. I know what I believe, what Sylvia believed, and what's going to be in the picture.' He shook his head, possibly in awe, possibly in fear. Maybe both. 'That was all that mattered to Sylvia. The picture. The idea that even if Morrow wasn't called out by name, the truth of what he did would still be up there on the screen. She wanted him to know somebody knew. She wanted the movie made even more than I did, and I *wrote* the goddamned thing. She told me more than once *Streetlight Story* would be the only justice she'd ever get. And the poor kid didn't live to see it.'

He pushed himself out of his chair and walked to the window to brood at the ocean. Edith sat worrying her napkin, doubtless appalled at the notion of untruths going into the world under the Paramount banner, while I remained stock still and tried not to cry.

Movies are what people remember, Sylvia had said that day in the drug store. *When you're sitting in the dark, you let yourself be vulnerable. You allow things in. And those things you carry with you.*

Josie clapped her hands. 'Well! Anyone for coffee?'

TWENTY-SIX

T he long drive from Malibu proceeded in stop-and-go fashion as Saturday beachgoers headed back to the city, some pulling over to buy hamburger sandwiches for children turned brown as berries by the sun. The rhythm of the ride was also thrown off by the many theories caroming around my brain. Edith and I had been largely silent on the trip out. Not so anymore.

'We know there's a fourth man, and Gene isn't him,' I said emphatically. 'Then who is it?'

'I'm considering the possibilities now.'

'Start with Clyde Fentress himself. I haven't ruled him out.' I realized to my chagrin I was almost yelling. 'He knows everybody involved with the robbery. He needs a hit movie and decides to turn the rumors about Gene into a script as his own private sick joke.'

'It's something of a risk, but I imagine he longs to get away from his wife.' Edith waved blithely to the caravanning family she almost sideswiped.

'Or it could be Bugsy Siegel.'

'Benjamin. Don't get in the habit of using that sobriquet.'

'He was in Los Angeles in 1936. He knew about the robbery when I mentioned it. And he could easily offload twenty grand with his gangland cronies.'

'Don't say "grand", either. Theoretically, Miss Ward could have told him about the robbery. On the other hand, given Mr Siegel's position in the criminal hierarchy, it's credible Mr Yates would feel "protected", as he allegedly told Mr Fentress.'

'Everything with Clyde is "allegedly". The only thing down on paper is his lousy script, and it's a tissue of lies.'

Another name occurred to me, but merely considering it made my heart flutter. Trying to speak it aloud brought an acrid taste to my mouth. This suspicion I couldn't yet share with Edith.

Suppose Fentress is correct, and the fourth man actually is with the LAPD. Only the machine in Clyde's head pulled a punch card casting the wrong cop in the role. Could the fourth man be you,

Captain Byron Frady? Would that account for your intense personal interest in the case, your dislike of Gene, your presence everywhere I turn? They say you're corrupt. How corrupt, exactly? Enough to plan and execute a robbery, with other men doing your bidding? You knew Giuseppe Bianchi. You arrested him yourself. Could you have sent him, and Hoyer and Yates, into the California Republic Bank? And just when a path to the police chief's office opened for you, this damned movie resurrected your crime. Now, you need to turn the script's fiction into fact, so an innocent man can pay for your sins.

I didn't dare give my wild surmise weight by voicing it. But I had to say *something*. 'What I don't understand is why, if Sylvia wasn't Clyde's mistress, she'd go to the trouble of dummying up those script pages.'

Edith leaned forward and squinted. 'Is there any sand left on the beach, or is it all on this windscreen? Those pages were for Mr Dolan. He's the writer Miss Ward was sleeping with. I daresay Mr Fentress didn't even know.'

I sat back in stark raving confusion as Edith rubbed futilely at the glass.

'Miss Ward knew the script would be extensively rewritten, and while Mr Fentress would have some say, much of that work would be done by Mr Dolan. You heard Mr Fentress. She regarded *Streetlight Story* as her sole chance at justice. She had to monitor the changes to the script and ensure the character based on Detective Morrow remained responsible for her father's death and was punished.' She glanced apologetically at me. 'She had a connection to Mr Fentress. She needed to forge one to Mr Dolan. To work her way into his affections, she began by convincing him she truly was an aspiring writer learning her craft from Mr Fentress. Mr Dolan may have been the only person who believed that story, partly because she fabricated those pages to augment the illusion for his benefit. He acknowledged he incorporated her suggestions as the script was revised.'

'OK,' I said slowly. 'But how do you get from that to Sylvia and Dolan sleeping together?'

'Simple,' Edith replied. 'He kept the pages.'

Late on Saturday afternoon, the Paramount lot was like an open-air cathedral, a place of stillness and grandeur. At least I saw it that way. Edith, as usual, viewed it pragmatically. 'Max is screening rushes from *Streetlight Story*. He wants to be reassured about the wardrobe and the overall look of the film. You're welcome to watch, if you'd like.'

'I'll be along shortly. I'd like to make a quick stop first. At George Dolan's office.'

I listened at the scribe's door until I heard a sound, a faint exhalation that could have been a sigh, or a sob, or a figment of my imagination. Only one way to find out.

He wore casual trousers and a mint green golfing shirt, as if he'd been dispatched to Wardrobe with the instruction 'Make him look like he's enjoying himself.' Feet propped on the windowsill, he watched the inactivity on the lot.

'First person I've seen in hours, and you don't even work here. I was hoping you were Clyde. Falling behind on this script since he up and vanished yesterday.'

'I just saw him.'

Dolan swung his chair toward me. 'Where is he?'

'With Josie.'

'I don't envy him, then.'

I had to agree with him on that score. 'He confirmed he wasn't sleeping with Sylvia.'

'Oh? Yeah, I always took that as so much chatter.'

'But someone else was.'

'*This* is what you and Clyde talked about? With Josie there?' I let the silence expand. 'I'll bite. Who was it?'

Bugsy – sorry, Benjamin Siegel, I thought, *but I'm not here to tell tales out of school.*

'You know who it was.'

Dolan pushed back from his typewriter. 'I have no idea what you're talking about.'

'Don't worry. Clyde doesn't suspect a thing. I understand if you don't want to talk about it. But the officers investigating Sylvia's death need to—'

'Ah, Jesus.' He hammered his fist onto the desk, his gaze fixed on the wall and likely some point in the past. As he moved, I caught a trace of a vaguely familiar odor, both fussy and masculine; a mixture of lotions from some luxe barber shop. With a start, I realized where I'd encountered the near-exact combination of fragrances before: on Ben Siegel.

Was that by design, Sylvia? Did you cajole poor, pliable Dolan, the budding California dandy, into using Bugsy's preferred products, so as not to carry the scent of one lover to the other? Oh, you clever, doomed girl.

'How could I have been such an idiot?' Dolan massaged his eyes. 'Actually, I know how. Not like it's complicated. A young girl hangs on your every word, laughs at your stories, finds excuses to be alone with you, it puts a charge in you. Even when you're happily married and not looking to stray. Sometimes, goddammit, it's just nice to be asked. Not that she was interested in me,' he added with a generous serving of self-pity.

'What was she interested in?'

'Writing.' Dolan pronounced his profession with contempt. 'All she wanted to talk about was *Streetlight Story*. What scenes was I thinking about, how about this piece of business, what did I plan to do with this character? I figured out she had a one-track mind and broke it off with her. It didn't change anything. She was still yammering at Clyde. He'd make script suggestions and I'd know they came from her.'

'When did you stop seeing her?'

'A few weeks ago. Around when *Streetlight Story*'s script was frozen.'

You mean around the time she didn't need you anymore, I thought, and wondered if their parting had in fact been mutual. If they'd parted at all; I only had his word for it.

'Anyway, it was for the best,' Dolan went on. 'I made a mistake. I don't want to hurt Gloria. That's my wife. She's done nothing to deserve this. Lord knows Sylvia didn't deserve what happened to her, either.'

Sylvia, who died believing the worst of Gene, and hating me for defending him. No, she didn't deserve that at all.

Dolan laughed bitterly as he picked his eyeglasses up from the desk. 'She was always pushing me to gussy myself up, Sylvia. New clothes, new cologne. I finally change my glasses and she's not here to admire them. Gloria doesn't like them.' He slipped on handsome horn-rimmed spectacles that didn't suit his face; point to Gloria. 'It's all such a waste. You read her pages. Sylvia was a good little writer. She could've gotten somewhere. Maybe farther than me.'

He still bought the balderdash Sylvia had handed him; she'd

played him completely for a fool. Once again, I didn't tell him the truth about Sylvia's script pages, this time out of respect for both her memory and her achievement. Maybe Dolan was right, and she did have a skill for telling stories. The one she'd spun for him, after all, still held up.

I stopped at a pay telephone and let the police know to expect George Dolan's call, and to get in touch with him if they didn't receive it. I hiked across the lot in the last of the late afternoon sunshine, accompanied by lengthening shadows and the echo of my footfalls. I could have been the only person at the studio and in the city of Los Angeles. The solitude was just fine by me.

The lights in the designated screening room were down. I slipped inside and eased the door shut. Turning, I slammed my shin into the closest chair and muttered an oath. So much for a seamless entrance.

In the projector's flickering light, I caught sight of a commotion in the front row. Max Ramsey clumsily untangled himself from Edith and vaulted two seats over, smoothing what remained of his hair. Edith fumbled with her glasses.

All the while I stood motionless. Thunderstruck. Like a child walking in on her parents putting out Santa's Christmas presents – or perhaps engaged in a more adult activity. My face flushed hot and bright. I calculated the odds of being able to exit the room before hell broke loose.

Then Max erupted. 'Lights!' he bellowed into the speaker connected to the projection booth, then wheeled around to glare at me. His crooked tie waved from beneath his askew collar. 'Who are you? What are you doing here?'

'I invited her, Max.' Edith spoke calmly while adjusting her hairpins.

'What on earth for? We're working here!'

'We can continue working.'

Max grunted. 'Not anymore. I'm not in the mood.' Noticing his tie and collar, he restored himself to his former dated elegance. 'We can discuss Brenda's wardrobe on Monday. I want to screen all the footage again. The pieces aren't coming together properly. Luddy's approach is too esoteric, too . . . European. I have to look at the story from a new angle so it makes sense. I need my writers, but Fentress has disappeared.'

'Mr Dolan is here,' I said, aiming to be helpful.

'I didn't ask you!' Max barked. Then, 'Is he? Hmm. We'll take this up on Monday, Edith. You have a pleasant evening.'

'Likewise, Max.'

He walked the length of the row so he could leave without having to pass me.

I sat down in the rear of the screening room – people stuck gum under the seats in here, too – while Edith finished setting her appearance to rights. An unruly tuft of hair poked out by her left ear, and I couldn't bring myself to tell her.

'Projectionists. They see all, and never breathe a word,' Edith said. 'Looks like my secret is out.'

'It's none of my business.'

'Then why were Max and I skulking around? Two unmarried people.' Edith pressed her fingers to her temples. 'The truth is, Max and I were engaged.'

'You were? When?'

'A few years ago.' Her answer caught me off guard, because until 1938 she had been married. Divining my thoughts, she said, 'Charles and I were still together. In name, anyway. Max said he wanted to marry me, and somehow that was enough. He didn't pressure me for a divorce. By the time Charles and I separated, Max and I had also drifted apart. This picture has thrown us back together.' She sighed. 'My emotions, I fear, are rather jumbled.'

'Mine always are.' We sat in silence a moment. 'There's nothing stopping the two of you from giving it a go now.'

'Yes, there is. I don't love him.' She smiled tightly, still showing no teeth. 'And a lot has changed. Max and I are at different places in our careers. He has history here, but he's barely hanging on. If I'm seen being involved with a man at the studio, it weakens my position. If he's a man on his way down, well . . .' She shrugged helplessly at the cruel indifference of the system.

I'd never heard Edith sound so cold-blooded, so mercenary. Worse, her words struck me as hypocritical after she'd taken me to task for continuing to see Simon. But then I didn't have to face the demands she did; I wasn't the sole woman in charge of an entire department at a major company. And it seemed petty to voice any disapproval when Edith seemed as vulnerable and exposed as she did now.

She cleared her throat. 'Would you mind watching the *Streetlight*

Story rushes anyway? Max is concerned about Brenda's wardrobe. And after learning about Sylvia's agenda, I confess I'm curious about the film.'

'So am I.'

Edith leaned over to the speaker. 'All right, Leo. Would you mind starting from the beginning?'

The lights dimmed. I waited for that giddy anticipatory thrill that ran through me the instant before a movie began, but it didn't come. Maybe I've felt it for the last time, I thought sadly. The price of learning how the sausage is made.

Rushes, the raw footage shot for a picture, were like peering at the mechanism of a film, peppered with glimpses of technicians hastening to their places and actors consulting with people off-camera. The sight of this behind-the-scenes magic produced a faint rush of pleasure. My love affair with the movies hadn't ended after all.

Luddy had filmed the early scene where Jim tries to persuade Arlene to help him talk her husband Eddie into working for him. He'd lit the nightclub set so the shadows around the stage were an almost Stygian black. Fred MacMurray and Brenda Baines were awash in light save for the final moments, when MacMurray stood with his face shrouded in darkness, only his wounded eyes visible, the lighting doing much of the work for him.

Sylvia, I thought, would have loathed the scene, because MacMurray – handsome, charming, everything I thought Gene was – proved so irresistible despite his obvious shadiness he won you over to his side. Luddy had been right; casting the hugely appealing actor as a heavy made an inspired choice.

I never should have let you get away. MacMurray said the line in take after take, modulating his inflection, gently boosting the hunger in each reading. In the last version, he reached out of the shadows to seize Brenda's forearm, and my heart leapt into my throat.

As for Brenda, she made Arlene bright and devoted without becoming cloying. *Plucky*, that was the word for her character, and for the actress herself. I liked her wardrobe, and told Edith so.

Her disembodied voice came out of the darkness. 'Thank you, Lillian.'

TWENTY-SEVEN

P alm Sunday ranked as one of my favorite dates on the liturgical calendar because you were given a prop, which made mass feel like show business. The service commemorated Jesus's entry into Jerusalem on the back of a donkey, the faithful cutting branches from the trees to lay down a path for him. My uncle Danny frowned on my affection for the day. 'Don't become one of those A&P Catholics, pet,' he'd tell me. 'Ashes and palms, only going to church when you get something. You've got to go to mass when you get nothing out of it.' His warnings didn't dim my enthusiasm. I never received an actual palm back in Flushing owing to the climate, just an acceptable facsimile. But in California, you got the McCoy.

This Palm Sunday began with disappointment. My favorite priest had yielded the pulpit to some mucky-muck from the archdiocese. Instead of one of Father Nugent's sprightly sermons complete with limericks and references to the latest movies, we were subjected to undiluted fire and brimstone from Monsignor Catlett about what Our Lord would be facing later in the week. The Monsignor cautioned us to be on guard for the Judases in our own lives, willing to betray us for thirty pieces of silver – or less, sounding like a used car dealer. The homily didn't go over well, judging from how many in the pews fanned themselves with their palm fronds like they were in a bargain-basement DeMille picture. Perhaps Monsignor Catlett should have previewed his effort in Pasadena. Father Nugent had done a whole bit as the donkey the year before, complete with funny voice, that had been gangbusters.

I walked home slowly, the Monsignor's foreboding words ringing in my head, letting passersby take note of my palms. I'd place them behind the crucifix hanging in my bedroom.

Simon's car waited outside Mrs Quigley's, the man himself reading a newspaper behind the wheel. He braced his hand against his left temple, concealing the puckered patch of skin on the side of his face. I lurked in the shadows of my building for a moment, watching him as I gathered my thoughts.

But I hadn't accounted for the car's mirrors. Without turning, Simon said, 'What's that in your hand? Have you come bearing gifts?'

Caught, I approached the car. A fifth of bourbon peeked out from under the sports section. 'It's Palm Sunday.'

'I have no idea what that is.' After I gave him a précis on the holy day, he asked, 'Do I wish you a Happy Palm Sunday?'

'I suppose. I'd hold off on Happy Good Friday, though.'

'I can see that. I didn't hear back from you yesterday. How did things go with your elusive quarry?'

'Very well, thanks entirely to you. I truly don't know what I would have done without you.'

'I'm always ready to help you. Even if doing so means I'm also helping Gene. How'd he take it?'

I brushed the palm fronds against the car's door. 'I haven't told him yet.'

'Why not?'

'I'm not sure how helpful what I found out is. I'm not even sure he wants my help.' I paused. 'Things have been a little fraught the last few weeks.'

'He's crazy if he doesn't want you in his corner. Speaking of that, I know I've been remiss lately. I want to tell you I'm changing my ways.'

'I'm glad to hear that.'

'I don't know that you're hearing it. Or, to be more precise, I don't know that I'm saying it properly.' He gripped the steering wheel as if it would help him concentrate. 'I want you to be with me, Lillian. I want you in my life. Every day.'

'Simon, I—'

'You don't have to answer. It's just when I was driving way to hell and gone to Malibu for you, I realized there's no one else on this earth I'd do that for. I decided that has to count for something, and I had to tell you.'

'I . . . I'm flattered.'

'And unimpressed, by the sound of it.' He smiled ruefully. 'That's understandable. I haven't been at my best. But as I said, I'm changing.'

I leaned into the car and nudged the sports section aside. Sunlight glinted off the bottle, making the bourbon within look warm and inviting. I could have used a slug of it myself.

Simon and I both considered the whiskey. 'I'm not drinking it,' he finally said.

'You hid it. Within arm's reach. In the middle of the day.'

'I was bored. It's a way of passing the time. You don't need to worry about it.'

'And here you said Gene was crazy not to accept my help.'

Simon stared at me as if my words had wounded him. Then he abruptly announced, 'You're right.' He snagged the bottle and launched himself out of the car. With a flourish he unscrewed the cap and poured the amber liquid into the gutter. He then pitched the empty vessel into a garbage can, the ringing clatter it made sullying the moment's effect. 'Unlike him, I have accepted your help.'

It was an audacious gesture. My time in Hollywood had taught me not to put stock in those. 'I appreciate that. You know there are stores where you can buy more.'

'I won't if you're beside me.'

'Don't say it like that. If liquor is a problem for you, you won't have any whether I'm beside you or not.'

'Then I won't have any. *Because* of you. I've learned what's worth protecting, what lengths I'm willing to go to for it. I'll go further than Malibu. But I had to drive all the way there to figure that out.'

He sounded sincere enough for me to want to believe him. I tried to determine if I did.

Simon rushed to fill the resulting silence. 'Can you eat on Palm Sunday, or do you have to fast or something?'

'You really don't know Catholics, do you? We're not a cult. We just don't have fish on Fridays during Lent. And on certain other days. And some people do fast, but that . . . Never mind. Are you asking me to lunch? Because I can have lunch. Just let me bring these palms upstairs.'

I shouted good afternoon to Mrs Quigley and nodded formally at Miss Sarah, in her usual lounging position in the lobby. Upstairs I put the palms on display and asked myself what exactly my feelings were for Simon. Our meetings could be tense, but he was open and honest with me, sharing his insecurities. While invulnerable Gene kept his own confidences and erected barriers between us. Simon's promise to go to great lengths for what was worth protecting whirled around the echoes of Monsignor Catlett's sermon, the words colliding with each other.

Until they detonated. And a horrible suspicion overtook me.

I sprinted to the street. Simon grinned, an offer on his lips. I couldn't allow myself to hear it.

'I'm sorry. Something's come up.'

'While you were inside?'

'It's partly your fault. What you said gave me an idea, not a good one, and now I have to test it.'

Simon nodded, reached for the ignition, started his car. 'Where do you have to test it?'

'Abigail's house, if she's home.'

'Get in. I'll take you there.'

'You don't have to do that.'

He gunned the motor. 'Didn't you hear what I said? I know how far I'll go for you now. Abigail's house is nothing.'

I had Simon drop me a block from Abigail's and told him not to wait. With a sober 'Yes, ma'am,' he drove off. On my brief walk I passed two women in beautiful spring hats carrying palms, and smiled at them.

Abigail did not seem surprised to see me, only embarrassed. She had a scarf wrapped around her hair, and wore a faded gray housedress. 'Sunday's chore day,' she explained. 'It's either clean or grade more homework, and frankly I'd rather scrub. Come in. It won't take a moment to fix some tea.'

I told her such largesse was unnecessary, but Abigail's innate sense of hospitality wouldn't be denied. Within minutes she'd spruced herself up and laid on a lovely afternoon spread of tea and sandwiches. 'It'll be Easter next week,' she said as she poured. 'Do you and Gene have plans?'

'I honestly don't know.' Nor did I have any idea how to broach the delicate subject that had occurred to me, an unholy combination of the Monsignor's early morning admonitions and Simon's protestations.

Who is the Judas in your midst? How far are you willing to go to protect what matters?

'It ended up being a lovely day,' Abigail said. 'What brings you here?'

'A sticky question.'

'I tell my students the best approach is simply to ask.'

'Fine,' I said. 'OK. Fine.'

Abigail smiled over the rim of her teacup, coaxing me. *You can do it.* She was undoubtedly a wonderful teacher. I could have learned a lot from her.

'It's about your husband. Teddy. I'm, I was just wondering. And I hate to ask this. But I have to.' A pause for breath, and to gauge the perspiration under my arms. Abigail had been correct: my only option was to spit it out. 'Again, I was wondering. If Teddy – I mean, you hear stories. Was he . . . on the level?'

I expected her to cry. Not jagged sobs, perhaps, but more stately, low-key tears. Certainly some outburst of emotion. What I did not anticipate was for Abigail to rise, smooth her dress, and quietly state, 'I'll be right back.'

She left before I could respond, darting away like a purposeful bird. A few seconds later, I heard the shifting of weight elsewhere in the house. She was searching for something. *Maybe her late husband's service revolver*, a chattering voice in my head suggested.

I called her name, asked if she needed help.

'I'm fine. Stay there, please.' The words spoken in firm, even tones. Her detention voice. *Now, Lillian, you understand why you had to be kept after school.*

It was another few minutes before she returned, lugging a leather satchel with worn handles. She had the blank, focused expression of someone who had one final rock to split before calling it a day, refusing to break concentration until the task was complete.

Her demeanor made me nervous. I started to talk.

Then she overturned the satchel, and silenced my babbling. A cascade of cash will do that to a person.

Thick bundles of money fell next to the teapot and the plate of sandwiches. One bounced off the table and hit the floor. Each packet of still-crisp bills wrapped with a now-faded label. I knew what would be printed on it before I picked up the fugitive bundle and read the words with my own eyes.

California Republic Bank

I had never seen twenty thousand dollars in cash before, never counted that much money in my life. But I could safely assume that's the amount I was looking at.

I had found the fourth man involved with the robbery. The man 'protecting' Borden Yates. The man who had turned savagely on his trio of partners. The Judas in their midst. And Abigail's. And Gene's.

Teddy Lomax.

I was still staring at the money when Gene spoke from the doorway. 'I guess you figured it out. Somehow I knew you would.'

TWENTY-EIGHT

W e put the kibosh on the tea and switched to bourbon highballs. Abigail cleared the sandwiches from the table. She left the money where it was.

Gene explained he'd already arranged a meeting with Abigail to discuss the DA's investigation. 'I thought there was lots to talk about before,' he said, attempting a wry smile. Then, with a wordless glance, he yielded the floor to Abigail.

'Teddy was a gambler,' she began. 'Everyone treats it as if it were a hobby, a roguish pastime. Teddy always with a tip on the horses. Even that movie script does it. And it was fun, for a while.'

Gene gently weighed in. 'Once he got married, he worried about money. He didn't think he could support a family on his salary.'

'Plenty of other men do,' Abigail said bluntly.

'Teddy wasn't interested in being like plenty of other men. You knew that when you married him.'

'It was partly *why* I married him.' Abigail nailed her wry smile on the first try. 'He sold some things that had been in my family. Heirlooms. Not behind my back. He told me he was doing it. The items from his family were the ones he hocked in secret. I noticed they were missing and didn't say anything.'

'He owed a lot of money,' Gene said. 'All over town.'

I couldn't help myself. 'Did he owe any to Bugsy Siegel?'

'I wouldn't be surprised.' From Gene's manner, I could tell he'd underlined my query.

'Things came to a head around Christmas in 1935,' Abigail said. 'Teddy had to admit we didn't have money to spend on presents. Which was fine. It's not like we had children, although that was the plan. But when he told me we couldn't afford to go visit my sister, I knew how bad it was. Then he started getting these phone calls. Nasty-sounding men calling at all hours, and he'd rush out telling me not to worry. We started fighting. He was drinking more. He struck me several times, which wasn't like Teddy at all. I didn't know what to do. So, I went to Gene.' She maintained her calm as she spoke, recounting the collapse of her marriage as if she were reading test questions to her class.

Gene took over the story. 'I immediately worried he'd turned crooked to cover his debts. I looked into it. Quietly, or so I thought. I put some words in Teddy's ear, hoping to get him to shape up. He did not appreciate my advice. He wasn't himself anymore. He sounded like a – what's the word? – a paranoiac, thinking everyone was against him. That's when Abigail and I began meeting, telling each other all we knew.'

'We were working together to save Teddy,' Abigail said.

I could imagine it easily. The two of them had known each other for decades. Gene had introduced Teddy to Abigail. It was like something out of a movie. Like *Streetlight Story*.

'But that's not how it looked to Teddy when he found out,' Gene said. 'He leapt to a different conclusion, and didn't believe us when we told him otherwise. What we didn't know was he'd already set a plan in motion to get clear of his debts. He just . . . rolled us into it.'

'He was an efficient man, my Teddy.' The last vestiges of pride resonated in Abigail's voice. 'Always killed as many birds with one stone as he could. That's a side of him they didn't get in that screenplay of theirs.' She drained her highball and set about building herself another one. I decided at that moment I liked Abigail very much indeed.

'What was the plan?' I prompted.

Gene waved his hand over the bonanza on the table. 'I assume he put together the crew, gave them their marching orders. Near as I can figure, Hoyer, Bianchi and Yates were to split up while Teddy held the scratch. Bianchi getting gunned down at the scene actually made it easier on Teddy. He met Hoyer at the rendezvous, likely finished him off, then took the cash. For his final trick, he'd get rid of both his remaining problems at once. Borden Yates. And me.'

A chill settled its weight on my shoulders, binding my chest. 'What are you saying?'

'Fentress actually had it right in that script. He just got the guilty party wrong.'

I looked at Abigail. She sipped her drink with an unearthly calm. 'You don't know that,' I said. 'You can't prove it.'

'Of course not. I only know what I know. And Teddy *knew* where Yates was holed up. Think about that. The department could have descended on that place in force. Yates already had a hand in killing one of our own. Easy enough in all that chaos for Teddy to make sure Yates didn't leave the house alive. But Teddy didn't do that. Instead, he suggested we check it out ourselves, on our way to grabbing a beer after work. "Probably nothing," he said. Just me and him. I can only assume he intended to kill me, then make it appear I'd died trying to capture Yates.'

'After which, he'd leave me.' Ice cubes rattled in Abigail's glass. 'Or stay and privately lord what he'd done over me, which is far worse.'

Gene grunted. 'Who knows why Yates got suspicious of Teddy? Maybe he always was. He came charging out of that house aiming at Teddy like I wasn't there. Teddy fell, and I shot Yates without thinking. He died never saying a word.'

With only his illegitimate daughter to avenge him, I thought.

I needed a moment to catch my breath and absorb what I'd heard. 'Then there were four men involved in the robbery. All of them dead. And nobody knowing the truth. Not even you.'

'Not at first,' Gene said. 'The one indisputable fact was the money. It hadn't been recovered. People wondered about that. I was spending time with Abigail, and people wondered about that, too.'

'They can be so cruel, so simple-minded,' Abigail said. 'At the time, Gene and I were convinced we'd failed Teddy, who died in the line of duty. We needed to console each other. We thought we were living with a secret. But Teddy had one more in store.'

I hefted a bundle of cash. Ran my thumb over its edge. The bills made a hugely appealing sound as they riffled past.

'You don't want to know how often I've done that,' Abigail said. 'After a few months, the rumors about us died down. Money, ha ha, was short – schoolteachers make even less than detectives – and I decided to sell a little fishing cabin Teddy owned up near Arrowhead Lake. It's the one thing he refused to part with, but he wasn't around to refuse anymore. I drove up to clean the place, and I found . . . that. Once again, I didn't know what to do. Once again, I called Gene.'

Redoubtable Gene. I'd summoned him in my hour of need once or thrice myself.

'We worked backward from that.' Gene again gestured at the

money. 'Figured what must have happened. This is the only explanation that makes sense.'

'But wait. You told Abigail *not* to report what she found?'

'Returning the cash only would have revived the rumors about us.'

'We could have weathered that storm.' Abigail spoke with a weariness indicating this ground had been trod many times.

'No, we couldn't. I can live with suspicion, rumor. Hell, that story may have even done my reputation some good, queer as that sounds. But once things become definite – once there are facts – you can't change them. This money is a fact. Your finding it is a fact.'

'What's that thing you keep saying? "Better an open question than a firm answer."'

'You know who taught me that?'

'Teddy. Who else would polish up that particular pearl of wisdom?' Abigail looked at me. 'I reluctantly agreed to go along with Gene's idea then. That was, what, September '36? And we've been living with it ever since.'

This was what Gene had been hiding. Not a tortured romance, long-buried passions at last surfacing. He and Abigail had been bound together by hate, by the shared knowledge the most important person in their lives had schemed to destroy them both, killing one while abandoning the other. And they had uncovered this truth only after grieving Teddy as a hero. I couldn't fathom the contortions they'd put themselves through. And I loathed myself for every misgiving I'd had about Gene, every begrudging thought I'd harbored about Abigail.

She looked at me, the relief in her eyes fused with a steely resolve. 'Do you know what I think? I think deep down – the subconscious, isn't that what they call it? – I wanted you to find out. I may even have urged you to keep digging without being aware of it. Only two people can share a secret. Once a third person knows, it's not a secret anymore.'

Abigail's statement plainly made Gene uncomfortable. 'So tell me. What gave the game away?'

'Nothing either of you said or did. Clyde Fentress told me a police officer was the fourth man. I suspected Captain Frady. I didn't think of Teddy until I talked to someone about what's worth protecting, and how far you'd go to do it.'

'I vote we've gone far enough.' Abigail sat back. 'I'm surrendering the money. It's all there. Every last penny.'

Gene exhaled. 'Abigail, no. Nothing's changed.'

'Only the calendar, which means everything's changed. It's been three years. If I say I found the money now, there'd be fewer rumors.'

'Not with this mayor. Not with the DA's investigation hanging over my head. It'll look like I turned in the cash to avoid prosecution.'

'You still have no idea what prompted the DA to reopen the case?' I asked.

'Not a clue. Somebody pushed him, but I don't know who or with what. Until I do, it makes sense to hang on to the money.'

I sided with Abigail, but chose to abstain. A silence settled over the table that even twenty thousand dollars in cash couldn't lift.

Abigail stood up. 'If you'll excuse me, it's time for my usual Sunday afternoon stroll.'

'Would you like company? We could—' Gene started to rise, but Abigail waved him into his seat with an indulgent smile. Silly Gene, unable to take the hint she wanted to give us time alone. As she left the room, I marveled at meek, amiable Abigail Lomax. I'd met many great ladies of the silver screen since moving to Los Angeles, but never had I encountered a better actress.

Another silence followed in Abigail's wake, broken when Gene said, 'You understand why I couldn't talk about this. Why I've been distant these last few days.'

So many emotions roiling, so many responses jockeying in my brain. In the end, I could only nod.

'And now that you know what happened, I hope this means you won't take any more foolish risks on my part.'

'I know exactly how far I'll go. Malibu.'

Gene's quizzical face made me regret the glib comment. *Always making with the jokes, Frost.*

'That's where Clyde Fentress was hiding out.'

'How'd you learn that?'

Dammit. After the frenzy of truth-telling, I had no choice but to make a clean breast of my use of Simon's assistance. Gene's brow puckered at the mention of his name.

'He calls me sometimes. We're friends. When I heard about Fentress, I couldn't think of anyone else who could do the job. I told him I needed his help so I could help you, and he agreed to do it.'

'Good to hear he's a big softy. I'll send him flowers.'

'Stop it. Look at what I've been doing for you. Working against the police and the district attorney's office, stirring up trouble for Edith and Paramount—'

'I didn't ask you to do any of that.' His words were sharp.

'You didn't have to. I wanted to do it.'

Gene nodded, not at me, but in agreement with the argument unfolding in his head. He must have swayed himself, because he reached for my hand. 'And I appreciate it. But you don't have to do any more. Except tell me why you asked about Bugsy Siegel.'

Dammit again. 'His name came up,' I answered weakly.

Gene's fingers tightened around my wrist, his grip like a handcuff. 'Came up how?'

I told him everything. As I spoke, Gene stalked over to the living room window. At one point he made an odd gesture I belatedly realized was a signal to Abigail to take another spin around the block.

When I finished, Gene said nothing for a long while, his gaze fixed on the street. Then he strode back to stand over me. 'Don't go near Siegel again. Understand?'

'I didn't. He came to me.'

'Don't split hairs either, Lillian. It's not the time. Siegel, that phony Countess, Virginia Hill, George goddamn Raft, give that whole crowd a wide berth. Do you understand me?'

He uttered each word of the question as a separate sentence. His voice radiated a cold fury I'd never heard before, his anger barely harnessed, a tranquilized beast beginning to stir. I nodded until I could compel myself to speak. 'Yes. Of course. I understand.'

I got to my feet and began clearing away our glasses, mainly to have something to do. Abigail returned and said a few quiet words to Gene, then joined me at the kitchen sink. 'We should decide what to do with the money.'

Drying my hands, I said, 'I'll leave that to you two. It's your decision. I'm going home.'

Gene stood in the doorway, trying to keep his aggression in check. 'Let me drive you.'

'No thanks. I could use the time to think.'

I kissed Gene goodbye, then wrapped my arms around Abigail at the front door. I couldn't shake the sensation I was truly seeing her for the first time. 'I have to say, lady, you're as tough as nails.'

'I could have told you that. I come from good stock.' She gave me one final squeeze.

I stepped into the sunshine. At the corner drug store, I telephoned

Addison's house. I hated to take advantage of him on a Sunday, but needs must when the devil – or, in this case, Rogers – drives. When Addison came on the line, I explained I also needed his chauffeur to come in a different car. Not the Cadillac.

Not anything Gene would recognize.

TWENTY-NINE

M oments for taking inventory of one's choices in life come upon us without warning. I didn't expect to engage in a rigorous self-appraisal on a Palm Sunday afternoon while cowering in a weedy alley opposite the home of a police widow, spying on the man I'd been romantically involved with for over a year. Yet the question rang in my mind: *What am I doing here?*

An answer came too readily. Gene's anger was new, his ease with it more frightening than its intensity. I feared he planned to do something rash, and prayed Rogers would arrive before he left.

The celestial switchboard was apparently jammed, because Gene was striding toward his car. He'd get behind the wheel and I'd lose him. Some detective I was. Torchy Blane never lost anybody. I knew, because I'd seen all the movies.

I edged backward into the alley as Gene's sedan rolled past. It rounded the corner only to swing in at the curb outside the drug store from which I'd telephoned Addison. Gene marched into the store and toward that very phone booth. I trotted up the street to a better vantage point, where I could see Gene end one call and begin another. When he hung up, he planted himself at the counter and was served a cup of coffee, which he proceeded to ignore in favor of staring at the telephone and willing it to ring.

It still hadn't when a red Lincoln slowed down in front of me. Rogers at least had the sense not to lean on the horn. I ran to the Lincoln, clambered inside, and instructed Rogers to circle until he found a spot where we could watch Gene's car.

'You had to bring this big red job?' I asked plaintively. 'Why not a float from the Tournament of Roses Parade?'

Rogers ran a hand through his hair, because as was always the case when he drove me he didn't bother with his chauffeur's cap.

'My orders weren't "Be inconspicuous." They were "Don't take the Cadillac."'

We pulled up a block from the drug store. 'When that car leaves, follow it,' I said. 'I suppose you'd like to know why.'

'I'm not paid to wonder why.'

'You're not even the least bit curious?'

Rogers eyed me in the rear-view mirror. 'Am I gonna get shot?'

'No!'

'Then I don't care.' With that, he took out his newspaper.

Twenty minutes later, Gene elbowed past the counterman to snatch up the pay telephone's receiver. By the time he bolted to his car, Rogers already had the Lincoln's engine purring. Gene miraculously didn't notice us in his wake, so focused was he on traveling at a Bonneville Salt Flats pace. Rogers, I realized, relished the opportunity to drive at such a clip.

When Gene's sedan shuddered to a stop opposite Howard Greer's boutique on Sunset Boulevard, I automatically assumed *he's buying me a trousseau*. But Gene never glanced at the shuttered salon. Instead he targeted his gaze at the closer building, the Hollywood Athletic Club. The nine-story tower atop the structure served as a bachelor hotel, home to actors, studio executives, and assorted well-heeled heels. The clubhouse on the lower floors, open to both genders, had been erected as a temple to physical fitness. Gene quick-stepped to the entrance. After asking Rogers to wait, I took up the pursuit anew. As I entered yet another Italianate building, I wondered if all of Rome was decorated in a style reminiscent of Pasadena. One of these days I'd have to get over there and find out.

I slipped into the club's lobby. No Gene, no attendant – *had Gene commandeered him?* – which meant for the nonce I had the run of the place. Signs pointed toward the men's and women's locker rooms. The nose-stinging scent of chlorine led the way to the swimming pool. I inched open a heavy door labeled *Gymnasium*.

The room beyond was large enough to accommodate multiple parties of people engaged in vigorous physical activity. Not that any of them needed the exercise; every individual in the gymnasium was already in peak condition, probably from climbing down off their pedestals in Athens. One familiar figure on the opposite side of the gym joked with a second man while throwing punches at a phantom opponent. His white T-shirt and black shorts appeared to have been painstakingly tailored.

Ben Siegel.

I shrank from the doorway, my worst fear realized. Gene had tracked down the gangster and intended to confront him – because of what I'd said. Briefly I toyed with warning Siegel, but decided that would only make the situation worse. I'd end up talking to Siegel again, and Gene might discover I'd followed him.

I noticed a spectator's balcony ringing the floor one flight up and sought the stairs. Whatever happened next, I would watch from on high.

The scents of perspiration and assorted liniments gathered at the upper elevation; a clothespin for my nose would have been welcome. Peering down, I could see a considerable gap separated Siegel and his workout partner from the others on the gymnasium floor, as if a magnetic field surrounded them. Siegel continued shadowboxing, his sidekick mimicking his every move slavishly. This second man had jet-black hair and the lean and hungry look I'd come to associate with studio executives.

Siegel threw a rapid-fire combination and spoke without sounding remotely winded. 'Better loosen up. Handball's a physical game. Tennis for savages, they call it. You a savage, Albert? I don't want any crying from you like last time.'

Albert laughed a little too long and too loud; definitely a studio man. 'Have no fear, Ben. I've been practicing for our rematch. Brought in an expert for private lessons.'

'The game's not about form. It's about instinct. Tell me something. This new picture, this Bible epic—'

'*The Story of Samson.*'

Siegel paused his routine to glare at Albert for daring to interrupt him. Albert busied himself with one of several nearby medicine balls, thumping it for ripeness. 'Yeah. You think Lodestar can make them as good as DeMille?'

'Absolutely. We brought over a director from Germany who did a picture there about—'

'Gonna need extras. These kind of pictures gotta have a big cast.'

'We're sparing no expense.'

'And sex. You've gotta put sex in it. Everybody sins, then they repent. Like DeMille, in *Sign of the Cross*, he put Claudette Colbert naked in that tub full of goat's milk or whatever it was. You've gotta get everybody riled up before the temple walls come tumbling down.

You make money on salvation, but you make even more with sin. That's why I love the picture business. Only racket ever figured out how to get a cut from both sides.'

Another histrionic laugh from Albert. I was wondering if Gene had gone into another building when the door beneath me banged open. Gene stalked in and saw Siegel. I tried to melt into the wall, hoping neither would look up.

'There you are,' Gene said, his voice pitched to bounce off the gym's walls. 'Guy told me you were upstairs playing handball. Should have just followed my nose. You reek like a New Orleans cathouse, friend.'

Siegel continued throwing punches, slow and easy. 'First, it's a Paris cathouse. Second, we're not friends, friend.'

'Let's you and I change that right now, Bugsy.'

The gym emptied so fast you'd think a fire alarm had been pulled. Albert stood stock-still. Maybe he'd read in the gangster guidebook that playing dead might save him. Siegel straightened up. Somehow, he looked more menacing out of his fighter's stance. 'What did you call me?'

'You heard me right. Otherwise you wouldn't be asking me to repeat myself.' With a smile, Gene held his detective's shield aloft. 'You see this?'

'Yeah? So you're a cop.'

His badge still in the air, Gene knocked on the gym door. A fearful attendant opened it. Gene tossed the badge to him, then turned back to Siegel. 'Now you see I don't have it. Because I'm not talking to you as a cop.'

'It don't wash off that easy, you know.' Siegel smirked.

'It'll have to do. I don't have a badge. And neither one of us has a gun.'

'Maybe my friend Albert here's packing heat.' Siegel pointed at Albert, who at that moment longed to vanish from the face of the earth. 'Christ, Albert, relax. You better sweat that much when we play handball. Fear not, copper. Albert's a nancy-boy studio man. Lodestar Pictures' finest.'

Gene walked slowly toward Siegel. When he stood paces away, he started talking – and Siegel immediately spoke over him. 'Are you a member of the club? Because if you're not here in an official capacity—'

'It won't take long to say my piece.' There was a faint tremor deep beneath the solid ground of Gene's voice; Siegel's gambit had thrown him.

'Then say it.'

'You accosted someone recently.'

'Who in particular?'

'Call this a blanket statement that applies to all of them.' Gene grinned, regaining some of his swagger. 'Keep to yourself. Don't pester those people again. Or you and I, Bugsy, will have business that can't be settled on a handball court.'

'Where, then? Boxing ring? Target range? Pistols at dawn, like in the pictures?' Siegel bent to retrieve one of the medicine balls, hefted it. 'I leave people alone when they leave me alone, Detective Morrow.'

As he pronounced Gene's name, he shoved the medicine ball with a swift flick of his hands. Gene, anticipating the move, dropped his own hands and caught it. I couldn't be certain from my position, but I thought he winced as he did it. Gene dropped the ball to the floor, where it landed with a meaty thud that echoed around the room.

'You're talking about the Frost woman,' Siegel said.

'You're the one who bothered her,' Gene replied.

'I asked her a question. It was not answered to my satisfaction. If I choose to ask her another one—'

'It goes through me. Consider me her representative.'

'You dance as well as her?'

'Try me, Bugsy. I'll lead. Until then, stay away from her.' He closed the distance between them and stared directly into Siegel's blue eyes.

Siegel stared right back. 'I feel threatened. I thought this city had reformed, turned over a new leaf. You seeing this, Albert?'

Albert, dismayed he hadn't been forgotten, cleared his throat. 'Now fellas, there's a bar upstairs—'

'I told you, I don't drink.' From Siegel's businesslike tone, you'd never guess he and Gene stood nose to nose. 'I don't appreciate being harassed in the middle of my exercises by a peace officer who's not a club member. Here I am trying to preserve my health and discuss business with a friend—'

'You mean pictures? I keep hearing you want to get into those.' Gene also maintained an even keel as he spoke. 'Yeah, I could see you playing a punk who dies one reel in.'

Siegel bristled, the comment irking him more than the use of his nickname. 'Not me. I stay alive right up to the weak ending Joe Breen makes 'em slap on the picture. No, my friend Albert Ryan here – you buy that Ryan nonsense? I mean, look at the schnozzola on that kid! – runs a profitable enterprise at Lodestar. I offer counsel to help keep it profitable. The landscape out there, it's tough to read, labor-wise. Unions all agitating for a piece, now you got the threat of a new one just for extras.'

Atmosphere players, I silently corrected from the heavens.

'Can't make a movie with a cast of thousands without those thousands,' Siegel continued amiably. 'I keep my ear to the ground, talk to both sides. At times of great unrest, people need friends. You and I, though, we're not gonna be friends.'

'No, we're not. Stay away from Lillian Frost, Bugsy. Anything happens to her, I'm holding you responsible.'

'What I hear, you're in no position to make threats. I get the sense the skids are under you and you just need a push.'

'Funny, I hear the same thing. Lucky I don't need a badge or any back-up to handle you. My best to your wife.' Gene turned on his heel and walked out. The door slammed behind him so loudly I feared the building would come crashing down around us.

A long, pregnant moment of silence, then Albert said with a strained laugh: 'What the hell was that?'

'Goddamned bum,' Siegel spat. 'Guy's as bent as they come. Money squirrelled away from years ago. He better not have thrown me off my form. I came here to tan your hide today.'

'You'll still thrash me, Ben, and no mistake.' Albert chuckled to chivvy the conversation in a different direction. 'Let me say, we all appreciate you using your influence behind the scenes.'

'The extras don't want their own union. They may not have lines to read, but they've still gotta eat. They'll listen to reason.' Siegel continued staring at the door, in case Gene made a surprise return. 'And I know you need the help. It's not just your Bible picture. You're working on the one about Andrew Jackson, right?'

'Just got a great script on it.' Albert preened a little. 'Ben Hecht knocked it out of the park.'

'Yeah, Hecht's good. And that horse-racing picture, too. Needed a good hundred extras on it last week, I hear.'

Albert frowned. 'It couldn't have been that many.'

'Yeah, it was. Check your records. Ninety-two atmosphere

players, twenty in fancy dress. Hell of a thing if they didn't show up. I wanted to ask you, Al. Things are tight.'

'You didn't actually ask me anything there, Ben.' A pause, then another of Albert's stilted laughs, then an even longer pause. 'What – what are you asking?'

'For a loan.'

'A loan. So you'll pay it back?'

Siegel finally turned toward him. 'You think I'm unfamiliar with what a loan is? I've got a rudimentary understanding of finance.'

'Sure you do, sure you – I just – how much did you want?'

'Five thousand oughta cover it. Rates here at the club have been going up.'

Albert's laugh was low on vinegar now, coming purely out of reflex. 'Have they? I haven't been keeping track.'

From the stairwell behind me came the soft tread of footfalls. When the attendant who had caught Gene's badge spotted me, his eyes popped out of his head. 'Miss? What are you doing here?'

Albert craned his neck to peer up at me. I scampered into the stairwell before Siegel could do likewise. 'I got turned around,' I said hurriedly. 'Trying to find the ladies' locker room.'

'Downstairs on your left. Are you a member of the club, miss?'

'Yes. I forgot my card. Let me go to my car.'

Ninety-two atmosphere players, twenty in fancy dress. There it was.

I ran through the lobby without looking back to see if Siegel had emerged from the gymnasium. I didn't stop running until I'd gotten into the Lincoln and barked at Rogers to drive. I didn't want him to stop, not even for a red light, until I had safely reached Mrs Quigley's, and had Edith on the phone, and could tell her I had not only solved the mystery of the California Republic bank robbery, but I also knew why District Attorney Fitts had reopened the investigation in the first place.

Not bad for a Sunday, and a Palm Sunday at that.

THIRTY

Florabel Muir couldn't join us until Monday afternoon, but when she did, she instantly transformed Edith's office into an extension of a newsroom. To complete the illusion we only needed a few copy boys, the thrum of the presses, and a fugitive murderer concealed in a rolltop desk.

The veteran reporter was on the telephone, her eyes fixed on the pearl stud earring she'd removed and placed in the center of Edith's desk. 'How are you, Mike?' she said down the wire. 'Now don't take this the wrong way, but I'm going to need to talk to the big fellow himself, or someone closer to Buron than you are. Nothing personal, you understand . . . Well, aren't you a charmer? I'm happy to tell you why. I'm about to solve two of the District Attorney's headaches at once and I want to make sure he knows where to address the great big favor he's going to owe me.'

I refilled Florabel's teacup as she continued haggling. The lateness of our appointment had allowed me to spend the morning putting the finishing touches on Addison's annual charity Easter egg hunt, which included tracking down the largest available *huevos* in Southern California so every child could easily find one. Sample hen fruit were being trucked in from Pacoima at that very moment. I also helped him unlearn all he'd been taught by Joan Crawford and Bette Davis during their acting lessons, replacing it with the only counsel I could think of: 'Don't look at the camera. Let the camera look at you.'

'The best advice you could have given him,' Edith reassured me, patting my hand. 'The nightclub scene will be shot on Wednesday morning. Will Mr Rice be ready?'

'No, but he'll be there. How was the rest of your weekend?'

'Not as busy as yours. I was here, finalizing Paulette Goddard's wardrobe for *The Cat and the Canary*. As if anyone will notice her clothes with Bob Hope's antics.'

Florabel, meanwhile, was growing steadily angrier. I could tell from the fact she took off her other earring, pinning the receiver against her shoulder as she did so. Clearly she wanted a sense of balance as she vented her spleen. 'Put him on, Mike. This is bigger than you, trust me . . . OK, fine. Got a pen and paper handy? Because you'll want to have these particulars down when you convey the news up the ladder.'

She winked at Edith and me, adjusted the pearl studs on the desktop, and let fly. 'I will be reporting that a young woman named Sylvia Ward – you've read about her, she was recently murdered – presented herself to the District Attorney and pressured him to reopen the 1936 California Republic bank robbery case with an eye toward investigating Los Angeles police detective Gene Morrow. Our good DA Mr Fitts is not in the habit of letting anyone who wanders in off the street dictate his office's operation, but the Ward woman offered him a deal too good to resist. "Investigate Morrow's role in the robbery and I'll deliver Benny Siegel on a silver platter with an apple in his mouth."' She paused while poor Mike asked a flurry of questions. 'I'm right, aren't I? I can tell by the panic in your voice. Care for additional salient details? Ambitious Benny is strong-arming the studios by claiming to have pull in the upcoming Screen Actors Guild's vote for a separate extras' union. The Ward woman knew about it because she was feeding him the inside dope he needed straight from Central Casting . . . Sure, I'll hold, Mike. You talk to whoever needs talking to. We don't need to start the presses rolling yet.'

She cupped her hand over the mouthpiece. 'It was easy enough to confirm Sylvia's role with my lower-level contacts in the DA's office, not that I'm about to tell Mike here that.'

'It was clever of you, piecing it all together,' Edith said to me.

'When I heard Siegel's encyclopedic knowledge of what pictures were in the works, especially which ones would require extras' – to hell with calling them atmosphere players; extras was shorter – 'I realized all that information went from the studios to Central Casting. Where Sylvia could pass it along to him.'

'That also explains Mr Fentress being taken aback by news of Miss Ward's relationship with Mr Siegel,' Edith said. 'She kept her plans completely separate. She wanted the movie to damn Detective Morrow's reputation, but once she got involved with Mr Siegel she understood she was in possession of information she could barter with the district attorney's office.'

'The pieces were all there,' I said. 'I didn't know how they were connected.'

'It's like Mr Ramsey said the other day in the screening room. Sometimes you have to look at the story from a new angle. I have to confess I'm still doing that.'

I didn't have time to ask Edith to expand on what she meant, or to dwell on the significance of Max Ramsey now being referred to in more formal terms. Florabel was rapping on Edith's desk, commanding our attention.

'Thank you, Mike. I applaud your sound judgment. Go ahead and put me through . . . And a good afternoon to you, Linus. I suppose Buron himself is indisposed? . . . You'll always suffice, Linus, and I assume as you're on the horn it means I'm on the money about this Sylvia Ward business. Considering how sadly she ended up, I'm also assuming your efforts to snare Benny Siegel have gone into a ditch . . . No, I can't help you land him, but I'll tell you what I *can* do. I will not only *not* write a story about how you botched this Siegel affair – he's shaking studio executives by their ankles personally, by the way, and keeping whatever change falls out of their pockets – I will wrap up the California Republic bank job for you once and for all. One beaming bundle, that's right.' She paused, a cobra's smile on her lips. 'I will return every last cent of the haul and exonerate an innocent LAPD officer, Detective Gene Morrow, in the process. It's a heartwarming tale if it's played right, and seeing as I'm writing it, it will be. Of course, another officer will have to take the fall in Morrow's place. But don't worry, this one's actually guilty. And even better, he's already dead, so he won't kick when you condemn him. The truth without fear of reprisal, which is the best truth there is . . . Oh, you bet I'll hold, Linus. I've nowhere else to be.'

This part of the arrangement set my guilt, custom-made for my every need by the Catholic Church, jangling. It required fudging the timeline of the money's discovery, a falsehood Florabel was unknowingly perpetuating. And it meant deceiving Gene about my role in his redemption. I had asked him if he and Abigail would be willing to surrender the cash if Florabel could clear his name and end the DA's investigation. I never let on I'd followed him to the Hollywood Athletic Club and eaves-dropped on his chivalrous confrontation with Siegel, thus tumbling to Siegel's racket. Gene's initial response to my pitch had been mixed, but an adamant Abigail insisted they go along with it.

I didn't mind if Florabel got the credit, as long as she sold the package to the DA.

She was doing so with tremendous persuasion. 'Take this deal, Linus,' she urged into the phone. 'Buron knows something is better than nothing. A photo of the recovered cash will look terrific in everyone's scrapbooks. You know where to reach me.'

She hung up the receiver looking like a lioness that had feasted on a herd of hapless gazelles. 'He'll play ball. Fitts is a fool, but he's no idiot.'

'There's still one issue,' Edith said slowly. 'We know what happened in 1936, but not in the past two weeks. Whoever killed Mr Conlin and Miss Ward did so for reasons that are, at best, peripheral to the bank robbery.'

'Were they murdered because of the movie?' I asked. 'That sounds crazy.'

'We have to at least consider the possibility.'

'You can. I'm not.' Florabel replaced her earrings. 'I don't know about pictures, but in real life, when there's a killer in your cast of characters, odds are he's the one who did it. Don't let the slick suits and fancy colognes fool you. Benny Siegel is a killer.'

Her certainty came close to clinching it for me. 'Why would he do it?'

'He found out Sylvia was talking to the DA.'

'And Mr Conlin?' Edith asked.

'If I had to guess, I'd say Nap's the one who told Benny what she was up to. Selling information was Nap's stock-in-trade. He went to Benny with what he thought was a hot item and got killed for it.'

It made sense to me. Edith, though, still seemed to be mulling it over, finding a fresh angle for the story. 'I can't believe all this mayhem is swirling around a Paramount picture. I'm indebted to you, Miss Muir, for clearing it up.'

'And I have to thank you ladies. Putting the California Republic caper to bed is a juicy story all on its own. I'll tell you, Edith, I could have used your expertise back in my early days. I was covering a murder in Salt Lake City, one involving the paper. A hefty fellow in the circulation department had married out of his league. His wife was some looker. He'd been driven so mad with jealousy he finally up and shot her. He's immediately stricken with remorse and uses the last bullet in his gun to join her in the Great Beyond. Only he louses up the job. Circulation department was a mess, too, now that I think about it. All he can find to finish himself off is a safety razor, but as I said he was a bit porcine in nature. He's got to hack at his wrists to get any traction.'

'My word,' Edith said, looking as green as I felt.

'The editor orders me to grab photos of the wife, so he can splash them all over the front page. Nothing sells papers like a beautiful dead woman. Only there's a cop outside the house. I slip around back, spy an open window, and swipe every picture of the missus I can find. Back out the window I go. I'm on the streetcar before I realize it.'

'Realize what?' I asked.

'The circulation man had good circulation in one respect. He'd staggered all over the house leaking blood trying to kill himself. Great pools of it everywhere.'

'And you'd walked through them,' Edith said. 'Leaving a trail of blood to the streetcar.'

'Forget the trail of blood. I was wearing my favorite shoes. Beautiful champagne kid slippers. Never wore anything so comfortable. Like walking in your bare feet. And I'd ruined them, thanks to this fat man's blood. I still think about those shoes. That's where your expertise comes in, Edith. For future reference, is there any way to get bloodstains out of kidskin?'

'You'd have to work quickly, before the blood dries. It was probably too late by the time you reached the streetcar.' Edith thought for a moment. 'You can never go wrong with soap and water. Lots of suds, of course. You also might try hydrogen peroxide.'

'There's a thought. It interacts with the blood.'

'And a mixture of cream of tartar and lemon juice can conceal a multitude of sins. But you've got to work fast and scrub hard. Even then, it may not be enough.'

'That's true of so much in life,' Florabel said.

'Isn't it?' Edith agreed.

San Bernardino Lamplighter   April 5, 1939

KATHERINE DAMBACH'S
SLIVERS OF THE SILVER SCREEN

Europe can't commandeer the front pages forever, as all Los Angeles is abuzz with the solution to a bank robbery and the discovery of $20,000 still stamped 'California Republic'. Turns out Detective Gene Morrow, the man on the Bulova end of the clock-cleaning dispensed by an ex-convict scenarist last week, was not the mastermind of the 1936 heist as some suspected. District Attorney Buron Fitts has pinned the blame on Morrow's late partner Edward 'Teddy' Lomax. But I'm willing to wager the proprietors of Paramount are turning purple from pique. Their *Streetlight Story*, now filming, points the finger at the wrong man . . . Get ready to giddyap! Astor Pictures will reissue William S. Hart's vintage 1925 western *Tumbleweeds* in May, with sound effects and a musical score. More than whinnies will fill the theater. For the first time audiences will hear the cowboy legend himself as Hart appears in an eight-minute forward filmed at his Horseshoe Ranch.

THIRTY-ONE

'Shall we dance? . . . Care to dance? . . . Shall *we* dance? . . . Shall we *dance*?' Addison half-whispered a half-dozen variations on a line no one had written for him and which he would never say. Occasionally he'd punctuate his dialogue with a mock rumba while seated in the rear of his Cadillac. He'd uttered scarcely a word to me all morning, and now we were within view of the Bronson Gate.

The big day having arrived, I would permit nothing to spoil it, least of all Kay's churlish column. She'd penned it out of spite,

I knew, because Florabel had scooped her on the bank robbery story. But Gene had his good name back. That was all that mattered.

He and I hadn't spoken aside from a fleeting Tuesday night telephone call, when he told me he'd been stood a round or five by fellow detectives who'd cold-shouldered him for years. I was thrilled for him. I was excited for Addison.

Why, then, did I remain in a blue funk?

Edith greeted us outside *Streetlight Story*'s soundstage, or to be precise, she greeted Addison. The tower of hatboxes I was transporting, along with several sets of evening wear, obscured me from view.

'I brought along some alternate looks,' Addison told Edith. 'I thought some variety might be helpful.'

'It always is. Though I doubt the hats are necessary. You're meant to have checked yours on the way into the club.'

'Yes, but I should be prepared in the event I'm needed to retrieve it. I also brought a tie I'm rather fond of. One that should make a statement on camera.' I couldn't see the object of his boast at the moment, but I was familiar with it, a bright green bowtie with a matching neon pocket square. I could hear Edith appraising it guardedly.

'That does indeed make a striking impression. My fear, Mr Rice, is that it might make *too* much of one, given you'll be in the background. This is more of a . . . star's tie.' She made a deliberative sound. 'Would you object terribly if I proposed to Robert Preston that he wear it in the scene later this afternoon?'

'A *star*'s tie, you say. Far be it from me to throw off the production's footing. Please, do as you wish.' Addison chuckled, inordinately pleased.

'Last chance, Lillian,' Edith said puckishly. 'Are you positive you don't want to join the cast?'

'Dead certain. You've heard about my screen test.'

'Indeed I have. Someone was describing it earlier today.'

'No, they weren't. Were they?' When I got no response, I peered around the spire of chapeaus and saw Edith leading Addison into the soundstage. I trotted after them.

She handed Addison and his wardrobe off to an assistant director. When he was gone, Edith returned his iridescent bowtie to me. 'I'm afraid it clashes with Mr Preston's ensemble.'

'It clashes with everything. But thank you.'

*   *   *

The Club Madrid existed in bits and pieces on the soundstage. Most of a bandstand, segments of dance floor, a scattering of tables. Only on camera would its world exist in full, a feat of everyday sorcery that still gave me chills. A clutch of dress extras was already assembled near the coffee, taking pains not to stain their Monday-through-Saturday best; I saw one woman in their number slip a buttered roll into her purse for later. Overhead, the lighting crew called to each other in their secret language. Luddy huddled with his cinematographer, handling the interruptions from script girls and assistants with good humor. He ran a disciplined, orderly set. I'd toiled in offices with more *Sturm und Drang*.

The only disturbance came courtesy of Clyde Fentress, pacing the edge of the soundstage and gesturing emphatically at George Dolan, who puffed insouciantly on a cigarette. Whatever had his partner agitated, Dolan found amusing. Edith extended a cheery 'Good morning!' to them both.

'What the hell's good about it?' Fentress rasped. 'The picture's doomed now.'

'For the last time, Clyde, it is *not* doomed.'

'The papers are making monkeys out of us. Our story is ass-backward. Turns out our good guy is actually the heavy.'

'Have to admit,' Dolan said to the tip of his cigarette, 'it's a neat twist.'

'Forgive me, Mr Fentress,' Edith ventured, 'but the picture was never going to be credited as based on a true story. These late developments don't affect it at all.'

Fentress ignored Edith, pointing over her at me. 'Bet you had something to do with this.'

I shrugged. 'Don't blame me. This is the work of the Fourth Estate.'

'Name the other three,' Dolan said.

I blinked three times, once for each estate, then Edith spoke up. 'The clergy, the nobility, and the common people.' Dolan stepped back in mock astonishment. 'I did study French,' she added.

A commotion by the coffee urn commanded our attention. It registered first as an explosion of color, a sudden profusion of vivid carmine red. Only after a moment did it resolve into the astonishing form of Virginia Hill, dressed in a strapless crepe gown. The dress's skirt hugged her form, sweeping up to gather in folds on her left hip. She sashayed past the extras, drinking in their stares, throwing her head back when she heard a wolf whistle from the catwalks above.

Edith and I moved toward her. Virginia stood arms akimbo, hands sheathed in long gloves, waiting to receive us. She bussed our cheeks, enveloping us in a cloud of perfume almost dense enough to be visible on camera. 'How are we today, ladies?'

'We are impressed,' Edith said. 'Another Howard original?'

'It's Greer or I go bare. And apparently this isn't that kind of picture, so I had no choice for my screen debut.'

The air pressure on the soundstage seemed to shift. I felt dizzy. 'You're going to be in *Streetlight Story*?'

'Only as an extra, but still! Ain't it exciting? You know, I thought about getting into pictures. Took a few acting classes when I came out here. Almost signed a contract with Universal, but it wasn't meant to be. Say, do they ever turn those goddamned lights off? I don't want to sweat through this dress.'

As I struggled to make sense of this development, I spied George Dolan dawdling nearby, listening in on our conversation with intent. Realizing he'd been caught, he raised his hands in surrender. As he drifted past, he whispered in my ear. 'Old newshound instincts die hard. Fill me in later.'

Edith assessed Virginia's attire anew. 'That is a stunning gown. I hope it's consistent with what everyone else will be wearing.'

'If it's not, make everyone else consistent with me. Class up the joint.'

Equilibrium regained, I asked, 'How did this happen?'

'Blame Benny. He set it up. He finally got his chance to be in a picture and he took it.'

Edith lowered her glasses. 'Mr Siegel will also be a background player?'

'Whatever Benny wants. Is this coffee for anybody?'

While Virginia helped herself to java – two different male extras raced to fix her a cup – Edith and I hurried over to Luddy. 'Edith! Surely your work here is done.'

'Yes, but I had a question. It's come to my—'

'Did you tell Bugsy Siegel he could be an extra?' I blurted.

'Has he arrived?' The director scanned the soundstage and seemed disappointed not to spot his latest discovery. 'Yes, I did. And it's my understanding he does not care for that name.'

'How did this come about?' Edith asked.

'Through serendipity, as so many inspirations do. I was dining with friends this weekend when the maître d' told me Mr Siegel wished to pay his respects. As it happens, he's an admirer of my work.'

I doubted Ben Siegel made a habit of watching German melodramas, but let the comment pass to spare Luddy's delicate Teutonic feelings.

'He asked if the recent reports were true, that the film is based on a real crime. As we chatted, I mentioned today's scene and invited him to participate.'

Edith nodded, trying to find a politic way of expressing her concern.

'I see you question the wisdom of my decision,' Luddy said with lordly benevolence. 'Rest assured, Mr Siegel poses no threat to anyone on set. But what he brings is incalculable.'

'And what exactly is that?' I couldn't keep the disdain from my voice. Truth be told, I didn't even try.

The gaze Luddy fixed me with should have chilled me to the bone, and on another day it might have. 'An authentic element of danger. A menace that cannot be faked. If the film is to have the requisite air of decadence, it must have the right characters. Not actors. Characters. I regularly did this in Berlin and it proved most successful. I once—'

He cocked an eyebrow. Edith and I turned to see Ben Siegel stride onto the soundstage, glad-handing grips and extras like it was Old Home Week. He looked pointedly in my direction but didn't approach. Maybe Gene's warning had been taken.

'There's certainly a change in the atmosphere,' Edith said. 'Will you introduce me?'

'Are you serious?'

'You heard Luddy. He can't very well harm anyone here. Of course, if you'd rather not—'

'Think nothing of it. Me and Benny are old pals.'

Luddy's casting technique might have had merit. An electric charge coursed through the soundstage as word spread about our special guest star. A crowd of rubberneckers was starting to build around Siegel, who'd fallen into conversation with Virginia Hill. She laughed with outsized force at something he'd said, slamming her hip into his side in mock-chastisement. Siegel seemed mesmerized by her, and slightly daunted by the spotlights. Edith and I cut a swath through the onlookers, even Clyde Fentress among them. I glanced around for George Dolan and saw the back of his jacket as he left the soundstage, probably to grab his camera and notepad.

Siegel girded himself as we approached. 'We meet again. Will our next dance be on camera?'

'I don't work on camera.'

'That's a shame. What if I insist?'

'Then you're out of luck. This is my friend Edith Head, who runs Paramount's costume department.'

Siegel bowed at the waist. 'A pleasure.'

'Mr Siegel. May I say I am a fan of your wardrobe, both in general and at present.'

'This old thing?' Siegel raised his arms to showcase a tuxedo different from the one he'd worn to the Countess's party. 'Just something I had lying around.'

'Oh, can it, Ben,' Virginia said with a giggle. 'How many tailors died in the night so you could have that ready for this morning?'

Siegel glowered at her until he understood she was joking, then smiled toothily.

'You and Miss Hill will be dancing together, then,' Edith said. 'Your attire complements each other's perfectly. I expect letters requesting a film about that well-dressed couple in the background.'

'We wouldn't want to disappoint our fans,' Virginia cooed.

A cocky young assistant director who clearly had no inkling who Siegel was waded into the center of the conversation. 'Break it up, people. We've got a picture to shoot. Background players, with me. Let's go.'

As the throng dispersed, I realized I'd somehow lost Edith. Had she left the set? Not sure of my proper place without her, I fled to the shadows, feeling as I did when I visited my uncle Danny at Paramount's studio in Astoria: like I was backstage at the magic show.

Half a dozen couples arranged themselves on the dance floor, their job to make the Club Madrid seem like the hottest ticket in town. Addison was the oldest figure in the fold by far, his partner a sloe-eyed blonde a few grades younger than me. I idly scripted their story in my head, Addison the out-of-town businessman destined to be rooked in the badger game by his seemingly naïve escort. She spoke cheerfully to Addison, who blinked sweat out of his eyes.

God help him, I thought, *the cameras aren't even rolling yet*. Siegel and Virginia, I noticed, had been positioned closest to the lens and seemed wholly nonchalant.

A musical recording started. The band pantomimed their playing as the dancers were steered through their paces. Addison made a few wrong turns and stepped on his partner's feet at least twice. Siegel, swinging Virginia past them, suggested they switch partners. Addison laughed good-humoredly, but the young girl in his arms looked as though she desired nothing more.

Addison had steadied the buffs by the second run-through, while Siegel and Virginia were dancing close enough to warrant their own Breen Office chaperone. An assistant director briefly had words with them, which led to a baleful gaze from Siegel. After that, they resumed tripping the light fantastic with enough space between them for, say, an envelope full of greenbacks.

At some point Fred MacMurray and Brenda Baines had arrived on set, MacMurray in a tuxedo nowhere near the equal of Ben Siegel's, while Brenda looked like a fugitive angel in the gown Edith had designed, its pink beads sparkling under the lights. Thinking about my recent exchanges with Abigail, I felt ashamed at how I'd treated her onscreen surrogate. I waved to her, a comically eager smile on my face. Brenda saw me, blanched, and averted her eyes. I supposed I had that coming.

The orchestra playback stopped. I darted onto the set with a handkerchief for Addison, carefully blotting his perspiration without damaging his make-up. 'This is my co-star Eileen,' he said of the woman in his arms. 'I'll be sending her to my podiatrist when this is all over.' He leaned in closer. 'How bad do I look?'

'You're a natural,' I said. 'Effortless.' Maybe I could act, after all.

Ten rehearsals of the number later, Luddy still wasn't happy.

'No, I want any couple, *this* couple' – he pointed at the most coordinated twosome on the floor – 'to guide the camera toward the shadows here.'

An assistant director nodded. 'Sure, Luddy. It just means starting the dancers off differently.'

'But it mustn't feel choreographed! We are not at MGM, this is not a musical.'

'Again, sure thing, Luddy. But it takes a moment to choreograph something that doesn't feel choreographed.'

They dithered as the dancers decorously wilted under the lights and the background players at the nightclub's tables amused themselves. I considered how hard they were working and how little they were being paid for their efforts, and decided they deserved their own union.

A shadow fell onto the soundstage floor next to me. I knew before I turned around it belonged to Ben Siegel. He didn't look at me, targeting his ire at the unsuspecting Luddy.

'Ridiculous,' he spat. 'Amount of time this takes.'

'They want to get it right,' I said as lightly as I could, each word landing like a Fatty Arbuckle pratfall in my ears.

'Right. What's right? Just let us dance around while the guy says his lines. I could be playing golf now.'

I forced myself to make eye contact with him. 'You can leave if you want.'

'I'm a member at Hillcrest. I can play whenever I like. I see your boyfriend made the papers. Twenty grand in the wind for three years. That's the real crime.' He nodded dismissively at MacMurray, consulting script pages alongside Brenda. 'This guy's the lead? He does comedies, plays the clarinet.'

'Saxophone,' I corrected. 'He's good in the part.'

'You'd know.'

The assistant director called for everyone to return to their places. 'Back to the salt mines,' Siegel said. 'Be sure to congratulate your friend for me on his newly sparkling record.'

I was still recovering from my exchange with Siegel when Edith returned. 'Sorry, my dear. Issues on several films this morning. Did I miss anything?'

'Just Luddy driving everyone mad.'

As if to prove the point, a new ruckus erupted as Fred MacMurray waved the director over. Luddy put a patronizing hand on MacMurray's arm and nodded at Brenda, the message plain: *get on with it*. MacMurray and Brenda read aloud from their pages, looks of confusion on their faces. Clyde Fentress loitered nearby, practically aboil with rage. MacMurray shook his head.

'I don't like the look of this,' Edith said, bolting toward the uproar.

'All I'm saying is the lines don't make sense.' Even when upset, MacMurray's voice maintained its pleasant timbre.

'I agree with Fred,' Brenda added. 'I can't make head or tail of this dialogue.'

'That's because it's only a partial rewrite.' Luddy's gaze was still on the shadows across the set. 'When the rest of the pages are in, all will be clear. But we must shoot this today.'

Fentress had had enough. He barreled his way into Luddy's line of sight, the expression of malice on his face so intense I expected a prison screw to blow his whistle. 'What the hell is this shit?'

'I wanted a scene rewritten,' Luddy replied blandly. 'It was rewritten.'

'Not by me, it wasn't.'

'You're hardly the only writer on this production. Or this lot. Writers, Mr Fentress, are not a scarcity.'

'I've had it with your high-hatting, *Ludwig*. We'll see about this.' Fentress pushed his way out of the crowd, extras and crew wobbling in his wake like pins in a bowling lane.

'If we could hear the lines again, please,' Luddy said, brooking no argument.

MacMurray gave Brenda a reassuring glance, then raised his script pages and dove in. 'Listen, baby, I can talk to this fella, make him back off.'

Brenda's lingering uncertainty added some texture to her line reading. 'He won't listen to you. Or to reason. He won't stop until he ruins me.'

'Don't talk crazy. Why would he do that? What does he know?'

'I . . . I can't tell you. It's something I've been carrying for so long it's become part of me. I can't—' Brenda gasped for air so suddenly I started.

MacMurray inched closer to her. Fierce longing shaded his words. 'I don't care what you've done. Whatever it is, it's behind us. I'll protect you.'

'Will you?'

'I promise. Have I ever lied to you?'

'Then you have to come with me. You have to talk to him.'

'Didn't I say I would?'

'And if words aren't enough?'

MacMurray faltered. 'What do you mean?'

'I mean what if I'm right and he won't listen to either of us? How far are you willing to go for me?'

Something in MacMurray's attitude made me think he'd seized Brenda by the shoulders, when in actuality he hadn't moved. 'All the way, baby. I'll go all the way down the line for you.'

He then wheeled toward his director again. 'Honestly, Luddy, I'm at sea here. Where does this scene come in the picture? Why are we shooting it in the nightclub now?'

'And who is Arlene talking about?' Brenda asked.

All good questions, I thought.

'Once more, please,' Luddy said in response.

They had just finished their encore and asked a new round of questions when Fentress elbowed his way through, dragging George Dolan behind him. 'I want you to hear these new lines,' Fentress said.

'Lines I didn't write,' Dolan added hotly.

Luddy signaled his actors. MacMurray folded his arms across his chest. 'How about we wait until the whole scene is written?' Brenda, I noticed, copied his defiant stance.

The director pursed his lips, preferring to issue edicts than make requests. Still, on his best behavior, he asked, 'If you wouldn't mind.'

MacMurray, shaking his head in bafflement, started in again. He and Brenda were halfway through their incomplete scene when George Dolan, his face ashen, began making his way toward the elephant doors.

He stopped when he noticed several newcomers standing there. Two uniformed police officers. A bemused Captain Byron Frady on one side of them. And Gene, amazingly, on the other. He had his arms folded MacMurray-style, his eyes on Dolan.

The scribe pivoted deftly only to come to a dead stop when he spotted Ben Siegel, his arm around Virginia's waist, waiting to go back to work. Dolan's mouth opened a few times, no words coming out, then he walked toward Frady. Edith nudged me, and I followed.

A sickly grin smeared across his face, Dolan said, 'Detectives. You have to arrest me.'

'Gladly.' Frady looked not at the contrite figure before him but at Edith. 'Suppose you tell us what for.'

'I killed Sylvia Ward. Together we killed that man Conlin.' He turned to Gene, throwing himself on his mercy. 'Please, you have to arrest me now. Before – before *he* finds out.' From the slight inclination of his head, it was obvious Dolan meant Ben Siegel.

'We always try to oblige.' Gene thumped him on the shoulder as if offering to buy him a beer. 'Let's talk outside.'

Luddy strutted over to Edith. 'Have I paid my debt to you and

Max? May we draw the curtain on this charade and return to the actual making of this picture?'

'Yes, of course, Luddy. Thank you for indulging me.'

Frady tucked a toothpick into his mouth solely so he could snap it in two with his teeth. Gene looked from Edith to me and back again. 'I suppose we might as well have you ladies come along for this portion of the show too,' he said, but his heart wasn't in it.

THIRTY-TWO

W e made a merry caravan, Edith paired with Frady, Gene keeping a downcast Dolan close at hand, me bringing up the rear. A few steps from the soundstage we came to an old wooden building that, judging from the punching bags dangling from the rafters, served as the studio gym. We stood on the structure's broad porch, out of the sunlight and the scrum of traffic. We could have been in Old California, waiting for a stagecoach.

At first Gene and Frady scrutinized each other as much as they did Dolan, unsure of the protocol in this lessening of hostilities between them. Frady told Dolan they'd be happy to hear whatever he had to say. Dolan glanced around in the vain hope of finding a rewrite man, then accepted his fate.

'I told you Sylvia and I were seeing each other.' An admission facilitated by Edith and me, not that anyone acknowledged it. 'She came to me on a Friday, I guess it was, and said she was being threatened by this fellow Nap Conlin. He had information he was blackmailing her with. I volunteered to help – and did it with better dialogue than what you just heard on the set.' He laughed. No one else joined in. 'The spirit of it was close, though. Where did those lines come from?'

'We'll get to that,' Gene said. 'You were going to help how?'

'By providing moral support.'

Gene and Frady shared a look, working together now. Dolan threw up his hands. 'All right. And muscle, I suppose you'd say. Sylvia was going to tell Conlin to blow, and she wanted someone there to protect her when she did it.'

'Meaning she did it,' Frady said.

'Yes. Saturday night, she and I went to his hotel. Squalid place. We didn't go in together. Sylvia kept saying I was only there in case things went wrong. She and Conlin went into his room. I waited in the hallway outside, as we'd planned.' His lips twitched into a grimace. 'I didn't think until later Sylvia only suggested that so I wouldn't hear what Conlin knew about her.'

'I can guess what happened next,' Frady said. 'Things went wrong.'

'She opened the door to his room and . . .' Dolan drew in a breath, the memory restored to full, lurid life before his eyes. 'I could see Conlin on the floor. Out cold, bleeding from the head. Sylvia said he'd attacked her and she'd struck him with an ashtray. It had split in two. She still had half of it in her hand. I moved to call the police, but Sylvia said it was too late, Conlin was dying and neither of us could afford to be found there. "Better to put him out of his misery."'

'This was a request she made,' Gene said. 'To you.'

'Yes. One I carried out before I could think about it. I still don't know why. I grabbed this statue from the hallway. Took it and the ashtray when we left.' Dolan wiped his eye with a knuckle. 'No one noticed a thing. Again, that kind of place. Self-defense by proxy, I thought. That's what it was.'

'You still didn't know what Conlin was blackmailing Sylvia over,' Frady said.

'No.'

'Did you ask her?'

'No. And believe me, I'm aware how ridiculous that sounds. You kill a man, you ought to know the reason. I assumed she would tell me. But all she said was we probably shouldn't see each other for a while. I saw the logic, but . . . my mind went to some dark places after that. A habit that comes with the trade.'

'What places?' Gene asked. 'How dark?'

'I started to suspect this hadn't been an impulsive act, and I'd been deliberately enlisted as accomplice.'

We listened to the distant clamor of crews on various soundstages. A breeze stirred a few scraps of paper on the gym's porch. I saw Edith gesturing to someone and turned to see Billy Wilder strolling toward Stage 13.

'I felt a strange sort of relief when you showed up a few days later.' Dolan flapped a tired hand at Frady. 'Followed by complete mystification when you asked *Clyde* about Conlin. I hadn't the foggiest they knew each other. I was flabbergasted. That meant *Streetlight Story* had to be at the heart of this somehow, so I said to hell with it and sought out Sylvia.'

'And?' Frady prompted.

'It took some doing to see her. She avoided me at first. Then she consented to meet.'

This time Frady merely cleared his throat.

'She told me everything. Probably felt she had to, in order to keep me close. That's my guess, anyway.'

'What exactly did she tell you?' Gene asked.

'That she'd been cooperating with the District Attorney's office in a bid to bring down Bugsy Siegel. Conlin found out, and was ready to spill the beans.'

'She also told you she was sleeping with Siegel.' Frady opened his tweed jacket, thrusting his stomach forward, letting it bully Dolan. 'Be honest now. That's what made you see red.'

'I wasn't pleased about that. But that wasn't it. I'd never been in her apartment before. She didn't have any books. I asked her, what kind of writer doesn't have books? She laughed at me. Said she wasn't a writer at all.' Dolan shook his head, aghast at his own credulity. 'She'd lied about everything. She'd used me from the outset, and now we were bound together.'

'Until you unbound yourself,' Gene said.

Dolan nodded, the way one does when the secretary pops her head in and asks if anyone wants coffee. For the first time, I could see George Dolan as a murderer. I stepped away from him, the board beneath me creaking.

'May I ask one question?' Edith said quietly. 'What did you throw on the floor of Miss Ward's apartment to conceal the remnants of your broken reading glasses?'

Dolan peered at her in mild surprise. It was Frady who regarded Edith as if she were a witch.

'A drinking glass,' Dolan said. 'My eyeglasses flew out of my pocket when I . . .' His hands unconsciously gripped a phantom length of cord, and I braced myself against one of the beams supporting the porch's roof. 'The lenses shattered. I couldn't hope to pick up every last sliver, so I threw a glass on top of them instead, hoping to confuse things. Did my new pair give me away?'

'More the fact that horn-rims don't complement your new

wardrobe. But when you require an immediate replacement, you purchase whatever is available in your prescription.'

'Sylvia did want me to get new glasses.' Dolan directed the comment at me. I wrapped both arms around the wooden beam. He then cast a nervous eye toward Stage 13. 'I don't want to tell you fellows how to do your job, but Siegel's on this lot to kill me. You have to get me away from here. Away from him.'

'That can be arranged,' Frady said. 'Gene, why don't you put Mr Dolan in the care of our officers?'

'I still want to know where that dialogue came from,' the writer said to Edith. 'You were behind that, yes? Can't miss with Shakespeare. "The play's the thing/wherein I'll catch the conscience of the king."'

Edith frowned. 'I confess that provenance didn't occur to me.'

'Might as well steal from the best. Working with Clyde taught me that. Everybody steals.' Dolan then wandered docilely off with Gene as if about to begin a studio tour.

Frady aimed his intimidating bulk at Edith. 'Suppose you tell me, Miss Head, how you knew that business about the eyeglasses without setting foot in the girl's apartment?'

She gazed placidly up at him. 'Lillian described the scene vividly, including the shards of glass. It wasn't until I noticed Mr Dolan's inappropriate new eyewear that I made the connection. As I'm sure your department already has. A cursory examination would reveal two different kinds of glass.'

From the way Frady worried his watch chain, I knew the glass had gone uninspected. 'Naturally,' he huffed. 'Did your interest in the shirt buttons we found in Conlin's room spark any similar insights?'

'Minor ones, to be sure. You said the buttons were like mother-of-pearl – abalone would be a good guess – and had been scattered on the floor as a result of a struggle. Meaning Mr Conlin had put on a fair quality shirt, which he took pains to fasten. From that we can deduce his guest was someone he aimed to impress, perhaps a woman. In this case, both. Miss Ward, lest we forget, was employed at Central Casting. Depending on the outcome of their conversation, she could still be a boon to his career. The serving of tea at that hour also strongly implied a female visitor, as I'm sure you've considered.'

Frady took out his frustration on his pocket watch, which he twirled furiously on its chain. 'Anything else?'

'Given the circumstances of the crime, it seemed odd Mr Conlin's killer would exit the room to seek a weapon. That fact alone raised the possibility of a confederate, which you've doubtless incorporated into your inquiry.'

His watch now a golden blur, Frady barked, 'And you didn't see fit to share these speculations with us?'

'Please, Captain Frady. I wouldn't presume to squander your time with guesswork.'

'Until this afternoon.'

'Circumstances demanded an exception, as I explained when I telephoned.'

'You called Morrow first, I noticed.'

'Detective Morrow and I have been acquainted for some time. And I felt it only right he be present, given his connection to *Streetlight Story*.'

Frady grunted. 'I won't begrudge him that. In fact, why don't I spell him so he can follow up with you ladies himself?' Tucking the watch into his pocket, he hotfooted away at a pace indicating he'd be happy never to set foot on Paramount soil again. I turned to Edith, now studying the structure behind us.

'This barn was the original Paramount building, you know. It used to be at the corner of Selma and Vine. Mr DeMille shot *The Squaw Man* there. The barn was moved here in 1926. So much history in these timbers. Shall we return to the soundstage?'

I held my tongue a good three steps before exploding. 'What happened back there? How did—'

We rounded the corner to Stage 13. Billy Wilder slouched against the building, arms folded, trilby tilted to shade his eyes. 'The operation was a success?'

'Indeed it was, Billy, thanks to you.'

Wilder nudged his hat back. 'I was not happy with my dialogue.'

'Don't be so hard on yourself. It was composed on the spur of the moment.'

'I tell myself that's when I'm at my best. It hurts to learn I'm not. Still, without context—'

'Wait a minute.' To Wilder I said, 'You wrote the dialogue that was just read on the soundstage?'

'At my behest,' Edith said.

'I can never resist a commission,' Wilder added.

'I was unsatisfied with Miss Muir's solution,' Edith explained. 'Yes, Mr Siegel was the most likely culprit, but I had doubts. The person with the most to fear from Mr Conlin, I reasoned, was Miss Ward, assuming Mr Conlin had learned of the rather dangerous game she was playing. As he sold information, she would want to silence him.'

'That's why he was on the lot the day I met him,' I said. 'He wanted to tell Fentress what Sylvia was up to.'

'Very likely. But while there were at least two viable suspects in Mr Conlin's murder, I couldn't think of anyone who would want to eliminate Miss Ward other than Mr Siegel. Then I saw Mr Siegel on our soundstage. More importantly, I saw Mr Dolan see him – and flee at once. Why would his journalistic instincts desert him at such a propitious hour, with an infamous gangster in his midst, unless he had reason to fear Mr Siegel?'

'Such as the fact he'd killed the woman Siegel was sleeping with,' I breathed.

'Not to mention relying on her for crucial information in his efforts to exploit the unrest involving the potential extras' union. I was reminded of Mr Ramsey's line about looking at the story from a new angle. The narrative made sense if Mr Dolan killed Miss Ward, and he would only have done that if he were at least impli-cated in Mr Conlin's murder. The trouble is—'

'You had no way of proving it,' I finished.

Edith nodded. 'It was a gamble, but I thought if Mr Dolan believed someone knew his secret – someone like Mr Fentress, who could have conceivably learned the truth – he might panic. I asked Billy to provide a script for the occasion.'

'Is it my turn? May I speak now?' Wilder smiled. 'I have no idea, of course, what either of you ladies is talking about. Edith knocked on my door and proposed my writing some dialogue. You told me what you wanted to say, and I said it. With a little more pizzazz, I hope.'

'You did so beautifully,' Edith reassured him.

'I heard a few of my lines when I snuck onto the stage. Serviceable, at best. But now my scene is over, so I will return to my office and my real script, where I can actually follow the story.' He glanced back at Stage 13. 'I hope Luddy knows what he's doing. He seems to be getting carried away with the shadows. I don't know the world is ready for such a film. Although MacMurray was surprisingly good playing a heel. A nice idea, casting him against type. He should do it in a better picture.' Wilder tipped his trilby at us and sauntered off.

THIRTY-THREE

Life on *Streetlight Story*'s set had stampeded along without us, our absence scarcely noted. Lives may have unraveled and mysteries been solved, but there was still a picture to be made. Addison, in his usual fashion, had become fast friends with his dance partner Eileen, the two of them laughing it up under the lights. He exchanged words with Siegel and Virginia. I resisted the urge to warn him away from them.

Brenda Baines had retreated to the relative privacy of a corner of the soundstage. She stood primly, careful to keep stray dust motes off her dress as she silently mouthed dialogue. I walked over to her, hoping not to intrude.

'Hi, Lillian,' she said a bit less brightly than on the other occasions we'd met, and who could blame her? 'Are you here with your boss? Someone pointed him out to me.'

'Yes. I'd be happy to introduce you. He loves meeting people in pictures. Especially when they're destined for big things. You handled that new dialogue very well.'

'Considering I couldn't understand it. It's like it came from some other picture entirely. I wonder when we're going to get the rest of that scene.'

'I heard it might be a while. You look lovely.'

'That's all Edith and the gang in the make-up department.'

'No. Clothes and cosmetics are finishing touches. You're the foundation.'

Brenda cocked her head, waiting to see if I was razzing her. 'Thank you so much.'

'I like your character. I think she's more complicated than she lets on.'

'Me too! That's how I've been playing her. Or trying to, anyway. Is it coming across?'

'Definitely. Now dish about Fred MacMurray.'

She chattered away excitedly as we watched the subject of our conversation consult with Luddy. He paused to speak with Addison, and Virginia interrupted to extend a hand.

'That woman reeks of danger,' Brenda said.

'You're not the first person to point that out.'

'Really? Someone else recognized the perfume?'

'Perfume?'

'Danger. It's by Ciro. I only know it because my beau gave me a bottle for Christmas.' Brenda wrinkled her nose. 'Smells like she filled a bathtub with it.'

'I'm only a little familiar with it myself,' I said slowly. 'Let me check on Addison before the cameras roll. I want to make sure he adds you to the guest list for his next party.'

Much as I hated seeing Addison deep in conversation with Ben Siegel – from the way they compared clothes, they were hashing out haberdasheries – the distraction meant I had Virginia to myself.

She waddled after me to a secluded spot. 'What goes on around here, sweetie? We're hearing all kinds of scuttlebutt. Something about one of the writers?'

'George Dolan. He was arrested. For killing Sylvia and helping her kill a man named Nap Conlin.'

Virginia clutched her throat. 'You're kidding!'

'If only I were.'

I hesitated, glancing around for Edith. She was huddled with a wardrobe girl. I couldn't wait for her. When crossing thin ice, the only approach is to move fast and hope it doesn't give way beneath you.

'Sylvia went to a lot of trouble to hide her relationship with Bugsy,' I began.

'Honey, I told you, he hates to be called that.'

'To hell with him.' I let the comment breathe a moment. It felt good to say it. 'The reason she kept it quiet is she was giving him up to the district attorney.'

'Wait. *That's* what she was doing?'

I barreled ahead, ignoring her interruption. 'Clyde Fentress had no idea she knew Siegel. Neither did George Dolan. The only person who knew about her and Bugsy was you, because you were – how did you put it? – members of the same club.'

'It's no small sorority, believe me. And it's the only one I'm ever likely to belong to.' She chuckled. Her perfume smelled divine –

spicy and dark, rich with roses – even though she'd doused herself with it. 'What's your point, Lillian?'

'I'm trying to figure out why Sylvia changed her mind and told Dolan about Bugsy.'

'And you think I'd know?'

'Yes, I do. I think Sylvia needed advice. Someone to turn to. Who better than another member of the sorority? A woman with the talent to live at night.'

'You mean me?' Virginia pressed a gloved palm to her chest. 'I wish she had sought me out. I'd have steered her right. I'm like a lawyer of the heart – and the pocketbook. Love and money are the only reasons I ever get into or out of bed, and that ain't hay or criminal.'

'Sylvia had been found out,' I said. 'And she *knew* she'd been found out. Nap Conlin learned she was talking to the DA, and he was making noise about telling Bugsy. She confided in you. But your advice wasn't on the level, was it?'

Virginia's expression had been flayed of all emotion. Her eyes appraised me indifferently now; I could no longer help her with either love or money, so I meant nothing to her. 'Why would you say a hurtful thing like that, darling?'

'You want Bugsy for yourself. When Sylvia told you she was working with the DA, you knew one of two things would happen. Either she gets Bugsy arrested, or Bugsy learns what she's up to and kills her. But suppose you told her to get rid of Nap Conlin instead. That would eliminate the immediate threat, while keeping Bugsy's hands clean. True, Sylvia's still talking to the DA, but you're on the inside now. Her trusted friend. Manipulating her. When her accomplice got squirrelly about what they'd done, she came to you again. And you suggested she tell Dolan everything. Another monkey wrench in Sylvia's plan under the guise of helpful advice. You probably never thought Dolan would kill her. You figured he'd put the fear of God in her and get her to stop cooperating with the DA.'

'I like this story. Beats the one in this lousy picture.' Virginia stepped closer, her fragrance overwhelming. 'But a story's all it is. There's no proof.'

'Only there is. Sylvia was relentless. Methodical. She was so careful she persuaded Dolan to use Bugsy's regimen of powders and lotions, so she'd never carry the scent of one married man she was sleeping with to the other. She certainly wouldn't wear perfume herself. There was none in her purse or her apartment. But I smelled some the night I found her body. I thought it was from a broken bottle on the floor, but I now know that's not the case.'

Virginia's eyes hardened, glittering like the diamonds around her neck.

'I used to work at Tremayne's Department Store. I learned a fascinating term there. *Sillage.* It means the extent a perfume lingers in the air when it's worn. Danger, by Ciro – what you're wearing now – has a strong *sillage*. I could still smell it when I arrived at Sylvia's apartment.'

'My signature fragrance,' Virginia said. 'Although I may change mine to Chanel No. 5. You should have one, too. It's no good for a girl to go through life smelling like the inside of a church.'

'You were there that night. Goading Sylvia into meeting with George Dolan and telling him everything. You're as responsible for her death and Nap Conlin's as if you'd pulled the trigger yourself.'

'Nobody pulled any triggers, sweetheart. Someone broke Nap Conlin's crown and yanked a cord around poor Sylvia's neck. I read all about it in the papers.' She leaned into my face, the perfume a bludgeon now. 'And I thought you meant legal proof. You know, evidence. There's no law against being a shoulder to cry on. And for what it's worth, I figured Dolan for the kind of fella who'd fold under pressure. Once Sylvia told me she'd gotten him to finish Nap off for her, I knew a push is all it would take. And Benny would be free and clear, without a drop of blood on his hands. Because here's the thing, Little Miss Choirgirl. Ben Siegel's gonna run this town one day. And I'm gonna be by his side when it happens. We're soulmates. Destined to be together. Our union written in the stars. All's I have to do is bide my time and clear the field.'

'That's monstrous. You can't—'

'OK, places, everybody!' The assistant director bellowed into a megaphone. 'We're taking the scene from the top.'

'Looks like I'm needed. Been nice knowing you, Lillian.' Virginia strode past me in queenly fashion, the blazing lights distilling her into a shapely silhouette. The aroma of her perfume wouldn't fade for some time.

Addison and Eileen donned their best poker faces, but merriment still sparkled in their eyes. I could see it from where I stood, well in back of the cameras, far from anyplace I could cause problems for the production. I wanted Addison's acting debut to go as smoothly as possible.

As Luddy made last-minute modifications, I noticed Gene working his way toward me. I tried to figure out how to summarize my conversation with Virginia, if it was even worth repeating. She was correct; she hadn't done anything wrong aside from bringing about the deaths of two people. And cursing me with the knowledge of same.

Gene stood alongside me, his eyes on the stir of activity on the set. Unhappiness radiated from me. I waited for Gene to sense it, to turn and ask what was the matter, to provide some measure of solace.

Instead he stared placidly ahead. 'You just had to keep helping me.'

All thoughts of Virginia fled my mind. 'What?'

'Even when I told you not to.'

'I – well, yes. I had to. I found out something that would put an end to all this, and I went to Florabel—'

'I told you I was dealing with the situation.'

'But I got rid of the situation. Now you don't have to deal with it at all. Nobody does.'

Gene shook his head. 'That's not the point.'

'Then please tell me the point. I don't understand. What you were going through wasn't fair. But what you were asking Abigail to do wasn't fair either, not to her. Pretending her husband was a saint when she knew the truth. She wanted it over with and you in the clear. That's what happened. I thought you'd be pleased.'

'I am pleased.'

'You could have fooled me.'

'Always a glib line. It's the Lillian Frost way.'

A follow-up wisecrack suggested itself, but tears sprang to my eyes first.

'I'd have solved this problem myself,' Gene said levelly. 'It might have taken longer, but I'd have gotten here. All under my own power.'

'Is that why you're upset? Because I helped you?'

'If that's how you want to see it. It'd be nice to have the lead role in my own life, that's all I'm saying.' He put on his hat, an extra tug on the brim drawing it closer to his eyes. 'Frady's expecting me.'

'I – OK. We'll talk later, won't we?'

But he'd already walked away.

'Action.' Luddy uttered the word with unexpected softness, like a benediction. The dancers moved around the floor, MacMurray and Brenda looking on from what I took to be the club's kitchen entrance. Addison had worked out a piece of business where he got to play the roué, Eileen sliding his hand up to the middle of her back. Ben Siegel and Virginia Hill danced a bit more stiffly, Bugsy shouldering his way close to the camera when it passed.

I thought of Addison watching himself on the screen at his house, and again my eyes moistened. What was happening to me today? Every nerve laid bare, vulnerable to be plucked at random.

'Cut!' This command Luddy barked. 'Very nice. Back to your starting positions, if you would, for one more.'

A figure strode out of the shadows. When he stepped into the soundstage's lights, Barney Groff, the studio's head of security, still carried darkness with him, a penumbra of gloom. He spoke to Luddy in harsh syllables, accompanied by emphatic hand movements. Luddy reared back and mounted an argument, but that only intensified Groff's conviction. The remarks became more clipped, the gestures more blunt. Groff spun to the assistant director and issued an order. The assistant turned to Luddy, abject in his helplessness.

I quickstepped to Edith. 'What's happening?'

'Nothing good,' Edith said under her breath.

Groff pointed a finger at the assistant, the motion serving as a decree. Luddy lowered his eyes to the soundstage floor. The assistant drew in his breath.

'Thank you, everyone,' he roared blandly. 'That's a wrap for today.'

After a moment of confusion, several extras moved toward the doors. A grumpy Siegel glared at Groff, who gave as good as he got. Virginia took Siegel's arm and pulled him away. Grips began weaving through the set, breaking it down. Luddy tried speaking to Groff again, but the studio man started for the elephant doors, now being cranked open, letting sunlight in to shatter the spell cast by the cameras.

Edith, braver than anyone else on the lot, planted herself in Groff's path. 'Mr Groff. Is there a problem?'

'There's always a problem. That's my job. Perpetual problem solver.' He absently smoothed his patent leather hair. 'I find one of our writers being hauled off the lot, charged with homicide. I come down here to find out what in blue blazes is going on and what do I see?' He raised his voice so his words would reverberate through the building. 'Bugsy goddamned Siegel waltzing past the camera! In a Paramount picture!' Another fearsome look at Luddy, too cowed to return it. 'Does that Kraut think we're running a flea circus? This is a major corporation, for Christ's sake. Anyway, it's over. We're shutting this picture down.'

'For the day,' Edith asked, 'or for—'

'For good. Paramount doesn't need the aggravation. And MacMurray's got better things to do. *Streetlight Story* never sees the light of day.' Groff's ferocious gaze fell upon me. 'I should've known you'd be here.' He brushed past and vanished into the sunlight.

'Poor Luddy,' Edith said. 'Poor everyone.' She placed an arm around my shoulders, and I was so relieved to be considered part of the multitude I almost started crying again.

Addison bounded over, exhausted and enthusiastic. 'The fun's over already?'

You don't know the half of it, I thought but didn't say.

Los Angeles Register   April 10, 1939

LORNA WHITCOMB'S
EYES ON HOLLYWOOD

That frosty air emanating from the Warner's lot isn't due to the filming of an Arctic epic, just the chill between Bette Davis and Miriam Hopkins. Seems the ladies are dueling for the best camera angles on the set of *The Old Maid* . . . The scuttling of *Streetlight Story* left some on the green and others in the rough. Fred MacMurray puts down the policeman's badge and picks up Madeleine Carroll in *Are Husbands Necessary?* We know how Fred's female fans would answer that question. Promising young actress Brenda Baines lands a role in Paramount's latest Jack Benny vehicle – a western of all things! On the minus side of the equation, we hear director Aaron 'Luddy' Ludwig is casting about for offers with no bites yet . . . It's not often we're able to report the Count and Countess di Frasso are in the same state, never mind the same stateroom, but that's what's in the works. The titled couple are heading to Italy to sell the Count's Roman palace to Mr Mussolini. Here's hoping memories of that 'hell ship' cruise don't keep Dottie awake those long nights at sea.

THIRTY-FOUR

Afternoon light didn't do much for Oblath's Café, still the top choice for anyone looking to play hooky from Paramount for a few martinis. It seemed like my last visit had been a year ago, not a little over two weeks. Perhaps because I was a different person then.

But some things remained eternal. Jerry the messenger had again claimed a table, his seductive spiel aimed this time at a redhead. 'Talent, especially talent like yours, is like a diamond,' he was saying.

'It needs the proper setting to shine. Which is where I come in.' The redhead, to her credit, looked skeptical. At least Jerry's timing was in his favor. He'd whisked the redhead into the café mere moments after the blonde who'd been his previous quarry had exited on the arm of an actual studio executive. Two weeks and the blonde already outranked poor Jerry, well on her way to becoming the next Brenda Baines. Still, Jerry was in there pitching. Points for persistence.

The aroma of frying meat had just compelled me to flag down a waitress when Edith hustled in to the restaurant. 'I'm not going to have much,' she said as she sat down. 'Cottage cheese with fresh fruit.'

'That sounds very healthy.' I handed my menu to the waitress. 'One hamburger sandwich. With onions.'

'That doesn't sound very healthy,' Edith said with her closed-mouth smile.

'I deserve it. I lost enough weight on Sunday chasing after children at Addison's Easter egg hunt.'

'How is Addison?'

'In the pink. He took the bad news about *Streetlight Story* in his stride. He thinks he's not cut out for acting. Although he has a standing offer from La Crawford to appear as an extra in her next picture.'

Edith sat back and appraised me across the table. 'If you don't mind my saying so, Lillian, you seem a touch down at the mouth.'

'Probably because I am. Looking at the Bronson Gate reminded me of Sylvia. She set this elaborate plan in motion to bring the true story of her father's death to light, and she never knew the guilty parties had already been punished. It's sad.'

'That it is.'

'Yet somehow it would have been even sadder if *Streetlight Story* had come out, with a false version of events. What's happening with Max Ramsey?'

'I fear the collapse of *Streetlight Story* reflects poorly on him as far as studio management is concerned. He'll be leaving Paramount. Steps are being taken to make it look like a mutual parting of the ways after Mr Ramsey's years of service here. He's putting a brave face on it, telling me he's looking forward to exploring opportunities as an independent producer.' She adjusted the silverware before her. 'Perhaps it's better for us personally as well. With all the demands running the department is making on my time, I'm content to be on my own for a while. And Bill Ihnen's always there should I desire an evening out.'

'Have you ever desired an evening out?'

'Once in a great while the mood comes over me. Let's talk about you. What's happening in your life?'

'I'm having lunch with Brenda next week before she starts on the Benny picture. And there's some news. Abigail accepted a teaching job in Oregon, where her sister lives. She'll move up there over the summer, begin work in the fall.'

'A change of scenery will do that poor girl a world of good.' She deliberately stirred cream into her coffee. 'And Detective Morrow?'

'Detective Morrow is currently on a fishing trip, all by his lonesome. It's kicking off a few weeks' deserved vacation. Which he will also be spending largely by his lonesome, if the tea leaves I've read are any indication.'

'I doubt that. Mark my words, a few days of solitude and he'll come around.'

Not sure if I shared this opinion, I said nothing.

'Have you seen your friend Mr Fischer?'

'Yes. I thanked Simon for his help and told him we'd get together for coffee on occasion. But that's all.'

'Then for the time being, we shall be alone together,' Edith declared.

I smiled. If a solo life was good enough for Edith . . .

We clinked coffee cups in solidarity. Edith then summoned our waitress. 'Nix on the fruit salad, my dear. I'll have a hamburger as well. Double onions.'

AUTHOR'S NOTE

We wanted *Script for Scandal* to have, as Max Ramsey would say, the stink of real life. A few words on liberties taken and sources used. Any errors are our own.

There were two 'jailbird screenwriters' in 1930s Hollywood. Ernest Booth returned to a life of crime. He was apprehended in the parking lot of Musso & Frank in March 1947 for his role in several bank robberies, and died serving his sentence in San Quentin. Robert Tasker married into society during his Hollywood heyday, then later wed the granddaughter of Costa Rica's former president. He was writing movies in Mexico when he was found dead in December 1944; the circumstances surrounding his apparent suicide, naturally, remain suspicious. We learned of this fascinating footnote in film history through an article in *Noir City*, the magazine of the Film Noir Foundation, by Philippe Garnier, who kindly elaborated on the subject for us. His article was excerpted from his 1996 book *Honni soit qui Malibu: quelques écrivains à Hollywood*, which also includes an invaluable section on the role bookstores, especially Stanley Rose's, played in the Los Angeles writing community. We're thrilled Philippe's singular book will at last receive an English translation, to be called *Scoundrels & Spitballers: Writers and Hollywood in the 1930s* (Black Pool Productions).

We had long been intrigued by Hollywood's glamorous gangster Bugsy – sorry, *Benjamin* Siegel, particularly by the oft-cited fact that he controlled the powerful extras union. We started researching and immediately found a red flag: there was no independent extras union until 1946, at which time Siegel was preoccupied with a certain real estate venture in Las Vegas. He was murdered the following year. We became even more curious about how this story became part of Siegel lore, and how Siegel might have exploited the campaign surrounding the May 1939 election in which extras voted by an overwhelming sixty-to-one margin to remain with the Screen Actors Guild.

Anyone wanting to know about atmosphere players should consult Kerry Segrave's *Extras of Early Hollywood: A History of the Crowd,*

1913–1945 and Anthony Slide's *Hollywood Unknowns: A History of Extras, Bit Players and Stand-Ins.* Mr Slide, a preeminent Hollywood historian, graciously answered our questions. We are also indebted to another book Mr Slide edited, *It's the Pictures That Got Small: Charles Brackett on Billy Wilder and Hollywood's Golden Age*, which captures the behind-the-scenes flavor of Paramount in the 1930s and '40s.

Astoundingly, no biographer has of yet tackled the life of Countess Dorothy di Frasso. (*Note to selves – potential project?*) One confirmed fact: her paramour Ben Siegel accompanied her on that April 1939 cruise to Italy. Their objective was to sell a new explosive called 'Atomite' to the Italian military, but the demonstration proved a bust. Of the Contessa's villa, Bugsy said 'half the guys she had hanging around were counts or dukes or kings out of a job,' and in later years he lamented not seizing the opportunity to whack two of her other houseguests, 'that fat bastard (Hermann) Göring' and 'that dirty (Joseph) Goebbels.' Siegel's claim of a potential Nazi-hunting party has since been discredited, but still, we're alerting the Paramount story department. While Virginia Hill does not appear in the 1941 film *Manpower* no matter what IMDb says, there are rumors she regularly mingled with extras whenever she and Siegel visited pals like George Raft on set in the hope of sneaking into a film. We haven't seen her in the background of any movies yet, but we'll keep looking.

Florabel Muir covered Hollywood high and low for decades; her memoir *Headline Happy* (1950) makes for hair-raising reading. We also recommend the 1951 autobiography of Edith Head's mentor Howard Greer, *Designing Male*. The description of his salon is taken from period accounts, and we're launching a campaign for it to be rebuilt according to those exact specifications.

The long-hidden tale of the studio-funded effort to track Nazi sympathizers in Southern California has now been told in two books, *Hollywood's Spies: The Undercover Surveillance of Nazis in Los Angeles* by Laura B. Rosenzweig and *Hitler in Los Angeles: How Jews Foiled Nazi Plots Against Hollywood and America* by Steven J. Ross, both published in 2017.

Edith Head's relationship with Max Ramsey is based on one she revealed to her biographer David Chierichetti. The Paulette Goddard incident is recounted in *Hollywood Magic*, an unpublished manuscript Edith co-wrote with Norma Lee Browning, now in the collection of the Academy of Motion Picture Arts and Sciences's Margaret Herrick Library. Miss Goddard would go on to have a sterling 1939. She was a late addition to the cast of *The Women*, appearing alongside Joan Crawford, and the box office success of *The Cat and the Canary* led to a lengthy Paramount career. In 1940, she reteamed with her then-husband Charlie Chaplin – yes, they were married – on *The Great Dictator*.

Shaun Considine's *Bette & Joan: The Divine Feud* admirably traces the lives of both of these actresses. Their voices ring through loud and clear in the books they wrote themselves.

Lastly, the Transogram Movie Millions game is real. We do not own a copy. Versions with the complete set of cards sometimes surface on eBay, at the cost of several hundred dollars, in the event you're preparing your Christmas list.